PRAISE FOR EMILY HOLLEMAN'S
CLEOPATRA'S SHADOWS

"Riveting."
—Steph Opitz, *Marie Claire*

"Holleman breaks free of the clichés dogging Cleopatra, the last great pharaoh of Ptolemaic Egypt, the better to see her fresh.... Arsinoe and Berenice could easily give the women of *Game of Thrones* a run for their money." —Alexandra Schwartz, *Salon*

"Vivid and page-turning."
—*Redbook*

"The rich, exotic world created by Emily Holleman in her debut novel, *Cleopatra's Shadows,* is mesmerizing. Intrigue, betrayal, and the near destruction of a dynasty follow in the wake of Cleopatra's little-known but ambitious sisters, Arsinoe and Berenice. A perfect marriage of dedicated research and passionately inventive story-telling." —Kathleen Kent, author of *The Outcasts*

"Holleman brings Alexandria to beautiful, spirited, and, at times, tragic life." —Mickey McAlary, *Brooklyn Magazine*

"Women have, throughout history, been secondary—often recorded (if at all) as complementary, or as muse to man's genius. But now, as modern societies are reappraising the value of women, so too are books evolving to match.... *Cleopatra's Shadows* reimagines Cleopatra's history through the perspective of her younger sister, Arsinoe. We want these stories more than ever." —Meredith Turits, *Vanity Fair*

"This historically detailed exploration of life on the Nile during the Ptolemy dynasty feels like a breath of fresh air after the *Downton*-inspired wave of twentieth-century historical fiction. Fans of Madeline Miller's *The Song of Achilles* should take note."   —*BookPage*

"The book for you if you're a historical fiction devotee who craves a lot from her read: multiple protagonists, lovely writing, and, of course, *drama*."   —*Bustle*

"We forget that Cleopatra was a Macedonian, her royal house a relic of the career of Alexander the Great. Where Cleopatra went to bed with Rome, her half sister Berenice, at nineteen, tried to hold the Egyptian throne against it, while her sister Arsinoe, still a child, fought to hang on in the margins. Prophetic dreams, fraying family bonds, and desperate development of strength in crisis define this affecting work of historical fiction."

   —Zachary Mason, author of *The Lost Books of the Odyssey*

"Holleman richly resuscitates this ancient world of danger, illuminating the lives of the women of one extraordinary lineage and their audacious, overt scrambles toward power."

   —Kara Cooney, author of *The Woman Who Would Be King*

"Breathes new life into these historical personalities. . . . Holleman offers a fresh take on the Ptolemy dynasty and has delivered what promises to be just the first in an exciting series about Arsinoe, youngest sister of Cleopatra."   —Jane Henriksen Baird, *Library Journal*

"Historically detailed and multilayered. . . . Holleman's imaginative, textured portraits of the lives and ambitions of these little-known heroines will appeal to readers of historical and literary fiction alike."   —*Publishers Weekly*

CLEOPATRA'S SHADOWS

A Novel

EMILY HOLLEMAN

BACK BAY BOOKS

Little, Brown and Company

New York Boston London

Copyright © 2015 by Emily Holleman
Questions and topics for discussion copyright © 2016 by Emily Holleman and Little, Brown and Company

Hachette Book Group supports the right to free expression and the value of copyright. The purpose of copyright is to encourage writers and artists to produce the creative works that enrich our culture.

The scanning, uploading, and distribution of this book without permission is a theft of the author's intellectual property. If you would like permission to use material from the book (other than for review purposes), please contact permissions@hbgusa.com. Thank you for your support of the author's rights.

Back Bay Books / Little, Brown and Company
Hachette Book Group
1290 Avenue of the Americas, New York, NY 10104
littlebrown.com

Originally published in hardcover by Little, Brown and Company, October 2015
First Back Bay trade paperback edition, July 2016

Back Bay Books is an imprint of Little, Brown and Company, a division of Hachette Book Group, Inc. The Back Bay Books name and logo are trademarks of Hachette Book Group, Inc.

The publisher is not responsible for websites (or their content) that are not owned by the publisher.

The Hachette Speakers Bureau provides a wide range of authors for speaking events. To find out more, go to hachettespeakersbureau.com or call (866) 376-6591.

ISBN 978-0-316-38298-4 (hc) / 978-0-316-38299-1 (pb)
LCCN 2015936837

10 9 8 7 6 5 4 3 2 1

RRD-C

Printed in the United States of America

For my sisters

But even on her the Fates
the gray everlasting Fates rode hard
—SOPHOCLES, *ANTIGONE*

THE HOUSE OF PTOLEMY

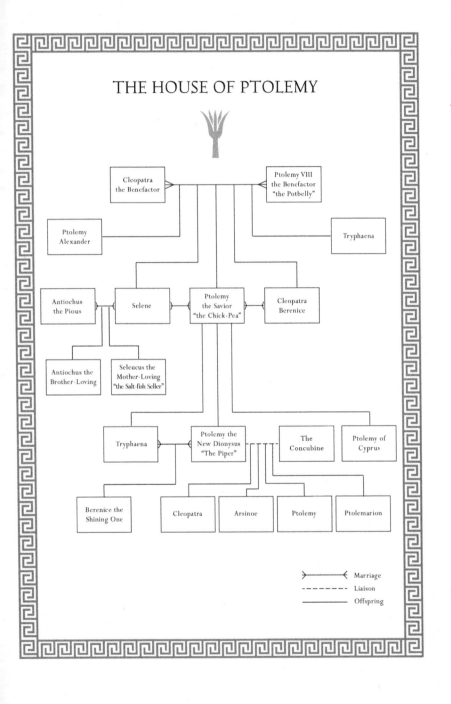

CLEOPATRA'S
SHADOWS

YOUNGER

She soared over the city, parched and desolate. Commoners writhed and withered on the boulevards. Rats scurried past their parents' corpses toward the dearer dead. Dipping between the temples, she traced their path. Alexander the Conqueror, stern in deathless marble, loomed, his sword thrust in the air. Blood leaked from his eyes, his lips, his thighs. The children cupped their greedy hands to drink.

"Arsinoe."

Wings stretched against the sun, she sailed onward, over bright sands, far from the arid Nile and its sins. Her feathers bristled in the breeze. The desert flamed beneath, and then folded to the sea.

"Arsinoe."

Thirst stung her throat. She circled down, toward the crashing waves. Her beak snapped against the salt.

"Arsinoe, my sweet. Awake."

She did not fly over the wine-dark sea. She lay small and shivering in her bed.

"Another night terror?" A gentle hand wiped damp hair from her brow.

Eyes sealed, Arsinoe clung to the wisps: her wings spread over the sands, the sticky seawater on her tongue. Had it been a tongue? Or did vultures taste by other means?

"No, it was . . . not a terror, no." She was nearly nine. Too old for fears that came at night.

"You could've fooled your old nurse." Myrrine clucked.

Arsinoe opened her eyes. Her nurse perched at the end of the bed, a few wisps of hair escaping her customary bun. With her full cheeks and unlined eyes, the woman had long preserved an almost ageless air—but now Arsinoe noticed the flecks of gray gathered at her temples. Beyond, the room was calm. The sewn muses danced about her walls in reds and golds, her silver basin brimmed with water, her clothes smoothed out for the coming day. But something was wrong. The light pouring through her windows was brash and dazzling. It was late. Long past dawn. She must have slept through the early hours. And on this day, this day—

Arsinoe sprang up from her bed. Her legs were weak and wobbly, as though her soaring dreams had stolen all landlocked memories.

"What's come over you, my child?"

She ignored her nurse's words and raced to the door. Knees cracking, Myrrine followed.

"Calm yourself, my dear. Where are you running off to?"

"I must go to the docks—or else I'll miss Cleopatra." She needed to say good-bye. She always said good-bye. That was the rule. "What we share is different, you and I," Cleopatra told her time and again. "We are sisters, and that bond cuts deeper than ordinary blood. No one—not Father, not anyone—will ever come between us." And so, since Arsinoe had been old enough to totter, she'd trailed her sister down to the river, and watched and waved as Cleopatra was borne away on their father's adventures. To witness the incarnation of the new Apis bull at Memphis, or to oversee the festival of Ammon-Re at Thebes, or as now to cross the waves to Rhodes, perhaps, or even as far as Rome. And then, alone, she would weep.

"You can't run to the ships in your underthings."

"My sister won't care what I wear."

"Your father will," her nurse said. "You must dress as fits a princess."

Dressing, bathing, combing—all that took too long. This wasn't some idle voyage up the Nile to check the river's rise; Cleopatra sailed over the sea. No one would tell her where. Or when her sister would return. It could be months. Arsinoe didn't have time for braids, and jewels, and other niceties. Grown-ups never understood these things.

"If you say I must..." She took a step, slow, tentative, toward Myrrine—and then she turned and bolted from the room.

"Arsinoe!" Myrrine's voice chased her. "Arsinoe!"

She slipped past her pair of sentries and ran down the stairs. Soldiers swarmed the small piazza below—the Sisters' Courtyard, she and Cleopatra called it. That ran in her favor. Their numbers would only swell when she reached the great courtyard. Achilles and Agamemnon, as she had named her two guards, were men grown; they'd catch her quickly in an open race, but they had no skill for obstacles. Weighed down by heft, by armor, and by age, they couldn't follow as she weaved through the gaps and bays of the crowd. She darted through the private porticoes onto the public ones, past beaming dryads and mauled lions, ax-wielding hunters and sneering sphinxes, until she raced through the eastern gate, and the whole world opened on the sands.

Breathless, she gazed over the beach, the docks, the sea. Against the squinting sun she spotted her prize: her father's round ship, crimson sails unfurled against the blue. At its prow, Thessalonike, the great Alexander's sister, transmuted to mermaid form, rose and fell upon the waves. The sand burned her soles, spurred her on.

Ahead, the docks stretched into the unending sea. The shore lay barren. Where were the dancers and pipers, the priests and soothsayers, the nobles and vagrants to see off the voyage? Only a tangle of aging soldiers, too old and worn to tend the king, stood by, spitting whispers over wooden posts.

"Wait!" Arsinoe cried out.

No one listened. A gruff man, fifty if he was a day, set his blade against the rope that bound her sister to the shore. Arsinoe ran to him, and yanked his hand away from the cord.

"Get off me, girl." Snarling, he wiped her fingers from his arm.

"I am no girl. I am the king's daughter."

"King Ptolemy's daughter is already on board. With the king."

Stunned, she fell silent. No one spoke to her that way. As though she wasn't even born of her father's seed. As though her blood counted for nothing. She wasn't the favorite—had never been, would never be; the king's third daughter and his last, she knew where she stood among her siblings. But commoners, courtiers, soldiers—they always treated her with deference.

"I've orders, girl," the man spat. His knife split the twine.

"Clea!" she screamed. "Cleopatra!"

Arsinoe scanned the ship. Guardsmen lingered by the prow, and farther aft a pair of sailors hastened to set the sheets to the wind. The deckhouse curtains were drawn; she couldn't see inside. Below, three sets of oars stroked the sea as one. All along the docks, the old men spurred their posts against the hull.

"Cleopatra!"

The waves crashed against her ears. On board, they'd sound all the louder against her sister's. There was no use in screeching. She wouldn't be heard.

"Arsinoe!"

And there she was, her sister, a vision on the prow. Clothed in rich sapphire, Cleopatra looked more a goddess than a girl. Even at eleven, she'd begun to take on the contours of a queen. At once, Arsinoe was ashamed of her own soiled garb, the clothes she'd slept and sweated in the preceding night.

"I wanted to come early, but Myrrine didn't wake me," she said to her sister in Macedonian, the private, ancient tongue of their family. Cleopatra had told her once that no one else spoke it anymore. Not anywhere in the wide world. They were the only ones who carried on the language of Alexander, the greatest of all kings. "I had the strangest—"

"I can't hear you," her sister yelled over the waves.

"Last night," Arsinoe shouted, "I had the—"

"Don't fret, little one. I'll return for you."

Cleopatra pressed her palm to her lips and blew a kiss along the breeze. Arsinoe caught it on her fingertips. And then she waved, and waved, and waved until her sister shrank into the sea.

"Arsinoe." A familiar voice greeted her. Her guard, her favorite. Her Achilles.

She could picture him behind her; his curls tumbled in the wind. She liked to pull on the one that always slipped out from beneath his helmet, liked to watch it spring back into place. But she wouldn't turn to face him—not now. Not with tears threatening.

"You've worried poor Myrrine half to death," he told her.

"I had to say good-bye."

His shadow dwarfed her own. But she didn't look back at him. She couldn't meet his eye. The water had escaped, streaming down her cheeks. Tears were for children.

"Come, princess. I must return you to your chambers."

She wiped the damp from her eyes and followed, but her mind lingered at the docks. It had been no king's departure. No trumpeters, no flamethrowers, no priests to spill sacrifices before the ship. The gruff man's words rang in her ears. "King Ptolemy's daughter is already on board."

The return trip was slower, though this time the soldiers parted to let her through. She couldn't make sense of their numbers: why did so many of them linger, clogging the courtyards? Usually, her father took the better part of his troops with him on his journeys. "A cautious man," her tutor, Ganymedes, called him, but she could catch a hint of mockery in the eunuch's voice.

Even the porticoes looked somehow dark and shrunken, though the sun burned as bright as ever. The laughing satyrs who graced the walls of the family colonnades had shed their customary joy. She could have sworn that the jolly red-maned one had sprung a tear on his bearded cheek. When she turned to check, she saw that it was only a glimmer, a trick of the light. Still, she felt that they, too, mourned Cleopatra's loss. Her sister's absences sucked the joy from the palace. Sometimes she wished that her own might have the same effect. But no one would notice if she vanished into air.

Myrrine chided her on her return. "Arsinoe, you mustn't run off like that!"

"I only went down to the docks."

"Only down to the docks? You could have been—there's no telling what might have happened."

"But nothing did. Nothing *ever* happens."

"Of course it didn't," the nurse's voice quavered. She knelt beside Arsinoe. Her eyes were red and swollen. She'd been weeping too. "But promise me that you won't go rushing off like that again."

"I promise," she lied.

Myrrine kissed her brow and folded her into her bosom. The nurse hugged Arsinoe so tightly that she could scarcely breathe.

"What is the matter?" she gasped when the woman released her. "Why have you been crying?"

"What nonsense, child," Myrrine said, laughing. "I haven't been crying."

Arsinoe didn't believe her. She'd borne witness to her mother's tears often enough, before her little brothers came screeching into the world, to recognize the signs. As her nurse bathed her, Myrrine filled the air with foolish tales of drunken gods and mistaken identities. But Arsinoe wasn't so easily fooled. She could feel the wrongness all around. The massing guards, the abandoned docks—none of it added up. And no one would tell her the truth. If only Cleopatra were here, she would help make sense of the goings-on.

By the time Achilles and Agamemnon trailed her to her lessons, the guards along the colonnades had thinned. She wondered where they'd all scurried off to; it was too late for them to follow her father across the waves. A second seafaring vessel hadn't even been prepared—at least she hadn't seen one on the beach. Around each bend, she expected to come across some new mass of armed men. But she never did, not even once she'd reached the library and turned off into the small reading room where Ganymedes waited. Usually, her royal companions would be gathered, gossiping and giggling around the table. But today she found only the eunuch, a hulking silhouette against the westward windows.

"Where are Aspasia and Hypatia?" Her voice trembled. It had been a dream, she reminded herself, only a dream that the statue of Alexander the Conqueror bled, that corpses lined the streets; it didn't mean anything at all.

"Elsewhere, it seems," Ganymedes answered. Cleopatra had first noted this, his calculated air of mystery, and now Arsinoe heard it in his every word. "But that's no excuse for wasting precious time. Go on, open your scroll."

With care, she stretched the papyrus across the table. Too many times she'd been admonished for tearing some musty work of Archimedes. *Histories,* it read. Polybius.

"I thought we were going to read *Antigone.*" She preferred the tragedies. The stories that unfolded in her mind and invaded her dreams. While epics and plays pulsed with life, histories were for the dead. "And besides, Polybius was a traitor. He betrayed Arcadia for Rome."

"Now isn't the time for stories." The eunuch's tone was sharp. "It's time for you to learn the truth about the world. And the importance of taking action in it. 'Can anyone be so indifferent or idle as not to care to know by what means, and under what kind of polity, almost the whole inhabited world was conquered and brought under the dominion of the single city of Rome, and that, too, within a period of not quite fifty-three years?'" Ganymedes knew the historian's words by heart, and Arsinoe had to dart her eyes down the page to keep up. "Are you idle, Arsinoe, or indifferent? Because you shouldn't be. Not on this day of all days."

"What's today?" She'd known something was the matter—her dream, the empty docks, her nurse's tears.

"Today is the day when it all changes. When you begin to learn why, after a hundred years—after Rome has fought and conquered a hundred more enemies—Polybius's words ring truer than they ever have." The eunuch paused and his voice grew gentle. "Tell me, child: have you noticed anything strange about the palace?"

She had noticed so many strange things, from the moment she awoke and rushed down to the sea.

"This morning," she began eagerly, "when I went to see Cleopatra off, the halls were swarmed by soldiers, but when I walked to the library, there were hardly any left at all."

"You were right to note that, because something strange is happening in the palace. You remember the fate of your uncle in Cyprus?"

She remembered her uncle well, though she'd seldom had the chance to see him. He'd seemed a good sort of man, jovial and gentle, easy with a smile. On those occasions when he came to Alexandria for feasts and other rituals, he'd paid her the attention her father never did, asking after her schooling and remarking on how she'd grown. It hurt to think of him dead. To think how that loss must torment her father, how it would destroy her if she lost Cleopatra.

"My uncle was killed fighting the Romans, defending the island my forefathers have ruled since the time of Alexander," she told the eunuch proudly.

"That's the story your father tells, but it is a lie. Your uncle poisoned himself rather than face Rome's legions. Marcus Cato, the one the Romans call the Younger, stole the island and its treasures without shedding a drop of Ptolemaic blood. Neither your father nor your uncle lifted a finger to stop him. Your father, I'm afraid, is a coward."

The words didn't sting; instead, Arsinoe felt a sort of dull ache in her belly. Shame, not anger, or even hurt. Too late, she opened her mouth to defend him: "My father is no such—"

"Your father is many things, but he's never been a brave man. Even you know that, in your heart of hearts."

She nodded. She did know. She'd heard enough servants whispering along the corridors, seen enough noblemen smirking at the sight of her father's pipe playing to know he wasn't revered, not as he should be. Not as a king. Not as a god.

"Don't follow his mistakes. It's always better to act than to do nothing. Even when your actions are futile, even when the Romans—as Polybius teaches—would still have conquered in the end. Which would you rather do: succumb to fate, or fight for your house, your dynasty?"

"I'd fight. Of course I'd fight." She and Cleopatra spoke of this at times, this need to fight, to defend what was theirs. After all, Rome *had* stolen the lands of Alexander's other generals. Even Mithradates, whose name still cropped up in murmurs, had lost the Pontic kingdom to that poisonous city. Theirs was the only one left.

"Good, because while you might forgive your father for his idleness, the Alexandrians never will. For weeks now they've been in near open revolt, clashing with his soldiers, setting fires in the street, though you wouldn't know it from how your father's carried on within the palace walls. Your sister Berenice, along with her mother, has enlisted the discontents in a coup—against your father and his womanly, Roman-appeasing rule. That's why your father flees, unattended, over the sea, to seek Rome's aid, and your mother has snuck her own path from the palace."

"My—my mother too?" Her father was forever whisking Cleopatra off, stealing her away on his escapades. She was his chosen one, his heir, and so she had to go see to the kingdom's concerns. One day they would be hers. But their mother usually remained, busying herself with her sons, sparing a small smile when Arsinoe passed her. Sometimes even a halfhearted kiss.

"Yes, my dear, your mother too. This morning she slipped away with your brothers."

Arsinoe's heart thudded in her ears. Her mother had forgotten her as well. Once again, her brothers had come first, as they came first in everything but birth. But couldn't her mother have taken her too? Would it have been so much more difficult, then, to sneak three children to safety instead of two? And besides, she might have helped with her little brothers. She sometimes played with them, and even though Ptolemy was a sullen, ill-tempered boy of three, she could always make him giggle. Her mother would even praise her for that. "How he loves his sister," she'd say with that strange smile playing on her lips.

"Is that why Myrrine didn't want me to go to the docks? Because my mother planned to bring me with her?" she asked, even though she knew better. But she wanted to hear, to be told fully and completely that her mother had abandoned her. To drink in the hurt.

"Perhaps that was the reason," the eunuch told her gently. But she heard another answer: *No.* She swallowed hard. She'd begged for this; she wouldn't weep.

"You do not cry. Most girls would shed tears over a mother's loss."

She answered—quietly, almost to herself—with the mantra that Cleopatra had seized on years ago, when her first brother had been born and their mother had lost interest in her girls: "'The one named mother is not the child's true parent but the nurturer of the newly sown seed. Man mounts to create life, whereas woman is a stranger fostering a stranger—'"

"Those are your sister's words, not your own."

"Those are Aeschylus's words, not Cleopatra's," Arsinoe quipped, blinking away her tears. Bereft of mother and father, sister and brothers, she felt a stab of loneliness. Only the eunuch and the nurse remained to her now.

"You have me, my dear." Ganymedes squeezed her hand. She

pulled away. His kindnesses alarmed her. He wasn't one for tenderness; he was harsh, impenetrable. And so when he reached for her, she knew how wholly her world had changed.

"Ganymedes." She took a deep breath. She couldn't mourn her mother, or her father, or the others who'd cut her away, leaving her untethered here in Alexandria. Not now, when she wanted so very much to be brave. "What must I do?"

"My dear, dear girl." His face softened. "You must return to your chambers at once. Tonight, after the moon has risen over the palace, I'll come for you. Make no preparations for our departure, and don't breathe a word of this to anyone."

"Not even to Myrrine?" She'd kept secrets from her nurse before, but they'd always been of her own making. Like when she and Cleopatra had broken the Minoan vase that had been gifted to her great-grandfather, and they'd blamed it on their baby brother, too young to speak up for himself.

"No, not to Myrrine, nor to your guards. Remember now, my dear: you can no longer distinguish friends from foes."

"Like Odysseus, when he returns to Ithaca and sees that many of his former friends court the faithful Penelope?" It helped to imagine herself as Odysseus, as a man grown and strong.

"Yes, precisely like that, Arsinoe."

She didn't smile at her guards as they escorted her back to her chambers. Usually, she'd make jokes, teasing them and trying to crack their stone faces with laughter. She'd tug at Achilles's curls or poke at the gaps in Agamemnon's armor, the place where his breastplate latched on either side. "I could pierce you with an arrow there," she'd giggle. But today she was quiet. They, too, might be enemies. With Myrrine, she was so taciturn that her nurse declared she must be ill and tucked her into bed long before the sea had swallowed the last rays of the long summer sun.

After Myrrine's steps had faded into the antechamber, Arsinoe rose. Quiet as a wildcat, she slipped across the room and pried open her great clothes chest. Her fingers lingered over the soft fabrics before she snatched one and yanked it out. Her pick wasn't poor: a sky-blue tunic edged in silver. She hurried about the chamber, grabbing a few treasures to tie up in the cloth: the first book of *The Odyssey,* which she kept furled by her pillow; the jade necklace Cleopatra had given her from far-off Nubia; the stuffed doll she slept with every night. This last item she labored over—she was too old for such toys. For years, she'd hidden the doll beneath her bed during the day, shielding her even from her closest friends. But she couldn't bring herself to part with her. Penelope had stayed with her always; Arsinoe couldn't abandon the doll to Berenice's men. She knotted the corners of the tunic's skirt to each sleeve as she had seen her friend Aspasia do once when she had explained how the children in the Upper Lands hawk their wares.

And then Arsinoe waited. She knew she should lie in her bed, pretend this night was the same as every other. But she couldn't trust herself to stay awake, and she didn't dare sleep. Instead, she sat on the hard floor and stared out the window, willing Selene to climb the sky, to pass beyond the palace gates and up over the roof. Her eyelids grew heavy, but she stayed vigilant, blinking them open every moment or two.

The door squealed on its hinges. Arsinoe jumped up in fear, bundle clutched to her chest. She let out her breath: it was Ganymedes.

"Leave that," the eunuch commanded. "I told you to bring nothing."

She opened her mouth to object, but she held her tongue. Gently, she placed the blanket on her bed. "Farewell, Penelope," she whispered. In silence, she followed the eunuch out into the antechamber. And there—there she met with horrors: Myrrine's divan lay empty, and Agamemnon was sprawled across the stone, his head wrenched to one side and his lips stained with wine. Drugged or dead, she couldn't tell. There was one goblet spilled, another upright, untouched. Her stomach turned and roiled, and she wanted to look away. He'd died. He'd died for *her.* And then she saw her other guard: Achilles stood upright, awake, alert. She gasped.

"It's all right," the eunuch told her. "You can trust him."

Ganymedes led her past the royal chambers and into the servants' passageways. Behind, her guard's familiar step assured her. At each corner, the eunuch held his hand to bring their retinue to a halt until he'd peered around the end. She didn't know how far they wandered through these lesser twists and turns.

The three fell into a marching step. Achilles, a soldier through and through, matched her eunuch's stride; it took her three paces to equal each one of theirs. And so their drum sounded its quiet, bleating rhythm: *hard, soft, soft, hard, soft, soft . . .* A second *hard* cut between her two *softs.* She strained her ears to listen. It was nothing, she promised herself, the chasings of a forgotten dream.

But then she heard the sound again—louder, closer, near at hand. And Ganymedes's step quickened. She raced to meet his new stride, but Achilles did not. His footfalls halted. The false ones did as well.

"Ganymedes," she breathed. A sword whistled through the night air.

"Don't look back," the eunuch whispered. Steel clashed against steel. She hurried on. A man groaned in agony—was it Achilles? Another clash. The squelch of metal into flesh. A body thudding to the stone. A second, darker moan. She turned—and there in the flickering candlelight lay her guard, her hero, her Achilles, twitching, a gash of blood spurting from his throat. The eunuch's hand covered her mouth, choked her bile and her scream.

"Stop!" one of their pursuers cried out. "Hand over the girl, or we'll kill you both."

"Run, Arsinoe," Ganymedes whispered.

And so she did. She ran through the servants' corridors, on into the workrooms and the kitchens, and out again into the great courtyard. Blood stained these walls, and bile too, but she didn't look at the faces of the dying men. She leapt over their bodies, and pretended they'd stir again in the light of day. But as she raced, a dark realization came to her: she didn't know where to run. And so her feet carried her back along her steps, back to her family's private plazas, back to her own rooms. Within: emptiness. Either Agamemnon had awoken or his body had already been cleared away. Discarded like refuse on the street. As though he'd never been a man, but some thing, some waste, to wash away. She almost wished that he remained; even a corpse was better company. And perhaps if his flesh lingered, his spirit would too.

Her bedchamber was in disarray. Her scrolls were strewn like so many corpses across the floor, and her bedclothes torn aside; her jewel box had been flung across the room, and her tunics tugged from their cypress chest. She searched for the bundle of her possessions, the one she had gathered with such care. But she could find no sign of it, nor of the riches she'd stowed within. Footfalls slammed behind her, and she slipped beneath her bed.

Shaking, she listened to the angry steps pace the colonnades. It sounded as though a thousand guards patrolled the royal halls. She'd been a fool to return here, a frightened, childish fool. She wondered what had happened to Ganymedes, whether the eunuch had lived or died. He lived, she reassured herself; he must. He was far too clever to be caught. He was the only one left to her. And he would come back. He had to.

The night was dark. The moon had sunk; only the gleam of Pharos, the great lighthouse of her forefathers, pierced the blindness. But Arsinoe refused to sleep.

The stale stench of urine stung her nose when she awoke. Stiff robes stuck to stiff limbs. With disgust, she realized she'd wet herself in the night, like some child of five. Even her brother Ptolemy hardly did that now, and he wasn't even four. Twisting her slight frame this way and that, Arsinoe struggled to peer out from beneath the bed.

Dawn had peeled away the night's terrors, painting the chamber rose. The nine muses danced along her bedside tapestry as they did each morning. She caught Kalliope's eye, gray with hints of blue and green and wine. The goddess of epics and adventures, she stroked her lute, her gaze intense and clear. She'd been spun into the cloth before she'd learned of her son Orpheus's death. No woman, not even one born of Zeus, could bear the loss of a boy. That's why Arsinoe's own mother had slipped her brothers away, and left her here alone. A daughter was disposable.

Still, that small part of her, the shrinking part, wanted to cry out for that woman who'd forsaken her. To weep and beg to be swept away as her brothers had been. To have the comfort of the warm embrace she'd known when she was small and sick, and her mother had not yet forgotten her. But more often, she knew, her nurse had been the one who had dried her tears and kissed her bruises. What good had a mother's love ever brought?

"Myrrine?" Arsinoe said, testing. No soft shuffle came in answer.

"Myrrine?" she tried again, louder this time. Quiet.

And once more: "Myrrine?"

The name rebounded off the stone. She clutched her knees to her chest, hands to her ears; she would shrink away to nothing. The Ptolemy who disappeared. But the ground didn't swallow her up. Soldiers didn't come. Only her stolen voice broke the silence: "Myrrine, Myrrine, Myrrine."

"Ganymedes?" she tried. But there was no sign of him either.

She sucked back her stomach's bile. "Better up than down," Myrrine always said. But the nurse had been taken from her too. No one would clean away her vomit or bathe her or dress her or change her coverlets.

Boots pounded beneath her bones. Each set kept a steady rhythm. None paused by her door. Her stomach growled angrily. Perhaps Berenice had forgotten her. After all, she'd never had much to do with her eldest sister. The daughter of Tryphaena, Berenice was already a woman grown. Too old to be her playmate, or even Cleopatra's. Some days from now, Arsinoe would be found, her body stained and rotting beneath the bed.

She wondered who would mourn her loss. Cleopatra would weep, of course. But would the others? Would her mother regret not stealing her away? Would that cruel guard remember barring her from her father's ship?

New feet shook the stone. A hand fumbled at the lock. The bolt screeched; the door swung wide to reveal a solitary guard. Her father's man. Or so he'd been once, guarding the king's person day and night. His beard bristled red; Arsinoe would have recognized it anywhere. Menelaus, she'd called him. She thought he'd sailed across the sea with Cleopatra and the rest. She couldn't trust him now; her father's men were turned or slain. Achilles's throat split open, blood draining to the floor, his curls dashed against the onyx. She shook the image from her mind.

The guard's gaze roamed from her writing table, to her hanging mirror of glinting silver, to her scattered scrolls, to her golden bed. Now was the time to scream. She opened her mouth but no sound escaped. She'd learned enough of war, of Troy, of Carthage, of Thermopylae, to know the fate of girls, even young ones, who met with men drunk on battle's haze. She held her breath until she thought her chest might burst, until her eyes and tongue bulged and begged for mercy. And then she held it longer.

The fire-bearded man removed his helm, a red crown rimmed with redder hair. He lifted a corner of his tunic to wipe his brow. Bloodstained, the cloth returned to his side. He crouched low, balancing his elbows on his knees, and waited. She wouldn't speak; she couldn't scream.

Some part of her, a crazed and agonizing part, wanted him to find her. It would be easier that way, and someday, after all, she'd have to be found. She was so weary, so very weary of hiding. And then, as though she'd spoken the words aloud, his eyes seized on her. He breathed easy now, and so did she. There was a relief in being caught. He removed a small parcel from his robes and placed it on her dressing table. Then, glancing about the room one final time, he stepped outside, and the creaking sound of iron against iron bolted her in.

Once his footsteps ebbed, Arsinoe struggled free and raced to the table. Unwrapping the bundle revealed a loaf of bread, a pair of dates, a cluster of green grapes. Her mouth watered. How she longed to stuff herself with bread and fruit. But she didn't dare. She'd never eaten anything that hadn't been tasted first, except for a few berries she and Cleopatra had picked from the garden on their own. She remembered how Democrates, her father's taster, had died, gasping and clawing at his throat. She wouldn't bring on her own death, not when she'd already survived that first night alone. She should throw the gifts out the window. But she couldn't do that either. Instead, she retreated beneath her bed, the guard's poison clutched tight against her chest.

ELDER

The crowds screamed. They screamed for her. For her, the least loved of Ptolemy the Piper's daughters. The shunted child of the shunted bride. For her, the humble phoenix rising from Egypt's smoldering ash. "Berenice Epiphaneia"—they cried her coronation name. "Berenice the Shining One."

Even as she drank in their chants, she couldn't shed her fears. Her coup had been too quick and too seamless. It had shown nothing of her strength. Her father had fled before real blood was drawn. The piping fool would have reached Rhodes by now. *And where to then, Father?* Even as her subjects shrieked for her, she knew that, in truth, they shrieked against him, against him and his brother, against their loss of Cyprus. That last, vanished vestige of her once great house.

Besides, it shouldn't be Alexandria that stretched before her but Memphis, the Balance of the Two Lands, with its sandstone halls and sphinx-lined avenues. That coronation would yoke her dynasty to the ones that had come before, to the ancient pharaohs who had ruled these lands as gods. *In time,* she promised herself. Her father had sat the throne for four years before he'd sailed up the Nile to the white-walled city to be blessed by Ptah and assume the double crown. And it was his priest, his beloved Psenptais, his so-called first prophet of the Lord of the Two Lands, who held sway there. It was too soon; she knew that. Better to let the dust settle. To secure her power here. The white steps snaked up the hillside, above the adoring crowd that flanked the city's sweeping boulevards. As she climbed, her breath ran thin and her heart pounded in her throat. Alexandria had seen kings, of course, who didn't deign to ascend on foot. Her great-grandfather had been among them. Ptolemy the Benefactor—or the Potbelly, as he'd been less kindly known—had commanded his litter bearers to hoist him up on their shoulders when he'd been restored to the throne. One had collapsed beneath his weight, sending king and litter in a tumbled heap on the marble. Another example that Berenice was eager not to emulate. The Potbelly had been the first to entrust Egypt's welfare to Rome, preferring to sign away his bloodlines' rights in a will rather than see the wrong son inherit. No, she'd follow in the footsteps of her first forebearers, the ones who'd expanded the realm's holdings, not stripped away the kingdom bit by bit.

Still, despite her plans, there was an emptiness to her victory. Now that she'd won, and easily, her hatred of her father grew worn, as though all the years of tending it had eroded the bile of his betrayal. When he'd cast her mother, cursing, into the streets, and turned his love to his younger, lesser children begotten on his concubine—then she'd thought she'd cling forever to her loathing. But what was left now, when she thought of him, was a mere man, not a monster—a foolish, selfish man who'd fallen in love with a woman who was not his sister. She almost pitied him.

The top of the temple pediment soared into view: bearded Serapis enthroned with three-headed Cerberus at his feet. As she climbed upward, the frieze opened to reveal the two nymphs, golden cornucopia in hand, flanked by a pair of splotched bulls. She should have been laughing at this cobbled-together god—part Osiris, part Dionysus, both Hades and Apis—but her skepticism failed her. Once she'd passed into the first colonnade, myrrh foiled the summer breeze. She could only imagine how the stench must already clog the inner sanctum's air. The priests rejoiced in this addling. She could see why: it stoked her own terrors.

Some deformity in the animal itself would taint her, no matter that these holy men tried to twist the omens in her favor. If the entrails were so perverted that any buffoon could see their ruin, she might lose the Alexandrians' support before she'd even had time to clinch it. Then she'd have no choice but to sail up the Nile at once—tomorrow, even—to fight to receive her blessings in Memphis and Thebes, and she'd need a military triumph to prove that the gods smiled on her reign. No, that was weakness: to fear things beyond her control. The incense had muddied her mind—no man would tremble before spilt entrails if his nostrils filled only with ocean breeze.

But tremble they did. Nobles clad in violet and coral and vermillion cluttered the courtyard, crowding among the statues to assess their peers, each keen to note who had arrived to greet the new queen, and who had stayed away, praying for the Piper's return. Stone and flesh both, these creatures remained aloof, untouched by the passion of their plebeian counterparts. Whatever allegiance they now pledged, they'd belonged to her father to a one. She hoped their loyalty to him would be as flimsy as his was to them.

As the sea of tunics parted, doubt nicked her heels. *You dare offer your name to the deathless gods?* Her mother's voice. She batted it aside. Why should she be plagued by misgivings? For all his faults, her father had no qualms about assuming the crown—a crown he wasn't owed. He'd never met a man or god who required his explanation. In his arrogance, he'd even named himself the New Dionysus, the most pompous of the Ptolemy epithets for the least impressive of its kings. And then she was at the altar steps, its ivory gates at last thrown open to her.

Steeling herself for whatever omens might come, she ascended to the sanctuary. Through the sodden air, she could make out only the god Serapis, glaring down from the altar, his beard and fruit basket trimmed with gold. He judged her harshly; perhaps he could smell her feeble faith. A shadow rippled beneath his gaze. She blinked until the high priest, his seven-pointed star dull in comparison, emerged from the incense-laden mist.

"Berenice the Shining One, daughter of Ptolemy the New Dionysus, son of Ptolemy the Savior, of the line of Alexander the Great, son of no lesser deity than Zeus Ammon himself," the voice boomed. "On this day, you stand before Serapis, who is called both Dionysus and Osiris, to be crowned Queen of the Upper and Lower Kingdoms."

She bent to kneel; the cold stone throbbed against her bones. In the corner of her gaze, a white heifer jerked her head against the lead. Dragged to her fate, the cow whined, wheezing through her nostrils. Berenice softened; dread rose in her throat too. So much rested on this moment. The twisting entrails might bless or damn her claim. Only the gods could curse her now and cast blackened guts in which any man would read poor fate. And then the city folk might turn against her rule—a woman's rule against which they might already chafe. Weak, she looked up to the gap-mouthed god, eyes blank, lips parted to reveal a fleshy tongue. *Serapis, first among the immortal ones,* she loathed herself for pleading, *don't let this priest of men stand between me and my birthright.*

"Great Serapis. We offer you this heifer, the loveliest of the royal herd, to bless your daughter's rule. We, your humble suppliants, pray that you might accept our sacrifice."

The cow strained her neck away from the silver blade; she moaned as her blood spilled to the stone. While her corpse still twitched, a white-robed attendant cut the beast's belly from sternum to udder, from left fore to right, from right hind to left. Skin peeled away, the entrails squirmed free. Berenice squinted at the pink coils; she could discern nothing unusual in them. Her clenched gut loosened. She'd heard of gruesome tellings, animals missing hearts or guts or ribs, but all the offerings she'd witnessed looked much like this: remarkable only for what was said about them.

The priest cleared his throat and cast his eyes around the

columned court. He looked to the heavens, and then down at the gathered fools. Finally, he spoke: "Glory to the gods. Serapis smiles upon this rule! The entrails are lush and red, the color of the bold, of the brave, of the great. Berenice the Shining One shall return Egypt to her days of glory!"

Relief flooded her veins; despite her mother's warnings, she would indeed be crowned—with blessings. Amid the smoke and guts, a second attendant entered from the inner sanctum bearing the insignia of rule: the white diadem and the golden scepter. She could still picture her father wearing his as he disembarked from his royal barge. He was younger in her vision, she no more than a girl of six. And overjoyed, she'd leapt into his arms.

"In the name of Serapis, I crown you, Queen Berenice the Shining One, Queen of the Two Lands."

The priest knotted the ivory ribbon tight about her brow. Her twin braids dug into her skull; she felt no pain. When she stood, she stood as queen.

The other ceremony, the one in Memphis—she wouldn't fret over that. The Upper Lands had lain quiet for a generation. Her grandfather had crushed their hopes of uprising once and for all, burning Thebes to ruin; the dangers were here in Alexandria. The city folk had torn more Ptolemies from their thrones than the natives ever had.

As she crossed the outer court a second time, she met with murmurs that coalesced into halfhearted cheers. That didn't worry her: the nobles would stand behind her. Their priest had blessed her claim, and besides, they'd no other choice. Her father had abandoned them. And when she descended back into the city, her subjects roared anew. Free of priests and nobles, entrails and omens, she delighted in this return march, in the drunken shouts of revelry, in the cool breeze lapping at her throat. She refused to be a cloistered queen, shut away in a gilded litter.

In the palace, her mother would be pacing the upper corridors;

from time to time, her eyes would glint over the bloated crowds. The unflappable Tryphaena, too weak to join her daughter's procession. "We can't have you hacking blood upon the queen's robes," her unyielding eunuch had chided. And her mother had groused, "Why not? It'll hardly add to the stain." Berenice knew her mother hadn't always been this way. There'd been a time, she reminded herself, when Tryphaena had held herself proud. Before her father had turned her out and bitterness had coalesced into fury gnawing away at her soul.

As Berenice passed through the royal gate, the world quieted. The palace, for one, looked unmoved by the day's events. The twin sphinxes that guarded either side of the marble entrance stared ahead with blank human faces. Above, the cobalt frieze of Alexander's defeat of the Persians gleamed in the sun. The great man himself, Medusa's head writhing on his breastplate, appeared as eager as ever to strike his opponent from his horse. She could divine a single welcome difference: one of the four statue nooks stood empty. Where her father's form had piped in marble remained only a barren block of granite. That was something, at least.

A gruff voice interrupted her thoughts. "A moment of your time, my queen."

"Dio." Berenice named the man before she turned. She was a great reader of voice and accent; the trick had often stunned her father's advisers when she was a girl. Sometimes he'd bring her out, blindfolded, to guess the origins of his guests. At the time, she'd nearly burst with pride at the attention, but now it seemed nothing more than another of his foolish capers. Still, it proved a useful gift. Even if she'd overheard just a whiff of a sentence, nineteen times out of twenty she could name the speaker, along with his city of origin. "It is a pleasure," she told Dio. "Walk with me a turn."

"Perhaps this isn't the proper time?" her adviser asked. He was a stout man, her Dio, with a bald pate ringed by a few dogged curls that refused to admit defeat. He had the look of a soldier gone to seed, the sort of man who enjoyed indulging in life's finer offerings as he worked his way through middle age. There must have been a powerful frame somewhere beneath that barrel of a belly, but only traces of it remained. She trusted him, more fully than she did any other man. After all, he'd been the first of the Alexandrian nobles to defy her father and sow discontent in the city streets.

"This moment suits me as well as any other," she told him as they passed along the public colonnades. Here and there, she'd catch sight of a servant shrinking from her sight. But perhaps she'd only imagined it. "Tell me, Dio: what is it that troubles you?" She slowed her pace, and looked him in the eye. "Your Alexandrians can't be displeased with me—not yet. The diadem's scarcely been knotted on my head."

"Oh, no, my queen. I assure you that my men are all quite content on this happy occasion. It's the culmination of all our prayers." His smile strained; his pate burned red. With Dio, that was the telltale sign of nerves.

"And yet?"

"And yet . . . your mother is proving difficult. It's been heard, my queen, that she intends to purge all those who were once loyal to Ptolemy the Piper. I don't need to tell you what damage that might do—"

"Then you have friends who support my father," she answered. It didn't surprise her.

"I might have friends who *supported* your father. But my friendships matter little. What matters is that nearly every man in this city has, at one point or another, tied himself to every Ptolemy who has sat the throne. It would be cruel indeed to cut off heads for such casual affiliations."

So he looked to her for assurances. Dio worried too much; she wasn't bloodthirsty. She could afford to be generous in victory. "Tell your friends that I don't intend to kill men who merely nodded in support of my father's reign."

"I knew you didn't, my queen, but it will soothe many hearts to hear the words all the same." He pressed her hand gently. As she watched him shuffle away, she wondered if there was some deeper root of his affections. She felt her face flush.

Upstairs, she returned to the Piper's—*her* chambers, the chambers of the king. The gold-framed mirrors, set at angles along each wall, blinded her, fracturing the finely wrought furniture into countless iterations. Everywhere she looked, a dozen sets of eyes stared back at her. The writing table, with its inlaid pearls blinking against its ebony slab, was the only surface unsheathed in gold. *The Piper sleeps in gilded chains*. And Berenice had thought her mother had exaggerated.

"I imagined I'd find you here." Pieton startled her as he often did. The eunuch had an uncanny way of entering rooms unnoticed.

"And I imagined my guards would block uninvited guests and leave me a few minutes of peace to enjoy my chambers." Despite herself, Berenice took comfort in his familiar presence. With him, at least, she knew what to expect. Teasing aside, he cared for her. And his regard couldn't be muddied.

"Your chambers? How quickly you appropriate your father's things. The diadem becomes you. No wonder you spend your hours in this hall of mirrors."

She smiled at the eunuch's mocking tone.

"These rooms must satisfy for a time," she answered.

"Meanwhile," Pieton trundled on, "Egypt accrues countless costs: your guards, your coins, your emissaries. And word from Memphis is that the Nile doesn't rise."

"Nor should it. Thoth doesn't start for another ten days. The Season of Inundation hasn't even begun."

"But it nears. And the priests of that city fret over the river's low measure."

"No doubt Psenptais stands first among the fretters." Her father had vanished across the sea, but his allies might still act in his name. Surely his prophet would be eager to stir sentiment against her.

"He does, my queen, but his provocation doesn't mean there's no cause for concern. A low flood means—"

"I *know* what a low flood means, Pieton." Children starving in the streets, men fomenting their hunger into rebellion. She would have to visit the Upper Lands and bring grain and comfort to the dying. "But let us, for the moment, celebrate. On this day of all days..." For too long, she'd waited for this. She snapped her fingers at the serving girl waiting by the door. "Wine for the queen and her adviser, her chief adviser, her minister of coin."

She found herself aching for the eunuch's smile, and he rewarded her. Even now, his moods pulled at hers, like the moon tugging at the tide. Throughout the long middling years of childhood, after her mother had been shunned and her father had forgotten her for Cleopatra, Pieton's grins, his kind words, proved her only nourishment. To the rest of the world, she'd shrunk away, an ungainly girl of nine, then ten or thirteen, discarded by the king. To everyone but Pieton. He'd coaxed her mind to fruition, stoking her interests and her hurts. His unyielding confidence had fueled her hopes, had persuaded her that someday, somehow, she might be queen. And now she was.

"To the double kingdom." She raised her glass. When she met Pieton's gaze, she saw no joy behind his smile. His mouth curled, but his eyes were dull slits in his girlish face. He twisted the goblet's stem between his fingers. The satyrs piped round and round.

"What else troubles you?" she asked quietly, doing her best to mask her disappointment. "Have you news of my father?"

"As far as our spies can tell, his course is set for Rhodes. He seeks a particular favorite of ours: Cato."

Cato—that stinking thief. He had stolen Cyprus in his Roman greed, and now her father would kneel before that man, beg for Roman arms to defeat her claim. She shouldn't be surprised: the kingdom had never mattered to the Piper. He'd been raised as a spare, she reminded herself, a bastard in far-off Syria, drinking in the favors of whatever king glanced his way. He'd viewed the throne as a gift, not an obligation. The loss of Cyprus still burned as salt in a wound, and her familiar fury sated the emptiness she'd felt. She couldn't undo her father's misdeeds in a day, but she had hoped he'd have pride enough not to seek aid from the very man who'd destroyed his legacy.

"Tell me: who else knows of the Piper's plans? Have your rats begun to spread the poison around the city?" This aspect of Pieton's power had long impressed her, his way of consorting with all manner of men, of blending seamlessly into palace and alley alike.

"Not yet, my queen. It's better to leave his friends in the dark a little longer. They think him fled; they know not where. Let them wonder at his cowardice for a time."

"There's much of it to wonder at." Her skin bristled. Her father's weakness baffled her. And how long she'd remained blind to it. She'd endured years of his scorn before she'd recognized the truth. It made no sense: her father had been born of Ptolemy the Savior's seed, just as her mother had been. But she couldn't imagine two dispositions more opposed. Did that same thinness run in her blood?

"You'll never be like him." Sometimes, the eunuch seemed to read her thoughts with disturbing ease. "You're cut from your mother's cloth, not his."

"I'm not sure that's a compliment." She grinned.

The wiry eunuch paused, assessing her. His teeth wore at his lower lip. "There's one more matter, of a rather delicate nature. The question of your sister."

Her sister. She thought she'd accounted for the children. The eldest, Cleopatra, would be with the Piper, and the concubine would whisk away the rest; she always imagined that would be the plan. The boys were barely out of changing clothes. And even Cleopatra was scarcely eleven—which would make Arsinoe younger still. Berenice tried to recall the child's face. The two daughters her father begot on his concubine blended in her mind. They were close in age, a scant two or three years apart. True siblings, the sort that had been stolen from her.

"I thought her mother took her from the palace."

"I thought so too. But it seems she has only the boys. This younger daughter appears less loved by both parents. A guard found her quaking beneath her bed during first watch last night."

"Surely she has some nurse or tutor who cares for her." It took Berenice a moment to realize why the eunuch was troubling her with this, to remember how her mother would react to find one of the Piper's younger children within her grasp. Her mother would want the girl dead.

"My mother, I presume, has other plans for the child," Berenice went on.

"She never did take a liking to your father's lesser children..."

"And what do you think, Pieton? What are your plans?" She hadn't wanted to involve the children—not if she could avoid it. But kindness, softness—she couldn't betray those either. They weren't the province of queens.

The eunuch's finger teased the fuzz along his upper lip. After all these years, he still needed to flaunt his vestigial traces of manhood. It saddened her. "I bear this Arsinoe no love," he said. "But the child is not universally disliked; among the servants she is something of a favorite. And there are those who worry that a city under Tryphaena's thrall will be a bloody one. The murder of an innocent girl would confirm those fears."

Berenice smiled. He had answered perfectly. This ability to cast her decisions in the most politic light was a special talent of his. "Perhaps, then," she answered, "it would be wiser for me to intervene on her behalf. Saving this poor, abandoned child might endear me to my subjects."

"I think it would reflect some wisdom, yes, and kindness too. That can work to your advantage."

Not a sentiment Tryphaena would ever credit. To her mother, kindness was softness, and softness was death.

After Pieton quit her chambers, Berenice let her thoughts wander to Arsinoe. The girl would be alone and terrified. At that age, she would have scarcely spent a night apart from her nurse, and now she'd measured two. And what could this child know of hunger pains and fear? The girl must be nine or so, the same age she'd been at Cleopatra's birth, when she'd watched her own mother cast from the palace and lain quaking in her room, waiting and wondering what would become of her. A stitch of sympathy twisted in her gut for the forgotten child.

YOUNGER

Arsinoe had run out of tears. Her fingers clutched the damp blanket, cold evidence of the recent flood. Now her eyes were dry as sand; she could hardly believe she'd authored such a deluge.

Half naked, shivering, she clutched her knees to her chest. She'd removed her soiled tunic and changed her underthings, but she'd no idea how to dress herself. That was never her job; that's what servants were for. A fool, she still hoped for Myrrine's return, for lavender-scented water, for cleansing hands. But no servant came to bathe or feed her, nor perfume the air or strip away her clothes. Even though she'd bundled them off in a corner, she could still taste their stench.

How she longed to creep from her chambers, and cross the corridor to her sister's rooms, to curl up beside Cleopatra in her bed. Her sister would whisper all the court's secrets in her ear. She would know what to do, and what to say, when to beg for mercy and when to stand with pride. But those chambers would be stripped and empty. That sister was far across the sea. In Rhodes? Athens? Rome? Arsinoe didn't even know where her father sailed. And what difference did that make? If he'd worried after her, he would've taken her along too. *King Ptolemy's daughter is already on board.*

Her palms cradled the fire-bearded soldier's gifts. Yesterday, her hunger had ebbed to a dull roar; hours had passed when she'd almost forgotten it entirely. But today her famine returned with a vengeance. Each breath brought a new pang in her gut. Starvation, too, could kill a girl, and not nearly so quick as poison. Democrates's end, when she thought of it now, didn't seem such a wretched one. Her left hand toyed with a grape, twisting it back and forth between her thumb and index finger. She brought the fruit to her lips. She kissed its cool skin. And so this was how her life would end: alone, abandoned by her mother and her father, by her sister and her friends. She clung to this moment, her very last, and then she sank her teeth into its flesh. The room spun as the juices dripped down her chin.

Death seemed a fair price to pay for such pleasure. So she ate another grape, and a third. She couldn't help herself. Soon she no longer ate them one by one but in handfuls, stuffing her cheeks until only a barren stem remained. A minute passed. And then another. She wondered what it would feel like as she died, whether it would be like falling asleep, or if—instead—it would hurt like something wretched. Like the time she'd caught the burning fever when she was six. How she'd shrieked and shivered in her bed, her head flaming and her mind possessed by dizzying dreams. Cleopatra had insisted on sleeping at her side, cradling her sweating form in her arms and whispering tales of Odysseus to soothe her each night. When their father had tried to banish Cleopatra from her chamber, fretting over the older girl's health, she'd fired back, "You have sons, Papa, and I won't live anyway, not without Arsinoe." But this felt different. No flames licked her cheeks; no hands cloyed at her throat. She could see straight and steady enough to count the Seven Sisters in the sky, fleeing from Orion's wooing sword. Her clenched fists uncoiled. She would live.

But rather than be sated, her hunger grew more forceful. She yearned for bread, as she'd never yearned for anything before. Only a bite, she promised herself, perhaps two, enough to tide her over to tomorrow's dawn, no more. Her teeth attacked the stale crust. And though she had to gnaw and gnash and tear, it tasted better than the softest, sweetest loaves in her father's hall. Before she knew it, she was licking the last crumbs from her fingers. The dates she wrapped up in the guard's cloth, and she slipped them beneath the bed.

That night, a hyena chased her through the palace halls. Her feet slipped against stone; she'd lost her sandals and the floor was cool beneath her toes. Her eyes scanned the walls for a door—any door—but there was none, only endless sheets of marble lined by statues: Apollo drawing back his bow, Athena helmed for war, the Three Gorgons struggling over a single eye. She rounded the corner to find shadows, shadows lurking, windows black. Ahead: nothing, nowhere to run, only solid stone. The beast snarled at her heels, and when she turned to face her enemy, she saw it was no natural animal. Instead, a bristled creature stood before her with a human face, the most wretched she could imagine: the bulging, bulbous eyes of Tryphaena glinted with hate. She gnashed her sharpened teeth. Arsinoe screamed.

She awoke, trembling. But slowly her panic recoiled as she took in her surroundings. The morning that greeted her wasn't so very different from ones that had come before her father fled: a tidy room cleared of soiled robes, blankets folded by the bed, even the curtains thrown open. And when she approached the window, she could see that a dark rain had washed away the bloodstained stones. And beyond, the light of Pharos called sailors to Alexandria's dawn. Perhaps Myrrine might even be returned to her. Eager, she paced the room to pass the time. Once, then twice, then thirty times. The sun inched higher on his path, but no servant came.

Arsinoe's stomach growled in protest, even after she'd eaten the dates. But someone had been in to tidy her room. That made her bold. She could demand food as well. She crossed to open the door, but it was bolted shut. Her fingers balled into a fist and rapped against it. She waited, but no one answered. Once more, she knocked, tightening her grip. Still silence. She banged a third time; her right fist joined her left, flailing harder and harder against the cedar. Her hands prickled with pain, and her right one snagged a splinter, but the hurt spurred on her fury. She beat against the door, against her father and her nurse, against her tutor and her mother, against her departed sister and the reigning one, until her hands were bruised and bloody, and her eyes stung with anger. Then she banged harder still. At last, defeated, Arsinoe sank to the floor, hunger consumed by rage.

When the sun had long since passed his apex and begun his slow descent into the sea, the door creaked. An unfamiliar maid, a girl perhaps a year or two her elder, darted in, bearing a plate of cheese and bread and olives.

"What's your name?" Arsinoe asked. There was a power in naming people and things. Cleopatra had taught her that too, when they'd encountered a strange woman lurking in the library. A vagrant of some sort, rooting through the scrolls. Arsinoe had shrunk away in fear, but Cleopatra had smiled sweetly and asked the woman's name. "If you call people by name, Arsinoe," she'd explained afterward, "they'll answer you." Arsinoe believed those words—fervently. The natives of this land even held that the first god, their Atum, spoke himself into existence, that he came into being from the water by conjuring his own name.

But the servant only shook her head, her gaze fixed on the floor. Arsinoe didn't know what this maid had to fear: *she* was the one who'd been abandoned, imprisoned in her rooms, and waited on by strangers. Arsinoe felt the tears building, the pressure clawing at her eyes, but she blinked them away. She kept her gaze trained on the girl, and an idea came to her: perhaps the maid wasn't Greek by birth. Her skin was burned a deep copper, darker than her own. There were some servants who traced their roots to the Upper Lands. Cleopatra's first milk mother had spoken only the local dialect. Not for the first time, Arsinoe wished she had her sister's tongue. Her own knowledge of the Egyptian language was dismal on the best of days. Her Persian, her Aramaic, even her shoddy Latin came more quickly to her lips. But she found the words, pronouncing each with painstaking care.

"What is your name?"

The girl's dark eyes grew wider still. Did she recognize the alien sounds, or fear them? Arsinoe couldn't tell. The maid rushed to the door.

Arsinoe switched back to Greek. "Please—I beg you. Do you know what's happened to my nurse, my dear Myrrine?"

The maid shoved the door open.

"Please—just stay. You needn't answer."

Wood slammed on stone, and Arsinoe was again alone. Still, she hoped the girl would return; otherwise, a more severe servant might come, one who wouldn't even glance in her direction. She walked her chamber, on ginger tiptoe, first in a straight line back and forth, and then round and round in restless circles until her head spun and her feet ached. The sun finally slipped into the sea, and Arsinoe flopped onto her divan. When the door opened, she lay still. Perhaps her questions had driven the servant away last time; maybe if she stayed quiet, the maid would linger.

This time, the girl approached her, cutting straight across the room. Arsinoe opened her mouth to speak, but the maid put up a finger to her lips: *Quiet*. The girl slipped a roll of papyrus into Arsinoe's hand before she scurried from the chamber.

Arsinoe unfurled the paper to find Ganymedes's script. Nonsense characters jostled together on the page. No matter how she stared at them, the symbols refused to coalesce into words. It must be a cipher, she realized. She tried to remember which code Ganymedes used. He'd told it to her once, in passing. First, she replaced each letter with the third following, but the corresponding words made no sense. That scheme belonged to her and Cleopatra. She tried again, this time swapping out the second, and then the fourth. *Xi* became *sigma,* and *pi* turned into *upsilon,* and slowly she hit upon the meaning: "You haven't been forgotten. Devise a visit with your sister. It's always better to act."

This message soothed her. Its words gave her a goal, though she couldn't imagine how she'd meet with Berenice. When she had memorized every word, every line, every curve of the eunuch's hand, she dangled the message over her oil lamp's spout and watched the papyrus curl into flames.

The days settled into a routine. In the mornings, she'd awake and dress all on her own. The first time she tried, she'd failed—pathetically. She'd taken out her favorite tunic, a turquoise one whose silver stitching matched its cinch, and stared at it awhile. Myrrine would tell her to lift her arms above her head and slip on the garment all at once. When she tried to put her head through first, her arms wouldn't cooperate—and more than once she'd ended up squirming from a tangled heap. But she didn't give up so easily; after all, she'd have to wear fresh clothes if she was ever to meet with Berenice.

After a few more attempts, she mastered it: by slipping her arms in first, she could then get the linen over her head. Dressed, she'd sit by the window, mouthing the words on the new scrolls the maid delivered: Ganymedes's steady diet of Sophocles and Euripides, Aeschylus and Homer. Thankfully, he sent only stories, her favorites among them. "In the spirit of action," the note on each scroll read. She hadn't puzzled out, precisely, how these works should teach her to act, but she gathered that she must prepare some sort of speech for her sister. And so she'd study them until late in the afternoon, when her silent servant came, bearing plates of bread and fruit and cheese.

She struggled through the first two Theban plays. The familiar tales of overweening fate, of cruel incest, and of dark love. She could never understand Oedipus's horror at his discoveries: he was a great king, not some ordinary man. Why should it matter if he'd slain his father, if he'd taken his mother to bed? Her own family history was riddled with more twisted stories. Her great-grandfather had coupled first with his sister, and then with that same sister's daughter by his brother. And her father's sister had been wed first to her uncle and then to that uncle's son. Oedipus's paucity of brides was more surprising than his choice of them.

Ganymedes always scolded her for such thinking: "The House of Ptolemy might abide by incest, but the rest of the civilized world does not." And she tried to take these matters seriously—she did. And once she'd buried blind and crippled Oedipus in his grave, she came upon the play that sparked her spirit: *Antigone*. In a desecrated city, one brother's body lies unburied, the other's celebrated and raised up to the gods. The words of caution echoed in her ears: "Now look at the two of us, left so alone.... Think what death we'll die, the worst of all if we violate the laws and override the fixed decree of the throne, its power—we must be sensible." She pleaded with Antigone just as Ismene did: "Why rush to extremes? It is madness, madness." How often she'd urged Cleopatra to caution: not to spur her horse so hard, not to swim so deep, not to provoke Ganymedes's rage. Sometimes Cleopatra would listen, but more often than not, she'd merely laugh and race her pony all the faster. And Ismene's words would echo in her head: "You're so rash—I am so afraid for you!"

Engrossed in the daughters' tales, Arsinoe didn't long for company. Her own travails paled against those of Antigone, the girl who shattered King Creon's uneasy peace. Arsinoe admired her righteousness, and feared it too. Sometimes she herself bristled with that firmness of conviction. And how weak and paltry lesser loves grew in comparison: Ismene's love, and Haemon's as well. They couldn't measure against Antigone's wild passion for justice, for the laws of the gods, no matter how Arsinoe wished they might sway the fated path. "Deserted so by loved ones, struck by fate..." Only in the evening, when her maid carried in her final meal, would she pry her eyes from the texts and repeat the practiced phrase, "I beg an audience with my beloved sister, the Shining Queen, Berenice."

As Arsinoe read on, Antigone's woes came to an end: she hanged dead as her weeping lover slammed his hands against the rock. And Ismene, sweet and kind and useless Ismene, was left to live on, knowing that she could neither change her sister's path nor share it. To Arsinoe, that always seemed saddest of all.

Her own trials wore on too. In her darker moments, she wondered whether she'd ever leave her chamber again. She cursed the eunuch, and his plans, with every dirty word Cleopatra had passed along from her long weeks on ships. How could she set up an audience with Berenice when no one spoke to her or remembered that she still lived? She was neither great nor brave nor bold. She was the ordinary daughter. That was why she'd been left behind. Not only by her father, who'd always whisked Cleopatra away, but also by her mother, who'd saved her brothers even though they were only dull babies.

One evening, instead of delivering another text from Ganymedes, her mute maid bore a different gift: a note sealed with an unfamiliar mark, the bloodred image of a woman crowned by the vulture headdress. A stiff hand informed, "The queen will grant you an audience tomorrow."

The words didn't frighten her, though she imagined that they should. Instead, the knot in her stomach loosened and she was overcome with a strange sense of calm. Arsinoe knew what she must do. She had to write, and act quickly. Somehow she had to convince Berenice to spare her. To prove to her sister that she didn't conspire with their father.

"My august and royal sister, the Shining Queen of the Upper and the Lower Lands..." Her quill scratched against the papyrus. "I beg not for my life." Her handwriting had grown straight and even with practice. She smiled at her work. "For who can twist the wrist of fate?" Over and over she scrawled and scorched each phrase until her hand ached and her fingers crisped. "I merely ask for mercy." She couldn't say why she burned each practice papyrus.

The childish part of her wished to hold on to them and show the neatness of her letters to Ganymedes. But torching them seemed somehow wiser than leaving them strewn about her chambers. Her eyes grew weary and watered at the flame. She rested her head on her hands, but only for a moment. And then dreams carried her far from Alexandria's palaces and across the great sea to Rome and her incumbent terrors: Cleopatra wounded, Cleopatra weeping, Cleopatra dead.

The sun had risen high by the time Arsinoe awoke, and in haste she scrubbed her face raw in her silver basin's cooled waters. She scoured her hands as well, but she couldn't rid herself of the grime between her bruised and bitten fingernails. When the maid entered, she hid her hands behind her back. Myrrine would have scolded her for them, but this new girl didn't seem to notice. In silence, she rooted through Arsinoe's chest of clothes until she pulled out a pale blue chiton.

Arsinoe would have rather worn her turquoise tunic—she almost would have rather dressed herself. She felt more comfortable in tunics; they were looser, easier for running about. But she didn't object. Instead, she matched the quiet mood and spread her arms wide to form a *tau* as the maid slipped the sheet over her head and buttoned it tightly along her underarms. It tickled, but she didn't laugh. It was a serious matter, this first meeting with her queen.

The great courtyard looked brighter than Arsinoe remembered. Even when she shielded her face with her hand, the light bouncing off the marble paths seared her eyes. Maybe it was just the emptiness that struck her. Usually this public court bustled with courtiers and bureaucrats, royal friends and servants. Now only sentinels lined its colonnades, tall and unfamiliar men so stiff in service that they, too, might have been made of stone.

"Keep up," one of her escorts snapped at her, and she nearly tripped over a trailing edge of her skirt as she hurried through the western colonnade. Here the soldiers grew thick in number, their eyes glaring at her even through their helms.

The first anteroom seemed to have overgrown itself in her absence. The granite arches sweeping upward toward the gods themselves and the twin sphinxes who guarded the atrium looked menacing. Even the one on her left, which she'd always imagined resembled her father, stared at her with an eerie, human gaze. She'd been called into the audience hall itself only on a few rare occasions. Once was when some Roman senator had come to town, and her father had wanted to show off his daughters. She'd been frightened then—Cleopatra had teased her that Romans ate little Macedonian girls for dinner—but she could not be frightened now.

She heard the herald announce her name: "Arsinoe, Princess of Egypt."

She was still a princess. That meant something. And with a deep breath, she walked past the sphinxes and into the hall. The chamber was quiet and nearly empty; perhaps half a dozen guards. Slowly, Arsinoe raised her eyes to Berenice.

Her sister sat bolt straight on her throne—their father's golden chair with its curved leopard-headed feet. It looked all wrong to see Berenice this way, the white diadem bound tight across her dark hair. At her right was Tryphaena, the stony-eyed monster who haunted Arsinoe's dreams. She remembered all too well the screaming scenes when she was small, before her father had banished his sister-wife from the royal lodgings. Returned to power, the woman appeared even more terrifying. Arsinoe glanced away, turning her gaze to her sister's eunuch, a skinny, almost graceful thing who from a distance could have passed for an uncut youth. In the far corner, a scribe, a squinting face familiar to her father's court, trembled over his papyrus.

Irreverently, Arsinoe hoped she wouldn't grow to look like Berenice, whose face betrayed all the lesser Ptolemy traits: the heavy brow, the hooked nose, the thin-lipped smile. "Medusa," she and Cleopatra had called her until, one day, Alexander, the odd boy among their royal set, had pointed out that the Gorgon herself had once been a beauty so ravishing that she'd been envied by the gods—and transformed into a monster. The fear of being changed themselves frightened them enough to drop the nickname.

"Approach," her sister told her.

Arsinoe obeyed, chasing disrespectful memories from her mind. What if Berenice could read them on her face? Cleopatra always knew precisely what she was thinking, and perhaps that was some skill of sisters, even ones she didn't know very well.

"You've begged an audience long enough, and given quite a fright to the poor girl who serves you." Berenice looked her in the eye. "What must you tell me?"

Arsinoe's hand twitched at her side, tracing words she'd practiced in the empty air, but her tongue stayed plastered to her teeth. Her mouth was dry and chafed; she couldn't dream of speech.

"I know you don't want to waste our time." Her sister's tone was nearly kind; perhaps Berenice didn't mean her harm.

"Perhaps the child doesn't talk," the eunuch offered with a shrug. "Shall I return her to her chambers?"

"Indeed," Tryphaena crackled in a hoarse voice. "Her mother could scarcely string a sentence together. I can't imagine why the pup would differ from the bitch."

The pup would differ from the bitch. The words ripped at Arsinoe's ear. And still, no words formed in her mouth.

"That's enough, Mother," Berenice said, clearing her throat loudly. Disappointment—or so Arsinoe thought—clouded her sister's eyes as she addressed her guards. "Return her to her chambers."

The moment ripened to the point of spoiling; she had to answer. She forced the syllables from her lips.

"My august and gracious sister, the Shining Queen of the Upper and the Lower Lands, it is an honor to be admitted to your presence."

Her rehearsed words came easily once she'd begun. "I beg not for my life, for who can twist the wrist of fate? I merely beg to pledge my allegiance to you, and ask for your mercy."

Her phrases flowed too quickly; the power of her rhetoric was lost, her painstaking words swallowed by her speed. Berenice, Tryphaena, Pieton—all stared at her blankly, as though she nattered on in some alien tongue. And her last phrase was met with deadened silence.

Tryphaena broke the quiet. "So she does speak, and rather prettily when she chooses, but that changes nothing. Her fate is sealed, Berenice. Her two bastard brothers live; you've no use for more pretenders to the throne."

"Mother, you'd have me hack off the head of my own shadow." Berenice smiled slightly, a flicker on her lips. "I am the only true-born child of Ptolemy the New Dionysus. I have no reason to fear the second daughter of a lesser wife. His favored Cleopatra, perhaps, or the two little boys, whose tiny pricks may pose a threat, but not this girl."

And there it stood, the unvarnished, devastating truth. She was no threat; she was nothing. Berenice wouldn't have her killed because she wasn't worth the bother. Arsinoe wasn't sure whether she should be grateful or ashamed.

When she returned to her rooms, she saw that they had been disturbed. Her heart pulsed in her throat. A certain smell, a familiar one, greeted her as well. She wasn't alone. Frightened, she rushed through her antechamber and into her bedroom. There stood the intruder, a figure shaking by her window. As the woman looked up, her face bruised, eyes red, it took Arsinoe a moment to recognize her nurse.

"Myrrine," she called out tentatively.

"My dear child," Myrrine whispered, and then she opened her arms to Arsinoe. "My dear, sweet child."

"Where have you been?" she asked, accusing.

"Never mind that." The woman's voice shook. "Come here, and let me hold you."

Arsinoe couldn't resist, and she raced across the room to wrap her arms around her nurse's neck. As she did so, her anger drained away.

"My dear, sweet child," Myrrine murmured in her ear. "How I worried about you. Who tended to you while I was gone?"

No one, Arsinoe wished to cry out. *No one at all.* But she held her tongue and wept only a few solitary tears.

ELDER

Berenice didn't like the feel of the white band tight about her head. But it proved a valuable reminder of what she had accomplished. Pieton teased her for wearing it at all hours. "I know why you sport it in the audience hall, but here . . . among your trusted councilors . . ." What trusted councilors? Dio had helped deliver her the city, and Pieton had proved instrumental too. But each insisted that she should be wary of the other. The Alexandrian couldn't abide any eunuchs, let alone ones schooled in courtly life. And the eunuch grew bitter whenever anyone drew too close to Berenice. He'd always clutched at these jealousies. Even when he'd been her tutor and she'd been no more than a disgraced girl, he'd hated when she'd confided too much in her companions. At the time, it had puzzled her, but now she understood: Pieton was alone. Why shouldn't she be too?

The same questions plagued her, even in her solitude. What did her father mean to accomplish in Rhodes? How long would Alexandria lend her support? And when, *when* would the Nile rise? That was most worrisome of all. If the natives of the Upper Lands grew hungry, they'd turn defiant—and look to Memphis or even to Rome for relief. She herself should travel up the Nile, bearing Alexandrian grain to placate the populace. Besides, a voyage to the Upper Lands would give her the chance to rally Egypt's far-flung soldiers. After years spent growing fat on their southern farms, they had to be reminded of their duty to their queen. She'd need them to launch her attack on Cyprus.

She heard a shriek outside. Her mother's. The woman would never, it seemed, tire of stalking her. Berenice preferred her father as her enemy, remote and unequivocal. Tryphaena was too messy and too near. She knew every tender point to press.

"Have the guards let her in," she told her herald.

The doors slammed in her mother's wake. Hair torn, eyes wide and wild, Tryphaena refused to enter quietly. "Women like us," her mother had often told her, "will forever be thrust aside when silent. We have no gift for meek beauty; that's what concubines are for." As a child, Berenice hoped, or feared, that her mother would diminish once the Piper swapped her birthright for a blushing mistress. Treachery had only ossified the old woman's resolve; she was her most formidable in defeat.

"Explain yourself, child."

The word irked her. She'd earned her victories, and she was weary of being treated as some girl.

"That's no way to address your queen." It was important to draw her lines now, even if they were in the shifting sand.

"You relish that unearned title, don't you, daughter of mine? How you love to listen to your coronation name ring out. But there's some small trifle that you seem to have forgotten amidst your celebrations."

"And what might that be?" She feigned ignorance, though it sounded childish to her as well. She hated how her mother's words reduced her to this. But she would not raise this issue, her mother's obsession over what it meant to share the throne.

"Don't be dull," her mother answered, chafing. "You know why I'm here. We were to be co-rulers, you and I."

"And so we shall be." Berenice smiled. Here she wouldn't give an inch.

"'Shall'?" Her mother hacked, her body buckling in on itself. As she straightened, Tryphaena looked at her with fresh contempt. "You think I will content myself with 'shall'?"

"You're sick, Mother, and you're tired. Sit down and rest. Alexandria has seen enough changes these past few days. Let the people adjust to one queen before we foist a second on them." Berenice tried to bring warmth into her words. Her mother *was* old and weary. And the woman had tried to protect her. Hadn't she, in her twisted way?

Tryphaena refused to sit, even as her veiny legs bent under her weight. "So, you imagine my illness makes me weak? You think I'll slink off in silence?"

"Mother, no one expects you to do anything in silence."

"My words don't shock you. A pity. With time, I'll overcome such disappointments. After all, they don't rank against the most disquieting discovery: that my daughter is a cowardly cunt."

Her mother's venom could not sting her; she wouldn't let it.

"Keep a civil tongue," Berenice ordered. "I might grant you leniency as my mother. My guards won't be so kind."

In truth, her men looked unperturbed. The thick-bearded one whose belly threatened to burst through his toga picked under his nails with a knife; the other, with a younger face marred by a crooked nose, stared blankly across the atrium, over Dionysus on his leopard and at the pair of gold leaf lions carved into the great ebony door. She wondered if he saw anything at all.

"Respect isn't earned in a day. Even if I grovel before you, they'll know what you are: a frightened child who dares not do what she must to protect her rightful seat."

"Enough, *Mother*," Berenice cracked. She should be planning her next moves, not arguing with her ailing mother who'd outgrown her usefulness. "You test my patience. I'm no longer that child of nine; I don't need to listen to your yapping."

"And you do not. Each day you seek to flout my will with your every move. For instance, that *girl*"—Tryphaena pronounced the word with disgust—"the one you call sister. What madness has possessed you to let the Piper's bastard daughter live? Surely

you haven't forgotten what that creature's mother did to me—
to us?"

No, she hadn't forgotten, but she would not twist herself with
hatred. She would not murder for murder's sake.

"She's but a child, Mother." Stripped of sentiment, the endear-
ment had become an incantation. *Mother, Mother, Mother.* She
clutched at that lingering notion of her girlhood: that this phrase,
this reminder of her mother's single act of womanhood, might lure
Tryphaena back to calm.

"A *child* who presents the most pressing threat to your rule."

"That distinction belongs to her brothers."

"Whom, I've no doubt, you'd welcome with open arms should
that concubine leave them soiled and sobbing at the royal gate."

They were babies, nothing more. Babies who shared the distinction and the curse of being born a Ptolemy. In time, she realized,
she might be forced to have them killed. The thought wormed its
way around her stomach, and there it purred as though she'd always
known the cold truth of it.

"You grow hysterical, Mother."

Berenice cast a second eye at her guards. His nails picked clean,
the first had returned his hands to his side. His thumb drummed
against his thigh. The second, to her surprise, had taken some interest in their conversation. That worried her.

"Leave us," she told them. "She's only a weak and weeping
woman. She's no threat to me, or anyone. Make sure no one dis-
turbs us."

As the soldiers filed through the lion-flanked door, her mother's
lips curled into a crooked smile, sharp and wide. Berenice winced;
she recalled the last time she'd seen that expression. A child of
five or six, she'd stumbled upon her mother cooing over a blanket.
When she approached, she saw that it was stained scarlet, and
within its folds lay not a babe but a scaly creature with shrunken
limbs. She shrieked, and her mother looked up at her with the same

grin. "Do you think you're any less hideous?" Tryphaena had hissed. "That is no way to speak to my beloved son, you useless girl."

Berenice shunted the image from her mind. "Does it please you? To mock me before my men?"

"It would please me if you slew the rat that creeps beneath your roof, growing fat on your misspent kindnesses. She may be young, she may not have the cleanest claim, but she's still a Ptolemy. Though you've forgotten what that means, I assure you that bastard girl has not."

"We hunt the boys. The girl means nothing. To kill her would be a needless act of cruelty."

"To kill her would show your strength. To do otherwise proves what your citizens already suspect: that you are a weak-willed woman. *Never show them you are soft.*"

This was her mother's anthem, the words she'd whispered over Berenice's cradle. Enfeebled, Tryphaena clung to them now, these straws of her once formidable self. And it nearly made Berenice weep.

"I've already sated the people's taste for blood. I've killed two dozen men, the closest compatriots of my father. I don't think anyone suspects me of softness. Not anyone but you."

"I see. You wish for me to coddle you. To soothe your fears with lies. You have a wet nurse and a eunuch for that. I'm your mother, and I won't shrink from that role. I raised you as I would have raised the boy I should have borne: to rule."

The boy I should have borne. What did her mother think of when she spoke those words? Did her heart ache for the lizard child she had cradled in her arms? Or the other stillborn boys she'd whelped each spring before the Piper banished her from his bed and palace? Beneath all her furies, did some tenderness linger? Perhaps Berenice gave Tryphaena too much credit for feeling. Her mother raged on, unperturbed, as though that reference to the sons that she might have had held no more weight than any other. "After all my years of sacrifice, I won't pale with meekness."

Berenice stoked herself with a deep breath. Even as queen, she remained subject to her mother's rages. Her eyes caught on the faience goblet on the ivory table to her left. How she longed to pick it up and toss the wine in Tryphaena's face, to watch shock widen the woman's eyes. Instead, she lifted the chalice to her lips; its sticky sweetness eased her anger. When she spoke, her voice was calm and collected. "I never ask for your meekness, Mother, nor your lies. And I haven't believed the many that you've offered up so eagerly."

"Believe this truth, then: Arsinoe must die. Or else one day you'll wake to find her allied with her father. You have enough traitors in your midst; you don't need to court another."

"I know I have enemies, Mother. I don't need you to name them for me."

The two stared at each other in silence. Tryphaena, for once, had run out of words, and so they had reached a draw of sorts. Berenice would not back down. As queen, she could at last take on this woman who'd never found her worthy of her love. From the corner of her eye, she saw a door creak open, and her eunuch stepped into the atrium.

"What's he doing here?" her mother spat.

"Apologies, my queen," Pieton replied coolly. "I didn't intend to disturb a familial parley."

A familial parley. The thought that Pieton wouldn't be included there was strange in and of itself. After all, he'd paid more heed to her than her mother ever had. It was Pieton—not Tryphaena—who'd taught her lessons and comforted her when she was sad. Wasn't that what family was—what other people's families were?

"That was precisely your intent," Tryphaena barked. "The guards told you I was within." She returned her fury to Berenice. "Watch your companions, my dear. This one's every word stinks of deceit."

"The two who stand watch told me they couldn't speak of the

queen's business," the eunuch answered. "I'd no idea who attended you here."

Berenice ignored her mother's glares. "What brings you to me, Pieton?"

"There are matters we must discuss involving Inundation in the Upper Lands."

Berenice pursed her lips. Inundation and the Upper Lands—business that concerned her and the double kingdom both. She'd already wasted too much time, mired in this feud.

"Do his lies blind you?" Tryphaena hissed. Her mother hated nothing more than being ignored. "Don't you see what he's doing? How he begrudges you all private counsel?"

"Don't flatter yourself, Mother. You're not my councilor—only a shrieking harpy upon whom I take pity in my weaker moments."

She didn't meet her mother's eye; she looked to the door instead.

"Guards," she cried out. "My mother requires an escort."

Tryphaena flailed against callous hands that gripped her shoulders and dragged her across the floor.

"Don't pretend I didn't warn you. Remember this day, child. Remember it. Perhaps you were right: the nearest threat isn't Arsinoe after all."

Hacking blocked Tryphaena's tongue as the guards pulled her away. Legs splayed before her, she looked not a hellhound but an aging mother, long past her prime, shielding her last living child. Her knees knocked; her flesh hung loose about her arms and throat. Berenice's heart grew weak but she steeled herself with her mother's words: *Never show them you are soft.*

In the days that followed, Berenice avoided her mother—a task that proved easier than she had imagined. As queen, she needn't answer to anyone, and perhaps her threats had frightened the old woman in the end. Rumors hummed that Tryphaena lay ill with coughs and quakes and shivers. The more dramatic among the slaves claimed that she was near death. Berenice didn't care. She had finished with her mother's games. Too many times throughout her childhood, Tryphaena would take to her bed—it was always a ruse, a desperate attempt to draw the Piper in. She would not fall for those same tired ploys.

Besides, she had more important matters to attend. To retake Cyprus, she would need knowledgeable advisers, ones who could muster troops and predict Rome's movements. Pieton had winnowed out what few of her father's men might be trusted—or at least kept in line—and so she called for them to be brought before the court. She wanted to see what she would make of these men herself.

"Is it necessary for you to leave Alexandria so soon?" Dio drummed his fingers against the cypress. Perhaps he worried that her support in the city would flag in her absence.

The eunuch glared at the question. "The local interloper," Pieton called Dio behind closed doors, as though the Alexandrian had no business concerning himself with matters of the throne. The more the eunuch objected, though, the more Berenice's fondness for the man grew.

"It's time for me to sail up the Nile to distribute grain. First to Memphis, and then on to Thebes. The locals should be reminded that they have a new queen, one who embraces her duties as their shepherd." The thought exhausted her; she'd never taken much joy in her journeys to Upper Egypt. But that was where too many of her armed men lay. Even reduced to an echo of its former self, Thebes remained a potent fantasy for the defiant masses: natives from the farthest reach of the Nile's waters all the way to Alexandria could hardly speak the city's name without a shiver of awe. Her presence, she hoped, would check any rebellious tendencies. She needed the town and its surrounding lands subdued if she was to recall the legions stationed there. "As queen, I will not let my people starve—any of my people."

"The solstice has scarcely come and gone. Surely the people are not starving yet," Dio argued with a light smile. "You shouldn't forget your beloved subjects in Alexandria either."

The eunuch eyed the man's broad belly with contempt. "Well, you're not starving, Dio. That much is evident."

Berenice smiled. Pieton's touchiness amused her. His loathing for Dio sprang from his affection for her, she realized, which she found comforting. It was a relief that someone loved her, her to the exclusion of all others.

"No, thank the good gods, I am not. I am merely jealous to be deprived the pleasure of the queen's company." He raised his goblet in her direction. "To Queen Berenice the Shining One."

Pieton raised his cup in return, grudgingly. That boded well; they'd need to find some way to work together. As she drained her glass, a knock sounded against the door.

"I present Nereus, son of Sostias; Dryton, son of Mentes; and Thais, son of Harmon," the herald proclaimed in his thunderous voice.

The first to enter was the last announced, a twitchy, beardless man whose balding pate was ringed by a dusting of chestnut curls. Unlike Dio, he did look nearly starved. This Thais was so skinny that his elbows stuck out at angles, as though a stiff breeze might knock him off his feet. He'd directed the farming of the southernmost lands under her father's rule. He was noted for neither loyalty nor bravery, but, she heard, he had a way of loading up the granaries with wheat.

"My—my queen," he stammered. "May the gods' blessings be upon you."

"There's no need for that, Thais," her eunuch sneered. "The priests have already said their words."

"It would be—it would be an honor to serve you, in whatever capacity you see fit. A—a great honor."

The man was terrified—that much was clear. Berenice had

already begun to tire of his shaking voice, and she turned her attention to his fellows behind: old Nereus leaning on a young man's—Dryton's—shoulder. Unlike Thais, neither appeared especially anxious.

"Or not to serve, if the queen prefers," Thais nattered on. "There can be honor in that as well. What—whatever the queen sees fit—"

"The queen would prefer your silence, Thais. She is likely too distracted by your stammering to see anything at all."

The reedy minister shrunk at the eunuch's words. He was a tall man but his shoulders hunched and his whole body looked as though it might collapse in on itself. Berenice smiled at Pieton. Snappish and ornery was how she liked him best. He served her well as a guard dog, her very own Cerberus.

Her gaze turned to Nereus. Among the oldest of the old guard, he'd gone almost completely bald. The hairs that once covered his head seemed to have migrated to his face, sprouting up in tufted eyebrows and bursting in thick clots from his nose. She'd never liked Nereus—she'd no reason to. After all, he'd advised her father to renounce her mother. He'd whispered poison in the Piper's ear: "Sons are what you need. And your wife only whelps dead ones." Or so Pieton had told her.

"Tell me, Nereus: why do you stand before me now?" This old man, despite his fickleness, required her courtesies. No one knew the inner workings of the army and the kingdom as well as he—and no one had more experience staving off the Romans. He still saw her as a girl, as helpless as on the day her father set aside her mother. But she'd show him otherwise. Spineless or not, he had his uses. As long as he learned his place.

His gray brow furrowed. He tried to read the wishes on her face. "Because, my queen, I have a reputation for serving the realm. I've served Alexandria since thirty years before your birth. I serve whoever rules. And you are the queen."

"While that's all very admirable, Nereus, we'll need more proof of loyalty than that," Pieton answered. "How are we to know that you won't send letters to the Piper? Even now, you might be telling him the inner workings of the palace."

"Very well, eunuch." The old man pinched at the sagging skin along his throat. He'd had a beard when Berenice was young—she couldn't fathom what foolishness had driven him to shave it off. "What would you ask of me to prove my loyalty?"

"The confidences between you and the Piper."

"You may have every letter that has passed between us two," Nereus rejoined solemnly. "I'll have my servant fetch them from my chambers at once."

"I knew you'd be cooperative." Berenice smiled, savoring each word. She'd let him squirm a while longer. "So I took the liberty of having my guards sort through your things."

Nereus's enormous eyebrows descended like great gray clouds over the sun, threatening to block his eyes entirely; perhaps he had more to hide than she had imagined. She would have her soldiers do a second sweep.

"Do you know where my father sails, Nereus?" she asked lightly.

"I know he is now in Rhodes," the old man replied with care. "But I don't know where he plans to go from there."

"I do," his young friend—Dryton—interjected. He had broad shoulders and a soldier's build. He wore his hair long as was the fashion among men her age, and he tossed an errant lock from his eyes before he continued. "I know your father, the Piper, sails to Rome. He told me so himself. He'll seek a favor from Pompey, a longtime friend of his. But he'll still have to beg his case before the Senate."

"Everyone knows that the Piper is in Rhodes, and any fool might surmise that he means to sail to Rome." Pieton yawned. "He entrusted his will to the Vestal Virgins of that city for safekeeping. And many a greater Ptolemy than he has asked for aid from the Republic." The eunuch toyed with him as a cat might with a mouse.

But Dryton was no mouse.

"I know more than that, my queen." His bright eyes fixed on hers, and he addressed his words to her alone. "I know the suit he'll make in front of Rome's senators. He discussed his arguments with me. I might sail to Rome myself, and make the counterplea."

Berenice kept her face blank. This man's offers were too shiny to be true, and though he could have some knowledge of her father's plans, she doubted that he had as much as he claimed. If he did, he might be a great deal more dangerous than she imagined. She wondered how one so young—he could not be more than twenty-five, perhaps not even that—had gained her father's confidence so easily. One way came to mind, but she pushed it from her thoughts. Her father was gone, and she wished to wash the city of his twisted proclivities, not dwell on them.

"You?" Pieton scoffed. "Sail to Rome? I wouldn't trust you as far as Memphis. Trust must be earned. A few choice phrases won't buy it."

Dryton started to object but thought better of it. "Of course, if that is—if that is what the queen desires."

"I'd prefer that you stay in Alexandria," Berenice said gently. Dryton knew her little; she'd let Pieton play the crueler part. "But you've been wise to tell us all you know. You'll relate my father's claims to Pieton and work to craft our argument."

Nereus spoke up. "But someone must go to Rome." He'd regained his footing, and he stood taller, as though a few years had slipped away. "A delegation must sail at once. Or perhaps one has already sailed. Pieton? Didn't you say that any fool might surmise that the Piper sails to Rome? Or are you not as clever as any fool?"

"Watch your step, old man," Pieton snapped. "I'm the only reason you are not already—"

"Silence. All of you." Berenice's voice brought quiet among these men who once had spoken over her without a second thought. This was what it was to have power. She savored it. This, she thought, would save her from emptiness; it would blossom in the place where all her hatreds lived.

"Dio shall lead the delegation to Rome," she announced with certainty.

Pieton tried to catch her eye; she ignored his efforts. She could hear his chiding voice inside her head: *Why reveal so much before these men you do not trust?* But now the eunuch wouldn't dare talk her out of her choice, not when she had marked it as her first command before her council.

Later, after that night's feasting had drawn to a close, Berenice eased back onto her dining couch. Weighed down with minted veal and honeyed duck, she felt as though her stomach might burst through her gown. Throughout the evening, the banqueting room had remained oddly bare. Too many of Alexandria's high nobles had vanished, either to their country villas or on her guards' spears. The rest were by and large too terrified to set foot in the palace. It didn't bother her; she liked the solitude. Great feasts marked her father's manner of conducting business, not her own. But she was still pleased when Dio slid onto the divan beside hers.

"I'm honored, my queen, that you'd send me to make your case in Rome." He grinned. His smile was the only handsome part of him: it revealed a dazzling set of teeth.

"I can't imagine a better emissary to represent my cause. There's no man in all of Alexandria who knows me as you do." Her voice grew flirtatious, despite herself. Dio brought out this side of her; he was too old, too plump, too lowborn, but it was his very home-liness that stoked her confidence. With pretty men, like Dryton, some part of her felt all knees and elbows, as though at nineteen she still hadn't grown into a woman.

"I worry about you here in Alexandria, surrounded by snakes." He scanned the chamber as though he expected to spot one slither-ing across the onyx floor.

"But my dear Dio, I won't be in Alexandria. I'll soon sail with

Pieton up the Nile to Thebes, to be worshipped by the adoring throngs."

She followed Dio's gaze to Nereus, old and drunk and crooning at the side of some young creature on the lute. From time to time, his hand crept higher up her leg, but the player paid his improprieties no mind. And then he turned his glance to Dryton, young and handsome and silent, watching every detail from his seat. He looked as though he had not touched a drop of wine.

"You trust these men to rule in your name, in your absence?"

"No, I don't trust them, nor that stammering Thais either, though I can't imagine he would have the balls to defy me." Berenice looked back at the man at her side. "But what other choice do I have?"

"Let me put off my voyage to Rome. Your father remains in Rhodes. For all we know, we have ample time to reach the Latium shore before he does. I can hold the palace in line until you return from the Upper Lands. And I can hound Dryton for all he knows about the Piper's plans."

A fervor reached his eyes, gleaming with the lamp's flame. She'd not seen that look before. There was an intensity to it that made her shiver. "Very well." She smiled. "Delay your voyage for two weeks. When my royal entourage passes through the city gates, you'll set sail."

As he stood, he clasped her hand and pressed it to his lips. An unfamiliar feeling stirred in her gut. Perhaps this is what her eunuch feared most of all: that Dio might offer something that he never could. *Nonsense,* she chided herself. *The man is as old as your father, and twice as fat.*

YOUNGER

Arsinoe slithered across grass and sand. She saw not with her eyes but with her tongue. A wolf, a hulking monster from a forgotten age, stalked ahead. He, too, hunted for blood. Her belly smoothed the prints left by his paws. A quail darted through the stalks, a fawn lingered at the shore, a peahen cocked her head. Everywhere she looked flashed lush and ample game. But the wolf ignored these delicacies. Hunger seized her, fang to tail. And then the blades opened to reveal his prey: a pair of foxes, one red and strong, the other white and withered.

Tail wagging, the wolf approached. He circled first his red cousin and then his white, round and round, the dance of fools. With each turn her hunger swelled, and her tongue tasted lies. Why was he toying with his food? And then the wolf's aspect changed: teeth bared, the fiend returned. He tore the fire fox's throat. Its mouth dripped with blood as the creature twisted in the yellow grass. In death, the creature's snout flattened into a human face—the red-crowned head of a familiar man. Her attention turned; her tongue caught another whiff of fear. Limping, the white fox fled—he fled toward her, and she hissed in pleasure. But at once the wolf was on him too, snapping his neck and tearing into his flesh. And then he turned his bloodshot eyes on her.

Dawn's rosy fingers stole her dream. Only cobwebs remained and soon those, too, were scraped away as Myrrine's deft hands plaited her locks for the new day. Out of the corner of her eye, she saw a figure lurking in the doorway. No, it wasn't possible. Arsinoe sprang from her stool; she could scarcely believe it. But there he was: her tutor with his narrow eyes and cracked nose.

"Ganymedes!" She ran across the chamber and threw her arms around the eunuch's neck. He remained—he hadn't abandoned her. She wanted suddenly, desperately, to be held.

"Calm yourself." He pried away her hands. "There's no need for such messy sentiment."

Hurt, she stepped back. Even here, he rejected her. This wasn't how their reunion was supposed to begin. The eunuch should have beamed with pride, and praised her for her wit, and wondered at her resolve. "The cleverest Ptolemy of all," he should have named her. She'd imagined it a thousand times: how he would lift her up and spin her around, as her father used to do with Cleopatra. One picture had lodged itself in Arsinoe's mind: their father, still clad in the trappings of the Upper Lands, the double crown perched upon his head, and her sister a blur of swirling crimson. Cleopatra had dressed herself as Isis, her eyes rimmed with kohl and her flowing garment knotted at the front. Arsinoe had thought it foolish, but when she saw the two together, the New Dionysus and his Isis, she'd changed her mind. They looked for all the world like a pair of gods, exalted in their twirling heaven. And this meeting was to mark her own triumph, her reward for all those quaking nights. The eunuch had spoiled it.

"Embrace her, Ganymedes. The girl's earned your approval." Myrrine prodded the tutor, breaking a dark hair from the comb's teeth.

"I don't seek anyone's approval. And I don't need my nursemaid to beg favors for me. Hold your tongue, Myrrine."

The servant frowned and looked away. Arsinoe wanted to unsay her own words, but she stayed quiet. She'd learned that skill.

"Come, my child," Ganymedes commanded, and she obeyed, trailing her tutor through the Sisters' Courtyard. The name itself stung; there were no sisters now. Or rather, it was the wrong two sisters: her and Berenice. But she brightened to see the water gushing from Arsinoe's fountain. It wasn't named for her, of course, but for one of her illustrious namesakes. Full-cheeked and full-bodied, the erstwhile queen stood between two columns, a half smile on her lips.

But Ganymedes was in no mood to stall. He tramped onward, his hulking form dwarfed by the soaring marble archways of the porticoes. The ancients, her tutor had told her once, had built their tombs this way to mimic the towering heavens. She felt small beneath, though she suspected that her father and her forefathers had emulated this style because they felt so very large. The scores of guards that flanked the columned walkways felt large as well. She could tell by their heavy steps, their hands resting on their hilts. She counted twenty, twenty-five, thirty guards before she tired of the task. And here and there, she caught a glimpse of spattered streaks, the dark end of the New Dionysus's rule.

Soon Arsinoe and Ganymedes passed into the courtyards that had been built long ago, by her great-grandfather Ptolemy the Pot-belly. The change was sharp. Gone were the twirling dryads and piping satyrs that her father preferred. Instead, the walls were carved with scenes from Alexander's life: first, the magnificent general loosening his sword to cut the Gordian knot, and later, spear drawn, galloping down upon the fleeing Persian army. Arsinoe saw her own father's face in place of Alexander's; she wondered how he would fare if faced by such adversaries. She couldn't be sure. The Persian king looked fierce in his chariot, whip in one hand, sword in the other. Would her father have stood and fought—or fled as he'd fled before her sister's men?

As she followed Ganymedes toward the library, the summer breeze blew away the flimsy ghosts of those bloody days. The grounds danced with the delights of summer, nymphs spat streams against their marble basins, roses peeked out from flower beds, figs unfolded green leaves against the blue of sky and sea. The world looked as though nothing had changed, as though the goings-on in the palace were mere child's play compared with the work of the undying gods.

"'I'm not ashamed to sail through trouble with you, to make your troubles mine,'" Arsinoe told Ganymedes, beaming. She'd prove that she merited his approval. She'd show him that she had studied the works he sent. And profited from each one.

"You look to Ismene now for inspiration? What happened to your beloved Odysseus?"

"I thought—since you asked me to read *Antigone*—and it was..." She paused to think, to make a careful measure of her words. "The war I fight isn't on the battlefield, but here in the palace."

"I wouldn't boast so loudly of your war," her tutor chided. "Especially as it seems to be a losing one like Ismene's. Ears linger at every bush."

Arsinoe spun her head this way and that, but she saw no evil eyes spying from the branches. Only the thick and carefree leaves of summer.

"It would be better to speak of what lessons lie ahead," the eunuch went on. "You've missed some weeks of schooling. I find you're very much behind in your learning."

"But I read," she protested. "I read many plays when I was confined. I read every word you sent me."

"I sent you nothing," the eunuch snapped.

Arsinoe nodded slowly; she could learn this lesson too, to never speak of what had come before. To pretend that this—whatever this proved to be—had always been her life. To forget that she'd ever had a mother and a father. To act as though she'd never been abandoned. As long as she could still hold on to Cleopatra. She refused to let go of her.

"I saw those scrolls piled in your room," said the eunuch. "What could you understand from them? Little and less, I'm afraid."

"I understood a great deal! I learned of duty, and of fate, and of mocking love."

"If you'd understood anything at all, I would hope it had come from Antigone."

"From Antigone?" she asked, curious. She hadn't expected this. She admired Antigone, admired her courage, her conviction. But the girl frightened her too. "But she's in love with death."

"And what attracts you to Ismene, then? Her love of life?"

Arsinoe shook her head. It wasn't that. Her thoughts returned to Cleopatra, to how, around this time of year, they might swim together in the sea, racing along the shore, masquerading as mermaids and other strange creatures of the ocean's depths. Girls had more freedom there beneath the waves. Once, her sister had dared her to venture out beyond the rocks, into the open sea, where the waves crashed unprotected, wild enough to swallow a child whole. But she'd done it, and without a trace of fear, because with Cleopatra at her side Arsinoe could do anything. Even die.

"No, it's her love of her sister," Ganymedes replied, reading her thoughts. "And where does it get her, all this loving of her sister? In the end, what is her love worth? It's not worth enough to bury Polynices."

It was true. Ismene had been too frightened to join Antigone, to bury their brother's body and pour libations over his flesh when their harsh uncle had forbidden it.

"But she regrets it, Ganymedes," Arsinoe protested. "And in the end, she understands. And she wishes that she'd helped Antigone."

"And what good is wishing?" Her tutor sighed. "What, my dear, does Antigone tell her? 'I have no love for a friend who loves in words alone.' And she is right. Didn't I warn you that it was better to act? How it is always better to act than to succumb to your fate?"

"But Antigone doesn't fight her fate—she embraces it."

"You have me there," Ganymedes said, laughing loud and deep. "But I'd hoped you might follow the greater point." His voice lowered to a whisper. "One that might advise you in your present state."

He was telling her to be brave, be bold, be Antigone. But she couldn't. Not now, not when the world had turned in on itself. It had been easy then, with Cleopatra. But all that courage had abandoned her along with her sister, sailing across the wine-dark sea. She didn't dare tell him that; she'd rather that Ganymedes think her dumb than spineless.

The eunuch, too, fell silent. And she hated the quiet more than his rebukes. He, too, had given up on her, she thought as she kicked each step against the stone. She stubbed her toe, hard, on an uneven bit but didn't cry out. Instead, she savored the pain; it distracted her from her aching loneliness. By the time she looked up, Ganymedes was far ahead, and she had to race across the plaza to catch him.

The palace entrance to the library loomed even grander than the one that opened to the street. Four arches sprouted from the ground, each guarded by a separate goddess: Arete, Episteme, Ennoia, and—her favorite—Sophia, with her turquoise eyes gazing up from her scroll. Arsinoe wanted to walk through Sophia's entry, but Ganymedes headed toward Arete's door. The goddess of virtue had always seemed cold and unforgiving, her face a stoic slab, with love for neither learning nor wisdom, and certainly none for girls who sought their favors there.

"No one's goddess." That's what she and her friends called Arete, for there were only three in Arsinoe's closely woven set. She had chosen wisdom and Sophia; Aspasia had claimed Ennoia, goddess of intelligence; and reluctantly, Hypatia had agreed to serve as Episteme, guardian of knowledge. They all three had eschewed virtue. Arete looked too daunting then as now.

"Will Aspasia and Hypatia join me for today's lessons?" she called after her tutor.

"Put your playmates from your mind."

Arsinoe said nothing. She didn't want her playmates anyway. She could renounce them if she must. She needed only Cleopatra. To her sister, Arsinoe might confess all, under the laurel tree in the forgotten gardens of Ptolemy the Potbelly. There they used to whisper away the afternoons, hidden from all interruptions. And she knew, with certainty, that Cleopatra would fix everything; she'd teach her how to impress the court. Her sister was the one who had convinced their father that Arsinoe needed a tutor of her own—that it wasn't fair to leave her behind with no one to teach her every time Cleopatra sailed.

But as it was, her sister was a memory, nothing more. Arsinoe had only Ganymedes, so she needed to show him, to prove how much she'd changed. If he lost faith in her, she'd have no one left. Except maybe her fire-bearded guard. And who knew what had become of him? She'd seen neither hide nor hair of her Menelaus since he'd left her food on that first frightful night. She'd been a fool to think her recent victories would be enough. Myrrine was to blame; the nurse had been too free in her encouragements, too eager to pretend that the way she'd met her trials had been remarkable. And now, though attended, she felt lonelier than she had before.

The interior of Alexandria's great library had been stripped bare of life. Arsinoe gasped at the metamorphosis. In the main gallery, where dozens of wizened scholars once bent, copying ancient scrolls to fresh ones, there sat nothing but rows upon rows of barren desks. Far across the sea, there must have been some parallel palace, bustling with all the disappeared: Aspasia and Hypatia; her two little brothers and her mother as well; her father's guards, though she could only picture them as headless corpses; and these departed sages, the kindly men who'd doted on her and, in happier days, allowed her to braid their winding beards.

"Take a seat, my child." Ganymedes guided her to an empty bench. Several scrolls were furled upon its companion table. They must have been abandoned as their readers fled. "Don't dwell on what's gone," her eunuch counseled. "Your lessons still must be learned; more histories await your eyes. I'll return with those scrolls in a moment."

The eunuch scuttled off toward the scholars' dormitories.

Arsinoe couldn't imagine what those chambers looked like now. Usually the building rattled with men drinking and eating and talking on divans, but she imagined that it, too, must lie empty, its cells and halls forsaken. Her eyes wandered over the scrolls; they were not ordinary texts but rolled with care and love and devotion onto rods of gold and silver and bronze. She traced a careful finger along one cold knob. A dark streak stained the metal; scholars flickered before her eyes, desperate in their flight. As one ancient ran, blood burgeoning on his tunic, he tripped and splayed his papers on the desk. Curiosity pressed her to unfurl the papyrus, to see what other evidence lay on the page, but she didn't. That was why Ganymedes had left them there: to tempt her. She wouldn't give him that satisfaction.

Her skin prickled. Someone was watching. She glanced about the gallery, half expecting to find a lingering fiend, blood-tried ax in hand, ready to kill her once and for all. Instead, a pair of familiar gray-green eyes stared back at her.

"Alexander!" She sprang up and rushed to embrace the boy. "My beloved Alexander!" she declared. Forgotten were the days when her entourage of girls had teased and taunted him. They'd called him Athena for his strange eyes and stranger presence in their female set. But that hardly mattered now. He was here, and he was *hers*. "Dioscorides didn't make you return home?"

"My father told me if you were safe within these walls, I'd be as well." Alexander shrugged his bony shoulders.

Her eyes narrowed at the boy. She recognized the rehearsal in his words; her own practiced phrases took on the same emphases, no matter how hard she tried to speak them plainly.

"And what of your mother, then?" she asked. "Didn't she want you to join her in the countryside?" Arsinoe could hardly imagine Cynane remaining alone within the city walls.

"She—my father's *wife*—doesn't much care what happens to me." He met her eyes, daring her to fling back insults.

Arsinoe chewed her lip. She'd forgotten that Alexander was born a bastard; she didn't put much stock in such distinctions. Least of all now, when Berenice had named her a bastard too. It was the father's blood that mattered, not the mother's.

"What have we here?" Ganymedes loosed a second set of scrolls onto the table. In the eunuch's presence, her friend transformed. His shoulders slumped, his knees trembled, his gaze fixed on the stone. Her tutor had this effect on many of her companions. They were frightened of him. She was not.

"Alexander's remained within the palace," Arsinoe replied with a touch of glee. "Not all my friends have left me. Sometimes, Ganymedes, even you are misinformed."

"You asked after Aspasia and Hypatia. I told you they were gone. This one's name never passed your lips. I assumed you didn't care whether he'd stayed or fled. Or died."

She laughed in answer. Ganymedes enjoyed teasing her play-mates, trying to turn them away from her. Besides, her own anger had turned against the eunuch—he'd wanted to make her feel lonely and forgotten. She pulled Alexander to sit beside her on the bench and bent to whisper loudly in his ear, "He wishes that we take him seriously. That is why he affects such low tones: he wants us to think him a man."

"That's enough, Arsinoe," the eunuch admonished. "Alexander, you've made enough mischief for one lesson. Go make yourself a nuisance elsewhere."

"If Alexander goes, then so do I."

Her companion's return had emboldened her. Her sister Berenice had power over her life and death, and might have her murdered as she slept, but what nastiness could Ganymedes—or any eunuch—inflict upon a Ptolemy? "If you wish to teach me, you must teach us both."

To her surprise, her tutor smirked at her insolence. "If you wish to study with him, so you may. But see that the boy remembers that

I'm no easy teacher. If he wants to learn beside one of the great members of the House of Ptolemy, he'll do it well, and to my satisfaction."

"I've learned beside her before," Alexander spoke up. Arsinoe smiled at her friend's retort. He sat taller now that she'd defended him, and he talked without a trace of the stammer that she and Aspasia had so often mocked. "The circumstances haven't changed so much."

"Then you were one of many, and if your recitations lagged behind some of the others—and believe me, boy, they did—it didn't make much difference. If I should teach you two alone, the role of inspiration falls all the heavier upon you."

The boy nodded solemnly, ready to accept the eunuch's terms. This irked Arsinoe, how easily everyone swam downstream. She wasn't so readily placated. She was itching, suddenly, for a fight. She'd been so pliant, so sweet; what good had it done her?

"If you keep taunting him, Alexander and I will simply go." She slapped her hand against the table. She hit it too hard, and the rough cypress stung her palm. She bit her lip hard enough to draw salty blood; she wouldn't succumb to tears. "Won't we, Alexander?"

Her friend fell dumb. The eunuch spoke instead. "Sit. Your trials don't excuse impudence. You aren't an entirely dull child. I'd hoped these recent days would help you realize the importance of your studies."

"He speaks the truth, Arsinoe," Alexander agreed readily.

"How would you know?" Her eyes flicked from Ganymedes to Alexander, and back again. "Were you imprisoned in your chambers, or were the lives of a tutor and a playmate not deemed worthy of such interruptions? Did you watch as your guards were hacked to pieces? Did you beg an audience with Berenice? I endured all that alone. I begged and wheedled for my life alone. And now you— both of you—dare tell me how I must act. As though I were still that pampered child who you knew under my father's reign."

"Alexander." The eunuch's voice dropped to a low growl. "Leave us a moment."

Her friend stood but he didn't inch away.

"No." Arsinoe took care to keep her own tone firm. She refused to sound like a whining child. "I told you, Ganymedes. Alexander stays."

"If that's what you prefer. I merely wanted to save you some embarrassment. If you'd prefer to flaunt your childish tempers for all of Alexandria to see, far be it from me to stop you."

"No matter how I act, you call me a child. I speak to my sister, I plead with wit and wisdom for my life, and still I'm nothing but a child to you. And so what does it matter if I now rave in front of you and Alexander and all the city too? What punishment can you give me that will match the harm Berenice might inflict at any moment?" She spat her words, her venom. But it didn't make her feel any better.

Ganymedes studied her for a long while. She refused to cower beneath his gaze. And then he spoke. "You wish that I would congratulate you, to pat your back and stroke your hair for not getting yourself killed. You wish me to tell you how wise and brave you must have been, how proud I am of my most brilliant student, whose remarkable knowledge of both the ancient texts and the human character has bought her life. You wish to bask in rosy words, my dear, and pretend that you live in some rosy world. I know that well."

Arsinoe's pride burned because the eunuch was right. She had wanted all that praise, and she wished she'd let Alexander run off that she might carry her shame alone. But when the boy squeezed his fingers around her wrist, she didn't pry them away.

"That, my dear," said the eunuch, continuing in this new vein, "would defeat the purpose. You've cleared one hurdle but a long race remains. To bask in each small triumph is not only foolish; it's dangerous. Your victories bring you something far dearer than my praise: your life. How would you rather spend your days: at leisure, wandering and learning nothing, like some craftsman's daughter, or with your nose buried deep in the great tragedies, your mind at work learning mathematics, and history, and Syrian and Hebrew and other tongues as well?"

She wanted to deny him, to banish him from her sight, to scorn him as he'd scorned her. To be alone, forever. But she could not. She needed what he offered. Education made queens. "I should like to continue my learning."

"Very well, then." The eunuch opened the first scroll. "We return to our study, then, of Polybius's *Histories,* of how the Romans conquered first Carthage, and then the Macedonians, and finally the Greeks. And what, from all those conquests, we here in Alexandria might learn today."

ELDER

The soot-faced woman balanced a babe on her hip as she spoke. Her other child, a boy, half of his face shielded by a filthy bandage, clung to her wrist. Perched on her provisional throne, Berenice struggled to catch the peasant's words. In Thebes, so many long stades up the Nile's stream, the accents grew thick, the men dark, the customs strange. Here she shed Alexandria's diadem and wore the heavy double crown: the white vulture nestled between the red cobra's coils.

Hordes from across the countryside had descended on the town to honor her arrival and heave home Alexandria's rich grain, swelling the population to near its mythic proportions. But crowds could not disguise the city's decay. The columns that rose along the avenue were charred, bleak reminders of her grandfather's efforts to burn the last bastion of native rebellion to the ground. Even along the main streets many of the buildings had been picked bare; every stray stone that could be moved had been carted away. Only foundations and outer walls remained, their burnt-faced god-kings crumbling beneath the sun. And so despite the prostrated forms that greeted her litter, Berenice had felt relieved to reach the gymnasium, with its glimmering two-decked portico. Constructed for her foreign mercenaries, it was relatively untouched by decay. But signs of the city's corrosion infested its walls too. Rot was written all over the face of the woman who pleaded for justice before her now.

Berenice believed that this peasant marked the fiftieth petitioner of the day, but she couldn't quite recall. This airing of grievances was important—she knew that; it promised to endear her to the local populace. But after hours of listening to squabbles over cattle and crops, neighbors and priests, the provincial stories bled together.

"They yanked the suckling babe from my breast." The woman's hand cupped her infant's head against her chest, as though to shield him from her words. The peasant went on in halting, careful Greek. "And they shoved me to my knees, and when I wouldn't serve them, they gave me this." She pointed to the bruise raised along her cheek. "And other marks I will not show before my royal queen. They forced themselves upon me and said I was lucky to be of use to the queen's men."

Berenice found herself nodding at the complaints. They didn't surprise her; the woman's boldness did. Usually it was the father or the husband, even the local priest, who voiced such accusations. "We avoid the messier scenes that way," her father had explained once, as he detailed what payments were warranted in such cases as these. A premium should be added if the woman was of Greek ancestry, he'd told her, or the crime was committed in Alexandria, or permanent damage had been inflicted. The hapless woman before her scored poorly on all accounts. "As often as not, they're making it up, or at the very least exaggerating," her father had said, chuckling. "I suppose even lowly whores must make their way in the world." Where had they been that day? Berenice must have been young, seven or perhaps eight. An only child and only heir, she'd been counseled in matters of rule. It had made her feel so important when her father had spoken to her as he might have to a woman grown. Before Cleopatra had usurped his love.

"Could you recognize these men? The ones who did this to you?" Berenice asked.

A hush fell as tension snared the guards who lined the eastern wall. They shifted in their sandals, these sometimes soldiers—the very ones she'd come to charm and whip into enthusiasm for her Cyprus campaign. Greek, Galatian, Syrian, their lineages mixed and muddied, mercenaries to a one who traded army stints for Egyptian grain and land. Could she trust them to fight Roman legions? She studied their bare faces. Not one man dared meet her eye. Good: they feared her, at least. They'd fight all the more fiercely when she called them to battle for Cyprus. The petitioner stood silent; across the gymnasium echoed only her babe's wails. The woman bounced the child to soothe it.

"Yes, I'd recognize them, my queen, daughter of the Sun." The woman spoke slowly, addressing Berenice by the Egyptian appellation. "I can point them out right now. All three stand there." She pried her wrist from her elder child's grasp and pointed to the line of soldiers. The impudence of the gesture sent the men into chaos. Mumbles erupted into yells. Above the other shouts one voice rang clear: "It was an honor for her. Her husband's got nothing that compares with this."

A few of his fellows broke into laughter. Berenice heard Pieton clear his throat, urging her toward caution, as he always did. That was a fair course for eunuchs, but not for queens. Thais, on her right, was no better: a taut and nervous grin spread quickly across his sunken cheeks. Though his fortunes had changed since Pieton had first summoned him before her, his manner remained stubbornly fixed. He flitted about as fearful as ever, as though the slightest sound might send him reeling back into disgrace. She wished Dio had come instead. She recalled the penetrating look in his eyes when she'd last seen him, as he'd lifted her hand to his lips—how her blood had bolted to her cheeks. She shook her head at the thought. It was better that he remain at a distance, that she surround herself with safe men like Thais, who trembled when she sneezed.

"You think you're amusing, don't you?" Her voice was calm and cold as she addressed the blustering offender. She'd come, after all, to make an impression and show her strength, not to serve up dull justice in her father's absence. "Arrest that man."

The soldiers quieted, but none moved to take up against their friend.

"Has farming my lands turned you all deaf to orders? I told you to arrest him."

An older guard shuffled forward to do her bidding. He didn't look like much of a match for his young comrade: his wispy hair had already begun to gray. Yet the loudmouth wilted at the soldier's touch. Marched before the queen by one of his own, he dropped his swagger. He was young—Berenice saw that now: scarcely old enough to grow a beard, and not for lack of trying. A few pathetic tufts puffed proudly from his chin.

"Was this one of the men?"

"Yes, my queen." The woman answered with a steady voice. She was braver than she looked.

"Can you pick out the other two?"

The petitioner pointed to a second beardless boy. He shook even more violently than his companion. His eyes welled, and Berenice feared that he might weep. These two were scarcely more than children. Perhaps her father was right: this woman had concocted a tale for a quick coin. Her husband could have just as easily given her those bruises.

"And the third?"

The woman clutched her babe closer to her breast. Her head jerked—a nod—but she made no move to point out the final soldier. Her elder child quaked, his fingers picking at the bandage on his cheek. Perhaps some injury had been inflicted on him too. Maybe he'd tried to shield his mother from the blows. Berenice's stomach churned at the thought, as did the bile that rose within it. Finally, the woman's finger rose and picked out the last guard, a stocky man well into his middle years. He chortled through crooked teeth, first at his victim and then at his queen.

"D'you think this'll make a difference?" he taunted his prey, this smug stain of a man who'd never been denied anything. "The queen'll pay you for your troubles. That won't help you sleep at night. I know where you fetch your water, and when your husband works the fields, and how your little boy shrieks when his mother sucks a fine Macedonian cock."

His strutting sickened her.

"Quiet," she told him. "I'm not some bureaucrat from Alexandria here to measure your crops. I am the Shining One, Queen of the Upper and the Lower Kingdoms, daughter of the Sun, Lady of Diadems, and you'll address me as such. Tell me: what is your name?"

"Agapios, my queen, the Shining One, Lady of Diadems." Smirking, he bent into a deep bow, so low that the crown of his head dipped past his buckled knees. "Your father never took such an interest in his men's business in the south. Perhaps you like what you see." He gestured to his body.

"I don't know if you're drunk or stupid or both. Honestly, I don't much care." Berenice turned back to Pieton and Thais. "Fifty lashes for each of the boys. And as for this creature, sever his right hand and relieve him of all duties and privileges of a soldier."

The soldiers quieted, their fear curdling. Even the petitioners who crowded the balconies and walkways stared in silent awe. The world grew still, as though she gripped Medusa's head and had turned her onlookers into stone. Their terror buoyed Berenice. They should be frightened.

"My queen," Pieton broke in. "May I have a word?"

At her nod, the eunuch approached to whisper in her ear. "Your actions may be noble but they aren't wise. These men expect certain rewards for their loyal service. And not merely the right to till some land in peacetime. They serve with the understanding that they might take what they please. Under your father, compensation to the woman was the standard and mutually amenable practice."

Slowly, Berenice shook her head—his words cloyed at her. She didn't need pleas to become more like her father. There were reasons that eunuchs could never rule. These soldiers had never re-spected the Piper—no one had. The answer, surely, wasn't to cast herself in his image.

"Do you think Agapios would serve me loyally on the battle-field?" she asked quietly. "That he wouldn't turn to Rome at a moment's notice? He'd treat me as he treated her if given half a chance. He insulted me before my own guards. I can't imagine he'd be more likely to esteem me as his commander." There were men, she knew, too many men who would bear her little respect, queen or no. Who would always see her as an interloper, a blushing flower, a naïf. But her father was the weak one, not she.

"He's a noxious creature," answered Pieton, "unworthy of the army, and you're right to punish him for his impudence—execute him, even. But don't punish him for this nonsense, or soon we'll have no soldiers at all."

She didn't believe that. She refused.

"And what of her?" Berenice looked to the woman, whose hands shook beneath the weight of her babe. Her older boy tried to com-fort her, wiping away her tears with the grubby hem of his tunic. He was naked underneath, but that didn't seem to bother him. That made sense, she supposed. She recalled that Egyptian children of that age rarely wore clothes at all. His mother had probably only forced him into an outfit for this occasion.

Pieton laughed, a hacking sound at the back of his throat. "You think she cares what happens to these men? She cares only for some coin, and even if there is some grain of truth in her story—and trust me, it's never more than a grain—she no doubt saw any molestation by the royal army as a stroke of luck. It's well and good to take note of the common folk's concerns, but don't make too much of them."

Berenice looked at the woman and her wounded child. The boy touched his bandage with tender fingers, as if to unstick the cloth from the oozing wound. His mother's hand batted his away. The silence had broken like a fever. The petitioners gossiped amongst themselves, servants jostled through the crowd, Thais crouched his bony shoulders over a fresh scroll. Only the soldiers remained quiet, eyeing the three plucked from their midst.

"I hear your point, Pieton, and I'll consider it carefully."

"You are wise, my queen," he murmured as he retreated with a slight bow. He held himself with grace and pride. Berenice was prepared to crush all that.

"My trusted adviser," she announced, "brings several important details to my attention. In addition to the punishments I've handed down against these criminals, the court of justice in Alexandria will provide a sum of fifty drachmas to the petitioner to compensate for her pains."

Poor Pieton. Poor, foolish Pieton. She almost pitied him as she caught sight of his deflated form in the corner of her eye. The eunuch thought she'd come only to soothe the starving throngs and to rally troops to fight her battles. But she wouldn't let her strings be pulled by men and eunuchs. She was a queen in her own right, like Hatshepsut of old. And she would prove it. As a child, she'd visited that woman's mortuary temple, its half a hundred columns glistening in crimson and ocher beneath the cliffs. "But where is the queen?" Berenice had whined to her father after she'd gazed at a half dozen reliefs of crowned men. "That's her," the Piper had rejoined, laughing. "Right there. And there. And there." He had pointed at each of the men carved into the wall. That had been her first taste of what it meant to rule: there were no queens in Egypt—only women who became kings.

Before her, here and now, one of the boys collapsed in tears; his friend stared dumb and silent at his fate. But the older man betrayed no nerves at all. "You'll lose your hand, you fool," Berenice cursed under her breath. He even smiled as her gaze lingered on him, as though this case was of no particular relevance to him, as though some other man had been condemned to a life of begging, unable to claw his way in the world.

His mockery whipped her irritation into fury. She'd been dismissed for too long, by too many men, by her father and all the idiots who followed him.

"Agapios, I see that you've ignored my warning. I said you were to be stripped of all rights and privileges of a soldier, and yet you stand there in your clothes. Royal coin paid for that tunic. You have no right to wear it."

"You want me to take off my tunic?" the man scoffed, pacing back and forth before his fellows, rallying passions to his cause.

"Yes," she snapped. "Now. Before I have my men do it for you."

The soldier gaped, speechless at last. Beside her, she heard Pieton inhale sharply. "If you want to retake Cyprus," he'd tell her, "you'd best show her men a touch more indulgence." She shrugged off his objections. If these men didn't trust her to be harsher than her father, then she'd show them what it meant to have a woman king. And if the eunuch didn't see her purpose, that was his folly.

"Guards!" she commanded. "Strip this man's tunic, unless the rest of you wish to throw your lot in with his."

Agapios didn't give them the chance. He gripped the collar of his shirt and tore it to expose his chest. The fabric strained and groaned as it split away.

"That too." Berenice pointed to the filthy loincloth belted about his waist. This time, one of the younger men stepped forward to loose the girdle, perhaps enjoying watching his superior get his due. As the linen fell away, Agapios shivered, and his cock shrank beneath his prodigious belly. A few of her guards sniggered. *Good. Let him know some humiliation.* The gods knew she'd been laughed at in her time. She still remembered the mockery she'd endured when her mother had been cast out of the palace. A girl of eight, she'd stood on the marble steps and watched, her stomach writhing with hatred. At that moment, she couldn't tell whom she loathed more: her father for elevating his concubine to wife, or her mother for letting him. In every day that followed, she'd felt the sharp sting of derision. Even the slaves snickered in her wake. *There walks the girl who thought she would be king.*

"Take him away. He ought to spend a few hours alone with his hand before he loses it at dawn. If he can find that fine Macedonian cock of his, he might even discover a use for it."

The man didn't struggle as he was dragged, naked, from the gymnasium. He went quietly now. The silence was maddening. They should cheer. Berenice looked back to the woman she had rescued. The creature looked as beaten as before, though her babe had stopped its howling. Peasants were never pleased.

"I'll see no more petitioners," she said. "Our time in Thebes is short, and we have other matters to address."

Such announcements were usually met with a certain degree of grumbling; no doubt those gathered had waited long months, even years, to bring their cases before their monarch. The Piper hadn't proved the most present of kings. Once, when she'd been a child attending her father on a rare journey to the Upper Lands, a doleful wretch had thrown himself before their litter, begging for his time before the king. "Please," he'd whispered. "I've waited so long." Without a second glance, her father had spat and ordered on the carrier. Berenice wondered what had become of that petitioner, whether he still waited somewhere to make his plea or if he'd grown old and died, unanswered. She wanted to push her father's foibles from her mind, but the harder she tried, the more they consumed her. It was as though that emptiness inside her, drained of her driving hatred, demanded to be sated by other thoughts of him, by this obsession of picking apart each failed aspect of his rule. As though he were someone else's father, someone else's enemy.

Here, now, the crowd had thinned, already dispersing through the western arches. The show had ended, and there was nothing more to see. Only a few lingered—old women, mostly—grousing to each other, and soon they, too, vanished. Berenice turned her attention to the soldiers who remained.

"You are angry," she told them, looking each man up and down, goading one to challenge her. "There's no use in denying it. The fury is written clearly on your faces. That's no concern of mine; rage is the better part of life. Perhaps you hate me. So be it. I don't need your love. But perhaps you think me weak and womanly. Perhaps you think it is because I have no cock that I took pity on that woman. Perhaps you think I wish to take away your spoils, the spoils for which you've fought so hard. To that I say, you are the ones who are coddled. You have grown weak tending your crops and hoarding your riches. I am not my father, and what loose laws he set upon you will not stand under my rule. When we conquer Cyprus, you may take what you like. There you will find your spoils. But don't confuse the women of Thebes with our enemies. When you've won battles, you'll reap the rewards. The easy work of tilling fields and counting coins merits no such prizes."

Her voice echoed through the hall. She drank in her rebounding words, the only sounds that pierced the air. She dared these soldiers to defy her, as she stared down each man in turn. But shorn of Agapios, the clerics grew subdued. Not one would look her in the eye, let alone speak out against her. They had a good lot, these men, with their farmlands and their slaves. The rules had changed—and they would heed them. They had no other choice.

The moment bloomed and passed. No one would challenge her now; their silence had lingered on too long. And so she nodded to her advisers, and quit the gymnasium.

Outside, the hot Theban sun scorched her face. The street before her swarmed with life. All those prostrated forms had risen, belongings and babies strapped to their backs. If her guard hadn't cleared the way before her, she could have scarcely squeezed through the teeming masses. They spilled off the sandstone pavement and clambered onto the sphinxes that lined the way. The statues saddened her, their golden faces flecked to reveal the ordinary stone underneath. Several figures had even lost their noses. And though she'd heard that their eyes had once been inlaid with lapis lazuli, they all now glared at her with blank sockets of granite. She shielded her own eyes with her hand and headed toward her litter. Suddenly, she hated this place. Its waning struck too close to her heart. The sooner she returned to the barge, to Alexandria, the better. She clambered into the carrier, and, with a jolt, her bearers lifted its poles.

"My queen." A shrill voice cut through the curtain.

Pieton. With an agile leap, he jumped into the litter. She didn't bother to tell him she wished to be alone; she was sure he wouldn't listen. The vehicle lurched forward.

"You can't appease these men with a few bold words," Pieton told her. "The punishments you've given out are too harsh for that."

"What's done is done." She hated his small-mindedness. Why couldn't he let the past lie in peace? She couldn't stand sitting still and dwelling on it all. It made the emptiness excruciating. She'd been forced to act, and so she had. She'd shown these men that she was strong and unflappable, worthy of a fight.

"You are strong," Pieton went on, to spite her, maybe. "And you rule well, but here you've stumbled. Your men serve as much from a desire for plunder as from loyalty."

"I'm not a fool," she snapped. "I know why my men serve. Just as I know that they must respect me if I expect them to fight for me, to wrench Cyprus from Rome's grasp."

The eunuch frowned. "They may not need to go as far as Cyprus to face the eagle standard. Your father has begun to curry favor in Rome."

Berenice stared, speechless, for a moment. The echo of fear thudded in her chest, but she ignored it.

"What?" She pursed her lips. And waited for the ax to swing.

"The Piper is poised to return. Your Dio sent a letter."

The name seared her ears. She missed him, her fat Alexandrian friend, but she'd hoped she hadn't been so obvious with her favors.

"*My* Dio?" she scoffed, as though she found the appellation absurd.

"I merely mean that you lean heavily on his counsel."

"Never mind," she muttered. Pieton's mockery, too, was a sign of pettiness—and defending Dio would only stoke the eunuch's jealousy. "What does he write? What news of that piping idiot who calls himself king?"

"Your father has reached Rome, where he's had an audience with Pompey, whom they call the Great."

"I see." She nodded slowly at the news, at the twist of her fate. Pompey could provide her father with legions that she might never match. The eunuch had been right: she'd been foolish and childish in her attempts to teach her soldiers a lesson. They would flock now to her father when he returned at the head of Rome's army.

Ahead, Berenice could see the sandstone temples of Karnak surging from the desert sands. She'd long admired those grand monuments to the ancient gods Mut and Ammon-Re and Mantu, the ones who ruled the earth before memory began. They'd stood for ages before her forebearers had set foot on this land—and they'd stand for ages to come. They cared little about who ruled: Berenice, her father, Rome.

There was no time to linger here, either with her thoughts or in some vain effort to repair the wreckage she left in her wake. If her father sailed across the sea, she needed to be at the shores to meet him, with any army she could muster.

"And so we must return to Alexandria at once."

"Precisely, which is why I urge you to mend your bridges. It would not—"

"If I shift course, I'll be called weak. I needn't teach you that," she told Pieton squarely. Whatever damage she might have caused, it would be worse to show herself changeable. "Don't speak to me of this again. It's done."

"As you say. But in the future, my queen, if you take rash actions, let them be ones that might win friends. They tend to be more valuable than enemies. And you already have plenty of the latter."

The eunuch was right, though she hated to admit it. Her rashness only painted her nearer her father's image. But forward, onward, no regret. For now, she would need friends, until she'd won her soldiers' hearts.

As the litter passed along the river, the lanes grew full of ugly sorrows: bloated children and twisted lepers and bedraggled cats, mewing at each passerby. No one paid them any mind, save a half-grown beggar boy who kicked a scrawny tabby aside when it rubbed against his calf.

"You know a city suffers when the cats starve," Berenice said. Even in Alexandria, much of the native populace worshipped the beasts—and many Greeks had taken up the practice too. Years ago, she'd watched a mob tear a Roman limb from limb for killing a cat. And in the heart of the Upper Kingdom, these creatures were held even dearer.

"Cats starve as people do," Pieton remarked. "There are no scraps to put out for strays. The town is even stripped of rats."

It was true. Even as they passed the heaps of refuse along the river, not one rodent stirred among the rot. Still, Berenice dreamed of Cyprus—even as she distributed grain, even as her own kingdom withered before her very eyes. She, too, was guilty of distraction, of her eyes widening beyond her powers. Was that the curse of being a Ptolemy?

"The street children eat the rats now," the eunuch went on. "And they aren't the only ones."

A filthy hand plunged through the curtains. "Please," bleated its filthy child, running alongside.

"Get away, you brat," one of the litter bearers hissed.

"Please," the boy repeated. "Please. I beg of you."

"Get him away," Berenice mouthed to Pieton. He sickened her, this reminder of collapse and degradation, of the kingdom's wilting. Besides, she'd refilled the granaries of her favored priests; it was up to them to dole out the wheat. Already, though, it was too late. A crowd had begun to gather along the street. She'd win no favors cursing at a child.

"Stop!" she commanded. The litter jolted to a halt. After bracing herself with breath—she didn't want to inhale the stink outside; it might pollute her further—she pushed aside the silk. Up close, the boy made an even more malignant sight. Sores oozed around his lips; it must have pained him even to speak. Berenice realized that her petitioners had been culled: only ones untouched by this plague had been allowed to enter. Even her vision of deprivation was skewed, directed by her advisers.

"Please, my—my queen," the boy stammered. He seemed to know no other Greek, for after that he babbled in his native tongue, one she'd no hope of understanding.

Berenice snatched a loaf of bread and a twist of grapes, the only food she had within. The boy grabbed them and bowed his head as he repeated, "My queen, my queen."

The crowd closed in on her. They disgusted her, these harbingers of famine and its devastations. They recalled the ruin her father had wrought and how much poorer the kingdom had grown under his decadence. It hadn't always been this way; when last she had visited the city, the streets had been clean and the farmers fed. A monument to times gone by, yes, but a well-kept one. But now the lingering sandstone facades were caked with dirt, ready to crumble at the slightest touch.

"Go on," she shouted as she jerked the curtains shut. "Go on."

Returned to the royal barge, Berenice ignored Leda's bath and dismissed her nurse. She wanted to be alone. The faces haunted her. And that boy, that pleading boy, with his filthy sores and filthy hands. She needed wine and food and sleep to sate her body and wash down those sights. Something caught her eye—a speck glittering on her coverlet. When she approached, she saw that it was an amulet. An iridescent vulture spread her wings along a golden chain. Beneath lay a piece of papyrus, creased over once. She unfolded it and read, "The mother goddess knows her friends." And though Berenice flipped the page over and back a dozen times, she could find no seal.

"Leda," she cried out. "Who cleaned these chambers?"

"I did myself, my queen," came the nurse's answer. Footfalls followed. "Is something the matter?"

"No. No, it's nothing. All is well." She turned the token over in her palm. "Only make sure everything is ready for our return to Alexandria."

"Yes, my queen."

Berenice listened for her nurse's receding steps. Then she crossed to her gilded trunk and flung open its lid. She rooted through the shawls and chitons and tunics until her hand struck cold, hard ivory. With care, she fished out the jewelry box. Across its lid a carved savage drew his bow. "It comes from Nubia," her father had told her when he'd given it to her on her eighth birthday, the last one before Cleopatra bulged in the concubine's belly. It was the only talisman Berenice had of his; if there'd been other gifts, she couldn't recall them. She couldn't say why she carried it on every voyage; in her softer moments, she feared that it was because she wished to remember the Piper as he'd been during her childhood—or rather, as she wished he'd been: an indulgent father who would break the royal coffers for his daughter's whims. On her stronger days, she knew that her reasons were quite different. The ivory box embossed with gold and turquoise proved the perfect souvenir of all she would never become: a king who cared more for trinkets than for armies.

The hinges squeaked as she opened the case; they needed oil to cure their rust. With care, she placed the vulture pendant inside. She would not lose it there.

YOUNGER

Arsinoe rocked from side to side. The bench swayed beneath her, but its pitching didn't disturb Alexander. His stylus stayed steady on the page, a serpent pouring from its point. She couldn't fathom his focus. Her own eyes darted over the reading room to the dog mosaic sprawled across the stone; she always thought the pup looked lonesome, staring up from the floor by an abandoned helmet, waiting listlessly for its master to return. She let her gaze drift over the twin columns with their snaking Medusa heads toward the door that framed the larger atrium beyond. Out there, a few scholars lingered, thumbing through the scroll nooks and spreading chosen ones across their cedar tables, bolstering some shred of the ordinary. She didn't recognize them, though, so she knew they belonged to her sister's reign. They looked too young to be learned men; no doubt they were only permitted near the royal reading room because their betters had all fled.

No sign of Ganymedes, though Arsinoe was sure he'd told her to come at this hour. If Cleopatra had been here—or even Aspasia or Hypatia—at least she would have had someone to talk to. But Alexander took no interest in her, only in the scribbles that he dashed on his papyrus. It felt strange how everything had settled into some semblance of normality now that Berenice had forgotten her. Ganymedes gave her lessons, Myrrine her baths. Her days took on the contours of those that had come before, in every way except this: she had no friends. Her one companion ignored her, and a pit grew in her stomach that threatened to swallow up her innards.

Alexander's scratching had sprouted fangs, black blood dripping from their tips. It looked alive, this creature, ripped from one of her dreams. And then, at once, talons seized its body; an eagle's form budded from those claws. Alexander inked rapidly now, filling in the men's faces staring up in awe.

"What are you drawing?" she asked.

"It's nothing," he murmured, and he put aside his quill, as though he'd been doing something shameful and had only now been caught at it. Her companions, Arsinoe recalled, had mocked him for his drawing. Hypatia, in particular, used to snatch away his papyrus and dangle it above the flames.

Arsinoe had shunned him too, in her way. Not that she'd been especially cruel—she didn't have to be. There were other girls, lesser girls, eager to inflict what jabs they could against those lower down the chain. And so it had been Aspasia who had teased him, calling him Athena for his gray-green eyes. And little Diana, a girl Arsinoe scarcely even spoke to, had taken to suggesting that Alexander actually wasn't a boy at all but a creature like Hermaphroditus of legend, neither male nor female, but some unnatural combination of the two. Arsinoe had never paid any of it much mind, but she wondered now if those whispers hurt him still. If that explained why he would hardly speak to her.

"Is that Agamemnon?" she asked Alexander, pointing to a man's face, a diadem cutting across his brow.

"No, it's Hector," the boy snapped. And then he paused, as if he were embarrassed by what he'd admitted, by what it might say about him. "It's the Trojan side, as they charge into battle, despite Zeus's bad omen."

Arsinoe nodded; that made sense to her. They were the better ones, the greater ones, the ones who had fought and died. The Greeks were cruel and pregnant with regrets, the Trojans merely doomed. "I like the Trojans better too."

"They're better fighters. Cleaner ones too." Alexander spoke in bursts. "And besides, the only reason Achilles can best Hector is because he has the gods on his side—all of them, and he's the son of a god himself. Hector's the better fighter by far. And he's the better man. The better man always loses."

"But not Odysseus," Arsinoe objected. The man of twists and turns remained her favorite of the Greeks. While Agamemnon and Achilles let the war drone on as they quarreled over their prizes of gold and women, the ruler of Ithaca put his mind to breaching Troy's impenetrable walls. Without his brilliant horse, where would the rest of the Achaeans be? In her mind, Odysseus always emerged as the best of the Greeks. "He finds his way home in the end."

Just as Cleopatra would, she promised herself. And her father too. She clung deeply to that belief, even though it would turn her world on edge once more. Because she knew that her sister—wherever she was—would be fighting to come back to her. After all, she'd said, as the ship sailed from the docks, "I'll return for you." And Arsinoe had believed it. Cleopatra never lied to her. Except when she was teasing, and she would dare Arsinoe to do something foolish like sneak into the scholars' dormitories. "No one will notice you—I promise." But that was different. That was joking.

"Pupils." Ganymedes interrupted her thoughts. She glanced up in surprise. She hadn't even heard the eunuch enter the room. It still amazed her how quiet he could be on his toes, despite his clumsy size. He smiled at her, and nodded to Alexander as well. A small concession, that. "We return today to Polybius."

Arsinoe sighed. She was sick of Polybius, of his tales of the Achaean cities falling one by one before Rome.

"It would behoove you not to lament your education, Arsinoe." The eunuch's tone was sharp. "You're lucky now, under Berenice's rule, to be receiving one at all. And I should think that *history* might interest you more than any other subject. Surely you can imagine some reasons why you should care about the story of Rome's rise."

Arsinoe nodded slowly. She thought of Cleopatra, across the sea, and her father carrying his business there. Now suddenly, palpably, she knew that they were en route to Rome. *That* was why Ganymedes was forcing her to read Polybius: to point her in the right direction. But what reception would they find? The Romans had no respect for the customs of others, and no qualms about inserting themselves in affairs abroad. She remembered being borne through the streets in the days after Cato had taken her uncle's island. The chants and curses hurled at the royal litter. The etchings that sprang up on the city's walls: her father beheaded, his genitals cut off as well—an echo of how the pharaohs of old had dealt with enemies.

"Alexander," Ganymedes snapped, and her friend glanced up from his scroll. "What is it that distracts you from the task at hand?"

The boy covered his sheet with his hand, trying to hide his markings from the eunuch's eyes. Ganymedes was no admirer of drawing; Arsinoe could scarcely count the times that he'd lectured her and her friends on how literature was the highest form of art: "Paintings are for the unread masses." But Alexander wasn't quick enough. Her tutor snatched away his page.

"What's this?" Ganymedes sneered, examining the lines on the paper.

"It's a sketch," the boy muttered, shamed.

"He drew it while we were waiting." It wasn't fair for Ganymedes to punish Alexander for that.

"And yet the boy dwells on it now." The eunuch held the papyrus over the oil lamp, the same one he'd carried to guide their way the night she had fled. The night she'd tried to flee. The flames licked its corner. Alexander winced as the yellow climbed the Trojans' backs, leaving only ash in its wake. The snake succumbed to fire too, and then the spark devoured the eagle's claws, its body, finally its wings. The bird exacted its revenge as the burn rushed up to meet the eunuch's fingertips. Stung, Ganymedes dropped the crumpled remains on the table, shaking his hand as though motion might rid him of the hurt.

"There," her tutor announced. "We'll have no more distractions as we learn of how Rome overcame the Greek cities, and the kingdom of Macedonia as well. You should pay special attention to that, Arsinoe." The eunuch glowered. "Perseus might have been the first of Alexander's heirs to surrender to Rome, but he was most assuredly not the last."

It sounded like a threat—against her, against Cleopatra, against all the Ptolemies and their blood. And so Arsinoe shivered. And she listened as Ganymedes read and lectured on the story of Perseus, and how his empire fell to Rome.

When Ganymedes left, Arsinoe comforted Alexander. He didn't understand what it was to be a Ptolemy. Though he was older, he still grew angry over childish things like drawings being burned to cinders. She knew better. But she felt glad for once to be the wiser one. And she even forgot for a moment or two how her heart ached for her sister.

As time drew on, if she ran fast enough, she could forget her longing for Cleopatra for whole afternoons. Even days.

She and Alexander raced, a pair of cruel and careless winds toppling saplings and unsuspecting brush. She pulled ahead, her stride stretching over grass and stone; he fell behind, lost among the trees. Her hand, caked with dirt, slapped against bark.

"Beat you again."

Alexander's head hung between his knees. "Because I let you."

"Liar."

It's because I'm nine now, she wanted to add as she slipped onto the ground. As though naming some difference would make it stick. All day, she'd been searching for some change within herself. Perhaps birthdays brought transformations only when they were celebrated. No one remembered whether she had seen eight winters, or nine, or twelve. They all assumed—Ganymedes, Myrrine, Alexander— that this was an afternoon like any other.

Did her mother remember what day it was? Arsinoe bit her lip to stop the tears. It seemed unlikely, anyway; even when the two were in the same palace, her mother hadn't always made note of the date, though Cleopatra never once forgot. What good were mothers, anyway? Hers had never cared for her, not after the boys were born, and Alexander's had little enough to do with him, even though he was a boy. "Our mother is jealous of us," Cleopatra would whisper, "because she doesn't have the Conqueror's blood." Only that didn't make sense. "Why isn't she jealous of Ptolemy, then?" Arsinoe would ask, but that would only make her sister laugh.

Arsinoe's mind wandered to her father, his blurred face bent over a flute, fingers kneading sweet notes from the instrument. She recoiled at the memory. Now—now she knew the truth: that other title, Auletes, the Piper, was never meant as a compliment for his songs. "A king," Ganymedes had growled at their latest session, "should be called the Savior, or the Thunderer, or the Great, not distinguished from his forebearers by his penchant for playing flutes."

Arsinoe peeled away these sticky remembrances. Her father was gone, her Cleopatra gone with him. Remembering changed nothing about that. She lay back against the scorched earth. The sky was bright and blue and cloudless, as it had been for months. The time, the time of her birth, the final days of Inundation, should bring rain to Alexandria, marble splattered with pregnant drops at dawn. But not this year. This month had been dry, dry as high summer. She squinted up at Alexander, silhouetted against the sun.

"Do you know what day it is?"

Her friend chewed his lip in thought. "The twenty-sixth day of Choiak."

"The twenty-seventh," she corrected him. Arsinoe studied his face for some recognition, but she could see that her words had no effect. "It's the day I was born."

"Oh," Alexander replied.

"I'm nine." She spoke the words with satisfaction. It was the first time she'd named her new age aloud. "How old are you, Alexander?"

"I was born in the middle of Emergence. I'll be eleven then, in Mechir."

"You are almost exactly of an age with Cleopatra," Arsinoe told him eagerly.

"I don't much care for Cleopatra," the boy said, shrugging. That bothered her. He might be her friend, but he didn't have the right to speak against her sister, a Ptolemy and an heir to the double kingdom.

"Why not? Why don't you like Cleopatra?" The thought wounded her, that anyone shouldn't like her sister.

"She wasn't very kind. At least not to me."

Tension tugged at Arsinoe. She should defend Cleopatra—she always did. But this was the freest thing she'd ever heard Alexander say. More often than not, the boy shut off his thoughts from her, as though he was frightened of what she might do, how she might react. And she wanted—desperately—for someone to be frank with her. As Cleopatra had always been. So she asked a question instead, one that plagued her from time to time. "Am I kind to you?"

"Kinder," he teased.

"Did you really let me win before?" This, too, had weighed on her. The question of who treated her differently—and for what reasons.

"No." He shook his head. "You beat me that time. I hadn't caught my breath."

"I'm accustomed to winning." Arsinoe used to think that was something to be proud of; now she didn't feel so sure.

"You wonder if the game is rigged."

She propped herself up on her elbows to take a look at this new Alexander, this daring one. What made him bold? she wondered. Was it because she'd let his words about Cleopatra slip? "I know the game is rigged. I'm not stupid. I know that people let me win because I'm the daughter of King Ptolemy."

"And why would I let you win now? Your father's in exile, and so is mine. What difference is there between them?"

Arsinoe sighed as she dropped back in the dirt. "Alexander. I was being serious."

"I was too." He lay down beside her. He rested his head on his hand and stared at her. Her cheeks burned but, brown with sun, wouldn't betray her. She didn't like it when people looked directly at her. She'd rather imagine she could disappear at any moment, and no one would be the wiser.

"Why are you still alive?" Alexander asked quietly. "You know the real reason. And it's not because of your father. It's because of you. You've proved what sort of blood courses through your body."

His finger traced the purple vein that twisted across the back of her hand. It tickled, but she didn't laugh.

"Sometimes I am still frightened, though." She said it so softly that she almost hoped he wouldn't hear.

He did, though. And his eyes widened. "You? Frightened? You're the bravest person I know. Braver than Antigone, even."

"I'm not so brave as all that," she whispered. "I'm frightened all the time. I'm frightened every morning when I wake up, and every evening when I go to bed."

Alexander studied her. Perhaps she'd said too much, and he would think her dull and stupid, a girl who jumped at the sight of her own shadow.

"I don't think that being unafraid is the same as being brave." He spoke with slow precision, as Ganymedes did when he wanted her to take note of a particular point. "I think bravery is when you go on even though you are frightened."

"What've you to be frightened of?" she asked. The boy winced. The question had come off crueler than she had intended. "I didn't—"

"It . . . there are . . . you don't know everything, Arsinoe." His voice had turned cold.

"I know one thing that frightens you." The words did not come properly; her tongue turned clumsy, thick, desperate. She didn't want to lose him—not now.

"What's that?"

"You're frightened that you won't be able to catch me."

She sprang to her feet and raced across the burnt grass, arms spread—a vulture took to the sky. *Don't fly so close, Arsinoe.* Only her own beating feet pierced the silence. No echoing footfalls called back. The emptiness stretched on, endless. She fought the urge to turn, to check. Like Orpheus rising from the dead, she knew better than to risk even a single glance. She could hear Alexander scramble up—the welcome sound of chase. Joy, mad and senseless, flooded her body, and she ran faster still. The speed of the pursued. But the footfalls behind her slopped and skidded. She cast a look back. Hands snatched her wrists away. She was caught.

"The very girl I seek." Ganymedes eyed her sullied tunic with disapproval. "Your sister, the Shining Queen, requires your presence."

Rebellion drained from Arsinoe's limbs. Her stomach lurched, and she winced at a memory, the pitiful child who'd wet herself in fear of looming death. No Ptolemy was she.

"The time for play is over. I'll return you to your chambers, and perhaps we might find something more suitable for you to wear before the queen."

All thoughts of games and birthdays faded from Arsinoe's mind. It didn't matter if she had changed; her position hadn't. She still lived at her sister's pleasure. And in a moment, she could die at it. The eunuch's face was grim. This new summoning didn't bode well for either of them.

As Ganymedes led her indoors, Arsinoe stole a glance at Alexander, his face pale, shoulders slouched, clothes caked with dirt. She wondered if she would ever see him again. If anyone would ever tell her that she was brave.

Unfriendly eyes followed her, the kind of eyes that darted when they were caught. Perhaps their owners heard whispers that she had not. Ganymedes remained silent, and Arsinoe knew enough to follow his example. Somehow his hand found hers. His tenderness made her more nervous still. As he delivered her to Myrrine, he squeezed her fingertips for luck.

"*Fortes fortuna adiuuat,*" he murmured in her ear.

Slippery words, even after she had worked them into Greek from the wretched Roman tongue: "Fortune favors the bold." Once in her chambers, Myrrine slipped the tunic over her head and led her toward her bath. Naked and shivering, she stood icy over the tub, trying to riddle out the meaning until her nurse urged her down into its depths.

Fortes fortuna adiuuat. Fortes fortuna adiuuat. The foreign syllables paced into an incantation. *Fortes fortuna adiuuat.* Comb in hand, deft Myrrine slipped and yanked at her scalp, but Arsinoe held her tongue. The slightest cry, or word of protest, might crumble her resolve and collapse her into childish tears.

As much as she hated baths, she dreaded this one's end. Rather than leap from the basin, she wallowed until the waters cooled and goose pimples sprouted on her arms. Quaking, she hunched over her knees and stared at her pruning toes.

Myrrine kissed her brow. "It will turn out all right in the end."

Dressed in her finest chiton, a bright sapphire one that made her skin glow like gold, Arsinoe was escorted into the public halls. She'd been a fool—she saw that now—to imagine that she'd been forgotten merely because the queen had been busy in the Upper Lands. She should have paid more heed to Ganymedes. He'd tried to warn her, with his readings of Polybius, that she should not forget that her life still hung in the balance. "You'll soon show what you are, worth your breeding, Ismene, or a coward—for all your royal blood." Antigone's taunts turned against her.

Stone-faced, heartless, the guards led Arsinoe to the royal

atrium. Would they brag or mourn when they told of how they de-livered the princess Arsinoe to her death? Why else would Berenice call her forward, unless she'd changed her mind?

The handles—two golden griffins guarding the queen—split open. Within, the joys and lightness of her father's court had been stripped away: no minstrels, no fools, no dancing maids. The mood here shunned laughter.

Nobles clustered in sets of four and five, like grapes on the vine. Some had familiar faces, but their names slipped Arsinoe's mind. And there, on her father's throne, sat Berenice. Her sister wore her hair twisted about her head, a pair of snaking braids gathered in a golden clasp at her nape, garnets and emeralds dripping from their tails. With her hair strung back so tightly, Berenice looked even more severe than she usually did. Beside the queen an aging crone reclined on a crimson divan. The old woman's clothes caught Arsi-noe's eye; they looked finer than even the queen's. Her violet chiton was embroidered with a thick border of golden lotuses around the hem and neck. Only when Arsinoe's gaze reached the woman's face did she recognize the creature glowering at her as Tryphaena.

"Arsinoe, my dear sister."

Arsinoe knelt in supplication. Head bowed, she felt as though she was offering her neck before an ax. She wasn't sure whether she should trust this sister who had once spared her life, or whether she should somehow try to cast her lot on her father's side.

"Blessings on you, noble queen, House of Ptolemy crowned with all your family. Blessings on you always!" The phrase leapt from her tongue with surprising ease. Later, she'd realize that it was some butchered line from Sophocles that had stuck in her head, the words of a messenger hailing Jocasta.

"There's no need for such formality between sisters." A slight smile crossed Berenice's face. "You may stand before me."

Arsinoe scrambled to her feet.

"You are kind, my dear," Tryphaena sneered, "to embrace the

natural child of your father with open arms, even as her full-blooded brothers plot your demise."

Berenice answered her mother lightly. "Why shouldn't I be kind to bastards, when both of my parents were born from the loins of Ptolemy the Savior's concubines?"

Arsinoe's own plaited hair weighed heavily on her scalp. The onyx beneath her feet looked inviting; perhaps she should remain there, fall back to the ground, a suppliant, and beg for mercy. *Fortes fortuna adiuuat.* Arsinoe kept her eyes fixed on her sister's as she approached the throne. She wasn't Ismene; she was Antigone. As Alexander had said.

"Tell me: do you know where your mother is?" Berenice asked. "Where your two brothers are hiding?"

"I do not." Her answer was slow, true.

"Do you think she'd answer honestly if she did? She's not as unnatural in her love as you." Tryphaena spat her words, first at her daughter and then at Arsinoe. "And do you claim to know nothing of your father's voyage to Rome?"

"I've heard nothing from my father since he sailed from Alexandria." Her words sounded far away, as though someone else had spoken them.

"I told you she knew nothing, Mother. Have you finished interrogating the child?"

"You believe those lies? You think those wide eyes prove her innocence?" Tryphaena wheezed. Blood spattered the woman's fingers. "You think she does not know that her father and her sister are in Rome? You think she hasn't been—" A fit of coughing interrupted Tryphaena's rage. Little specks of crimson spotted against the stone.

"That's enough, Mother. Your hacking won't point her toward the truth."

The two women spoke over her, around her, as if she didn't exist at all.

"I'm not lying," Arsinoe broke in. "My brothers are nothing to me. My father and mother have both abandoned me. I'm at your mercy."

"I suppose you are, my dear. Although I hope your time hasn't been so bleak as that. Tell me, my child: what lessons have you learned of late? I wouldn't want my sister to go untaught." Berenice smiled again. It softened her appearance, even with her hair drawn back, but did little else to improve it. Kingdoms, like horses, shy from ugly riders, Arsinoe had once heard. She raked her mind for an answer here; what *had* she learned? That Alexander was far bolder than she'd ever dreamt, and that Polybius thought they were all doomed in the face of Rome. But neither seemed the sort of thing she should mention here.

"Has a cat stolen your tongue?" Berenice teased.

A few of the nobles snickered in appreciation. Arsinoe realized, suddenly, why they looked familiar: these were the same men who had attended her father, men who smiled at his jokes a scant year past, men whose loyalty she'd never questioned, men she'd thought would sooner die than shed their allegiances.

One in particular stood out. Nereus, that gray-bearded man who had known her from the cradle, the dearest of her father's friends, blinked at her with cold eyes. She hated him with a deep loathing, this man who'd betrayed her father, who'd turned on her. She wanted to taunt him, as he taunted her. *Fortes fortuna adiuuat.*

"I'm learning a monologue from Sophocles," Arsinoe began. It was risky, but hadn't Ganymedes told her to embrace risk? Snakes and liars surrounded her sister, choking out the truth. This—this was what she could offer Berenice. What none of these men dared: an honest look at the creatures who poisoned the court.

"And whose speech is that?" asked Berenice. "Jocasta's? Or Deianeira's, perhaps?"

"It's the one Antigone gives to explain why she must bury her brother Polynices." She'd committed to the path now, this path of bravery, of truth. Her heart drummed in her throat.

"And what reason does she have?" Berenice asked, indulgent.

" 'It wasn't Zeus, not in the least, who made this proclamation—not to me. Nor did that Justice, dwelling with the gods beneath the earth, ordain such laws for men. Nor did I think your edict had such force that you, a mere mortal, could override the gods, the great unwritten, unshakeable traditions.' "

"Those are well-spoken words. But I wonder if you know their meaning."

Berenice's voice was stern—and it gave Arsinoe an escape. She could back down from this plan, could lie and concoct some dull excuse. Pretend to be a foolish girl who parroted lines blindly. No, she'd press on.

"Antigone means that there are certain laws, laws of the gods, 'the great unwritten, unshakeable traditions,' that no man should flout, not even if he's commanded to do so by a king."

Berenice looked at her with interest. "Indeed. And what, little one, do these 'traditions' concern? I must admit that I'm not over-joyed to hear that you'd give men leave to flout my laws."

Again, a forced chuckle of approval echoed across the atrium.

"The customs concerning burial, for one." Arsinoe threw herself into the performance, remembering how Cleopatra would draw attention to herself when reciting a monologue. She stood straight and let her voice build upward from her gut. "And also, I believe that for Antigone, at least, another aspect plays a role: loyalty."

The word quieted the murmuring men, all the way to the soldiers who lined the lotus-laced arches that led into the great courtyard.

"And what has Antigone taught you of loyalty?"

She paused and gave a pointed look to Nereus. "That it's much more prized by Sophocles than by the Alexandrian Court."

Silence drowned fickle fortune's favored boldness. Arsinoe's throat tightened, and her heart raced. Her die was cast.

"Your so-called sister shows little respect, my dear," Tryphaena hissed in her hoarse whisper.

"No." The queen chuckled lightly. "The girl offers me something of much greater value than that: a bit of humor and honesty in this bitter palace."

The knot in Arsinoe's stomach loosened; her head spun. She'd charmed her sister. She had won.

"My—my queen," Nereus stammered. "You forget that—"

"Who among us hasn't wondered at all my father's friends who have so promptly embraced my rule? I know I have." With a smile, Berenice surveyed the nobles standing before her. "I'll impede your studies no further, little sister. Return to your tutor now."

Arsinoe had no need to be dismissed twice. She quit the chamber with measured and dignified steps. Beneath the forgiving sky, she broke into a run. Panting, she found Alexander in the garden. Frozen in the spot where she had left him. Waiting, even, for her return.

"You were right." She gasped, breathless, pleased. "I am the bravest person you've ever known."

ELDER

Poseidon's winds beat against her face, teasing strands from the golden clasps of her diadem and whipping them across her cheeks. Cold idled in the air despite the bright afternoon sun, and Berenice wrapped her woolen mantle more tightly around her shoulders. She stepped lightly over the thick grass. All around her, acacia trees sprang up, their stalks spindling into the blue until their branches burst forth in a spurt of olive. Here and there, Berenice caught sight of one of the menagerie's lingering denizens: a giraffe stretching his neck to munch idly on the leaves, or a peacock dragging his luxurious tail through the high-grown lawn. Otherwise, she was alone. Or as alone as she could ever be. Two guards trailed some twenty paces back, silent yet obtrusive.

As a child, she'd loved this forgotten isle cast off the royal harbor. Her father's hapless uncle, Ptolemy Alexander, had built a palace here during his first reign some fifty years ago, among the rocky crags of the northern beach, but it had long since fallen into ruin, its gold and marble pilfered by his more fortunate successors. In the years that followed, the island had given itself over to wilder passions. The glimmer of the past gleamed sharper along the southern shore: the limestone avenues cracked with stubborn grass, the Isis temple with its shrinking coterie of priests. The rest had been overtaken by the Piper's ever-growing collection of exotic creatures. Amid the birds and beasts of far-flung lands, Berenice would lose herself in wonder. Here she could forget the tensions of the court, her mother's scheming, and her father's decadent feasts.

And it was here that she'd first learned of love and death: the wolf who leapt to greet her each day until the day he rose on his paws no more. "Don't weep for your foolish pets"—Tryphaena's words. Those had been long and solitary years for her mother, years of welcoming and burying babes each spring as she tried and failed to bear a living son.

As Berenice left the acacia grove behind and crossed onto the limestone that snaked toward the Temple of Isis on the island's southern end, the grounds grew more ordered. Between the granite statues of her forefathers in sphinx form, each cloaked face virtually indistinguishable from the next, stood the cages of her father's more fearsome beasts. Most of the pens lay empty; the Piper had taken great joy in acquiring creatures but little interest in their care. The albino tiger of her childhood remained, lying listless on his belly. He raised his head and growled halfheartedly at her step. In his youth, he'd paced until his tread wore through the iron floor of his crate. Now he was still; only his tail flicked from time to time. Pieton would have her kill the creature. "A powerful example, the death of the most prized piece of your father's collection," the eunuch told her. Her mother urged the animal's execution too. But Berenice needed him, this creature paled to an imitation of his former majesty. He reminded her of her father, of all she herself refused to become. The tiger's claws, yellowing with years, relaxed; his growls calmed to a purr.

By the time she reached the Temple of Isis, its frieze of the bare-breasted goddess suckling her fatherless babe brilliant in the afternoon glow, the sundial's shadow stretched long. She should return to the other shore, to her royal palace and all the irritations that waited there. What was she searching for here? Did she believe that she could sate the cold hole in her stomach? That was childish. Besides, her absence would have already turned the bureaucrats and petitioners restless. She had to tread with care to appease the people and their priests. Word of her antics in the Upper Lands had spread—and the Alexandrians were capricious characters. She couldn't risk another such display. Not if she wanted to capture Cyprus. Not if she wanted to fend off her father's armies.

A scuffle scattered her thoughts, and she turned toward the upset: her men grasped a breathless boy between them. The larger guard seized the child's wrists in one hand; the other pointed his sword at the interloper's neck.

"Caught a likely assassin, have you?" Berenice scoffed. It was their job, their duty—she understood that. But she wondered why they'd grabbed a child with such ferocity. Did they think her so weak and womanly as to be endangered by that wisp of a boy?

His knees buckled, collapsing him forward toward the limestone lane. She almost pitied this pathetic messenger. The broader soldier jerked him to stand. The smaller, the sword-wielder, spat in disgust at the child's cowardice.

"Come, come. Let's see what he has to say for himself before you bruise him too badly." It was strange that he should come to the island at all. Who would know that she lingered here? "You ought to know better than to race through the royal menagerie," she told the boy. "As you've now learned, there are those who might mistrust your motives. What brings you here at such reckless speed?"

"My master, Sophos, sent me." His voice cracked and he took a moment to gather himself. "Sophos, who cares for your mother."

This tired tale again—her mother feigning some sickness to gain her attention. "I know who he is. Why did he send you?"

"Her illness . . ." The boy's tongue stuck in his throat.

"What now of her famed illness?"

"H-her illness," he stuttered. "Her illness has taken a bad turn. Sophos bids you to come at once. She has little time, the doctor said."

The renowned physician should know better than to send some slave every time her mother feigned worsening symptoms. But her men's eyes lay accusations on her. Perhaps they had mothers they hadn't yet learned to hate, and so, for their sakes—not for her own worries, no—she followed the boy back to her father's palace.

The moment she entered her mother's apartments, she was overwhelmed by the stench: dusty myrrh pricked with the treacly smell of honey. Another odor wafted, sick and sour, as though the dulled silver incense burners lining her mother's ivory-embossed table were meant to cover up some far more frightful smell. Berenice resisted the urge to cover her nose with her hand. Instead, she stepped carefully across Medusa's pebbled head and toward her mother's bedchamber.

Within, the doctor bent over a withered crone. All bones, skin, and elbows, no flesh on her at all. That creature with paper skin and twisted veins could not be her mother. Berenice refused to believe it. Tryphaena could not have grown so small. And yet as she thought back on the past weeks . . . Her mother's absences had stretched on from one week to the next. Berenice had scarcely laid eyes on Tryphaena since her return to Alexandria, and her mother had never been quick to remove herself from court. When Sophos looked up from his shriveled patient, Berenice shrank to a girl of six coming upon her mother's bed of child death.

"My queen. I'm glad you have come."

"Is she awake?" Berenice's whisper caught in her throat. She hadn't prepared herself for this scene. It was a scene, though, she reminded herself. Her mother's curled form and the physician looming over her, the faience figure of bare-breasted Isis on the mantel and the half dozen incense burners scattered about the room—each detail had been chosen to craft a death tableau. Berenice could scarcely believe that her mother had turned religious in her final days. Tryphaena would no sooner take to lighting scented sticks to beg the goddess's mercy than she would give up her dream of ruling.

"For the moment, she sleeps," Sophos answered. "Only the gods may say whether she'll wake again."

"It can't be as grave as that."

"My queen, she's suffered for months. This latest turn comes as no shock."

Her mother didn't suffer; she prevailed. She manipulated ailments the way lesser women manipulated costumes: with ease and calculated malice. She wouldn't be felled by some plebeian illness—an infection of the throat and nasal passages.

"Shall I leave you two alone, my queen?"

Berenice nodded despite herself. She hadn't expected to see Tryphaena so pale and feeble. Her mother was fading—but not dying, no. Berenice couldn't believe that. Her mother thrived on attention—this, too, would be part of some ploy. She wouldn't be taken in. The cloying stench of incense wouldn't cloud her senses here.

"Call for me if her condition worsens," Sophos told her gently.

The door thudded shut, and the two were alone, free of the eyes of physicians and servants. And now her mother should spring up at once, with renewed and fearsome vigor. Laughing at how she'd tricked her daughter—*soft*. But the body on the cedar bed didn't so much as twitch.

Berenice cleared her throat, and kept her voice cold. "You may drop the theatrics, Mother. We're alone now."

Still, the body didn't stir.

"Isn't luring me here victory enough?"

Berenice approached the sleeping woman. Beneath her mother's bracelets, chapped sores had cropped up on Tryphaena's paper skin. Foolish, careless slaves. When her mother grew strong, her rage would mount and they'd come to regret their negligence. Berenice took the old woman's hand in hers. Its palm was clammy; its fingers nearly slipped from her grasp.

"Berenice." Tryphaena's voice scratched in her throat. "You've come to me at last."

"I weary of these antics, Mother. If you wanted an audience, you might have petitioned like anyone else."

Tryphaena's laughter choked into a cough. It wrenched her frame, ripping the hand from Berenice's hold. An act, she reminded herself. A good one.

"Even now you deny me. What sort of unnatural daughter doesn't mourn her mother's death?"

"I've witnessed this particular ruse too many times. If you brought me here only to berate me, I'll go at once." Berenice straightened in anger. She'd grown weak; she'd nearly been blinded by her mother's theatrics the way she'd been as a girl. But now she was a grown woman—a queen, not a fool.

"No, no, my child," Tryphaena whispered, her voice weak. "I bid you to sit. I didn't mean to lose my temper. There are—there are things I must say to you before my soul abandons this world for the next. You must accept the truth, child. I am dying."

Something in her tone made Berenice pause. Her mother sounded meek, her voice shorn of conniving undertones. Had she herself been so unbending as to miss the truth? That Tryphaena, the impenetrable woman who'd borne her and raised her and plotted for her and connived for her, was dying? Her stomach twisted at the thought. For all her bitterness, Berenice had never imagined what life would be without her mother. Without Tryphaena as her spine. The hardness her mother had clung to had shielded her. Permitted her foibles. Her knees wobbled—traitors. And so, no matter what her mother had done, Berenice couldn't abandon her, not at the end. Not the way her father had when he sent Tryphaena from the palace, and crowned that concubine his queen. The shrunken woman reached out to her. Berenice took the proffered hand and squeezed it.

"My child, tell me: what will you do when your father returns at the head of a Roman army?"

Even now, even in her final breaths, her mother worried after her rule. There was a sort of caring in that. Maybe it wasn't the caring that she'd wanted. But it was the sort that her mother had to give. She'd take it now.

"He won't gain an army," Berenice told Tryphaena softly, in a tone she might use with a child. "We have our own men in Rome. They tell us he hasn't swayed the Senate. Pieton says—"

"'Pieton says,' 'Pieton says.' What do I care about his words?" Tryphaena spoke so quietly that Berenice could scarcely hear the venom. "May the gods damn the day I sent him to tutor you. You trust too easily."

"That's neither fair nor true, Mother."

"But this eunuch." Her mother's voice shook. Berenice bent close to make out the words. They were important, or at least her mother thought they were. She should listen. "Do not...do not trust the eunuch. He's no Ptolemy. He will..."

Her lips twitched but no other sound escaped. And then the twitching stopped too. No. Her mother wouldn't fade from her this way, leaving her to grasp at a new mystery. Berenice cleared her throat to cry for Sophos, to bring him running to revive the woman who'd given her life. But as she watched Tryphaena's uneven inhales, she knew it was too late. Berenice's fingers tightened on the woman's fingers as though her grip might bind her mother to this life. *Please.*

The rasping stopped. Her mother's form collapsed, empty, and no air came to fill it whole. She squeezed her mother's hand tighter, until she feared that she'd crush Tryphaena's fingers with her clutch. It wasn't possible—not now, not yet. Berenice counted the pacing of her own lungs: *seven...eight...nine...* But still, still her mother's chest didn't rise.

"Mother?" she pleaded, her voice edged with a child's belief in magic. Again, she tried. "Mother?"

The old woman didn't answer. Berenice slipped her fingers to her mother's wrist to check the beat of blood. But as she ran her hand up Tryphaena's veins, there was only stillness. Desperate, Berenice put her fingers to her mother's temple, her throat, and finally her chest, but no heartbeat matched her own.

"Sophos!" she called out, and then again: "Sophos!"

The long moments stretched on as she listened to his steps, his prying open of the door. Her mother's skin felt clammy and cool. She pulled her hands away.

"She has passed, then," the doctor said softly from the threshold.

Berenice didn't shout at him, nor at the servants who flooded in, the very ones who'd ignored her mother's peeling skin. Instead, she stared at the empty face before her. Tryphaena looked at peace; death had stolen the mad vigor that had defined her life. As Berenice stared at that face, the quiet face of an old woman—lips chapped, eyelids wrinkled—she knew that her mother would not return. Yet something anchored her to the spot as maids bustled in and out, as the breathless boy whispered in his master's ear. She paid their murmurings no mind, and she didn't object when the ebony-clad priestesses came to remove the body. To bathe and dress and care for it as she, the daughter, was supposed to do. The servants dispersed, and the sun sank into the sea.

A quiet knocking echoed in her ears. She ignored it. She was queen, and if she wanted solitude, the world should grant her that. But the banging didn't yield. It grew louder, more insistent; it demanded a response.

"Leave me," she shouted. Her voice was too loud, too angry. She regretted it at once. She didn't want anyone to imagine that her mother's death had an effect on her. *It didn't,* she told herself firmly. *It doesn't touch me.*

"Please, my queen," a trilling voice said. "Let me join you."

"I told you to leave," Berenice repeated.

But the door opened, and a girl slipped in. Berenice recognized her, but barely. It was the accent that had tipped her off, that lilting of the Upper Lands. The girl, she thought, had joined her entourage in the days after her return from Thebes.

"Get out," she mouthed. She could breathe no sound into the words.

And so the servant lingered. In time, she even ventured to speak again. "Your mother is truly gone, then."

"So it would seem," Berenice answered dully, swallowing the lump rising in her throat. She had not—would not—shed tears. But somehow it soothed her to talk. "I thought she'd outlive us all. My father and my bastard siblings and I would be dead and buried, but she would thrive, sowing some new generation against another."

"I, too, believed my mother would live forever. If fourteen child-births could not kill a woman, what could?"

"What did?"

"A soldier."

The next morning, Berenice awoke to a world unchanged. The morning sun spilled through her eastern window, lighting the char-ioteers who raced along her wall. She studied their faces, the inky black of their eyes and the earthy red of their hair, to see if she could detect any difference. But each seemed as eager to spur on his horse as he had the day before. Her mother hadn't risen from the dead, and the palace itself seemed not to care at all. When she called for Leda to come and dress her, her nurse didn't even mention the pre-vious day's events. The woman smiled brightly through her rotten teeth as she gently pinned the violet chiton along Berenice's under-arms.

Perhaps that was the way of it. She should ignore the emptiness wearing at her gut, and go about her business. When Leda offered a mirror, a heavy handheld one inlaid with ivory, to check her face, Berenice even smiled at the kohl-eyed woman who met her gaze. She held her head high as she crossed through the great courtyard and into the royal atrium. At first, the gold overwhelmed her: the leaf embossed atop the head of each column, the specks ingrained in the Dionysus mosaic on the floor, the whole hunk molded to form the throne. But no one else—not Dryton nor Nereus nor Pieton—seemed to notice the glaring incongruity of it all. That the palace remained untouched by her mother's death, as though Tryphaena had been just some other feckless resident, of no more consequence than a slave.

The moment Berenice took her seat, the nattering began. Each of her advisers seemed to hold a strong opinion on the necessary rites and rituals. None of them appeared the least surprised— they'd all known this day would come. She alone, Berenice realized, had imagined that her mother would live forever. These men had foreseen Tryphaena's death; they thought it natural. To them, she'd been nothing more than a weak old woman. How had Berenice been so blind?

"And then we must decide what items she should bring to the next life," Nereus droned. "Her furniture, of course—what little is left of it—and all the jewels given to her by the king. I imagine the set of heirloom scarabs from Ptolemy the Benefactor would do nicely as well."

The recommendations scratched like rough-spun wool against her skin. The thought of her mother buried among golden diadems dripping with enamel and faience cosmetic boxes embossed with ivory irked her. Berenice knew that these were the standard fare for women of her mother's station, far removed from the actual items that Tryphaena valued in life. No one thought to include the copy of Herodotus's beloved histories that her mother had pored over each evening, nor the switch she had used upon her horse, nor the dagger she had kept tucked under her bed. *In death, we all become concubines.*

"The embalming will require—"

"That's enough," she interrupted. "My family has been buried in the same manner in these same lands for three hundred years. I trust you four will be able to execute it to my satisfaction. But the world doesn't pause for death, not even for Tryphaena's." Thrashing around desperately for some fresh topic, something innocuous to divert her mind from her mother's passing, from the emptiness that lingered in place of rage against not one parent but two, she turned to Thais. "Tell me, Thais: how fares Dio in Rome?"

"We've had no word of him for some weeks now," he replied. "But we do know he and his party have put their case before the Senate."

"What use is that news to me?" She tried to laugh, but it sounded more like a cough. She pressed onward—always onward. "I need to know how the proceedings went, not that they occurred. If I'd known that Dio would prove such a dismal correspondent, I'd have sent someone else in his place."

"Don't blame poor Dio," her eunuch said.

She didn't like these kindly words from Pieton. He'd never liked the Alexandrian, and she didn't want to imagine what might bring him to speak gently of the man now.

"It isn't good to heap aspersions on the dead, my queen."

The dead. Not him too. It wasn't possible. She couldn't believe that her dearest adviser, her most trusted, had been snatched from this world. She thought of Dio the last time she'd seen him, vibrant and full of life, his broad smile spread across his round face. The smile that had somehow made him handsome. A tightness gripped her chest. She ignored it; she couldn't spare her tears for Dio either. Tears were weakness. Weakness and death.

"Why didn't I hear of this at once?" She hated when the eunuch kept things from her.

"The message came earlier this morning." Pieton waved a piece of parchment before the council. "There was no time to break the news quietly."

"So the Romans are now so bold as to murder Alexandrian citizens in the street?" That fury, sweet and familiar, filled Berenice with heat; she relished it. It made her feel as though she might swell to the far reaches of the atrium, her head cresting the red granite that arched above. "Have we sunk so low in their regard that our men might be hunted as boars?"

"I don't think it fair, my queen, to blame the Romans for this trouble," Pieton told her. "It was, by all accounts, your father's doing." He glanced down at the letter and read: "'As we returned to the inn, we were ambushed by half a dozen men. At first, we assumed they wanted our purses, but when we handed over our coin, they told us no money would be adequate to appease their master. And when they spoke, it was with an Alexandrian accent. I can scarcely write what happened next without weeping. The tallest among our attackers, a great brute of a man, lunged at Dio with a knife.' Or so writes our Laomedon, one of the few delegates who survived the attack by your father's ruffians. Poor boy . . .'"

Her father had murdered Dio. Berenice's fury twitched in her spleen.

"'Poor boy'? Perhaps you're to blame for this, Pieton, for sending boys when you should have sent men." Her rage displaced her sorrow. It relieved her—she wanted the fury to swallow her whole.

"My queen, it was merely a figure of speech. What I meant to say—"

Berenice cut him off. "What is it they say about eunuchs, Nereus?" Her anger flickered. The rage wasn't self-sustaining, not as it once had been; it appeared a glimmer of its former self. That frightened her. Once it had been all she needed to raze Alexandria and take the throne. "About how eunuchs' tongues wag where their balls can't."

Old Nereus let out a hearty laugh, as did Thais. But their amusement irked her too, almost as much as her own forced lightness did. Her mother was dead. Dio was dead. Even in Rome her father stretched his hand to steal back his crown, to erase the hard work she'd done governing the lands he'd failed. She'd put Alexandria's granaries to good use, distributing wheat to the starving Upper Kingdom and putting aside the rest rather than selling it to Rome for more gold. She'd raised the levies on the farmers and ensured a surplus of food for this year as well. And now that the Nile had risen high this season, she could promise that there would be grain enough to save and sell. With that certainty, she'd been sure that she could buy enough mercenaries to reclaim Cyprus and begin to seize her dynasty's lost lands.

Unmoved, Pieton remarked, "I believe the saying goes, 'A eunuch's tongue is endowed where his cock is not.' But in this particular instance I feel a different reference might be more apt: 'A eunuch hears when other men merely listen.'"

"You aren't wrong there," she told Pieton, searching for an answer. Despite herself, her heart ached for Dio, for the one man who'd sought her out, and never bent to the Piper's will. She couldn't trust her rage, or her levity either. It was too polluted by her grief. She'd cast about for distraction—and instead, she'd found this. It was Cyprus she should be planning for, not her father's return. Why did it all fall to dust, all at once? "And you, you wise men before me, had no idea of the goings-on in Rome. We must send another delegation."

"We send more men to the slaughter, then?" Dryton said. Her minister of war didn't often speak, but when he did, he silenced the room. "What we should be doing is finding allies, not sending more men to die at your father's hands."

The quiet ached against her ears, but not as it must have ached against Dryton's. As she glared at him, his pretty face twisted with regret, and his mouth contorted to justify himself.

Dio—foolish, foolish Dio. What had he been thinking, staying at an unprotected inn? Surely he could have taken more precautions while in Rome. And without anyone to plead Berenice's case, her father would certainly bring the Senate to heel. Strong though her Alexandrian support was, she could imagine how easily Rome's citizens might be swayed by her father's tale. And these daft men, her pathetic excuses for councilors, had no advice to offer at all. What she needed was to be alone.

"Get out," she ordered. "Get out, all of you. I'll think over what you've said. And whether I can wrest some fresh allies from the stones."

It calmed her to watch the effects of her words. Thais was the first to flee, wrenching his reedy body from his chair and rushing toward the door. And pretty, flustered Dryton hurried out as well. He liked to give the impression that he was both wiser and busier than any of her other advisers. It was how he justified his insolence. Perhaps he believed in all honesty that the kingdom couldn't run without his caustic advice and sticky fingers.

Pieton and Nereus stayed seated, settling into a stubborn war for her attention. The eunuch drummed his fingers on the table, his impatience palpable in every tap. But the old man paid him no mind. A word from her would resolve the matter, but she could take some pleasure in watching these petty power struggles play out.

Pieton cleared his throat. Scarcely two feet to his right, Nereus made no answer. Berenice suspected that the old man feigned deafness to suit his purposes. She would have to recall that skill when she grew old and faint of mind. If she should live that long.

The eunuch cleared his throat. "Nereus, my friend, the queen requested your absence."

"And yours as well, eunuch."

Pieton didn't look at her; he knew better than to appeal for her favors. But Nereus had no such cautions. "My queen, I beg a word with you in private."

Why not? The old man was easy; she could handle whatever he tossed her way. With her former tutor, though, her emotions might boil to the surface. He knew her too well, read her too well. She didn't dare speak to him alone. Not now, when more than ever she needed to be strong. "Go on, Pieton. Leave us awhile."

The eunuch cocked his head in surprise. He wasn't accustomed to dismissals. He looked very nearly wounded, his eyes shrunk and twitching. But then he shrugged and bowed, and did as he was bid without objection.

"Very well, Nereus. Now that you have bested Pieton"—she smiled; if she didn't smile, she was afraid that she'd rage into madness, or tears—"tell me what bothers you."

"It pains me, my queen—" Nereus's voice caught. He cleared his throat loudly to continue. "I, too, worry for the future of our lands. And though my nephew sounds like a firebrand at times, he does, I am afraid, address an important point."

Dryton was his nephew, then. She'd make a note of that. It helped to focus on the minutiae of these lesser men's lives. How they built one upon the other to claw closer to the crown.

Nereus spoke quietly. "We don't have the swords to defeat Rome. But there is another path to victory."

Berenice knew what he would propose before he spoke the words. But she wouldn't heed them. Pieton, too, would urge a similar course if she gave him half a chance, the course that confounded every woman at one point or another: marriage. Not even for Cyprus would she sink to that. She'd witnessed the consequences of wedding, how it had destroyed her mother.

"Long before you were born—nay, even long before I was born; yes, even as long ago as that—your ancestors kept the Romans at bay by wedding allies, uniting the descendants of Alexander against the Republic," the old man continued.

"That's all very well. When my foremothers didn't bed their uncles and their brothers, they bedded the great kings of Asia. It was a good strategy then. But tell me: what allies might I wed? Do you have some Attalid, some Cyrenian picked out?" Berenice laughed. This, too, was forced. But forced emotions were better than the effortless ones that might otherwise leak out. Even fury she couldn't trust; it was too changeable for her to harness. "Those kingdoms, I don't need to remind you, fell to Rome long ago, before even you were born. Mine is the last dynasty of Alexander's crumbled empire. There are no such fine friends for me to marry."

Nereus's eyes lit up. "Begging your pardon, my queen, but the Seleucids—"

"The Seleucids?" She laughed, cold, cruel. "Have you lost your mind, old man? Pompey murdered the last of those kings—Antiochus died some half dozen years ago." Destroyed by Rome. To a one. Her own kingdom's future—if her father had his way.

"But my queen, Antiochus was not his father's only son." The old man rubbed the loose skin along his gullet. That twitch of his sickened Berenice; it made her think of death.

"It doesn't matter if the elder Antiochus had a hundred sons. Many men have sons. It's kingdoms that prove rare."

"Begging your pardon, my queen, but you have a kingdom, a double kingdom. What you seek, I believe, are more spears to defend it."

She looked hard at the old man. It had been years since she'd heard such determination in his voice—not since he had whispered poison in her father's ear, urging him to put aside her mother, his lawful wife, in favor of that whore. Old wounds. The scars ran deep.

"And this boy," Nereus went on firmly, "this younger son of Antiochus heads a legion of some ten thousand men along the Syrian coast. Men who loathe the Romans as much as you do, led by a general who despises the Republic all the more. They killed his brother, they stole his crown, they sow his lands with blood and chaos."

When did the Romans do anything else? Berenice thought of Cyprus, the peaceful, sheltered island where she'd wintered as a girl, shredded and shorn. "And you believe this hate might be turned to my advantage. That he would be eager to fight any Romans—say, the Romans who back my father?"

"If you wed him, yes. You, my queen, are wise beyond your years."

She disliked that particular compliment. Nothing in her life had convinced her that age brought much in the way of wisdom. Her father grew more a fool with each passing day, and her mother died a withered shadow of her former self, vulnerable and soft. Wisdom unchanged.

"And what is his name, then, this younger, lesser brother of Antiochus?"

"Seleucus, named for the first of his dynasty, my queen."

She'd always thought it would be one of her brothers that her advisers would be urging her to wed. She could still picture her mother, crooning over another shriveled babe: "He could have been your husband. If only you'd proved worthy of him." And why? What good had it done her mother, marrying her brother? She'd been discarded and disgraced. Cast off like the monsters she'd cast from her womb. No, she'd wed no baby brothers—not now, not ever. Only horror arose from that. But there could be some benefit to wedding a man who brought an army.

"I will think it over, Nereus. You did right to bring this to me alone. Let's keep this idea between the two of us."

"Of course, my queen," the old man said, wheezing, as he hobbled from the chamber.

Berenice studied him with cold eyes. With each passing day, her suspicions sharpened. She grew sure that he played up these maladies; beneath that trembling facade lurked a strong and able man. She wished, suddenly, that she hadn't sent her councilors away. It was worse, by far, to be shorn of them, surrounded only by distant guards. Worse to recall her mother's shrunken form, the dull smile on her face. At peace—and finally alone.

YOUNGER

Arsinoe slipped her toes into the fountain's waters and slid her heels across the stone. Ahead stood Aphrodite, stark naked in white marble with her hands raised over her head, twisting at her long, gold-plaited hair. She crept toward the statue; the best hiding place was behind the pale scallop shell rising at the goddess's side. Roughly, she shoved her shoulder against the stone and struggled to squeeze the rest of herself in; she was nearly too big to fit. She wouldn't be a little girl forever. Her limbs would grow and betray her too. Footfalls squelched the grass, and she jammed herself behind the statue.

But the steps didn't belong to Alexander. Boots—angry even on the dirt—belonged to guards, guards who hunted her still. She'd never escape their pounding. No, she soothed herself, they were merely Berenice's men. They meant her no harm; she was safe. She counted three pairs of footsteps. Two sounded the standard march, but the final set fell at odd intervals: a stomp answered by a scrape. A gimp, she imagined, dragging a withered leg behind the strong.

A voice, weak and reedy, reached her. "A place like this'll be full o' ears." The words, she felt certain, came from the cripple.

"There are none. I'm sure. The queen favors the menagerie for her walks. The rest will be too busy with preparations for Tryphaena's funeral."

She knew that voice. She'd recognize it anywhere, among a thousand crying in the night. It belonged to the fire-bearded guard, her savior from those early days, the one who had brought her dates as she hid beneath her bed—Menelaus. The one who'd told Ganymedes of her plight. Or so she gathered. How else would the eunuch have learned she was alive? And have known to send his cryptic advice?

She strained her ears to hear.

"Yes, I imagine they are. A dead Ptolemy requires a thousand times more care than a living man," a third voice replied. It was deeper and harsher than the other two. Arsinoe didn't know it.

"We should act soon. The court is distracted. It will be easy to steal a child from the palace."

Her friend. His voice comforted her, and his words as well. He spoke of her, of her rescue—he must be speaking of her. What other child might be stolen from the palace? No one would go through such trouble for Alexander. He was nothing; he had no royal blood.

"I don't wish to be callous, but someone has to ask: is a mere girl worth the risk?" The gimp had caught his breath.

He shouldn't speak that way. A girl, King Ptolemy's daughter, even his forgotten one, was worth ten crippled men. Or more. The water sent chills up and down her spine. But she didn't fidget. "It's too cold, Arsinoe," Alexander had told her. "Too cold for outdoor games." He'd come around in the end.

"I don't want to lose a hand," the gimp whined. "You two are young and hearty men, but even a few dozen lashes don't feel so light on this back of mine."

"She's no mere girl. She's a Ptolemy." Her Menelaus defended her.

"I know she's a Ptolemy. But she's a girl Ptolemy with two brothers, alive and well. What d'you think, Lykos?"

Lykos, "wolf." That name recalled a dream that stalked Arsinoe's nights, not once but many times. She shut her eyes to summon it.

"And who'd we give her to, if we get her out?" the gimp went on. "Her mother took the two boys with her; we've got no proof that she wants the set."

There'd been a wolf in the dream, an enormous wolf; she'd never seen a beast that size in waking life. Black as the ocean after a storm. A wolf with gleaming teeth, a bristled tail. A wolf pretending to be a fox.

"Of course she'll want the girl," said Menelaus. "She is her mother."

"Let me ask you, Amadokos," interjected the wolf. "Have you heard from the Piper's wife, even once? Have you any proof that we would be thanked for our efforts? I don't think any of us want to be stuck with a fugitive on our hands."

No, that wasn't right. The wolf had been among two foxes: a red one and a white.

"Of course you'd ask that. Why did I expect you to understand natural sympathies?"

The black beast circled the two smaller ones, sniffing, sniffing. Arsinoe had wondered as she slithered, *What does a wolf want to do with foxes?*

And her fire-bearded guard—Amadokos, they called him, not Menelaus, as she did—went on: "You'll be well rewarded when the king returns."

"You play more to your own sentiment than his. You've taken pity on the girl. Don't let it bring about your death."

The wisps congealed. The wolf lunged at the fox, tearing its red fur with gnashing teeth.

"But tell me, Amadokos: who will help us in this act? Have you talked to her nurse, at least? We must have a way to slip into the girl's chambers undisturbed . . ."

"I've not spoken to her servant, no. But I'm certain she'll be of help."

The white fox fled.

"And what of Ganymedes? The girl's tutor. Perhaps he's given you some insight into our plot?"

"I haven't discussed it with him directly, but he must know of our plans. I imagine that the king wrote to him as well."

But he couldn't flee fast enough. Both foxes, red and white, drenched in blood. The red fox wore her Menelaus's face.

"Yes, you must be right. His letter to me implied as much." There was a threat in his voice. "What did he write to you?"

"Don't answer," Arsinoe whispered. She knew now why she'd dreamt of a wolf feeding on his friends. It had been of this moment—the gods had sent her this vision, this sight. Lykos would kill them both. *Don't answer,* she repeated in her head, louder, as loudly as she could. Her mind shouted. But not loudly enough.

"Merely that he felt confident that Pompey would back his claim," her friend replied. "And that his forces had overcome Dio and his men."

"And where would one so low as you keep such a kingly letter?" The tone had transformed into poison. She could hear the gimp's sloppy paces creeping back. But the deep-voiced man would ignore him. He was not the prize. "I suppose it would be on your person. There's no safer place."

"I'd watch your words if I were you."

"And I'd think twice before I betrayed the queen."

A scramble of hard steps. Arsinoe couldn't see the men, but she shut her eyes just the same. She wished she could shut her ears against the sound as well. But her sightlessness heightened her other senses. The clash of steel on steel, the gulp of steel on flesh. The fire-bearded guard's cry, the thud of his body against the earth. And the gimp, leg dragging through the yellowed grass, and then his begging words.

"I got no letter from the king—from the imposter, I mean. I haven't done nothing, nothing at all. Take me before the queen—anything. Jus' let me live."

It sickened her to hear these pleas, a grown man weeping for his life. "Be strong," she whispered to the wind. She had been; she would be. And a sword splicing through skin, a cry of anguish, and then a moan, a low, unearthly cry, that filled the air long after the man had drawn his final breath. She listened as the murderer circled about his kills, as he checked their weapons, as his steps faded in retreat.

Her eyes opened on stillness. Shivering, she crept out from behind Aphrodite's legs. Her gaze fixed on the fountain's waters, the circles upon circles upon circles that her toes formed with each step. But she couldn't keep her eyes innocent forever. She looked up. The vision made her gasp.

Her guard lay strewn against the earth; his blood stained the yellow grass. His eyes, blue as crystals, stared unblinking at the sun. With artful steps—she didn't drop her heels; it was bad luck to wake the dead, and worse still, to wake those she'd murdered in her sleep—Arsinoe approached the corpse. She'd seen Achilles's corpse—and many others too these past moons—but none like this, none near enough to touch. Robes dripping, she knelt beside the body, and her fingers slid his eyelids shut.

"Thank you," she whispered. "For everything. I'm sorry."

She wished she had a coin to slip beneath his tongue, so she'd know that he could pay the rower's fare. That was how the common folk made their way to the reaches of the underworld: aboard Charon's boat across the River Styx. Tryphaena would not need a coin. Her body would be bathed and beautified before her burial, but no one would take such kind care of her friend. The first one, the only one, who'd tried to help her after her father fled.

Her eyes welled with tears, but she wiped them away in anger. "Many men will die for you," Ganymedes had told her. The firebearded guard was not the first; he wouldn't be the last. But much as she urged herself to be hard, steadfast, she lingered by the dead man's side and clasped his cooling hands in hers. She pressed a kiss on his forehead, as she'd seen Cleopatra do once years ago, when they'd visited a home for the dying. She wondered what her sister would do now, in her place. What there was to do other than kiss—and weep. Then her eyes searched out the body of his friend.

The gimp had fallen some twenty paces off—he'd made it farther than she'd imagined. His gray tunic was stained brown; the rest of his body would soon join his leg in rot. She walked to his corpse. Even if he was a coward, he, too, had died for her. That was enough. She knelt beside him and laid her hand on his shoulder. She strained to roll his body over; his lame leg had fattened the rest of him. At last the corpse yielded and flopped onto its back. Arsinoe winced, wishing she'd managed to move him with more dignity. His eyes, the same narrow slits in death that she'd imagined in life, glazed open, and she shut these eyes as well. As she stood, she smoothed her robes and her hands came back bloody. And then, dumbly, she stared at the bodies. If only she'd listened more to the rituals, to the preparation of the dead.

"There you are," Alexander cried out. "I've been searching for you for hours—"

His voice cut off. He must have seen the horrors, but she didn't turn. She couldn't let go of her men so easily, no matter what Ganymedes said.

"Arsinoe. Arsinoe." He repeated her name dully.

"They are dead."

"I see that." He grabbed her wrist.

"They died for me." Her voice scratched in her throat.

"Come back inside." The boy's hand tugged at her, but she kept her feet planted.

"We must bury them." The realization came sharp and quick. Arsinoe didn't know the libations by heart, but she could remember enough.

"Arsinoe, we must go. Now."

"You go, Alexander. I must bury them."

The slap came from nowhere, stinging hard across her cheek.

"You're as brave as Antigone, but you can't be as foolish. I won't let you. We must leave before someone starts asking questions."

Alexander jerked her arm and pulled her back toward the

palace. She dug her heels into the stone. He yanked her hand, hard, but she didn't budge.

"Arsinoe," he hissed. "You're soaked in blood."

"You can't tell me what I must and mustn't do." She wrenched her fingers from his grip and rushed through the columns of the great plaza and past the Arsinoe fountain in the Sisters' Courtyard, and up the stairs to her own chambers.

Myrrine gasped when Arsinoe stumbled in. "My dear child! What happened to you? Are you all right?"

"It's nothing," she lied. This came easier each day. "A cut. That's all."

"Where is it?" her nurse asked, taking hold of Arsinoe's wrists.

"It doesn't matter." She snatched her wrists away.

"As you wish, my sweet." Myrrine shook her head slowly. "Come here. Let me help you with those clothes."

As her nurse lifted her tunic over her head, Arsinoe ached to confess, to tell her all, to relate every detail of what had happened—both in the flesh and in her dreams. How the foxes had turned into dead men. But she held her tongue. Alexander was right: no one should know what she'd seen.

"Eirene! Layla!" her nurse cried out. "Bring hot water for the basin. The princess must bathe before the funeral."

The two girls appeared: the mute maid who, having served Arsinoe since Berenice's coup, had slowly regained her tongue, and the dark one from the Upper Lands. Each carried a bucket of steaming water for her bath. Arsinoe pictured them dead, as she'd seen the fire-bearded guard. Everyone who loved her, protected her, ended up in a pool of blood. A lump rose in her throat, and no matter how hard she swallowed, she couldn't shrink it away.

"Do you believe in dreams, Myrrine?" Arsinoe asked as she slipped into the tub. In her heart, she wanted to speak of her dreams only to Cleopatra. But now she knew that she couldn't wait until her sister returned. She needed an answer before more people died. Before she killed them. "In visions and omens and other evils that come to us in the night? Do you believe they come true?"

"They're not evil, my dear. These are gifts. 'Dreams as well can come our way from Zeus.'"

"But what if there are bad things that happen in the dreams?" *What if my dreams make bad things happen?* That was the question she wanted to ask, but she didn't dare. "Is there a way to stop them from coming to pass?"

"If the gods send us dreams of what's to be, then there's not a thing we can do to change them." Her nurse patted her head gently. "And even if the dreams are bad, good may come of them. All the greatest kings and queens in the world—Alexander the Conqueror himself—consult seers and soothsayers and dream tellers. Who'm I to question that?"

Myrrine scrubbed the dried blood from Arsinoe's knees. The cloth stung but she said nothing. She leaned into the pain. It was a small price to pay.

When Ganymedes came to take her to the funeral, Myrrine pulled her aside. "My dear," her servant whispered away from the eunuch's ears. "What worries you? What can your poor nurse do to comfort your sorrows?"

"I've no sorrows," Arsinoe answered, forcing a smile along her lips. Myrrine would be no help, not if she thought dreams couldn't be stopped and changed and twisted. It was better, then, to keep her secrets to herself.

Outside, she found a city shrouded in black. Thick along the marble avenue, mourners wailed. Their hair was already thinned from years of tearing, and still they ripped the remnants. One mourner, a girl only a few years older than Arsinoe, split open her rough-spun tunic and dug her nails into her breasts. Three crimson streams trickled in her fingers' wake.

"Even here?" she asked Ganymedes. "I thought the corpse lay in the Sema." That was where all her ancestors had been buried, from the magnificent Alexander to the uncle who'd lost Cyprus to the Romans.

"It does. But when you are mother to a queen, your mourners stretch the length of every street. So it shall be upon your death."

And what of those other deaths, of the fire-bearded guard and the gimp? Men had died for her that day, men far braver and kinder than Tryphaena. But for them, there would be no mourners, no weeping, no libations. Their souls would wander lost and helpless through the world as listless shades, stripped of life yet unable to pass into the undergloom. Would he haunt her dreams, her Menelaus? Would she see him around each bend, only to find him vanished when she looked again? Or would he merely come to her as the red fox, as he already had?

The wails echoed against wind and sea. They sounded as one now, a united cry for the death of Tryphaena. In olden times—so she'd been told—the women of the house not only prepared the body but performed the mourning rites as well. There'd been no hired wailers, no underclass of women born to tear their hair.

"Arsinoe," the eunuch whispered. "When you enter the Sema, you must be silent, and respectful. Bow only to the queen and then retreat. Don't make a nuisance of yourself."

"I know how I must behave." She shrugged Ganymedes's hand from her shoulder.

As they drew deeper into the city, the moans joined in a dirge, long and low and mournful. Here the criers were of a higher class—singers, not mere rippers of hair. Arsinoe was jealous of their madness, of their mutilations. And angered by their weeping too. Her father's sister didn't deserve such honors. She deserved no distinctions at all.

A line snaked outside the Sema, the imposing marble mausoleum that contained Alexander's tomb and the tombs of all her forebearers. Hundreds upon hundreds of nobles had come to pay their respects. With ease, Ganymedes steered Arsinoe through the gathered men. If they recognized her she couldn't tell, but whatever their reasons, they parted before her step. "But Death overtakes even the man who runs from the battle..." These words hummed in her ears.

A hundred wailers dotted the outer colonnade, with its columns of red-streaked onyx; subjects passed between these pillars to see the fallen Tryphaena. The Alexandrians were stoic and stern-faced. Perhaps they didn't care so very much for Berenice's mother—or for the queen herself. As Arsinoe entered the sanctuary, the dirges grew louder, but she felt a hush fall over the gathered lords. Perhaps they, too, were frightened of the unrisen Ptolemies who flanked each side. She shivered at the first: a sapphire-tinted cast bore the likeness of her uncle, his wide nose and fleshy cheeks, though she knew that his true body had been lost in Cyprus. She peeled her eyes away, fixing them above the altar. There, dwarfed by the goat-headed columns that marked the entrance to Alexander's shrine, she saw Berenice, quiet and regal, no trace of sadness in her eyes. Arsinoe understood her stoicism. She wasn't sure if she would weep if it were her own mother who lay dead.

All at once, a fear gripped her: what if Tryphaena hadn't died at all? Too many grown-ups stood between her and the corpse; she couldn't make out the body. And if she didn't see it, how could she know this wasn't some elaborate ruse? Arsinoe long had her doubts: the woman was too monstrous to meet such an ordinary fate as death. Ganymedes, at Arsinoe's side, gripped her hand tightly, as if he could smell her thoughts.

She wrenched her fingers from the eunuch's and darted through the crowd, past the earlier Ptolemies, the Potbelly and the Savior too, their glass faces staring at the vaulted ceiling. And then at last she saw her: Tryphaena reduced to a shrunken, weak-willed body draped in white and laden with gold hanging from her ears, her wrists, her varicose throat. No more dangerous than a spider squished beneath a heel. Arsinoe rushed toward the hateful corpse, dodging the legs of men who'd come to pay their respects. This woman—this creature—had a thousand mourners. Her Menelaus had none. There was no fairness in that.

Arsinoe's fingers clawed her tunic and tore it open. Her nails ripped away her flesh in gashes as she shrieked and wailed and moaned. One mourner would remember her fire-bearded friend.

The dirges echoed louder as her fingers plowed into her skin. In her mind they sang for him. *Menelaus, kindest of the Argives and of the Alexandrians too*...Eyes fixed on her—the gathered men, the high priest, even her sister Berenice. Arsinoe dug her nails into her scalp and clawed at her hair. And then Ganymedes caught her hand.

"My queen, I beg you, forgive this child," the eunuch pleaded. "She doesn't know herself for grief. She forgets the proper place of a royal princess."

"No." Berenice spoke in a queer and unfamiliar voice. It seemed to tremble. She looked Arsinoe directly in the eye. "No, indeed, she recalls it better than any other here today. She knows what it is to mourn, though I can't imagine for whom she grieves."

"For your mother, my queen," Arsinoe's tutor answered seamlessly.

"Don't lie to me, Ganymedes. I have my own eunuch for that."

As her tutor led her away from corpse and queen, Arsinoe smiled. He would be remembered, her Menelaus, because she wouldn't forget this day. This day the whole of Alexandria had paused to watch her, wrenching their eyes from that wretched corpse.

"Don't look so pleased," Ganymedes scolded her.

"Why shouldn't I be pleased?"

"I know you think it great fun to make a spectacle of yourself, to remind the people of the Piper's forgotten daughter," he whispered. "And perhaps it is great fun for now: you are but a girl, and many things might be forgiven. But one day you'll appear a true threat, Arsinoe, and on that day you'll go too far."

"But *fortes fortuna adiuuat*. It was you who told me that, Ganymedes."

"Yes, fortune favors the bold, little one. That's how the saying goes. But neither fate nor fortune favors the foolhardy."

She swallowed her protests. Even though she wanted to argue, she knew that she couldn't. She *had* been foolhardy, but she wasn't old or wise or brave enough to admit it aloud.

The eunuch walked too quickly up the avenue, as if he wanted to outpace her steps and leave her to her fate.

"Ganymedes." She raced to catch up. "Ganymedes, there is—I know—there is something that has been troubling me."

He looked back at her. His eyes weren't unkind.

"Go on."

Arsinoe hesitated. She wasn't sure how to phrase her question. How to explain that the visions that haunted her at night became true in the light of day. But she couldn't wait any longer; she had to know if he would offer her more comfort than Myrrine had. "Do you believe in dreams?"

The eunuch laughed. "What do you mean by such a question?"

Her voice dropped to a murmur. "Do you believe in visions?" Her eyes darted to see if anybody watched them. But all eyes were on the mourners and the musicians and the maidens on the temple steps. No one among them paid any mind to a girl and her eunuch. "Do you believe in the sort of dreams that predict what is to come?"

"My dear, we all have dreams. And we all have minds that read our desires into our dreams."

Desires? Had she wanted to see Menelaus slain? Had she, like Antigone, fallen in love with death? "I'm not speaking of those sorts of dreams. I mean the sorts where bad things happen. And then happen again in life."

The eunuch studied her. His hand twitched at his side. "You believe that you have had such dreams."

Arsinoe nodded, gnawing at her lip.

"Let me give you some advice, my child. Put such thoughts from your mind, and don't speak of them again. They are nonsense. Only fools believe in such madness—priests and witches and lunatics. The sort who think that you can brew magic from some amalgam of roots and body parts. Commoners and idiots, Arsinoe. You wouldn't want anyone to think you are among them."

His hand jerked madly at his side. Arsinoe couldn't remember a time when she'd seen Ganymedes so unnerved. And though they walked back to the palace together, her tutor didn't speak another word.

ELDER

The atrium was close and sticky, even though the doors and shutters had been flung open. It seemed the very air meant to thwart her. Nereus certainly appeared determined to. Claiming fresh reports from abroad, the old man had requested a meeting of the councilors, and so Berenice found herself shut away with Pieton, Thais, and Dryton as the old man held his haughty court. She stared at her aging adviser as he twisted his signet ring back and forth across a gnarled knuckle, spewing forth his relentless news.

"Our spies in Rome tell us that Pompey supports your father's claim," he went on. "And he has urged the Senate to give the Piper the men he requests. Without Dio to counter, it seems almost sure that he will gain a Roman army."

The words struck hard, as if the blow was intended. *Your mother is dead,* they threatened. *Your father will descend on Alexandria. Your rule will crumble.*

"My queen." The old man's voice grew strained. "I know you have suffered great losses, but you must listen."

"I do listen, Nereus, and I've not suffered such losses as that," she snapped, gathering her attention up, cloaking it around her grief. There would be an escape from this too. Even if her father gained a Roman army, there would be ample time before the legions arrived. Berenice had already called up her troops from all across the Upper Lands. She was prepared to fight. Keen to, in fact.

"And tell me, Nereus: how will these legions arrive from Rome?" she asked.

"By ship, I imagine, my queen."

There lay her glimmer of hope. Her ten-oared galleys would outmatch Roman sixes with ease. The Republic's guard would either have to make a long journey by land or face her royal warships on the sea. In landlocked Rome, men loathed battling aboard ships; they preferred to fight in the field. That was to her advantage: flanked by a great river, lake, and sea, Alexandria suckled her soldiers on the water.

"The Romans won't seek a naval battle," she said with certainty. "And it will take some months to reach Alexandria from Rome, or even Asia, by land."

Nereus cleared his throat, rubbing at his pockmarked chin. It seemed he could not bear to stand completely still. "It is possible, my queen, that—"

She interrupted the old man. "Tell me, Nereus: how many victories has the great and glorious Pompey enjoyed upon the waves? Or even that younger general who's busy gallivanting about among the Gauls?"

"Julius Caesar," Thais cut in, simpering. "I believe that is—"

"His name doesn't matter to me. The point is this, Nereus: how often do the Romans—any of them—seek an engagement on the sea?"

"The wars against Carthage—"

"I meant in recent times, not stories that might have frightened my grandfather's grandfather." In her agitation, Berenice felt the sweat pooling in the sticky crevices of her knees and elbows. The weather had grown unseasonably warm, and her dark woolen mourning garb trapped the heat against her skin.

"Not often, I admit," Nereus answered, "but I would point out that Pompey did win some great sea battles when he cleared the waters of the Cilicians."

"The Cilicians were pirates—skilled, but pirates nonetheless," she reminded the old man. "You might not value our soldiers highly, but even you must think our two hundred war galleys more formidable than that."

Nereus swallowed at the bobbing apple in his throat and argued no further.

These men irked Berenice, but they no longer seemed fearsome. They'd been her father's councilors before they'd been hers—and they were a fickle group. Except for Pieton, she could not be sure where any of their loyalties lay. How many of them secretly longed for the Piper's return?

"Pieton." She cleared her throat at the eunuch. He was now leaning back on the silken pillows of his divan, his fingers dangling near one of the couch's lion-crested feet. She'd noticed that Pieton looked overly comfortable during these sessions, as though he already knew how each part would play out, what her advisers would say, and how she would respond. She deserved his full attention. "How many clerics have we recalled to mount our Cypriot attack? We must divert these soldiers to prepare to fight my father instead."

Pieton straightened up, folding his legs neatly over the side of the settee. "We have perhaps ten thousand now in arms. But the harvest has been poor thus far, my queen, which should come as no surprise. The Nile ran low this year—too low. We nearly emptied the granaries seeing that the Upper Lands didn't starve. I don't imagine we could pay for more than another ten, fifteen thousand at most."

"Twenty-five thousand on foot, then," she interjected, lumping all the infantry together. It sounded like more that way, though far from enough. Ten thousand might have been equal to taking Cyprus unaware—but this? To battle a rested set of Roman legions? "And how many on horse?"

"We didn't recruit horses for Cyprus, but we might muster three thousand," Pieton answered. "Perhaps fewer. Our equestrian order has been greatly depleted. The upkeep of charges costs more than that of men."

"How can there be so few?" Berenice shook her head in frustration. The fault lay with her as well. Her father had been absent for nearly a year—and what had she accomplished? Not nearly enough. Her plan to keep Rome neutral had failed. Dio was dead. She'd shored up some support among the natives in the Upper Lands, but she'd cemented enemies as well. She needed to act now—and quickly.

"The time has come for me to wed." She spat the words as much as spoke them, thrusting them from her lips quickly, so they could not be unsaid.

"An excellent notion," Pieton chimed, all attention now. His ready agreement disappointed Berenice; she'd hoped that he might for once be shocked. "It's high time you wed the elder of your two younger brothers."

Her stomach churned at the notion. She'd seen what little good wedding her brother had done for her mother, how she'd ended up whelping monsters year after year, ruined and betrayed. She'd known that someone would suggest it, but not Pieton—he'd seen what the Piper had done to Tryphaena, what the Piper had done to *her*.

"What benefit would that bring?" she replied coolly, as though she spoke of only the politics. There were men here she didn't trust—and she wouldn't show them she was soft. "He is a child; he has no men, no arms, no horses unless you count his piebald pony."

"The way I see it, my queen," Pieton pressed on, "you have two choices: you either fight the Romans or convince them you are the rightful ruler of Egypt. The Senate won't send legions against a reigning brother-sister pair. They'd be mad to."

From the corner of her eye, Berenice could see Thais's nodding, bowing head, splashed with the afternoon light pouring from the window. His chin always inclined to the last opinion spoken. It disgusted her. And she would not become her mother, no matter what the eunuch said.

"Begging your pardon, my dear friend," Nereus cut in. "But how do you propose the queen wed her brother Ptolemy? I was under the impression that—despite our exhaustive searches—no man had seen hide nor hair of the boys. Unless you're privy to some secret knowledge?"

That she couldn't believe. It wasn't possible: Pieton wouldn't think of speaking to the concubine, to the woman who'd stolen her father's love and wrecked her own claim to the throne. But when she looked to the eunuch and saw his fingers twitching at his chin, stroking his imagined beard . . . Perhaps he had. This was a nervous habit of his. Did Nereus's accusation contain some slip of truth?

"I have no special knowledge," Pieton answered, "but I am confident that there are ways, Nereus, of getting word to the mother of those children. And she would surely approve of the idea. She worries more for her boys' safety than for her husband's."

Dryton joined in, chewing at the discord like a wild dog. "Strange, Pieton, that you know so much of these children's whereabouts, of their mother's state of mind . . ."

Sometimes Berenice thought they all spoke merely to provoke her, to drive her shrieking to her grave. She'd listen to no more of this—that wasn't why she'd broached the topic.

"Enough bickering," she told them firmly, as she might a roomful of children. "My mother's body is hardly cold. I won't disgrace her memory by marrying one of the Piper's bastard sons."

The eunuch's eyes narrowed to slits cut across his gaunt face. "Whom, then, shall you marry? I thought you meant to wed for pragmatic reasons."

She ignored the jab. They both knew she wouldn't wed for pleasure—what pleasure had she ever witnessed in a marriage? At least he'd backed away from the sickening idea that she wed one of those little boys.

"There are others I might marry for greater gain," Berenice told the eunuch. "My house has long wed queens not only to their brothers but also to form alliances with other sworn enemies of Rome."

"Rome, my queen," Pieton replied softly, "has few enemies these days. Unless you plan to wed some uncouth Gaul."

"Rome has one enemy left, and a great one too." Nereus had planted the notion, and now Berenice clutched at it, echoing his words. "Seleucus, the last remaining son of the Seleucid dynasty, loathes Rome—and he has many legions who follow him, men who would be glad to do battle with the Republic."

Dryton laughed. "Seleucus? The one they call the Salt-Fish Seller?"

Berenice glanced at the old man. In the midst of his eager attempt to bring her around to his plan, to sell her on the son of Antiochus, he'd neglected that detail. But Nereus said nothing in his prospect's defense. She supposed she should be thankful for his silence. Pieton would be more likely to agree if the old man didn't argue in favor of it.

"Or perhaps you meant to neglect your favorite's name?" Dryton said, mocking Nereus. "Oh, yes, this is what the great son of Antiochus the Pious has been reduced to: a petty *merchant*—"

The eunuch cleared his throat. "He is no merchant. At times, he has been known to traffic goods across the sea. But I fear none of us could say we are innocent of that. And his parentage is remarkable for another reason. He is the son of your grandfather's sister. Do you remember her, the less favored one who was called Selene?"

She did. Of course. The one who had tried to steal her father's throne and name her own sons as kings over both the Seleucid and Ptolemaic kingdoms. Berenice had a feeling she might have liked the woman, if history hadn't set their claims at odds.

"Well, I suppose we are meant to think this Seleucus is her last living son," the eunuch continued.

"It's not a rumor, Pieton; it's the truth," Nereus croaked.

"There's no need to cast aspersions on his birth. He is indeed the son of Selene. And a union between these two would serve to unite those feuding branches of the family."

"I am less concerned with familial concord than I am with soldiers," Berenice said, smiling wanly. The conversation had shifted; it edged in her direction now. She could snatch control of it. "Tell them, Nereus: how many men will Seleucus bring?"

"He would bring five thousand on foot, perhaps another thousand on horse. Good fighting men, my queen."

Five thousand sounded paltry now that the moment had come and Berenice had to choose whether to sell herself. So very few soldiers in exchange for her hand and nearly half of her throne. But she'd said she'd wed, and so she would. Better Seleucus than her brother. Better anyone than him.

"Send word to Seleucus, then, that he should come to Alexandria but leave his armies outside the city gates. I'll not have foreigners marching into our capital." The Alexandrians would never stand with her after that. Foreigners were foreigners, whether Roman or Seleucid. And should a strange army tramp through the Canopic Gate, there was no telling how quickly the mob might rise into an angry wave.

"As you wish, my queen."

Pieton nodded in agreement, and Thais as well. Only Dryton, sneering and scoffing loudly into his hand, gave no sign of approval.

"Is there something you'd like to add?" Berenice asked him sharply. "Do you mean to counsel me against this marriage?"

"No, my queen," Dryton replied, straightening on his cushions.

"But I heard you. I believe we all heard you when I announced my plan. Thais." She prodded her least courageous adviser. "Did you hear Dryton make a noise, a noise perhaps of disapproval at my words?"

"I—" Her reedy adviser gulped. "I did indeed, my queen."

"And you, Nereus? Did Thais and I imagine some noxious commentary on the part of our dear Dryton?"

"You imagined nothing, my queen." The old man's tone was civil. This response, more than any other, made Berenice realize that she'd gained his favor that day. More often than not, Nereus expressed displeasure when she picked at Dryton's scabs.

"And so, Dryton, why don't you tell us what amused you so?" Berenice smiled as sweetly as she could. "I've been known to enjoy a good laugh."

"I merely thought, my queen . . . five thousand men. It seems so few to buy the throne of Egypt."

And she did laugh. It was her best weapon. There was nothing like a woman's laughter to unman the cockiest of men. "Oh, is five thousand troops so few? Should I wed you instead, my master of armies? Should you serve as my king? Tell me: how many soldiers would you add to Egypt's fleets?"

To her delight, her councilor turned a bright red, a hue that only lowborn Thracians from the craggy north could achieve. Dryton didn't look so handsome now that he'd been shamed. His family might have served hers for generations, but royalty wasn't bred by proximity.

"No, my queen. I would never—" Dryton sputtered.

"Of course you wouldn't. For all your service to the realm, you are a commoner, of no royal blood nor of any other particularity to recommend you except your loyalty. Don't forget that."

"No, my queen, I won't—I won't forget. I'll keep that at the very forefront of my mind."

After Berenice sent away her advisers, the eunuch lagged. At first he collected the scrolls he'd laid across the golden table, furling each one with care. Once he had finished and stacked them with precision in his arms, he stared across the table and out to the sea below. His patience set him apart. When Berenice was a child, Pieton used to sit in silence for whole afternoons, waiting until she stumbled onto the right answer on her own. Once or twice, she'd tried to match his quiet, but she'd never been able to hold her tongue for long. As she watched him now, her anger dissipated. He could be callous, her eunuch, but he didn't—he couldn't mean to betray her.

"Am I wrong?" She broke first; she always did. But before whom could she break if not him? "Am I wrong to accept him for so few men?"

"I wouldn't say you are wrong. This Seleucus may bring you much: arms, an heir, and fresh Ptolemaic blood. There's no more that you can ask from a husband. And besides: the more men he brings, the heavier his hand in rule, my queen. Isn't that another of your concerns?"

She nodded; that did worry her. Sometimes she thought he could steal her thoughts. "I want you to handle the particulars here. I don't trust Nereus."

"I would mistrust him too." The eunuch smiled, as she'd imagined he would. After years of practice, she knew how to charm him, how to win him to her way of seeing things. He might be the more patient, but he had his weaknesses and vanities as well. "He's rather eager to see you wed. And I do recall some rumors from the old regime, rumors about his relations with Selene—"

"I trust you to be the master of all rumors, Pieton," she told him. "But don't trouble me with ones from ancient times. Not now, when I must look ahead with clear eyes."

Days bled readily into weeks, and Seleucus followed on their tide. The maids whispered at his arrival: "He's handsome—and such a royal bearing. A wonder that he should wed one so ugly as the queen." Berenice, too, had marked the beauty of this man who haunted her court, peddling his smiles. Despite his attempts to arrange an audience, she refused to speak to him before the wedding. Sentiment would only sully her decision. If she liked him, then she might be accused of wedding him for that reason; if she loathed him, well, there wasn't much that could be done in that case. The fact that he was a well-formed man, with a cunning face and piercing eyes, was no matter. If she wished, she could have a dozen such men—queens took their liberties as well. She wouldn't be ruled by false stirrings as her father had been, with his actors, musicians, and concubines. A pretty man's cock would be much like any other, she imagined.

The morning of the wedding ceremony dawned, and with it fruitless hours of preparations: primps and curls, oils and paints. Two dozen women flooded in and out of the royal apartments. With each new player, Leda would whisper some astonishing detail in a hushed voice. "This woman has dressed the hair of every queen and priestess from Antioch to Rome." Or "The queen of Nubia refuses to attend a royal function unless that one draws her eyes." Or "Pompey's wife will let no other servant clip her toenails."

Berenice would give a slight nod of encouragement and let these women go about their duties, until the last one—who came to trim her nails and paint her lips—had melted from her chambers. But when Leda gestured to the serpent-headed mirror that hung above her dressing table, Berenice looked away. She'd endure this duty, but she didn't wish to see herself. She knew she made a poor imitation of an eager bride: eyelids sunk with kohl, lips swollen crimson, cheekbones burnished coral. She was accustomed to the stylized makeup of state, not the lush cosmetics of lust, and her fingers longed to wipe away this altered face. Pieton had insisted on it all: the embroidered chiton, the lapis earrings, the gold armlets. "Half of Alexandria will care only for your costume. Give the ladies what they wish to see." He was right. Her own delicacies shouldn't interfere with that.

"I don't suppose my husband-to-be is undergoing such a dramatic transformation." Berenice had meant it as a joke, but the words tasted bitter on her tongue. It struck her as more than a bit unfair that she should be the one to be painted, she who brought a throne when the princeling would contribute nothing but a few thousand armed men and a pair of practiced balls. Of that she'd been assured. "He's sired at least three bastards that we've found," Thais had informed her with delight. Her trembling minister of grain took a strange pleasure in all this chatter of husbands—she couldn't quite understand it.

"I'm sure he's just as eager to impress," Leda prattled on. "Grooms always are."

Those words surprised Berenice, and she looked at her nurse with fresh eyes, at her worn breasts and belly. The body of a mother and a wife. Berenice had never given much thought to her nurse's life outside her service. But it might avail her now. Leda, after all, had fed her and bathed her and loved her since she was a girl. Berenice knew that the servant would never breathe a word to anyone about her questions. The woman had been a mother to her, the gentle, nurturing sort. "You've been married, haven't you, Leda?"

"Oh, yes, my queen, four times in all." The nurse busied herself with final touches: sharpening the lines that blacked her mistress's eyes, capturing stray hairs with an ivory comb, smoothing the folds of her violet skirts.

"Four husbands. That's no mean feat."

"Yes, and ten children among them all, though only six lived long enough to name."

Berenice wondered idly where those half dozen were now, whether they, too, made their way as servants, or if one or two had managed to break from that life, and if Leda ever saw them.

"You must know quite a bit about men," Berenice pressed. The words sounded foolish to her ears, but it made no difference. She hadn't much time; it was best to get in her questions while she could. Besides, she'd heard rumors about commoners: that they knew all sorts of bedroom secrets—the type that proper nobles would blush to mention.

"Why, my dear, are you nervous?" Leda's hand stalled and her face wrinkled with concern.

Berenice laughed. "No, I am not that."

"Many a bride is. And the gods know my own nerves were trembling before I wed the first time. And you a maiden too."

"I know well enough how it works."

As a girl sailing down the Nile with her father, she had seen bulls mount heifers more times than she could count. And peasant women from the Upper Lands to the cold islands beyond Gaul managed the task with stunning frequency; the brats they churned out each season were proof of that. How much skill could be involved? But still, there might be an advantage she could work. Perhaps, where her looks failed, she could beguile Seleucus with sex. Already, she'd noticed the glances he cast at pretty maids; it would be simpler, surely, if he sought his pleasure in her bed. She had enough bastards to contend with. She refused to share her mother's fate.

Berenice forced herself to continue. "But there must be more to it than rutting cows. Loveliness can't be the only power a woman has in the bedroom."

"I daresay it's not. I'd have myself in a right bit of trouble if it was." Leda's words burst forth eagerly—as though she'd long awaited this very moment to offer her queen counsel. "There are . . . well, my fourth husband strays only on the high feast days, and I've seen nearly sixty summers. I'm no blushing flower."

"And I'll never be." Berenice smiled. "Go on. Don't spare me. I won't be a maiden for long. What can I do?"

"Well." Leda's voice took on a conspiratorial tone. All at once, Berenice saw how Leda must have been as a girl of fifteen, full of life and mischief, before age and disappointment had weighed her down. "You might try mounting him. It'll surprise him, to be sure, but most men like a change."

She liked that idea. Mounting sounded more appealing than lying motionless beneath some rutting beast.

"There's one other thing that'll please him for a certainty, in particular if he's having a bit of difficulty," Leda went on, though

Berenice didn't follow her meaning. The nurse must have caught her puzzled look for she hurried to explain herself. "You know, sometimes, when they've had a bit of wine, their parts don't always work proper. And if that happens"—her voice hushed to a whisper—"take it in your mouth until it hardens. I've never had a husband who didn't like that."

"In my mouth?" Berenice repeated, stunned. Though she tried, she couldn't mask her disgust. She should have heeded the nattering of her childhood playmates. Penelope, for instance, was always blushing over some boy or another, and Berenice recalled that Eurodike had been wed in a hurry. Surely they would have given similar advice, but she'd never thought to pay attention to their youthful swoons. At the time, she couldn't imagine how those girls would ever be of any interest.

"Yes, that's right," the nurse whispered back, reddening to her ears. Berenice hid a laugh behind her hand; it was strange to see her old servant blush over bedroom talk.

A trumpet blared to mark the start of the procession. "It's nearly time, my queen." Leda patted her hand. "And I know you've no nerves, but drink a spot of wine. It'll calm you, and perhaps you might even have a bit of fun."

Berenice noticed her nurse's shaking fingers as she poured from a golden pitcher into a goblet, stray droplets splattering on the table. She'd grown so very old, Berenice realized with a shock; before her eyes, the woman had transformed from ample mother into bent crone. A rush of tenderness came over Berenice, and a mad part of her wished to guide those withered hands.

"Here, my dear." Leda pushed the wine on her.

Berenice brought the goblet to her lips and drank deeply. The liquid sloshed down her throat so fast she nearly spit it back up. She forced herself to swallow and gave Leda what she hoped was a captivating smile.

"That's the spirit. Weddings are joyful occasions, after all." The nurse dabbed a damp cloth to wipe the dregs from Berenice's lips. "You look lovely, my dear. A true queen."

"Loveliness is not the business of queens," her mother would have snapped. Berenice agreed, but she didn't begrudge her nurse the pleasure of admiring her handiwork.

"I won't forget your advice." Berenice smiled as she stepped from the chambers.

Flanked by her honor guard, she crossed through the refurbished colonnades. She marked the glorious decorations: the great hanging carpets and polished silver mirrors, the retouched murals and dazzling mosaics. It was like crossing through a fevered dream, every piece familiar but somehow more vivid than it ever was in life. The repainted nymphs danced in flamboyant reds and greens along the walls, and the lion-headed mosaic had been polished until his mane gleamed gold. The great statue of Isis stared out with new intensity: fresh emeralds had been set in her all-seeing eyes. As the procession wound through the gates, she caught sight of the churning mob— children hoisted on their fathers' shoulders, sweethearts clutching their beloveds' hands, crones hunched over canes—and her heart quickened.

The last time she'd performed this pilgrimage, she'd walked to take her crown. Then she'd rejoiced at every face, each one a mark against her father's ledger. The mob had snaked all the way up Pan's hill and onto the step of the goat god's temple—anywhere to steal a glimpse of the new queen. But now Berenice watched her subjects with apprehension. Who would they belong to now: her or the handsome Seleucid?

Too soon she reached the carved pillars of Serapis's temple, gleaming gold and emerald in the Harvest sun. From the great pediment, the god himself stared down, flanked by his attendant nymphs and bulls. Berenice could never tell whether the deities stared at her in kindness or cruelty. By now, her scented robes were soaked through with nervous sweat. So much for the fresh and eager bride.

Across the plaza, she stole a glance at her husband-to-be. Beneath the archway, Seleucus shone. His skin glowed beneath a golden tunic, and his hair glistened with reflected sunlight. While she'd pursed her lips, he had smiled and waved at the adoring crowd. Tall and broad and bold, he looked everything a king ought to. She felt a jealous twinge in her spleen.

She forced a smile as she climbed the temple steps and marched through the lines of priests and nobles in festive garb. Her feet struggled to obey her will, turned heavy and stubborn. Too much wine, too much sun. She nearly tripped over her trailing chiton; her hands hastened to lift her skirts and clear her path. These efforts consumed her energies: she must not, could not fall. When she reached Seleucus and placed her fingers on his sturdy arm, she felt her innards unclench in relief.

The temple quieted as they approached the altar. An onyx Serapis loomed as implacable as the one who sat beside his wife on the building's facade. The high priest joined the betrotheds' hands; Seleucus's, like her own, was slippery with sweat. She took comfort in that. Perhaps Leda had been right: he, too, might be nervous.

"I give myself to you." She loathed these words, the verb "give." But at least her father didn't speak them for her. The fact that the two were at war rendered the traditional call-and-response between father and husband rather difficult. Instead, she and Seleucus met as equals: wife and husband each speaking with an independent voice. A small victory. "That I might bring into this world children born in wedlock."

"I accept you," Seleucus replied in kind.

"I agree that you shall rule beside me on the throne of Egypt."

"I accept that too—with pleasure."

Seleucus's eyes, dark and fierce, fixed upon her; her own wandered. Even this closeness made her more nervous than she cared to admit. The crowds, she realized as she gazed over the gathered men, didn't rival those of her coronation day. That soothed her furies:

even if he looked a king, they wouldn't love him as one. The first rows were crowded with nobles and their wives—Berenice could tell them by their resplendent robes and inlaid jewels. But beyond those ranks the colors dimmed. Pieton must have found merchants, even peasants, to warm the farther benches. Among them, surrounded by a set of serving women, she spotted little Arsinoe, bold and brash in a sapphire chiton. The girl caught her eye and grinned; Berenice couldn't help but grin in return.

"Before the great god Serapis," the priest called out, "I join these two suppliants in body, in spirit, and in mind. Their union shall be blessed by sons, sons who will rule Egypt until the day Serapis rises from the dead."

Cheering erupted, but it sounded halfhearted to her ears. It didn't matter: the ceremony was over, the marriage sealed with the god's blessing. Or at least his priest's. Berenice ventured a glance at her husband, but Seleucus no longer tried to meet her eye. His own drank up the cries of commoners and nobles alike. There was something almost sweet in that. He'd never been worshipped before.

"Soon we shall give them more to celebrate," he whispered in her ear as he led her back through the reeling crowds. "A realm loves nothing more than a beaming baby boy."

He was no idiot, at least. He knew that his place depended on his showing as a stud. Berenice could admire that. Despite herself, she wanted to find traits she might admire, to fill a small part of her emptiness with something sweeter than hate. Esteem, perhaps. She clutched his hand and smiled. She could play this game as well as he could—after all, it was hardly the first time she'd been displayed before adoring throngs. Long ago, when she was small, before Cleopatra had stolen the Piper's heart, her father had brought her with him on his fleeting trips up and down the Nile, offering her as breathing, kicking proof of his line's vitality. She knew what it was to be venerated.

Entering the palace by the southern gate, Berenice was overwhelmed by the sticky scent of flowers. During the ceremony, thousands upon thousands of blossoms had been set up around the entrance courtyard, to the point of foolishness. Great silver vases carved with marital scenes of the gods—Ariadne and Dionysus, Hera and Zeus, frightened Persephone and gloomy Hades— bloomed with rich roses and pale lilies and golden-bellied narcissi. Even the granite statues of her forefathers suffered the same motif: a veil of pink lotus buds draped Arsinoe the Brother-Loving's gold-plated hair, and a crown of hyacinths knotted around her beloved brother's diadem.

But the procession pressed relentlessly forward—Berenice had no time to ponder the floral arrangements in the first courtyard or mark the alterations in the great one that opened before them. Already her herald's voice boomed to announce their entrance into the great banquet hall: "Berenice the Shining One, Queen of the Upper and Lower Lands of Egypt, and Seleucus the Mother-Loving, King of Syria."

King of Syria. Berenice covered her laugh. The audacity of the claim: Syria was Roman territory, ruled by the stern hand of some Latin governor. But she felt generous as she glanced at the man by her side. The former Salt-Fish Seller was welcome to the title now, in the safety of her realm.

Within the great banquet hall, the smell of smoking meat made Berenice groggy once more. Her head spun as she crossed the chamber with Seleucus. The golden tables blinked like lesser moons in the lamplight. She found herself gripping Seleucus's shoulder as she stepped up the marble lip to where their twinned dining couches stood. The two gold-encrusted pieces were set head-to-head so she and her now-husband would share a single table. Her hand dropped away from him, and she sank down into the silken pillows with relief.

The evening ebbed as the courses came and went—the crabs seasoned with rosemary and thyme, the game hen stuffed with Illyrian truffles and sweetened with honey, the roasted boar overflowing with duck and prunes. Berenice scarcely touched her food, save to split a rib bone with her husband and suck away at the fatty innards. Her husband shared her lack of appetite—he sated himself with conversation. First, he addressed himself to nearby Dryton and Thais, asking after their families and allegiances. When he'd drunk his fill of their tales, he took it upon himself to tour the lesser dining couches, addressing the various members of the noble families who'd come in their finest purple silks to pay their respects. As she watched him, forever ready with a kind word or a joke, Berenice realized that he was charming—despite all his mad claims to glory. She strained her ears to listen to his conversations, his careful small talk into which he slipped knowledge of Egypt and her double lands.

Nearer at hand, old Nereus had devoted himself to savoring the feast. He cracked each bone and drained it dry, the milky marrow dripping from the corners of his mouth. It disgusted Berenice, the way the sticky juice of prunes and blood and wine stained his chin. There was an odd relish to his face as he carried on with some Seleucid, a robust-looking man with a nose that looked to have been broken in several spots. The two grew rowdy as the night carried on. Once, the Seleucid slapped Nereus so heartily on the back that it sent her old adviser sprawling to the onyx floor. She had to bite her lip to keep from laughing. But even this amusement lost its charms, and she began to fear that the procession of plates would go on forever—until Serapis himself rose from the dead. But slowly, surely, the feast died down. The young ladies retreated to their chambers, and the men picked fights with their neighbors or snored, drooling onto their plates. Seleucus, she noticed, studied the scene as well.

"Come, my love." His hand was on her shoulder. She'd had too much wine, she realized as she stood, and she was glad to have his arm to grip.

The bridal chamber hung with new tapestries, scenes of lustful maidens chased by raunchy satyrs and the goddess Isis with the Horus babe at her teat replacing the ordinary ones of Alexander's great battle against the Persians, as though these fresh images of fertility would set a babe kicking in her belly. Each corner was marked by squat statues of Bes, the gape-mouthed dwarf staggering beneath his enormous cock. Seleucus vanished, and an unfamiliar maid—his?—helped her stumble free of her clothes. Stripped, Berenice perched at the edge of the bed, searching for steadiness, though she knew she'd had too much wine for that. When her husband returned, naked too, his cock hard—at least she needn't put it in her mouth—she even managed to smile. He returned the favor. That seemed a promising start.

"That was quite a feast," he said. "They don't exaggerate the Ptolemy opulence."

She nodded, though his words sounded like a condemnation. He stared at her, expectant; she wasn't so drunk as to think his gaze was touched by lust.

"What's the matter?"

"Well, lie down," he directed. "On your back."

Surprised, Berenice obeyed. It felt good to lie down. Once she stretched out on the bed, Seleucus straddled her and kissed her. Hard. His tongue pried into her mouth, and she fought the urge to bite it off. As far as she could tell, he didn't much enjoy it either: his sex seemed to soften against her thigh. But soon he opened her legs, his fingers sticking up inside her.

"Wait." Berenice struggled under his heft. Leda's words rang in her ears; she might at least try to please him here, even if it was distasteful. It could reap its rewards.

"Don't tell me you've grown shy."

"Not in the slightest," she returned—jaunty, almost. Heady confidence flooded her form. She wriggled from beneath him, and he made no move to pin her back. She climbed on top, placing her knees on either side of his.

"Do you think this is an Athenian whorehouse?" Seleucus's face twisted in disgust. He no longer looked so handsome as the world claimed. But Berenice refused to be so easily cowed. Clumsily, she wrapped her fingers about his cock. Who knew what a man might like once a thing had begun?

"Stop it." He clamped a hand onto her wrist. "Lie still."

Seleucus flipped her roughly onto her back, and with his fury roused, she felt his full strength. He was a hardened warrior, she—much as she hated to admit it—a woman. She leaned up to kiss him; perhaps closeness would salvage matters. But he showed no interest in that now. His body grew rough, hardening once more, and though she knew better, she fought against it. The slash of a fingernail cut across her breast, another against her thigh. She sank her teeth into his chest, hard—and he cried out in anger. The flat of his hand struck her face. Warm blood ran down her cheek, but she could scarcely feel the pain.

"I told you to lie still," he hissed. "Neither of us seeks pleasure here."

And so she let him thrust away, an animal in heat. The shame was enough to make her sympathize with Medea, the child-killer: "Surely, of all creatures that have life and will, we women are the most wretched. When, for an extravagant sum, we have bought a husband, we must then accept him as possessor of our body." His body twitched, and he was finished. Shamed, she fell into wine-drenched sleep.

When Berenice awoke, she was alone. The hour was late; a midmorning sun spilled in arches through the windows. To her surprise, she found that the mat was dressed in fresh white covers. The ravaged ones had disappeared. Bloodstains displayed elsewhere. The new sheets burned rough against her skin.

Her head pounded from drink. Between her legs ached too. When she looked down, she saw that her thighs were stained a dark and murky brown. She swallowed back bile and the child's desire to shout for Leda. She wasn't some girl at first blood. Instead, she surveyed the other damages: a crimson welt raised across her swollen breast, a purple bruise marking her knee, a set of four scratch marks spanning her arm.

She'd seen toms come out of fights looking more bedraggled, but she hadn't thought rutting should bring equal scars. *Women do battle in the bedroom.* Her mother hated that saying, but Berenice had always assumed that was only because Tryphaena had lost hers. With care, Berenice tried to stand, but that, too, was a mistake. The motion hastened new aches, and she collapsed back on the bed.

The door creaked and two maids heaved in with slopping buckets for her bath. The younger, a girl of eight or ten, gasped at the sight of Berenice and let her pail crash to the ground, leaving the pair sopping in the threshold. Her companion was the copper-faced maid from the Upper Lands, the one who'd comforted her and led her from her mother's death chambers. Another life. The older girl hushed the little one, whispering a few words in the child's ear that sent her scurrying on her way. With surprising ease, the remaining maid lifted both buckets—her own, still brimming, and its half-empty partner—and carried them across the room. She gave Berenice a shy smile as she poured their steaming contents into the silver basin.

When the second servant returned, she managed to balance her pails without further incident. With care, she poured her buckets into the bath, looking to the older girl for approval after each pour. Loneliness knotted Berenice's belly as she watched the pair, watched how the little one bristled with admiration for the elder, glowing at the slightest encouragement. Much as she'd scorned her royal comrades in her younger days, Berenice also missed them. They'd been stolen from her after her mother's fall from grace. Nobles had preferred to have children wait on the exalted infant Cleopatra than befriend the shunned elder child. In that way, Cleopatra had taken everything.

The basin full, the copper-faced maid dismissed the younger attendant. Then her eyes turned to Berenice, shimmering with that strange boldness.

"What is it, girl?" Berenice teased. It took her mind from the pain. "You stare as if you want to bite me. You should mind your manners before your queen."

"My deepest apologies, my queen, daughter of the Sun." The girl looked to the floor. "Your bath is ready."

Berenice nodded. With soft fingers, the maid helped her to the basin, and soothed her as she slid her body into the scorching silver. The girl washed her thighs and did not pale as the water ran red. Next she rubbed Berenice's wounded breast, and though Berenice winced, the maid kept scrubbing until the dirt had bled away.

"You aren't squeamish, at least, even if you are impudent," Berenice told her.

The girl smiled. "I've seen men do much worse than this. Husbands can be cruel."

An idea sprouted in Berenice's mind. "And what should become of these men who do worse to their wives?" she asked.

The maid studied her for a moment, eyeing her face and her wounds. "There are ways . . . of dealing with that too. Widows, for instance, don't have to suffer men's brutalities."

Berenice sighed, disappointed. "Your solution seems to place a great deal of faith on the gods."

"The gods aren't the only ones who make widows," the maid whispered with a flustered intensity. Was it true, Berenice wondered, that women enjoyed great powers in the Upper Lands? Had the Egyptian laws of old provided for such problems—allowed wives even to dole out death? She'd heard such rumors, but she'd never put much stock in them.

"Tell me, child: do you speak from experience?" Berenice pressed. "Do you know so very much of men?"

The girl's face flushed. Berenice felt foolish; she'd misread this nervousness. The girl, she supposed, was merely at the age—fourteen, perhaps—when men in the abstract and those in the flesh proved different beasts. "No, my queen."

As the water restored vitality to her limbs and liver, Berenice grew anxious to dress and return to the audience hall. The longer she lingered with her wounds, the greater his victory would appear. She must retake the public rooms at once. She would emerge from these chambers reborn, not an eager bride but a formidable queen.

She stood, sending sprinkles of water across the floor. The girl pinned the cloth beneath her arms and let it fall to her sides. Berenice had settled on a deep purple chiton embroidered with a simple emerald stitch, covered by a gold shawl. Far humbler garb than she'd worn the day before. She nearly felt herself in it.

"My queen." The girl boldly met her eye; whatever fire Berenice had seen burned all the brighter now. "Forgive my impudence, but should there ever come a time... Should there ever come a time..."

She stared at the girl in disbelief, and the maid's voice slipped away.

"You speak dangerously out of turn," Berenice told her firmly. The new fury ate away at the holes that had blossomed inside her. The thought of what it would be like to kill—she couldn't think of that. Not now. Not when her father would soon march a Roman army to her gates.

YOUNGER

Arsinoe watched her sister's hands. They trembled, full of rings, ruby-eyed snakes and sardonyx cameos jangling against one another. It was a symptom of matrimony, this quaking. Before Berenice wed Seleucus, Arsinoe had never seen her sister shake. And now Berenice couldn't stop shivering. It should be she, Arsinoe, who was shivering—she was the one who had been summoned to the royal atrium. She didn't see what Berenice had to be frightened of. Slyly, Arsinoe stole a glance at her sister's husband. Eirene and Layla, the maids who cleaned her chambers and poured her baths, spun tales about him. They called him "handsome," "heroic," "strong." But Arsinoe saw nothing so remarkable in the man. Then and there, she decided that she would never marry. Not now that she'd seen what weaknesses matrimony begot.

Old Nereus, her father's changed adviser, spoke. "My queen, news of the Piper grows ever more disturbing. He allies himself with Pompey. He murders Alexandrians in the streets of Rome. He parcels off our kingdoms to the highest bidder. It's past time for us to question the serpent lurking in our reeds."

Berenice laughed behind shaking hands. "And what secrets might this child, this so-called serpent, possess? Does the Piper send fleets of pigeons to carry her messages each night? I hoped my mother's death might bring an end to these daft accusations—"

"My love, my queen," Seleucus broke in. His wide-set eyes feasted on Arsinoe. "Who can say what messengers your father employs? This girl is no ordinary child. How could she be? The same blood courses through her veins as yours—and mine. The same blood of the House of Ptolemy. Your adviser has a point."

Her sister sucked air through her teeth. It made a hissing sound, like a snake. "Since it pleases you, my dear husband, I'll let him proceed. Go on, Nereus. Ask the girl your questions."

Arsinoe braced herself. Now it had come to it, and she would have to answer for something, though she still couldn't say for what.

"Thank you, my queen," the old man murmured. "I assure you, I intended no offense—"

"Enough." The queen sighed and looked at Arsinoe. "My ever wise and *constant* councilor wants to know what knowledge you have of our father's plans. You haven't had any letters or messengers—that much we know. But perhaps you're blessed with sight, or you've flown as a vulture to Delphi, or maybe Athena has appeared to you to whisper the Piper's plots?"

As a vulture. Did Berenice suspect her dreams? Had Arsinoe betrayed herself, cawing out her secrets in the night? Or perhaps there was some tacit understanding between the two? Berenice was her sister, after all. Just as Cleopatra was. Well, not as Cleopatra was, but still: there was a closeness in that bond. Did the queen share her night terrors? Arsinoe struggled to wrench a clever answer from the ether. None came.

"See? The child is as puzzled as I am by this nonsense." Berenice turned back to Nereus. "But perhaps, dear friend, I've forgotten some other likely scenarios. Might you list them for us?"

"My love, my queen." Berenice bristled at the sound of her husband's voice. "Nereus doesn't merit your mockery. The child said nothing; that hardly proves her innocence. She must know things she's not letting on."

She did know things—a great many things—but not the sorts these men imagined. Whispers she'd caught while racing along the colonnades and sneaking through kitchens and soaking in her bath. Just as men paid no mind to their attendants, servants didn't seal their lips before her, a royal child stripped of favor. From the fat baker, Arsinoe had learned that her father had "throngs of supporters, chomping to rally to his side." And that the city wearied of the "brash and ugly queen." Eirene, loose-lipped now, had said that borrowed coin might pay for sixty thousand Roman legions, drawn from the world's most fearsome gladiators. But Layla had shot back her rebuke as she mended Arsinoe's tunic: "Their soothsaying Sybil does not favor giving aid to Egypt's kings."

"Go on," Berenice urged. "Tell us, Arsinoe: what secrets do you know from Rome?"

Arsinoe brought her eyes to meet Berenice's. This question was an easy one. She knew the right answer. "My queen." She kept her voice calm and steady. "I've had no word from our coward father. Nor from Athena either. My loyalties are with you."

"The child lies too easily," Nereus murmured.

She hated the old man with a deep and violent loathing. It was his fault, she realized; he'd stirred these suspicions against her. Her fists clenched at her side. In her mind, she drew one across a bow and sent a poison-dipped arrow into his sunken chest.

"What loyalty does she owe you? She enjoys no royal favors." His accusations railed on. "Once she reaped the benefits of your father's indulgence, and now she is permitted merely to live. How can such a diminution please her? Her loyalty is to her father—her father who adored her—and not to you. You are too generous with her, my queen."

That's not true, Arsinoe wanted to shout. She shouldn't have to die for favors she'd never enjoyed. If her father had loved her, surely he would have brought her with him. But he'd never cared for her, not as he did for Cleopatra, whom he wanted always at his side. Arsinoe had been abandoned here by him and by the woman she'd called mother. Even Cleopatra had left her, and with each passing day, she lost more faith in her sister's fading promise of return.

"She is a Ptolemy," Seleucus added, dry and cold. "She can't be the meek lamb she appears."

Somewhere, a heart flailed against her ribs. It belonged to another. She felt no fear. Some greater spirit seized her, like the one that had taken hold in the Sema, the one that bade her tear her hair and claw her face in the memory of her fire-bearded friend.

"We hear on good authority, my queen, that there was a plot to steal the girl from the palace," Nereus rambled on, tugging at his sagging gullet. "A plot that would have succeeded, if Lykos hadn't intervened."

Lykos. Arsinoe's fingernails pierced her palms. How she loathed that man, loathed that very name. The name of a murderer.

But who, she wondered, was the greater murderer: the one who killed or the one who sent the killer? As she drank in Nereus's words, it became clear to her: Nereus had orchestrated that murder too. He'd killed the fire-bearded guard as surely as Lykos had. And her anger at the old man thickened. She didn't dare look up. Her fury threatened to outpace her sense.

"Lykos takes a generous view of his own importance," Berenice answered. "Whatever plot there might have been, the girl's eunuch would know, perhaps her nurse. But what idiot would involve a child in such matters?"

"I did—I knew about the plan," Arsinoe whispered. Her voice brought the others to heel. Regret nudged her for a moment, but she buried the feeling deep in her belly. It was better, by far, to betray the dead than to turn on those who lived and breathed and prayed. "They didn't tell me of it. But I overheard them in the gardens."

"The girl, as you see, my queen, changes her story yet again," the old man muttered. "Perhaps she'd find it easier to keep her lies straight if she didn't tell so many of them."

Again, her anger flared, menaced.

"I didn't lie!" she yelled, louder than she had meant to. "Begging your pardon, my queen, but I did not. I've heard nothing from my father, not since the coward fled Alexandria. I'm not certain that the guards who meant to kidnap me had word from him either." That wasn't true: the fire-bearded guard had said he'd received some letter. But Arsinoe doubted that it mentioned her. "In fact, they were mostly worried that no one would want me once they'd stolen me away."

"My queen, my love." Seleucus spoke again, savoring the room's attention. Arsinoe wondered if his repetition of that phrase wore on Berenice's ears as it wore on her own. "Despite all your kindness, the girl still betrayed you. She tells of her treachery without a hint of remorse."

Arsinoe's stomach clenched. "My queen," she pleaded, "you are my adored sister, though I do not call you 'my love.'"

A few snickers erupted at her words. Berenice made no attempt to silence them. Even here in the royal atrium, the provenance of advisers and friends, some did not hew to this Seleucid's telling of the world.

Flush with their approval, Arsinoe carried on. "And what loyalty could I possibly owe my father, the very father who left me here to die? When I was abandoned, it was you, my dear sister, you alone who took pity on me, who protected me, who treated me only with kindness. Why would I lie to you?"

Berenice studied her carefully. At last, her hands were still. "Very well, Arsinoe. Did you know about this plot?"

"Not until I learned of it in the garden," she answered. The truth again stood at her side. "I'd never even seen those men before. I've told you everything I know. I promise I would never do anything to betray your trust."

"No," Berenice replied thoughtfully. "No, I don't believe you would. You may run along, little one."

Seleucus's voice strained against the air. "You can't mean to show this traitor more benevolence?"

"She's done nothing." Berenice's voice was sharp. "I wonder

at your interest in her, my love. How does the Piper's youngest daughter concern you?"

"She has all but confessed that she's heard from the Bastard—"

"Mind what epithets you fling at my father. He might be a coward—he is certainly a traitor—but don't call him 'bastard' in my presence."

Arsinoe didn't wait to hear the rest. She was too frightened by the boldness, by the rage Nereus brought on in her. She might say something, something that didn't charm her sister. And so she raced from the royal atrium. She could run faster than her anger and her fear.

The summer winds tossed her hair as she outpaced the ugliness inside her. Arsinoe closed her earthly eyes and let the third one carry her across the waters to Rome, where her father and sister might gaze over the echoes of these waves. Beneath her feet the grass choked and gave way to rush and cracked earth and finally to the soothing burn of white sand. Her soles scorched until the mud grew soggy beneath her toes. Only when she'd splashed up to her ankles did she open her eyes and stare across the abyss, squinting first west to Poseidon wielding his trident atop the white lighthouse and then north over the sea that stretched, it seemed, to the very ends of the earth.

On such afternoons as this, the water burned the eyes, so intensely did it mirror the unflinching sun. Arsinoe squinted into the distance. If she squinted hard enough, she could almost make out Roman sails, a whole fleet heralding Cleopatra's return. She mouthed a silent prayer to Poseidon: *Please, Lord of the Seaways, bring my sister safe across the waves.* She no longer included her mother or her father in her prayers. She hadn't lied, she realized, when she told Berenice that she owed her father no loyalty. Nor had she made it up on the spot. Indeed, in her heart, she'd long known that to be true. *King Ptolemy's daughter is already on board. With the king.*

The days grew darker after that, though the sun shone yellow in the sky. Arsinoe no longer tried to escape her loathing, the heavy hatred that curdled in her chest. She nursed the fury there, whispering to it in the darkness, promising that she would exact revenge, first against Nereus. The old man had become her locus, her center. After all, he—she was convinced—bore responsibility for her fire-bearded guard's death, and for that simpering idiot at her sister's side who'd transformed her into some wretched, trembling creature.

Alexander didn't understand. *Forget about Nereus,* he had told her. *What does that old man matter?* But she couldn't forget; she didn't want to. So rather than spend time with her friend, playing children's games and sneaking sweets from the kitchens, she avoided company, reveling in her anger. She'd taken to wandering north along the shore and lingering in the forgotten courtyards of Ptolemy the Benefactor. Seleucus's men had been installed in her great-grandfather's lodges, among his wasting fountains and mossy stones. Perhaps if she waited long enough, she'd catch Nereus at some mischief there. And when she did, she felt certain, she'd win Berenice's confidence. Perhaps even enough to convince her to allow Cleopatra to return . . . Arsinoe pushed that thought from her mind. It was childish.

Sometimes she grew bored, waiting on her own, watching Seleucus's men march back and forth along the marble avenue that linked the main palace complex and this one. On occasion, she caught sight of Lykos, and her heart thrashed with new loathing. But she didn't need to bother with him: he wasn't worth her efforts. It was Nereus who'd corrupted Berenice, who'd poisoned her with this marriage. And he was the one who mattered. Still, she wished that Alexander would join her vigil, but she was too proud to ask him. He'd already told her she should be avoiding trouble, not looking for it.

Arsinoe was almost ready to give up—it was nearly time to return to the library for her afternoon lessons—when she caught sight of someone coming down the path from the palace. An old man, he leaned over a cane as Nereus often did on longer walks. Her heart pounding in her ears, Arsinoe squinted down the road. The figure's face clarified. Those scrunched eyes, that sagging chin—those features belonged to Nereus. She froze a moment and then recovered herself, squatting behind a dittany bush.

Gingerly, Arsinoe peered out between the sticky branches as Nereus hobbled past her, groping with his cane before each step. She'd expected him to climb the portico, but instead, he continued onward, toward the abandoned gardens of her great-grandfather's palace. Overgrown and deserted, the grounds were the perfect place for private talks and confidences. She knew that soon Ganymedes would be expecting her, that even now he prepared her lesson, but her curiosity had embedded itself too deeply. She felt as though she'd changed into the snake of her dreams, writhing after its prey. She had to follow, to see what treachery Nereus plotted.

And so, quietly, Arsinoe crept along the side of the path, keeping her head low beneath the bushes. Nereus muttered softly to himself as he passed through the first two gardens, skirting about their central pools and hugging the bushes that guarded their edges. If his murmuring included words, she couldn't make them out. Perhaps he wasn't meeting anyone at all; he might merely be stealing a few moments to himself.

The thought of Ganymedes waiting for her, and of Alexander too, nagged at her. She could turn back and get away with a mere scolding from the eunuch. But as she passed into the third field, she saw the reason for the old man's expedition. There, beneath the great laurel tree, stood a dark-haired man, sneering and impatient. She couldn't place his face, but she recognized him at once as a Seleucid. His red tunic was cut too high up his thigh. No self-respecting Alexandrian would wear it so short. Her heart pounded all the faster. She'd been right: there was some treachery here. There was no other reason for Nereus to meet with one of Seleucus's men in secret. She squatted back on her heels behind the brush at the entrance to the gardens, watching, waiting.

As Nereus poked his way through the flush grass, leaning heavily on his cane, the Seleucid made no move to help him. Arsinoe almost felt sorry for the man, nearing his second infancy, so old that he walked now on three legs instead of two.

"So this is it, then?" the young man snorted. An eastern accent tainted his Greek, and his face twisted into a grimace of disgust.

Nereus answered him, but Arsinoe couldn't make out the words. And then the Seleucid lowered his voice as well. Here they were, scheming—and she couldn't hear a word. She needed, somehow, to get closer. The best hiding spot would be behind the far wall of the crumbling fountain, long since mossed over with disuse. Nimbly, she unlaced her sandals and knotted one around each wrist—she'd be quieter on bare feet.

Her eyes scanned the distance that separated her from the two men. The cover was sparse: a few straggly bushes and a hunk of granite that, she'd heard ages ago from Cleopatra, had once served as a pedestal for a solid gold statue of the Benefactor himself, a statue that had long since been melted down for coin. Crouching to stay out of sight, Arsinoe scampered to the first bush, and then the second. As she drew nearer to Nereus and his Seleucid companion, she began to catch a few dull words: "my master," "my mistress," "the palace," "the sea." She'd need to get closer to hear full sentences. The block lay about ten feet off—mere strides from the two men. She took a deep breath and broke into a run. A bramble caught on her arm and she yanked back, hard, as she dashed toward the stone. Only when she'd ducked behind it, resting her head against its cool edge, did she realize what she'd left in her wake. One of her sandals had caught on a branch, and now it dangled by a lace, for all the world to see.

"I tell you." Nereus's voice snapped sharply against her ears. She prayed that neither man would glance her way. "The first attempt didn't go well. And now the queen appears set against it." Arsinoe could hear his every word. Her gut pinched with hatred.

"And whose fault is that?" the young man growled. "My master tells me—"

That would be Seleucus, Arsinoe told herself.

"I've already put myself too much at risk. I wash my hands of this business."

Her heart pounded—this was it. Her moment. The trouble she'd been looking for.

"We've come too far for that, old man."

She didn't breathe. She couldn't twitch even a muscle. They were close, perhaps only a few yards away. And she didn't dare move, not even to retrieve her sandal.

"What? Do you threaten me now? Here? Here in my own city?"

"It is not your city. It's the queen's."

"What would you have me do? Berenice has taken a liking to the girl. I can't say why—nor can I understand why your master is so concerned with her. She is a *daughter*, the *youngest* daughter."

Arsinoe felt her pulse beating in her throat. They were talking about her. Nereus had been plotting against her, as she'd suspected. But why did Seleucus hate her so much that he would send one of his companions to get rid of her?

"And her father was the *youngest* son, a *bastard*. We all know how easily elder children might be . . . lost. What my master doesn't understand is why the queen would fatten up a rival. He only wishes to ensure that his own children, when they arrive, inherit in due course."

"I don't care anymore for Seleucus's wishes," Nereus growled. "I tell you, the queen is willful. Drop the matter for the moment, before it rains destruction on us all. And besides, in all likelihood the Piper—"

"The Bastard, you mean?"

"You know what Ptolemy I mean. And when he returns with a Roman army, we'll have graver problems to attend to."

The two men had grown angry. They no longer bothered to modulate their voices. And Arsinoe could hear one of them—the young one, she imagined—pacing back and forth in front of the tree. She'd been stupid, she realized. Foolhardy, not brave. One false glance could reveal her now, her shoe dangling in plain sight. She clung to the hope—the vain hope of a child—that her own blindness would turn others blind to her as well.

"To think that Seleucus was so certain he'd find an ally in you. You were, as I recall, a dear friend of his mother's in her youth . . ."

"That was in another life."

"And these intervening years have convinced you that baseborn blood outmatches that of trueborn heirs? I can see why: Alexandria has certainly flourished under the reign of the Bastard and his brethren. Cyprus stolen away, and soon the whole kingdom will bow to Rome."

Arsinoe swallowed her fears. She'd come, and there was no changing that. She focused on parsing their words. Who was Seleucus's mother? And how had Nereus known her in his youth? It was strange to think of the old man as having been young at all. But he must have been once.

"I didn't say—I don't need to justify my loyalties to you. I was fighting for this dynasty before you were a twinkle in your father's eye."

"Ah, I see the way of it, then. Now you're old and weak and spent, and so you give up the battle, you abandon Selene's dying wish, when it's so close to fruition."

Selene. Her grandfather's sister. He had two, and he was wed to both at different times. Selene, the younger, had later married the other brother too—and later still . . . Arsinoe quieted her breath and sifted through her remembered lessons. Some king, but she couldn't say which land he had ruled.

"This matter no longer concerns her."

"I know. It's a touchy subject for you. Rumors abound—"

"I don't care about rumors, neither then nor now. I won't listen to a pup natter on about a subject he knows nothing of."

"So be it. I'll keep my thoughts on that matter to myself. But I don't need to remind you that your goal is very near at hand: her son sits on the throne."

Idiot. Arsinoe cursed herself. Selene had married Antiochus—the name had come racing back to her. A whole series of Antiochi: Antiochus the Hook-Nosed, and his brother Antiochus the Cyzican, and then the first's son, Antiochus the Pious, though Arsinoe couldn't remember what, if anything, had been particularly pious about him. Of course Seleucus would want her dead: he thought he had his own claim to the throne. He might even plot against Berenice as well. Any true Ptolemy stood as an obstacle.

"Sits *by* the throne. And what these intervening years have taught me is that he's nothing like his mother. Nothing. Tell me: what interest did he take in Alexandria before his listless brother lost his empire?"

"Ah, yes, of course. Your famed Alexandrian pride is wounded. You'd have had Seleucus take on the Bastard in a fight some twenty years ago? A mere child matched against a king."

"I did not—"

"Quiet." The stranger's voice turned cruel. The pacing stopped; Arsinoe couldn't see him, but she could nearly feel his stare. "My, my. What have we here?"

Her stomach sank into a pit. He hadn't seen her—only her sandal. If she stayed still, very still... She prayed that the ground would swallow her, belch her into the land of the dead. It was no use. She felt his eyes on her, burning.

"It seems, Nereus, that we aren't quite so alone after all. I thought you said this grove would be safe from prying ears."

"It is. It should be."

"Come out, little one." Arsinoe heard him thud toward her. He'd guessed where she was. His feet sounded heavy even on the grass.

His voice turned sickening and sweet. "You've been caught. And you know the punishment for eavesdropping."

She thought to run, to leap, to fly. But to what end? Nereus she might outrun, but Seleucus's man—he was young, agile. He'd catch her in a moment.

"You should've come out the first time I called."

The Seleucid grabbed her by the wrist and jerked her up until she stood.

"Tell me, child, and tell me true: what did you hear?"

"I—I heard nothing," she stammered.

"You are quite the little liar," he spat. "What a knack you have for catching conversations that were better left unheard." He hit her hard across the face. Her head spun as she fell, and she could taste the hot iron of blood. She watched his fist recoil, the ring that had split her lip dripping red.

"I don't—I didn't hear a word. I promise you." Her words swirled, as though her swelling mouth had grown too big for them.

"Oh, you promise, do you? And what, Nereus, do you make of the child's promises? Should we trust them?"

The old man said nothing; he wouldn't even meet her eye. He wouldn't protect her, then. He didn't care if she lived or died.

"What ails you?" her attacker sneered at Nereus. "True, we didn't wish to be overheard, but this is a stroke of luck, if we merely turn it to our favor."

"I don't know what's taught in Antioch," the old man replied, "but in Alexandria it's considered poor form to play with one's food."

"Oh, yes, you vaunted Alexandrians have quite the reputation for manners and civility. No doubt that's why they so often murder your kings."

Arsinoe stilled her breath; she ignored the stabbing behind her eyes, the aching of her jaw. Perhaps the men would fight each other first. It wouldn't buy much time—the old man wouldn't hold out long. But even a small distraction might be enough to allow her to flee to more peopled grounds.

"Don't think about trying to escape." The younger man stepped on her wrist, digging his boot into her skin. Arsinoe shrieked in pain. "You'll not leave until I've finished with you."

"I haven't heard anything. I promise you." In her terror, she repeated her words as if on a spool, the same piece of wool spun over and over again. "I promise you. I haven't heard anything. I won't repeat a word. Not any of it."

"Not any of what?" he mocked. "I thought you said you didn't hear a word."

"I—I—I didn't." She hated when she stammered.

This time, it was his boot that came slamming toward her face. She rolled to the side, letting it smash against her stomach instead. The pain pulsed angrily in her chest, her head, her wrist. And then, finally, Arsinoe thought to scream.

"Shut your mouth!" he yelled over her screams. "Shut up!"

And still her voice carried on the wind. He grabbed her tunic's neck and yanked her to her feet. His blade kissed her throat, and she fell quiet. She dug her teeth into her lips to keep from crying out.

"There." He grinned. His teeth were mossy. His breath stank. "That's better."

"Enough," Nereus snapped. His eyes squinted around the grove. "You've scared her. Now let her go."

"What good will that do? You're too soft, old man. Too soft. What tales Selene once told of you . . . your great bravery. Be grateful she's passed on to the next world. She'd be shamed to see what a craven fool you've turned out to be."

Seleucus's man shoved Arsinoe against her tree, her favorite laurel. His forearm knocked her shoulders into the bark. Her blood throbbed against the dagger. And so this would be the end. Here she would meet her death.

A cry of agony. His—not her own. And the knife dropped

away. Arsinoe collapsed beside it. The Seleucid flung his arm against a boy.

"Get your hands off her," yelled Alexander, who'd been struck to the ground. He'd come to rescue her. But when the man spun around to face her friend, she realized that she'd been a fool to hope. The Seleucid dwarfed Alexander in height and breadth— there was no chance of an even fight. She tried to shout out, to warn the boy, but her voice caught in her throat. From the corner of her eye, she saw Nereus moving toward her. A boot smashed against her temple, and she saw only black.

Feathers danced on the breeze. She flew over the river's banks. Past the stone sphinxes of Thebes and the great pyramids of Memphis. She left the Nile, and sailed toward the setting sun until the farms gave way to white sands. A keen hunger drove her forth, a hunger that goats and heifers and lambs could not quench. And there, at last, she saw her prize: a carcass dark against the desert. She circled, dipping lower with each rotation. A child's bones, not yet picked dry. She alighted at the corpse's side. Its eyes were fresh and open, staring up a bright gray-green. The face looked both familiar and transformed, a face from another life. She cocked her head to study its contours, its chapped lips and high cheeks. *Alexander.* The word echoed. *That had been the boy's name.* And then she plunged her beak into its flesh.

Arsinoe awoke to a strange calm. A warm cloth dabbed her brow. Her nurse cooed over her. The muses danced slowly round and round. But something nagged at her. There was poison in the air.

"Where is he?" Her voice sounded distant, spoken underwater. "Where is he? What've you done with him?"

"Hush, my dear." Myrrine smoothed her sweat-soaked hair. "You need to sleep. The doctor said you shouldn't upset yourself."

"No, tell me, Myrrine." Arsinoe swatted away her nurse's soothing hands. "You must tell me. What happened to him?"

"Calm down, little one. Take deep breaths." Myrrine stroked her hand. "Speak slowly and clearly. What must I tell you? What happened to whom?"

"To Alexander." Arsinoe sat up violently. Her eyes darted about the room, but she saw no sign of her friend. "Where is he?"

"Hush, my dear, there's time to talk of that later. Now you must rest."

"I'm plenty rested." Her head throbbed. "Tell me what happened to Alexander!"

"Only if you promise me you'll go to sleep when I am done."

Arsinoe nodded frantically.

Her nurse sighed, reluctant. When her words came, they came slowly, as though she was speaking to an idiot or an invalid. "I'm not sure what you remember, my dear, but that man, that Seleucid—gods only know what came over him—beat you black and bloody. Nereus says the monster might have killed you, if he and Alexander hadn't come upon you two. The boy attacked that barbarian, dug his teeth into his hand. He's only a child—no match for a grown man—but he made such a commotion that half a dozen soldiers came running." The nurse paused. "You know, little one, you shouldn't wander so far on your own."

"But—but—Alexander. He didn't—he is well?" She'd dragged him into this, into her foolishness. And now she could hardly remember why it had been so important to follow Nereus, to listen to what it was he had to say.

"I wouldn't say he's well." Myrrine gave her a hard look. Harder than she deserved. It hadn't been her fault she'd been attacked. "He suffered more blows than you did. It'll be some time before he's healed. The boy took quite the beating for you. I hope you remember that, my dear. The Fates don't often send friends such as that."

But the Fates had sent her other gifts too: men eager for her death, and her own reckless, angry search for them. And dreams that sometimes gave a glimpse into the future, and sometimes told her nothing at all.

Arsinoe shied from Nereus when she saw him in the halls, and looked on Seleucus with new loathing. They plotted something—she remembered that much—but each time her thoughts crept closer to the answer, it flitted away in the wind. Bits and pieces came back to her. Murmurs of honor and trueborn children, and a woman named Selene... When she thought of it, she'd tell Berenice. She had to tell the queen, because their plot was aimed against her rule. She'd clung to the wisps of her father long enough; he wasn't coming back. Not for her.

ELDER

The god-raised stars hung heavy in the sky, and Berenice lay awake. Her husband's snores killed any chance of sleep. With every grating inhale, an image flickered in her mind: a pillow sealed over his mouth, a twitching corpse, and then blissful silence.

She hadn't expected Seleucus to come to her that night, stinking of sour booze and the stale sweat of whores. It seemed that he employed a whole army of them. But they couldn't give him what he needed. And so he raided her chambers, speech slurring with threats of "wife" and "heir" and "duty." Rough hands bruised her flesh, and her body acquiesced to his.

Sleep soothed the demon. Traces of a sweet-faced child emerged, a dimple at his left cheek, a curl falling over his brow, parted teeth between parted lips. Desire sated, he lay helpless, and a maternal feeling awoke in Berenice's breast. But she wasn't a fool. Men like him could be tamed only by great beauty or great lust. Her own looks were ordinary at best, and on their wedding night, he'd made it quite clear that she lacked the skill to break him by other means.

Berenice rolled onto her side, pressing her face into her pillow, clamping bedclothes over her ears. Between her legs dripped a pink and milky substance, spilt seed congealed with spilt blood. "A hardy woman like you," he'd sneered. "I didn't think I'd have to be gentle when I took my marriage rites." The remembrance nearly made her gag. She pushed the tender thoughts of motherhood from her mind.

At last, his breathing quieted and Berenice closed her eyes. She prayed for auspicious dreams, but she awoke to a blank and empty mind. His arms had wrapped around her in the night and she struggled to be free of the unwelcome weight.

"Hush," Seleucus whispered. "Lie a moment with me."

"Why?" Whatever yearning she'd had for closeness had been razed. She'd embrace the balm of hatred and purpose. Strength, not softness.

"I thought we might waste some gentle moments together before the rush of day."

"You've already wasted my night of sleep. I won't sacrifice my morning too." Berenice twisted from his grasp.

"Life shouldn't be torture between us, my dear. We're cousins, not siblings. We don't need to share your parents' woes. The gods don't frown upon our union."

His eyes played over her breasts, her belly, her hips. Berenice wrenched the bedclothes from him and wrapped them tightly around her form.

"What's made you shy?" He teased the fabric from her fingers. "I've seen your body bare and bloody. I like it well enough. I appreciate women of all shapes."

"Last night you certainly appreciated a great number. Though I can't speak to their shapes."

"Does that bother you?" His fingers pinched her waist. "I hadn't pictured you the jealous sort. I thought you were too high and mighty on your throne to bother with petty envies. But it seems I was wrong. All women, even queens, are the same in that respect."

She hated him, with even more venom than when he was rutting on top of her.

"If I thought your whores would keep you from my bed, I'd welcome them as warmly as babes born of my own womb. But no matter how often you visit them, they don't quench your desires."

It wasn't true. She almost wished it were.

"And you think you do? Such a romantic heart, Berenice." He

laughed. "I came to your bed so I might sire a child with you. A rightful heir to the Ptolemaic line, born to the last trueborn descendant of Ptolemy the Benefactor—"

"You put too much stock in your tangled blood. My father ruled Egypt for twenty years. Your mother ruled for none. You may consider the double kingdom your birthright, but Alexandria sees you for what you are: a Seleucid whose brother lost his empire."

"And how do they see you?" The man in her bed smiled. His eyes were large and striking, with the delicate lashes of a child. Berenice could see how they might have been comely if they didn't brim with such malice. "Are you lauded as the Ptolemy whose father lost his empire?"

"No, my husband, because I'm not known for my father, nor for my storied line, but for my own deeds. I am the Ptolemy who seized the throne from the Piper and saved the double kingdom from Roman rule. Don't lecture me on dynasties. Your blood marks you as a passable consort. Your deeds mark you as nothing."

"Last night you didn't speak so rudely. You need another lesson in manners." He sat up suddenly, as if his lurching could bend her to submission.

"The sun's risen." Berenice shrugged. "Soon my maids will come to bathe and dress me for court, where I dictate how my lands are run. A word from me and my guards will arrest you. At night, I may keep the secrets of this marriage bed, but once dawn breaks, the world changes. If you lift a finger against me in the light of day, I will scream. And I promise, you don't want to see what happens when I scream."

She hoped her threat sounded convincing—it yielded the desired effect. Seleucus's lips parted and a touch of fear flickered in his eyes. *Good.* And then he chuckled. "I've rarely met a woman who matched your feistiness. I'll grant you that."

"You should have tried that tactic earlier. No woman is immune to flattery. But the time is long over for such tricks."

Loudly, she crossed to her dressing table, praying that her maids would hurry in. Before she'd wed, any sound of stirring would bring them rushing to her door, but these days the girls hung back. It was as though they wished to punish her. Even they couldn't be so daft as to think she took pleasure here.

"My love," he called out. He wouldn't let up the game, no matter how many times she brushed away his words. "There's no need for this coldness. We're of a blood, you and I. A great and gloried blood. And we have long years before us. In time, I'll father many children upon you. Some tenderness might be welcome. I fear we've begun on an unlucky foot."

Berenice bit her lip, hard. What kind of fool did he take her for? "How easily these sweet words come to you this morning. Last night you'd little enough concern for tenderness. Yet now that I've reminded you of your position, you're full of kindly urges. A strange coincidence, isn't it?"

"A man unfamiliar with our situation might hear a threat in that, but as we both know, I've six thousand men at my command who'd fight for me if I come to any harm."

Berenice squinted at this man, her husband, until his features grew as sharp as her childhood sight would have rendered them. She wanted to see whether he was formidable, if any true strength lurked behind his blows and bluster. She suspected not; he seemed to be formed of little more than charms and artifice, the sort that might fool his soldiers but not her.

"No, I don't know that," she said slowly. "For once you're dead—should someone wish you dead—your men will have no reason to fight. What hope do they have of retaking the lands that Rome has seized from them without the great Seleucus, descendant of both the House of Ptolemy and Seleucus, the incomparable Salt-Fish Seller? You die, and their hopes of victory die too. They'll diminish, and return, and serve Rome. Younger brothers with no heirs are little use to anyone dead."

Her taunts finally roused him: Seleucus stood, his member shrunken in the morning light. Trembling with anger, he slipped his tunic over his naked form.

Rid of her husband, Berenice returned to bed and sealed her eyes against the sun. She hoped she might steal a few moments of slumber now, but sleep refused to come. Everywhere she turned reeked of him. The stale stench of drink and sweat hung over her skin and bedclothes alike. Soon she gave up and rose again. This time, the servants scampered in at the first falls of her feet.

Bathed, dressed, and scented with so many perfumes that her head had begun to spin, Berenice descended the slick onyx steps that led from her apartments to the court below. When her father had ruled, he'd insisted that all the columns be hewn from purple marble, as though the very color might imbue the royal apartments with power. She'd always thought that the rich hues clashed with the lotus flowers that emerged from each capital in dull gold relief. To complete the misshapen idyll, the walls were plastered with her father's preferred images of Dionysus—the flame-haired god riding naked upon his leopard's back and leaning on a satyr's shoulder—which almost made her wonder whether the Piper had chosen violet because it reminded him of wine. But that had been the way with everything her father built: one symbol jumbled atop the next, with little consideration for the whole.

She quickened her pace as she passed by the last of the god's revelries. With any luck, she might reach the great atrium before Seleucus. Now that her moments of ruling alone were in short supply, she cherished them all the more, even on mere matters of resolving tax complaints. The threat of losing any stitch of her authority made her cling to it all the more tightly. Besides, taxes were needed to raise armies, whether to fight for Cyprus or to defend Alexandria.

As she crossed the blue wave mosaics of the great courtyard's central path, Berenice nearly broke into a run. She was so distracted by her thoughts that she didn't notice the small body hurtling toward her.

One of her guards did and seized Arsinoe's arm so hard that the child shrieked like some harpy of legend.

"They wouldn't let me see you," the girl gasped, flailing against the soldier's hands.

"The queen has more important matters to attend," the guard told her gruffly.

It was true. Seleucus had, Berenice hoped, returned to his own chambers, but he wouldn't sleep forever. And she needed to milk every moment in his absence. Each decision that she made without his hovering reminded Alexandria that power rested with her alone.

"Arsinoe, he's right," she chided. "Wait until next I summon you."

As Berenice turned away, the girl, her sister, cried out, "Wait, my queen. I beg you. There's something I must tell you. At once."

The child had certainly inherited their father's flair for the dramatic. And Berenice was about to send her off, but then her eye caught on something strange. The girl had a scabbed cut across her cheek, and her wrist was bound as though the bone had snapped. No wonder she'd shrieked so loudly when the guard grabbed her.

"What happened here?" Berenice took Arsinoe's bandaged arm in her hand. The girl flinched but didn't weep.

"Please," she begged. "Just let me speak to you alone. I'll be quick. I promise."

That was curious. Her sister had never demanded anything of her before. And so Berenice had Arsinoe escorted to her apartments. Though the child eyed the guards suspiciously, Berenice didn't dismiss them. She didn't want them to think that she catered too extravagantly to the girl's whims.

"Tell me now, and quickly, Arsinoe," Berenice said once they'd both settled in her small antechamber. "What's the meaning of this display?"

A strange story poured from the girl's lips. She'd been playing behind a stone of sorts, it seemed, when she'd overheard Nereus talking to some Seleucid. Arsinoe had always struck her as a smart child, a survivor, but Berenice still couldn't understand what had brought her little sister rushing to her side. The girl should know better; she'd been raised in court, after all. An irksome thought entered Berenice's mind: maybe Tryphaena had been right. Perhaps her affection for the child had made her too careless with her favors toward her sister.

"And then," the breathless girl went on, "the Seleucid called Nereus a fool for giving up when they were so close to getting what they wanted, when her son was already on the throne."

That sounded peculiar. Maybe Arsinoe had heard something worth repeating after all. "Whose son?"

"Selene's," her sister replied, earnest and exasperated, as though she'd explained it a thousand times before.

"And what happened next?" Berenice asked, urging her on. "How did Nereus respond?" Some small part of her was almost impressed that Nereus had tricked her, at his age—that he had the energy, the fortitude, to pull the wool over her eyes. To fight for something against all hope of triumph. There was a twisted sort of honor in that.

"He said he wasn't old or weak but he was sure that Seleucus was nothing like his mother." Arsinoe raced through these words as well. Now that she was finished, she took a deep breath and looked utterly pleased with herself.

Berenice studied her sister with fresh eyes. What else did this child overhear, this girl with such open rein over the palace? "Did you learn anything else? Any indication of what treachery they plan next?"

Arsinoe furrowed her brow and thought for a moment, but then she shook her head. "They found me after that." The girl gnawed angrily at her swollen lip, so fiercely that Berenice feared she might draw blood. "And so I didn't hear anymore. But I thought—I thought you should know."

"You were right to tell me, sister." Berenice smiled. After all, each was the only family the other had left. "I'll take your words to heart."

Arsinoe glanced back when she reached the chamber door. There, framed by the golden latticework of vines, she dug her heels into the stone, flouting the guard who tried to hurry her along.

"So you'll kill him, then?" she asked, bright and hopeful, as though she were requesting a new trinket. In that brief moment, her sister reminded Berenice strangely of Tryphaena.

She laughed. "You're too young to be so bloodthirsty."

But the question weighed on Berenice all throughout the petitioners' pleas, and the bureaucrats' presentations about the new taxes to be levied for the army. She studied Nereus with care, but the old man betrayed no hint of nerves as he questioned each plan and how many talents it would draw. *Even a man such as this can be blinded by love...* She'd heard rumors of his affair with Selene, but she'd never put much stock in them. Perhaps that wasn't fair. Nereus, too, had been young once. And foolish to this day.

It was Pieton, not the old man, who later sought her out in her antechamber. As the eunuch ran his finger over the amber tortoise-shell inlay of her father's desk, he looked rather more self-satisfied than usual. He smiled from ear to ear.

"You seem to be in a cheerful mood for someone who has spent the day listening to whining peasants and nagging officials," Berenice teased.

"The great glue that holds our kingdom together," he said with his lopsided grin. "Although I do admit I've had some news that might lift even your spirits."

Berenice wondered what could lift her spirits. News of more coin to pay another ten thousand Galatian recruits? Word that Rome had fallen to the Gauls? Neither prospect seemed likely.

"I doubt that," she answered.

"I think you'll find I'm full of surprises today." Pieton paused grandly for effect. "Your father sails to Ephesus."

"To—to Ephesus?" Berenice stammered. That did surprise her. "What business can he have there?"

"I imagine he has the business of licking his wounds. His friends don't yield such great power in Rome after all. The Senate denied his claim. They'll loan him no men to retake Alexandria."

Her mind stumbled. Her father had failed in Rome. This was victory. It wasn't the magnificent triumph she'd dreamt of, but it was welcome just the same. Her father's loss would spare her troops—it would even give her a second opportunity to secure Cyprus. The Piper would not return at the head of a Roman horde; he'd sail to Ephesus and wither away his remaining years, praying that Artemis might deliver him to the throne. "And without Dio, or any other convincing? What swayed their minds?"

"Rome has, to our advantage, spread herself too thin," the eunuch mused. "I imagine it's all those costly foreign wars. She's overextended in the East. And the Gauls stir up trouble along her borders. The days are gone when she could afford to lend men to every king who bends a knee and weeps."

For once, Fortune, that capricious goddess, was smiling on Berenice. She was almost afraid to hear more, for fear that on closer inspection it would all wither away to dust.

"Who else knows of this?"

"No one, my queen. My source is speedy and tight-lipped and already en route to Athens. Shall I make the preparations, then, for a feast to celebrate your triumph?" His eyes tested her.

She saw what the eunuch was poking at. He knew her far too well. Her father's defeat could spare her more than armies: it could spare her Seleucus. She would no longer have to endure his cruelties, his drunken weight bearing down on her. If she wanted, she could have him killed. The thought made her shiver. She'd held lives in her grasp before, surely, but not ones that were so closely inter-twined with her own.

He'd been cruel to her, rough with his hands and his words, but many men did the same. Did that mean he deserved death? He had his charms and uses. And in her softer moments, she even hoped he felt toward her some shadow of tenderness. Perhaps she was think-ing of it the wrong way around. Perhaps it was more important to ask, Did he deserve life?

She'd been reared among men like Seleucus, men who thought the world owed them merely for the twig between their legs. Her father had been such a man, and he'd nearly drunk his kingdom to the ground. Her brothers, babes though they were now, would grow up to be such men. And what sort of world had they brought forth through their misplaced confidence? One that was ruled in all but name by Rome. Her husband and his ilk had already received far more than they deserved.

"No preparations just yet," Berenice told the eunuch. "Let's keep this happy news between us two."

Pieton bowed his head low before her, his loose curls flapping over his eyes. "I thought as much, but I must warn you, my queen: take care. The palace has ears. And when things such as this must be done, they should be done quickly, and with discretion."

Suddenly, she became acutely aware of the sound of her own heart thudding in her chest, as though Pieton's plea for prudence had somehow sealed her husband's death. She could not turn from her choice now.

"So it will be done as I do all things." Berenice nodded. As Pieton turned to leave, she felt the uncontrollable urge to call him back. The moment between them had passed too quickly, and she wanted—no, needed—his comfort.

"One more thing, Pieton," she cried out, against her better judg-ment.

"Yes, my queen? What is it?" As he stood, quiet and unmoved, she realized that there was nothing he could say. She couldn't let him see her suffering. She was no longer a child begging for her tutor's affection.

"A small matter," she answered stiffly. "Have someone keep an eye on Nereus."

"Nereus?" the eunuch echoed. That had caught his interest. "Any particular reason?"

"Not in the slightest. I merely don't like the look of the man." She swallowed. The eunuch had his secrets; she should keep hers too.

"As you command, my queen."

That night, Berenice asked Leda to send the copper-faced maid, that child of the Upper Lands, to dress her for bed. As she waited, Berenice ran a comb through her hair. Its ivory teeth caught on a tangle. She jerked hard against the knot.

"My queen," her maid cried out from the threshold. "Let me. Your hands are made for finer things than combs."

The girl's fingers were deft. Berenice barely felt the biting teeth spinning her hair into smooth spools.

"Where did you learn such artistry?" Berenice applied the compliment with care. The maid had offered much, more surely than her advisers did, but Berenice still couldn't say why it was she trusted her.

"I learned many skills in Thebes. How to twist hair, how to speak your tongue, how to please men."

"And how to kill?" Berenice's voice barely scratched above a whisper.

"Yes, that too," the maid said as she twisted the comb through her tangles. "The priestesses schooled us in all ancient arts."

Berenice had ordered men dead a hundred times in those heady days after she claimed the throne, but this was different. Time ticked by, relentless. If news spread of her father's defeat in Rome, the suspicion would fall all the more heavily on her. "It must happen tonight."

The girl's eyes widened, but she didn't object. "And so it will, my queen."

"Wake me when it's done."

She needn't have asked to be roused. Sleep refused to come to her that night, though she was alone, untroubled by her ill-fated husband. She nearly wished that Seleucus would enter, that she might do the deed herself. She, too, could find the strength—she didn't need a slave to carry out her killings. She wasn't soft. But it would be reckless for him to die in her bed. A thousand more suspicions thrown her way.

Every noise she mistook for footfalls, and each time the ghost steps echoed in her ear, she shot straight up in bed. But they came to nothing. The moon rose—and the maid did not return.

Perhaps the girl had lied. Perhaps she'd no intention of taking a knife to Seleucus's throat. Perhaps she was Seleucus's spy. Berenice had been a fool to trust her. How often her mother had warned her against such credulity—and here she was, asking some cretin of the Upper Lands to commit her murders.

Berenice slipped from her bed. She cast aside the curtains and breathed in the night sea. The moon was but a sliver over Pharos's gleaming beacon. At times, the lighthouse threatened the very stars. She wondered if the gods grew jealous, if they planned one day to tear it down and curse the foolish men who challenged nature's grandeur.

"My queen."

She spun around to face her servant. For all her pained listening, she hadn't heard the girl's approach. Wreathed in lamplight, the maid looked more spirit than flesh. There was something otherworldly about her, standing there half dressed, her pupils alive with flame.

"It is done," the maid whispered.

Berenice waited for her heart to steady. It was over: Seleucus was dead. His hands could not touch her now, and she would reign in peace. All the relief she'd longed for evaporated. Not even a taste. Only another wave of emptiness, another life excised from her own. Perhaps that was what it meant to rule: to cut away one tie after another. Her father, her mother, her husband. All natural affiliations obliterated.

"Take me to him." Suddenly, Berenice needed to see him. She'd sent someone else to kill him, but she should bear witness to the destruction she'd uttered.

"My queen." The girl crossed to her. "It's not wise—"

"I decide what's wise." Wisdom didn't dictate her decision here. Not even power, nor politics. Her softness drew her to the dead man. It was as relentless as the drive that called a pigeon home.

The girl's eyes grew large. Then she nodded. "Of course, my queen. We should take the servants' corridor. It will be safer."

Safer. How strange to picture herself hiding from her own guards. But Berenice meekly acquiesced and followed the maid out of her bedchamber, passing through the dark corridor that led toward her father's private banquet hall. She'd scarcely ventured into the space since she'd taken possession of her father's apartments, and it felt odd to see it now, precisely as the Piper had left it.

Though smaller than the dining rooms that flanked the palace's great courtyard, this hall was far more lavish. Not only the tables but the frames of the dining couches were cut from solid gold, and each divan was softened with thick cushions shrouded in red Chinese silk. Whereas the other rooms were merely painted, deep friezes had been cut into the chamber's marble walls, scenes of goat-legged Pan, his horns and beard flaked with gold, playing his flute and chasing maidens, his arms and cock outstretched. Berenice had heard rumors, of course, of the other sort of business that her father had indulged in. Her stomach twisted to think of the drink and sex that had no doubt filled this room. She felt a welcome flood of relief when her guide pulled on a clutch of grapes hanging on the far wall. A well-disguised door creaked open to reveal a servants' entryway.

The staircase they descended was narrow and drab, all the more so for its nearness to her father's luxuries. Even the smells were of a different nature, as though the incense and perfumes that laced the air in the king's apartments couldn't permeate the divide between the royals and their slaves. The light from her maid's lamp was so dim that Berenice had to run her fingers along the wall to guide her steps. If she should fall and cry out—nothing would implicate her more than being discovered here, sneaking through the back corridors with a serving girl.

When at last they stumbled into her husband's rooms, Berenice felt the blood throbbing in her throat as though it meant to burst the vessels that bound it. She took a deep breath and, shrugging the maid's warning hand from her shoulder, stepped into Seleucus's bedchamber. Within, his body lay bathed in Selene's ghost light. Berenice approached, her feet bare and silent on the onyx floor.

His form was warm, as though life still lingered in his veins. Her finger traced the purple bruise around his neck, residue from the silken scarf that had stopped his breath. The bedclothes reeked of sweat and shit and sex.

A palm clasped over her nose and mouth, Berenice used her free hand to peel away the soiled sheets. The arms that had once pinned her to her place lay limp. His cock was no mighty weapon now, a pink and meaty worm drooping from his groin. Soon his body would be cleaned and clothed in fineries, stench and soil scrubbed from his skin, all evidence of life erased. She'd seen her mother's corpse transformed that way. At burial, Tryphaena was reborn a demented deity—a father-loving, brother-loving goddess, her face caked in kohl and ruby, her limbs pumped with immortal bile, her body decked in gold and turquoise and lapis lazuli. Humanity wiped clean.

But not here. Seleucus's eyes stared blankly upward, empty of the vigor that had marked them in life. He was a man, and he was mortal. And now he was dead. No subterfuge to mask his end. Berenice leaned forward and gently placed a finger on each of his eyelids, pulling them shut. That was better; he looked almost peaceful. If she ignored the smell, she might even imagine that he slept. Some keening part of her, deep in the pit of her stomach, yearned for his love. Unbidden, her left hand had come to rest on her belly; even now her womb might quicken with his seed. Leda would know ways to rid a woman of an unwanted child. Berenice didn't wish to bear a dead man's son, but as she looked at his face now, it saddened her to think that no child would ever reflect its contours.

The maid's gentle hand pressed hers. Berenice didn't look up; her fingers lingered on his sharp cheekbones, his parched lips, the small cleft in his chin. To peel away her gaze would be to admit her guilt. *Never show them you are soft.*

"We should leave him now, my queen."

Berenice swallowed her nostalgia. No one—not even her parents, who'd been compelled to do so by blood—had ever loved her. It was foolish to have expected her husband to be any different. There was something deep inside her that made her impossible to love. It was the same quality that made her strong. Their bodies had come together, nothing more—a paltry imitation of closeness. Love and beauty were for concubines. He'd surely begotten many a kid upon many a whore, and once winter had come and gone, she'd scarcely be able to walk ten paces without setting eyes on some brat who shared his father's dimpled cheek.

She glanced up from Seleucus's corpse and drank in the maid's beauty: her lush hair, her rising breasts, the glowing copper of her skin. How many times had her husband taken this creature to his bed? What a thrill for him, that she'd come to him willingly this once. How eager he must have been to spill his seed into her cunt.

Seleucus took what he liked; she could no longer begrudge him that. Berenice smiled. Two women hovering over the body of a false lover: did the gods know a staler tale?

"My queen, you shouldn't be found beside his corpse."

Berenice said nothing. The artifice grew feeble in the fading night. It would be no secret who'd ordered her husband's death. All of Alexandria would know the truth by dawn, though the wiser ones would deny it. Seleucus's dying moments strung out before her eyes: moans coalescing into desperate gasps as the beauty tightened the deceitful silk about his throat. Such dainty hands. They didn't look as though they had the strength for murder.

Those same hands urged Berenice to her feet, and she bid a silent farewell to his wasted form. He would not overcome the nighttime trials to take his place among the gods; he'd drift aimless, useless in the undergloom. A common fate for a common life.

"There's so much death."

"There is, my queen, but no more or less than there has ever been. Bloody gods birth bloody creatures."

Berenice nodded at these words. They even passed for wisdom. At least in her experience, life was filled with only blood and fury. And if the gods were to blame—well, then her mother would be contented in the afterlife.

"Who will tend to him?" She'd see that gentle hands bathed his form—she owed him that little. He'd given her his seed and his soldiers, though the first she would cast out.

"I can prepare the body, my queen, if it pleases you. But first you must return to your chambers."

Berenice let the maid guide her through the darkened corridors once more. Leda did not wake at the creaking of the first door, nor did she stir as the pair crept through the antechamber. The old nurse's breathing stalled as Berenice pushed open the door to her bedchamber, but soon her snores returned.

Inside, the girl lit a lantern, her eyes washed crimson in the glow, and her fingers trembled. These shaking hands untied Berenice's chiton, unwrapped its loosened folds, and then slipped a fresh tunic over her head.

The maid seemed rattled, more so than before. "What frightens you?" Berenice asked.

"Me?" the maid replied. "Nothing on this earth."

"Then why do you tremble?"

The girl took a deep breath, gulping up so much air that Berenice wondered how such a small body could contain it.

"It's weary work to take a life." She paused and considered her mistress with consuming eyes. Dark irises floated in milky whites, and Berenice recalled an old tale warning against such features. *Don't trust eyes adrift in ivory.* "But I'm glad to do so in the service of my queen."

"Did you care for him?" Berenice knew she could have asked the same question of herself—why else did her mind turn to thoughts of sons that she might have borne? Had she longed for that, as her mother had, no matter the cost?

"You mean because I lay with him?" The girl turned the question against her. "Not once, but many times?"

Berenice could have sworn she caught a hint of amusement in the maid's firelit pupils.

"No, I didn't care for him. He wished to lie with me. It was easier to agree. And I thought in time it might prove useful."

"And so it did." Berenice allowed herself a smile. The girl was clever, cleverer even than she'd suspected. "What's your name? I've never heard the servants call you anything but the beauty of Upper Egypt."

"My name is not Berenice nor Arsinoe nor Cleopatra." She answered softly. "So it can be of little importance to anyone. But you may call me Merytmut, if it pleases you."

"Merytmut," Berenice repeated. Merytmut—beloved of the mother goddess, in the girl's stranger tongue. She knew the power of giving names and choosing them. "What brings you to Alexandria?"

"You take an unusual interest in your servants."

"Most of my servants don't share your skills."

"I told you: I learned my skills in Thebes," the girl rejoined quietly. "And everyone in the palace knows I am from the Upper Lands. There they find me ordinary enough. Perhaps someday you might linger in the southern kingdom, as you've grown to admire its people so."

An edge had slipped into Merytmut's voice, so slight that Berenice scarcely noticed it at first. As a girl, Berenice had been weaned on tales of native resentment, stories of failed rebellions and fallen egos, but she'd never imagined that she would encounter this hatred within her own walls. The rebellions, she knew, were real enough, but she'd always assumed they were to do more with low floods than with any deeper malice. That part she'd supposed was a mere rumor that eunuchs told their Macedonian charges to stoke their nightmares.

Berenice kept her tone light. "Why come to Alexandria if you hold my house in such contempt?"

"I don't hold you in contempt, my queen. Although I admit I was curious to see Alexandria and her masters for myself." Her words grew reckless now, as though Seleucus's murder had granted her rights to freer speech. " 'The usurpers,' my father always called your ilk, as though he himself could remember a time when Greeks didn't rule the twin lands."

The girl's voice faltered; she began to tremble once more. She proved both craven and courageous. Perhaps every brave woman had to battle the coward the world made her out to be. Berenice dismissed the thought. The words sounded too much like her mother's. If she wanted to be brave and strong and never soft, she would be.

Berenice broke the taut silence. "And so you fancy yourself a fighter for your people's freedom? I'd have thought you wiser than that."

"I've told it to you all wrong. My father wants to shake the Ptolemy yoke, but my father is useless and a drunk. I am neither." Merytmut spoke quickly now; her nerves had caught up with her. "What difference does it make to me whether a Greek man or an Egyptian rules? The power would still lie far from the goddesses of old, far from mothers and daughters and wives. The priestesses taught me that as well."

"I see."

"And they've come to favor you," the girl added, almost shyly. "You'll always be welcome in Thebes, among the priestesses of Mut. But you know that already."

Berenice laughed. Mut's priestesses. Why hadn't she thought of that before? She supposed she imagined them as shrunken as their goddess. All but drained from the earth. "And they were the ones who left me that vulture amulet? That token of their esteem?"

"The vulture is the mother's symbol, my queen."

"So it is," Berenice replied thoughtfully. "So it is."

When at last she returned to bed, Berenice fell asleep at once. A deep sleep bursting with propitious dreams.

YOUNGER

Ganymedes squatted with unaccustomed grace, feet flush against the stone. His eyes slipped over the garden, the dancing nymphs, the purple columns, the cypress colonnade. Arsinoe had rarely seen him look so grave. But these were grave days: Seleucus was dead, and his men clashed with Berenice's in the alleys and on the battlements. At night, Arsinoe heard their fighting too.

And it was her fault. She hadn't meant for Berenice to kill her husband. It was Nereus that Arsinoe had wanted dead, in vengeance for Alexander. And that's why she'd left out bits. She hadn't told her sister that the Seleucids plotted to kill her. Besides, who would have believed her then? But now blood was spilling, splashing, spurting in the streets—because of her and her alone. At least this time it was no fault of her dreams.

Her tutor spoke at last. "I'm afraid I have bad news." Arsinoe drank in his words with relief; she'd feared that he would come to chide her about her audience with Berenice. "You reveal too much," he'd scold, and leave her to wonder at his meaning.

Alexander said nothing. He'd been quiet of late, and she avoided him, despite her nurse's advice. He looked at Arsinoe but she couldn't meet his eyes. Not now, when he'd already been bloodied by her recklessness. Not when she'd seen him dead and feasted on his flesh. The gods cursed her; she knew that with certainty. And curses had a nasty way of rubbing off on the people she loved most.

"What sort of bad news?" She wondered dully what had happened this time, whether matters could indeed get worse.

"Your father has failed." The eunuch's voice scarcely reached a whisper. "He can't buy a Roman army. He won't retake the throne."

Her stomach fell away, sinking into the ground where she could not follow. She should scream and cry and wail as she had at Tryphaena's funeral, but she felt nothing. Her father belonged to a different world, a dream world where she had been a princess. But that dream was dead and gone. What she had now was Berenice. But somewhere, far away, her other sister lived and died on their father's fortunes.

"And Cleopatra—is she well?" Arsinoe ventured, though she dreaded the answer.

"As far as I know, both your father and your sister are in good health. They sail now to Ephesus."

Her tutor squeezed her hand. She didn't feel the pressure. The hand masquerading as her own at her arm's end belonged to another girl. "It will turn out. You've done well under your sister's rule. I would not fret."

Arsinoe nodded. She would not fret.

"What of Seleucus's men?"

The eunuch raised his brow. "What of them?"

"Will they take the palace?"

Ganymedes laughed, but not unkindly. "I daresay they will not. There will be scuffles, yes, but no more than that. Who would lead them in a palace coup? Their king is dead, and his storied empire dies with him. They'll engage with the queen's men, perhaps a few days longer. Some among them might even gather longer still and whisper words of revenge. But Berenice will root them out. The others will choose new masters, either the queen or the Romans who rule their lost lands. There are those who were born to lead, Arsinoe, and those who are meant to follow."

So that was how it worked: the common folk were formed

differently. Soldiers knew only how to follow. She wanted to ask another question, to ask what would happen to the man who'd attacked her and Alexander, the man she'd heard plotting with Nereus. But she didn't dare. Any mention might remind Ganymedes of her visit with her sister. And she'd no intention of sitting through another lecture on the difference between rashness and boldness.

"Until our lesson, then, my dear." The eunuch's knees cracked as he stood. She watched him shuffle off to the palace.

"Arsinoe." Alexander's whisper tore the air. "I'm sorry."

She wanted to turn back to him, to throw her arms about his neck and weep. She wanted, more than anything, to be comforted. But she had to be strong. She knew—she knew with certainty— what her dreams meant. She hadn't merely seen Alexander's death: she'd played a part in it. The closer they grew—the more their lives knit into each other's—the more danger she put him in.

She held strong; she didn't turn. Cruel, harsh, she answered, "Why?"

It shouldn't be so difficult to drive away his love—she'd destroyed everyone else's. Or else, perhaps, she'd never had it at all.

"I'm sorry that your father did not get his army."

She shrugged and walked away. She would cast no more corpses.

As the weeks slid by, Alexander still sought her out to play, dogging her steps. But Arsinoe remained cold as ice, though at night she wept from loneliness. In time, he grew tired of her distance, and took to ducking her as well. She saw less and less of him outside their lessons, when she was forced to encounter those wounded gray-green eyes.

One afternoon, once Ganymedes had concluded a discussion of Plato's early dialogues, Alexander left, again in silence. He'd turned so quickly on his heels that Arsinoe couldn't have stopped him if she'd tried. Not that she would have tried. A child's tears stung her eyes, and she buried her head in her hands. She dug the heels of her palms deep into her pupils. She wouldn't succumb to weeping.

"Come now, my dear," the eunuch said, placing a soothing hand on her elbow. "What's this between you and Alexander that brings you so much grief?"

"What do you care? You've never liked him." She didn't trust Ganymedes's pity.

"Your moping wearies me. It's nearly impossible to teach two children who won't so much as look each other in the eye."

Arsinoe looked up and studied her tutor's face, the worn lines along his eyes and mouth. Perhaps she could tell him after all. Maybe he would understand. She longed to confide in him—to confide in someone. If Cleopatra were here . . . But Cleopatra wasn't here and never would be. Her sister had vanished across the wine-dark sea without so much as a letter of regret. Arsinoe did not know if she'd see her again. It was foolishness to seek her tutor's counsel; she knew too well what he thought of visions. The delusions of madmen and fools.

"We're not as close as we once were." She shrugged. "That's all. I don't know why."

Ganymedes's expression softened; the lines smoothed along his brow. "My poor child. My poor, lonely girl. How many summers have you seen?"

"I'll be ten soon," she answered proudly. "Before the Nile falls."

"And Alexander?"

"He turns twelve not long after."

Her tutor gave her a sad smile, revealing only the tips of his broken teeth. "You see, my dear, this is why I wish Aspasia and Hypatia had remained. When you're too young to tell the difference, a boy serves as well as a girl. But now—"

"What do you mean 'too young to tell the difference'?" Did Ganymedes think her daft? She'd heard servants talk. She'd read the plays of Euripides. She knew what happened between a man and a woman.

"Someday, my dear, you'll grow into a woman—"

"I know that!" She blushed roundly just the same. It was strange to hear Ganymedes talk of such things, all the more so since the eunuch would never grow into a man.

"And Alexander into a man," her tutor went on. "And that day is no longer so very far off. He can't remain your innocent childhood companion forever. At nearly twelve, he already begins to change. And these differences will only grow more . . . troublesome."

Ganymedes was wrong. That wasn't the way it would be with her and Alexander. What had sprouted up between them, between two abandoned children, had grown thicker, tougher than ordinary friendships. That was why she had to cut Alexander off. "You don't understand. That isn't what is happening."

"What is it, then? If it's not the natural separation of man from woman? You said that you yourself weren't sure." She heard the pity in her tutor's voice. And hated it.

"I'm sure it's not *that*. Our friendship's made of firmer stuff. The silly sentiments that crop up between man and woman can't spoil it. Alexander would follow me to the ends of the earth, down even to the depths of hell to capture Cerberus if I asked him."

"Perhaps he would. But if that's the case, you must ask yourself, Why does he slink away in silence? What drives this stake between you two, the best and greatest of friends?"

Arsinoe chewed on her thumbnail. She couldn't tell whether the eunuch mocked her. If he even believed in friendship. After all, he didn't have friends. He only had her.

"The truth isn't gentle, little one," her tutor said. "But I don't tell it to wound you. I wish only to warn you of the changes to come."

"But Ganymedes." Her tongue battled her wiser nature. *Only fools believe in such madness—priests and witches and lunatics.* "There was—there is. There is something else. I had a dream—"

The eunuch's hand trembled. He curled his lips and snapped, "Dreams are but the afflictions of a sick and troubled mind—nothing more. I told you not to mention such things to me again."

That night, again she couldn't sleep. Arsinoe didn't dare close her eyes; otherwise, some wretched dream would come to haunt her. Myrrine thought they were blessings that foretold the truth. Ganymedes thought her mad. *The afflictions of a sick and troubled mind.* She tossed and turned and tossed again until she'd wrenched the coverlet clean off her mat. As she blinked at Pharos's beacon, calling the sailors home, she knew what she must do.

It was not the first time she'd snuck from her rooms. When she'd been a frightened girl, she'd often crawled to Cleopatra's bed on dark nights when the moon had shrunk to a sliver. Her sister would wrap her arms around her and keep her safe from Tryphaena's shrieks. But this was different. She passed not only out of her chambers but into the cool sea air. Escape—if she could call it that—was easy. Myrrine slept as she always did: soundly and with snores so loud that they sometimes cracked Arsinoe's fragile dreams. Luck ran in her favor: the day was dedicated to Apollo, and the guards had drunk more than their fill. They didn't stir at a barefoot child's steps.

The wind blew harshly as she tiptoed along the darkened shore. She cupped a hand around her flame. The storehouses swelled, giants hunched against the sea. The fifth one, she recalled from a trip with Ganymedes, held the medical scrolls. They frightened her, these lurching edifices, even in the sunlight. There, she imagined, was where the scholars had been slain. But she'd been a shrinking child then, and now she was Antigone—brave. Brave enough to seek an audience with the queen and whisper her secrets in Berenice's ear. What were haunted buildings set against that?

Within the storehouse, her oil lamp barely dented the darkness. The night transformed the dank interiors, but the smell, the scent of yellowing papyrus, stirred her senses. With care, she retraced her steps. Ganymedes had first guided her right, and then down some half dozen rows, and again to the left. There she'd find the works of Hippocrates and Aristotle, Herophilos and Erasistratus.

Arsinoe shrank beneath the shelves, anxious not to stray from her shy ring of light. As she wandered deeper into the black, the scholars' ghosts haunted more brazenly—one spirit nearly passed through her outstretched arm. She ignored them. She pressed onward through rows upon rows of scrolls. Parchment and papyrus curled snug about itself; a few grander ones spun on rods of brass and silver and gold. She found comfort in these sights; perhaps the philosophers' shades did too. She couldn't begrudge them that.

As she made her way through the labyrinth, a thick layer of dust rose beneath her toes. Her torch caught upon stray cobwebs stretched between the nooks, and a plump rat scurried along one wall. Ganymedes often told her that the great library was long past its prime. As she explored these lost corners, Arsinoe saw the truth of his words. Once scholars had bustled throughout every inch of this complex, seeking out new works, new discoveries, new ideas. If she were ever queen, it would be that way again.

Her fears grew bolder in the darkness. As she turned a corner, she nearly thought she saw her sisters' faces—Berenice and Cleopatra both, rotted in poison sleep. Arsinoe blinked. It was the reflection of her candle in a pair of abandoned oil lamps—nothing more. Berenice lived, and despite the chaos the queen had caused, Ganymedes promised that the Seleucids would fail. No ill could befall her sister in Ephesus. Cleopatra would be safe among the priestesses.

"They're not real," she said aloud. "Nightmares, not portents."

Tryphaena had died—and no dream had foretold that. The murder of her fire-bearded knight could be mere coincidence. She'd obsessed too much over the link between the foxes and the wolves, and the men of flesh and blood, dying and moaning before her eyes.

The visions—fantasies—were an ailment, and like any other ailment they could be cured. Arsinoe would not be Cassandra to Alexander's Hector. She was too young to be cursed by the gods. There was a physical explanation for her sights, and she would find it. Her fingers tapped over bronze and silver knobs until she reached the golden ones belonging to the medical scrolls. The first Ptolemy the Benefactor, not the fat one, had had them bound this way when he'd sent for the originals from Athens some generations back. He'd kept them for his collections and returned the copies. But then the library had been grand, the envy of the world. He'd never imagined that the scrolls would be hidden here amid a gathering of dust.

The Hippocratic works alone filled two dozen nooks. Arsinoe would never read them all, not even if she slipped from her bed each night until the Nile rose and fell again. Her lamp placed firmly on the ground, she worked one scroll free from its fellows, careful not to let the rest fall. And then, gently, she unfurled the aging parchment across the floor.

"It appears to me a most excellent thing for the physician to cultivate Prognosis; for by foreseeing and foretelling, in the presence of the sick, the present, the past, and the future . . . ." Arsinoe skipped ahead, winding and furling through the text. One book, two, three. She'd no interest in reading about why doctors might want to "cultivate Prognosis" for various sicknesses; she wanted to know what sorts of illnesses brought nightmares. She read with a heavy tongue, stumbling over whispered words like "inflanunation" and "phrenitis."

While the language was unfamiliar, the work focused on patients with the most plebeian of symptoms: fevers and cold sweats, icy feet and swollen ankles. No premonitions shook these patients' fragile minds. Arsinoe searched on, clinging to the hope that the work might discuss other conditions, specifically men cursed by dreams. Finally, she furled the scroll. This one wouldn't help her.

Arsinoe stood and surveyed the rows of texts. Eyes closed, she picked another at random and slipped it from the others. *"On the Sacred Disease,"* it began. That sounded promising. "Men regard its nature and cause as divine from ignorance and wonder, because it is not at all like to the other diseases . . ." She'd found it. This surely—this sacred disease—must be her ailment. And this text would detail her cure. She read on hungrily. But though she studied each word with care, she couldn't discover what, precisely, the sacred disease was. Nor could she find any mention of a cure. "But this disease seems to me to be no more divine than others; but it has its nature such as other diseases have, and a cause whence it originates—"

"Arsinoe."

Ganymedes's voice. She wound the scroll shut. Only now did she notice the round shadow he cast over her flame. How long had he been watching her? She could hardly believe she'd been so careless, so absorbed, as to miss his approach.

"I'd no idea you took such an interest in Hippocrates. But there's no shame in your desire to study medicine. You might even do so in the light of day, if the passion moves you."

His voice teased, but when Arsinoe looked up at his eyes, she found softness there. She expected him to admonish her for being out of bed, out of the palace. Instead, he sank to the floor beside her.

"There was a time, my dear," Ganymedes began slowly, "when I, too, sought out medical texts in secret, desperate for a cure for my own unspeakable illness. Of course, I didn't have access to a grand library such as this. But curiosity always seeks out its satisfaction. Several of the men in my traveling troupe carried a single text or two with them on our journeys. They weren't doctors, but I'd seen more than one act the part for a talent before an unsuspecting patient. I suppose they found a bit of knowledge useful for such tricks. My search began by rooting through their trunks. I stumbled over each and every work I could find. I didn't know my letters well back then, and so my frenzied reading proved both a hardship and an accomplishment."

Arsinoe nodded eagerly. The eunuch never spoke of his early life. In her mind, he'd sprung fully formed into the palace, like Athena from Zeus's head.

"In time, I found that I'd rooted out every volume and devoured them all. Yet I'd discovered nothing of use. I hadn't come across a single case that resembled mine, never mind met with any text that proposed a cure. And so my desperation grew. At night, I snuck into the homes and shops of local apothecaries. As we traveled often, these visits exposed me to a vast range of new works.

"One night, perhaps a year after I'd begun my quest, I broke into the home of a learned man, a physician. I sat at his table, a fine piece carved from a single oak, and pored over a scroll. It was one I hadn't seen before, in all my nights of searching. It was the second of Hippocrates's volumes on disease. I'd consumed the first long before, and I was convinced that here, in the second of the great doctor's works on ailments, I'd find the cure for my despair. I read ferociously. By this time I'd grown accustomed to mouthing over the complex terms "ulcerate," "dysuria," and "bilious." And though the work began with a discussion on various injuries and illnesses of the head, I soon became so engrossed that I didn't notice that the doctor, the master of the house, was watching me. I looked up with a start to find him, a well-muscled man but a few years past his prime, looming over me.

"Remember, now, that I was but a boy then, a plump and frightened boy, and I began to tremble. I thought he'd rage and strike me—and he would have had every right to do so—but instead he put a gentle hand on my shoulder and said, 'My poor, poor child. I grieve for you, but these texts won't bring you comfort. They've no answer for what it is that ails you.' And I couldn't help myself—I wept. For years I'd clung to this notion: that if I read enough, knew enough, I could overcome my pain. I could regain what I'd lost. And the man, he rubbed my shoulders and comforted me. When my tears had dried and my breath returned, he told me something I remember to this day. He said, 'You may mourn your differences, but remember that the gods give mysterious gifts. There may come a time when your affliction seems an advantage, not a shortcoming.'"

The eunuch paused; the lamp licked his face, but it didn't reach his weary eyes. Those looked as dark and forlorn as Arsinoe had ever seen them. She didn't speak; she didn't wish to break the spell. She wanted the candlelit Ganymedes to go on, to tell her of what happened with his ailment and what had become of the kindly physician. But the eunuch kept his silence, too absorbed by his own story to note her anxious eyes. When he spoke again, it was in a different vein.

"And so tell me, Arsinoe, daughter of gods, descendant of Alexander the Great: why do you wish to rid yourself of visions?"

"I don't even know if they *are* visions." Now that her surface had cracked, her secrets spilled out swiftly. "I often see things that never come to pass. I can't tell what is real and what's not, who's dead and who will die and who will breathe another day. And I dreamed of Alexander. I was feasting on his flesh. Ganymedes, I can't—" Tears choked her words. Furious, she brushed them away.

"You're allowed to cry, my dear." Ganymedes took her fingers in his own. "I wouldn't put too much stock in all these grave sights. Dark dreams have many causes. They aren't always sent by gods to reveal the untarnished truth."

"But some are true, aren't they?" What of the foxes? What of her Menelaus's death?

Ganymedes took a deep breath. "There are many false seers, but yes, we've all heard tales of true ones too."

"Will you teach me to know which visions will come to pass? And which I may simply forget?" She pleaded with him now—she needed desperately to understand, to know, which dreams would come true.

"I'll help you, my child, as I always seek to do. But I'm no seer, and I'm afraid this isn't the sort of thing that can be taught. It must be learned in its own way, and in its own time. In the meantime, I wouldn't dwell too much on these dreams."

"I don't wish to dwell on them. I wish that I might forget them all."

"But you will not," the eunuch said sadly.

"No, I will not." She hesitated. "I thought you'd be angry."

"Angry?" Her tutor laughed. "Where would you get such a notion?"

"I know you loathe priests and sorceresses. You always have." She paused, wondering if it was better to leave these thoughts unsaid. The eunuch's open face made her bold. The time had come for confessions. "I thought that you hated them because they saw things you couldn't."

Ganymedes's eyes clouded. Arsinoe hoped that he would cry, that his tears would avert her own.

"No, my sweet child. That's not the reason. Though you're quite wise to notice my aversion to such magic, I've no need for the gods to show me what is to come. There are other ways of finding out the future. Kinder ways. And if there are those who do see such things, I imagine it's more a burden than a blessing."

Arsinoe wanted to ask why, then, he hated seers and magic, both of which seemed such useful things to her, but a yawn stole away her words. She rushed to cover it with her hand, but she wasn't quick enough.

"It's late." The eunuch's tone was firm and final. "Long past time for you to return to your bed. What will Myrrine think when she discovers I've kept her charge out of her chambers into the wee hours of the morning?"

"But I'm not sleepy," Arsinoe protested, though her eyes felt heavy. "I want to talk more."

"We'll talk tomorrow. For now, we must both get some rest."

Her tutor scooped her up in his fleshy arms, and Arsinoe wrapped hers about his neck. The return journey passed quickly, her mind dipping into quiet dreams. Soon the eunuch was carrying her across the gardens. The clouds had cleared and the moon shone through the great laurel leaves, wine-dark in Selene's soft light.

Already, Ganymedes was slipping her into her bed. Myrrine wasn't there—she must not have stirred from the antechamber. Only her tutor had noticed her absence. There was a lesson there . . . Arsinoe's heavy lids grew cumbersome. She blinked them open.

"Did you ever come to see it as a gift?" she whispered as her tutor made his way toward her door.

Ganymedes stopped and turned back to her. "Did I ever come to see what as a gift?"

"Your ailment. The physician said you might one day see it as a gift from the gods. Did you?"

Ganymedes smiled. "Well, it brought me here, did it not?"

Long after the eunuch left, Arsinoe wondered what he'd meant by those words. And what illness had afflicted him. And how it had brought him to the palace. And then her limbs weighed her down, and she sailed into the sky.

ELDER

Helmed, on horseback, Berenice squeezed the reins until the leather plowed into her palms and her charger slowed. She glanced out over the gathered soldiers. The infantrymen who formed the central phalanx wore red pleated tunics cut midthigh—the traditional battle garb of the Seleucids. Their lines stretched the length of the dusty practice field between the two single-story barracks that flanked either end. Sensible buildings, they lacked all ornament save a flaking layer of gold paint on their columns—a stark contrast to the opulent monuments that her father had constructed for himself. Still, the edifices were strong and solid—loyal. Unlike the men drawn up between them who'd clogged her canals with corpses. They didn't seem so fearsome now. The rows on foot reached only halfway to the sandy beach beyond, which was dotted with marooned ships. Boys and old men, for the most part, not battle-ready soldiers. It was hard to believe that they numbered six thousand. On horse, Berenice could count perhaps five hundred, though she'd been promised twice that. Nereus, it seemed, had lied on several fronts.

Her sworn men formed a neat column dividing the traitors from the shore. A scant thousand, though most were mounted, which granted an advantage. Enough to guard against an escape by sea. Seleucus's soldiers would be dead before they reached their boats. "Don't be rash," Pieton had warned her as she was boosted to the saddle. "They'll never cleave to a woman's rule." But she had no choice. Bold or brazen, she'd bind these men to her.

"You grieve your general's death," she began. The winds whipped to steal her words. She'd conquer them too, Aeolus's unruly charges. "And I, too, grieve his loss. But your grief has curdled into mislaid fury. Fury that you turn against me, your queen. Fury that brings you to attack my soldiers, not as men but as craven boys, in brothels and back streets. Fury that is rooted in a treacherous rumor. Because in your hearts, you know the truth: Seleucus's death is a tragedy, but not one of my making."

The breeze carried murmurs of disbelief. The footmen shifted in the dirt. More than one pair of eyes floated to their ships and the formidable guards who blocked that route. None of that concerned Berenice. She didn't need to turn their hearts—only their swords and their tongues.

"And whose grief is greater than my own? You lost a brilliant general, but I lost so much more: my cherished husband, bound to me by blood and vows. His life was marked with bravery, passion, and, above all else, devotion to his subjects. I have never met a man more driven to avenge his realm's wounds. In his final breath, he bade me, 'Berenice, my queen, my love,' his hand clutched in mine, 'don't let Rome steal the double kingdom as it stole my own.'"

Without thinking, she parroted the tone and timbre of Seleucus's voice. His men ceased their grumbles. Their eyes fixed not on escape but on her alone. They held still and silent. No man adjusted his shield or fidgeted with his spear. Even their horses were frozen in the sand.

"You're free to go," she told them. "Throw down your weapons, if you will, and slink back to bow to your Roman overlords. My men won't keep you from your ships."

One shield, and then another, clattered to the earth. A javelin, its point glinting in the morning sun, joined them. Somewhere down the line a sword unfastened from its belt. Then silence. The other spears gleamed fierce against the sky. Why not? Here they were fed and housed and fucked. Who knew what sort of reception they'd get in Antioch? Given the choice, ninety-nine men of a hundred would stay the familiar course.

"Let those cowards flee. Be glad of it. I'd never ask a soldier of mine to fight beside such cravens. You who remain will be rewarded, granted lands and moneys and wives for your services to Egypt. And what are lands beside the greatest prize of all: the glory of carrying on your king's fight against Rome, against the wretched Republic that rapes your land and your daughters?"

Only the wind and the waves echoed her words. Had she spoken too openly? Too brashly? Too soon? Perhaps she should have drawn out her praise of Seleucus. Now that he was dead, she had little trouble stomaching his lies. The blood pulsed in her fists. Her horse kicked at caked earth until, at last, a sputtered cry.

"To Queen Berenice the Shining One!" A man had called out her coronation name—some old, bedraggled soldier with a wispy beard and wrinkled brow. Such a supporter might hurt her cause more than help it: some wouldn't want to join their voices to one who looked so near death's door. The second silence drowned her. Pieton had been right, with all his gnawing doubts. These men thought no more of her than their master had. No number of choice words would ply them to her side.

"May the gods shine their glory on the Queen of the Upper and Lower Lands," a second voice answered.

This enthusiast had a more promising look: he was a well-built youth with dark curls to his chin, his javelin kissed by the sun. The soldiers around him regarded him with interest. A third shout followed, this one from a mounted man, and then another until both armies roared together, louder even than at her crowning: "Queen Berenice the Shining One."

On horseback, she was her best: bright and graceful. She'd remember to make better use of that. She had been haunted by her mother's fears for so long, and for what? Here she appeared hardened, never soft. Whenever she addressed her fighting men, it should be from this perch, where they'd see her not as a failed woman but as some sort of hybrid creature born to lead. She scratched her stallion's mane; he whinnied in appreciation.

The soldiers carried on with their shouting, even after she'd raised her hand in acknowledgment and eased her charger back toward the palace. Their cries echoed in her ears as she dismounted and handed off her steed. Victory spun her thoughts. She even admired her father's details: the ivory gates curled with vultures and lions and men-at-arms. Serapis stared down at her, and for once it wasn't with foreboding. She could swear a smile twitched on his stone lips.

"My queen." Dryton cleared his throat at her side. He seemed twitchy too, his cockiness worn away. "My queen, you were—you are magnificent."

Once, such a compliment from him would have made her flush with pleasure. No more. One pretty man's praises hardly made an impression.

"I'm surprised at you, Dryton. You're not a man given to sycophancy. Out with it, then. What favor do you beg? Has some golden trinket caught your eye, some girl you wish to wed or bed?" His good looks and self-assured smiles had no effect on her. Berenice knew what such a man was worth. He died as easily as any other.

"I ask—I ask nothing," he stammered. "I don't, perhaps, flatter as swiftly as other men. But your speech—your speech was brilliant. I've never heard your father give one so inspiring as that. If there was a time I underestimated you..." He trailed off. "Well, I was wrong to do so."

A king, she strode through the colonnades. Hatshepsut on the temple walls. Fair news traveled fast: the eyes of guards and servants and noblemen trailed her with wonder. She tasted it in the air. This was what it felt like to be loved—and feared. It was intoxicating. She could grow used to this spinning of her head and heart. No holes remained now, no emptiness lingered inside her, no worry about what might take fury's place. Only triumph, and bliss.

Her royal atrium, though, was filled with small men with small minds. They didn't care for her triumphs. Muttering to himself, Nereus hunched over a map of the Upper Lands. Reedy Thais whispered at his side. The old man pretended not to notice. She wondered if he realized that she knew about his lies, that his life trembled on a thread. She might merely reach over and cut it at any instant.

Pieton sat apart, staring down another scroll. He'd a dour look about him.

Berenice cast a smile at Dryton. "Come. Look at our stern eunuch. Perhaps he hasn't heard the good news?"

"She was magnificent," her minister of war repeated at her right.

"That's lofty praise indeed, considering the source," Pieton replied. "And though I hate to bear bad tidings, there was, you may recall, another matter neglected as you charmed the Seleucids. A certain petitioner was kept waiting for some long hours. He wasn't pleased by the delay, especially given all the previous postponements."

Psenptais. The high priest of Ptah. Her father's priest, his *prophet*. Pieton had caught her: this rendezvous had slipped her mind. Or rather, for days she'd been doing her best to forget that he'd sailed down from Memphis at all. Whatever his business here, her father's creature, it didn't bode well. The god's priests rarely ventured to Alexandria; she didn't like his newfound interest in her goings-on. But perhaps she should be flattered: traveling here showed that he recognized her rule.

"I'll see him now." She snapped her fingers at a passing servant, who scurried on to carry out her words. After all, she had nothing to fear from Psenptais anymore—her father had failed in Rome. She was the last remaining Ptolemy, and she ruled alone.

"Psenptais, son of Psenptais, high priest of Ptah, prophet of the

Lord of the Two Lands," Berenice's herald called from the center archway.

The words smarted in her ears. That he dared to announce by that title, when the man who had bestowed it was cowering behind Artemis's skirts in Ephesus. Berenice remembered this Psenptais only slightly, in bits and pieces that sprang more from the tales that she'd heard of him than from actual recollections. There was the famed story of how at thirteen he'd crowned her father, then a nervous but precocious boy. But that was years ago, well before her birth. The priest who emerged before her was a man grown.

And a handsome one, even, despite his shaved pate and simple linen robes. The two boys who attended him looked young—too young even to grow beards. Psenptais gave her a long look, expectant, as though he thought that she—*his queen*—should speak first. She said nothing. This man could sway little now.

"Troubles plague the double kingdom," he murmured. He spoke Greek well, almost as if it was a native tongue, but with a strange formality common to Upper Landers. And he didn't deign to address her as queen.

"What troubles, Psenptais? The Nile rose high this Inundation, which promises a prosperous Emergence. Last year, our farms were barren, but this season they will grow lush and green. I see few troubles there."

"I speak of troubles of a higher sort. Events that shock both gods and men. Events that are of great interest to Ptah, and to every god. Events here in Alexandria." He paused to clear his throat. "Marriage is a divine rite, a rite that should not be undertaken with ill intent. Our idols are none other than the great Serapis and his unwavering wife, Isis."

Berenice's hand hid a smile. Had he come to lecture her on marital devotion? Her, a Ptolemy? Her eyes slipped to Pieton. His face was a mask of stone. She could read no amusement on his pursed lips. A pity. He should laugh more. Why not? Triumph tasted sweet.

"When I heard that you were to marry Seleucus, it gladdened my heart. The gods prefer a man—any man—to rule. But other news, troubling news, reaches Memphis. And when I heard that so soon after your wedding day Seleucus lay dead, dead not at a brother's hand but at a wife's——"

"Mind your words, Psenptais," Pieton's voice cut in. "You don't mean to accuse your queen of murder."

Berenice held up a ringed palm. "Silence, my friend. Let the good priest go on."

But the eunuch's words had called the man back to his senses. Psenptais's eyes sprang furrows; he realized that he didn't stand before Ptah, or before her meek father, but before a far more fearsome judge. Berenice was no child who'd listen to his lectures on marriage and divinity.

"Psenptais, go on. I beg you," she goaded him. "You were, I believe, about to blame me for my husband's death, a tragedy that pains me beyond measure. I'm sure you know what fate awaits those who levy false accusations against the queen."

"I am not—I am the high priest of Ptah, master of justice. Threats won't sway me from the truth." His head was held high; his lip twitched.

"Tell me, Psenptais: how does Ptah anoint his high priests?" Threats would sway him—Berenice was quite sure—as long as they were clearly made. "You are, as you say, but a servant to the great deity. In dire times, surely, a god might select another priest, a servant who would be more willing to fulfill his duties here on this earth. Mortal lives are only brief flickers before the deathless ones." She smiled lightly at the priest. He didn't look so frightful now— a tall man, and powerfully built, but a mere ant before her. And to remember how he'd frightened her, how he might have refused to crown her queen. He would refuse her nothing.

"Ptah yields mighty powers. He must and shall do as he pleases."

"It does ease my mind to hear that." Her voice held light and airy—she had no reason to fear. He'd come to chide her, but by do-ing so he'd conferred approval on her rule. Priests held sway when rulers fought amongst themselves, or when the Nile failed to flood and crops were low. Not when the gods smiled on their earthly agent as they smiled on her. "Your Ptah's temple might serve as a good place to reflect on my words—unless you'd prefer that we ar-range accommodations for you here."

"Your offer is kind, my queen, but you are right. My own hum-ble rooms will serve well for such reflections." He kept his tone steady. A last attempt at dignity.

The carved ebony doors beneath the ivory-enameled arch swung open and swallowed the man of god and his attendants. The atrium didn't stir, except with the sound of some ibis calling in the dis-tance. Thais and Nereus, Dryton and Pieton, were joined for once in silence. Fear glinted in their eyes—fear mingled with respect.

"My queen." Pieton disturbed the peace. "A word in private?"

His scolding tired Berenice. The eunuch was bitter because she'd defied his advice and charmed Seleucus's men. It was his own fault. He'd thought her incapable of such magic.

"What could be more private than here, before my trusted coun-cilors?" She wouldn't dismiss her advisers on the eunuch's whim. She was queen; neither man nor god threatened her rule. She'd dis-patched the one creature who'd dared profane her body. Uncoupled from his Seleucid friends, Nereus proved no threat.

"As you wish," said the eunuch, glowering. "Though I hate to question your judgment, I must ask: is it wise to speak such harsh words to the high priest of Ptah? I know you hold his counsel in low esteem, but the common folk—"

"The common folk are happy that the Nile rises and their ba-bies eat," Berenice interjected in her most didactic tone. "They don't care for the worries of their betters. I believe you taught me that."

"On the greater part, I agree. But my queen, the gods breed

madness. The high priest still holds sway over this city. Should he decide to turn the hearts of Memphis against your reign—"

She cut off his mewling words. "Where would he turn their hearts? My father and his sons have fled. The natives haven't risen against Alexandria in a generation. I've heard enough."

Pieton sucked in his breath through his teeth and looked away. In another life, she would have begged for forgiveness. She didn't need a eunuch's approval, not now that whole men shouted for her in the streets and on the battlements. She had finished waiting, wheedling for love and acceptance. The throne was hers and hers alone. Even the soldiers who had scuffled in the alleys cried out her name. The time had come to solidify her power, to retake Cyprus, perhaps even to seize parts of her unlucky husband's splintered empire. Her army spoiled for war—and so did she. All she needed to do was wait for high harvest to arrive, and then she'd make her move. In the meantime, she'd garner more support—and lure more troops to her cause.

"We've another, more pressing matter to discuss. I've decided to wed once more." She'd been foolish to shirk marriage before— it was a bargaining chip, a useful one. This time, she'd wed her own choice, at her leisure.

"An excellent notion," Thais chimed in, eyes bright. A taut quiet met his words. He'd spoken too fast, and too soon. He flailed, anxious to correct his error. "After a suitable period of mourning, of course, my queen."

"I am stricken over Seleucus's death. But in these dark times we must all find the strength deep within ourselves to carry on. Tell me, Thais: what man should I wed?"

Her adviser paled at her words. But then he paled at most words.

"Don't fret, my friend. It's no punishment. I mean to ask you each in turn." Berenice was especially eager to ask Nereus. What would he say now that his favorite, his Selene's son, had been slain? How would he try to turn this changed course to his advantage?

Meanwhile, brow bent in thought, Thais looked as wise as she'd ever seen him. Perhaps he possessed some untapped knowledge of the princes and kings of Asia. Somewhere in his dull-witted mind, he must have a passing opinion on some relevant matter.

"Ariobarzanes of Cappadocia has two sons, neither of whom is wed, and both of whom would bring some number of loyal soldiers," her minister of lands told her slowly.

Berenice cared little for the kings of Cappadocia. In Mithradates's wars, they'd proved themselves to be weak, no more than puppets beholden to Rome, fleeing at the slightest sign of defeat.

"And then," her reedy councilor went on, "there are the sons of Antiochus of Commagene."

Nereus scoffed. "And how old are those boys? The elder can't be more than twelve."

"Twelve is old enough to wed—"

"For a girl, perhaps," the old man sneered.

"That's enough, Nereus." Berenice smiled. She took joy in mocking him. At last, she could show this fickle man how small he truly was. "What would you suggest? I recall you had some rather strong opinions when last we broached this matter."

Nereus coughed into his hand. His face reddened beneath his palm. "I'm sure there are many worthy men . . ." His voice faded away.

"But none so worthy, it seems, as Seleucus," she taunted. The old man's eyes grew wide and frightened. His fingers tugged at the sagging skin along his gullet. "Nor with so grand a Ptolemaic pedigree. Did you know, Nereus, that there are those who thought Seleucus's claim to the throne outweighed my own? My dear husband often reminded me that my father is called Bastard for a reason. But perhaps you were not familiar with that particular appellation . . ."

"It's the father's blood that matters most," the old man replied.

"And that's why you were so eager to see Seleucus crowned: so that my children would have the proper blood—a father's blood." She drew out each syllable willfully, watching Nereus squirm.

"My queen, if I've done something to offend—"

"Offend?" Berenice laughed brightly. "No, never that."

Nereus bit back his tongue and stared. She could read each passing fear flicker across his face. She savored that for a moment before returning her attentions to the rest of the set.

"Each of you is to draw up a list of suitable men along with the number of soldiers and the amount of gold they're likely to bring. We'll go about this in a sensible manner, as we should any weighty decision for the realm."

Berenice's words cut as they were meant to. But much as she blamed Nereus's treachery, she knew her own naïveté had been at fault as well. Trusting had been her downfall. Hounded by her fear of the Piper's rise in Rome, she'd panicked and wed too soon. She wouldn't make that mistake again.

Pieton looked up from his scroll for the first time. "I don't need to make a list. I can tell you now whom you should wed: your brother Ptolemy. Take him as your husband. Your father lies low for the moment, but he won't stay quiet forever. And Rome would never dare depose a united brother-sister pair."

This tick again. Berenice clenched her fists. Why did Pieton harp on the notion? He knew that she would never wed her brothers, that she needed soldiers to take Cyprus. But she didn't want to air these arguments. Nereus had no inkling of those plans. Best to keep it that way.

"And how, pray tell, might I heed your advice?" she asked with false sweetness. "My two brothers fled some time ago. And, you may recall, we've encountered certain difficulties in finding them."

The eunuch's face glowed; he always reveled in his trump moves. "I've discovered them, or at the very least discovered a means of contacting their mother. She won't refuse you; she wouldn't dare. And you'll find no more malleable consort than a young boy."

Berenice's stomach churned. He'd had some contact with the concubine, then. The very thought sickened her. She remembered the first time she saw the woman, young and lush and beautiful—everything her mother wasn't—sitting at her father's side. She'd fed him grapes and laughed at his jokes and whispered treason in his ear. How could the eunuch speak to that creature? Suggest again that she wed one of that woman's sons?

"Today, perhaps, and tomorrow he'll be malleable," Berenice answered through gritted teeth. "But what of in ten years? He'll grow into a man—I hear even the youngest of boys do that in time—and one who some will believe has a claim equal to my own."

"My queen makes a point," Dryton seconded, and she felt a distinct warmth for the pretty man. "There's a poor history for queens who rule alongside brothers."

"Berenice." The eunuch's tenor strained. "I'd urge you to worry about holding the throne for the next ten weeks, never mind the next ten years. The Piper might be waylaid in Ephesus, but he will find an army, one way or another. Your brother appears to be a hardy boy of five, but who can say what the Fates have in store for him? He might not see another ten floods."

Berenice raised her voice, her sense of calm shattered. "I will not wed my brother." She hated the eunuch at that moment for foisting horrors at her feet. She would not repeat her mother's mistakes. Her life would not be marked by birthing monsters year after year. Had Tryphaena ever stared at one of her strange and stillborn babes and wondered at their shape? A godly punishment for bedding her brother, for daring what only immortals do. At least with Seleucus's seed Berenice might have borne healthy children, perhaps even handsome ones, to carry on her house.

"If I were you, I'd come up with a list after all, Pieton," she added, reining in her anger as best she could. "See that it's a good one."

Her advisers hurried off; not even the eunuch lingered. Doubt clouded her mind. Why did Pieton press her brother's claim? Wasn't it enough that Nereus had betrayed her? Must she suspect the eunuch too, the tutor who'd raised her and shielded her more carefully than either of her parents had? She dug her claws into her hair, loosing clumps from their net. Pieton had lobbied for it the first time as well, though he knew better than the others how she loathed the idea. Did he plot in secret with the concubine? Berenice had never imagined him capable of betrayal. For years, she'd held that eunuchs were less changeable than other men. But now Tryphaena's enigmatic warning rang in her ears. Berenice shouldn't have dismissed those words so lightly. Perhaps they were more than symptoms of her mother's delusions. *Do not trust the eunuch. He's no Ptolemy. He will . . .*

"He will *what,* Mother?" Berenice asked aloud.

YOUNGER

S he had terrible dreams, terror stalked her nights, she shook with fear. . . . She dreamed she gave birth to a snake." Arsinoe read with hunger. She knew what would happen, how the Fates would unfold before her eyes. She'd drunk in these tales a hundred times, first with Ganymedes alone, and then with Ganymedes and Alexander, and then over and over and over again on her own. Myrrine teased her each time she asked for the text: "Arsinoe, it isn't natural for girls to stay cooped up reading indoors."

Arsinoe ignored the taunts. What mattered was that she read on.

"Aeschylus again, I see."

Ganymedes. Arsinoe looked up eagerly. The eunuch didn't often visit her in her chambers. Perhaps—she hoped, she prayed—he'd come to discuss her dreams. In the days after their meeting in the library, she'd tiptoed around him, praying that if she was very good, the eunuch might speak to her in confidence again. She'd almost given up hope, but now—perhaps in her private rooms? After all, her tutor could hardly bring up their conversation before Alexander. Or she certainly hoped he wouldn't. She couldn't imagine trying to talk about the deaths she'd seen in front of her friend.

He smiled. "I have a surprise for you, little one." He called her that in his gentler moods.

"A surprise?" Arsinoe's limbs lightened. She bounced up from the floor. "What is it?"

"Follow me, and I'll show you."

Arsinoe did as she was told. She trailed the eunuch out of her rooms and into the familiar corridor, with its shining frescoes of the first Ptolemy the Benefactor's victories in Asia. They passed the cedar staircase that curved down to the courtyard below, and instead continued on toward the nursery.

She felt a stab of sickness in her spleen as the eunuch opened the door. What sort of surprise could this room hold? Empty of children, the chamber felt dank and dismal. The walls themselves, with their brightly painted panels of hyenas circling one another and baboons bounding through the grass, seemed to have dimmed. As a girl, she'd traveled down the Nile with these images, picturing herself lounging in the rounded skiff as fish leapt about her toes. Each time Cleopatra returned with their father from the Upper Lands, Arsinoe would quiz her on which of the exotic animals she'd glimpsed: a rock python, a sphinx monkey, a rhinoceros? Many of their names were painted below their depictions, and those words marked some of the first that she'd learned to read. It all seemed foolish now. A child's world of guessing games and imaginings.

Arsinoe glanced around the rest of the room; she might as well look for Ganymedes's surprise. But all she saw were the scattered remnants of her brothers' toys. The boys were long since gone, but their mess remained. In the far corner, a pair of hobbyhorses leaned against the wall, as if waiting for some ghost children to return. A chill ran down her spine. She didn't like it here. The nursery reeked of death and fear.

She dragged her feet at the door. "Why did you bring me here?"

"Go to the window. Look."

She crossed the hunted stag mosaic on her toes. Indoors, she preferred to walk this way, drinking in her silent steps. Below the window stretched the Sisters' Courtyard. There, two different girls, one dark and one fair, whispered beneath a laurel. Their gold-hemmed tunics glinted in the sun. Their faces were familiar, players from Arsinoe's other life—the life before her father had fled. The dark girl held a doll; the fair one reached for it.

"Let me brush her hair awhile, Aspasia."

"She's mine. I'll let you when I choose." Their voices carried on the wind.

Arsinoe turned from the scene. "I'm too old to play with dolls."

"I thought you'd be pleased. Your friends have returned."

"You brought them here," she replied dully.

"I did indeed. And Berenice was kind enough to agree. It seems your antics have won you some favors on that front." The eunuch clucked at her frown. "I thought it would make you smile, little one. You longed for girls who shared your age and birth."

"No one shares my birth." *No one except Cleopatra.* The longing for her sister washed over her in heady waves. For weeks, even, she wouldn't pine for Cleopatra, and then the feeling would strike Arsinoe so hard that it knocked her wind away, and she was left gulping, hungry for her sister, for the blood and whispers that they shared. But Cleopatra was in Ephesus, she reminded herself harshly; she might already be a novice before the goddess Artemis. She wouldn't return, and Arsinoe wouldn't embrace these paltry substitutes.

"Of course they don't, my princess." Ganymedes smiled.

Arsinoe chafed at his mockery. What did it mean, to be a princess now? Was she Berenice's heir because she'd told her of Nereus's plot? Did her sister even care about that? Nereus, as far as she could tell, was alive and well and favored.

"But they're noble girls of noble blood, Arsinoe. Proper companions for a Ptolemy."

"Alexander is of noble blood." She should know. She'd feasted on it in her dreams.

"He is. On his father's side, at least."

"That's the only side that matters." She didn't like to think of her own mother. She refused to consider his.

"In your case, yes. But not in Alexander's—"

"I won't listen to you cast aspersions on his blood." Fury clawed at Arsinoe's cheeks.

"Noble-blooded or not, my dear, Alexander isn't speaking to you."

She winced at the words. It hurt more that they were true.

"Or perhaps it's you who aren't speaking to him." Her tutor sighed. "I don't know, my dear, but I do know it isn't healthful for a girl your age to spend so much time alone, to lose herself in scrolls."

That wasn't fair. She shouldn't be chided for reading. "I read Aeschylus, the oldest of Athens's tragedians," she protested. "You can't object to that." Nothing she did was good enough. Not now, not ever.

"You need companionship," Ganymedes said quietly. "The sort of companionship I can't provide. But these girls—they can."

"I'd rather be alone." That wasn't fully true, but it was true enough.

The eunuch's voice hardened. "You don't have that luxury. I've worked hard to return these girls to you. I begged their fathers. I told them that their daughters were your particular favorites. 'Arsinoe asks for Hypatia and Aspasia every night,' I told them. 'She yearns for these, her dearest friends.' They've taken a great risk in returning their children to you. With your future so uncertain."

"My *blood* is not uncertain." She hated how everyone forgot that: blood didn't change. Even separated from Cleopatra, from her father, it wouldn't atrophy. Would it?

"No, it's not. That's why these men send their daughters despite their better judgment. Because your blood is divine. And they hope that might buy favors in good time. When the winds turn, even the most stubborn reed will bend. Surely you who are too old for dolls and childish playthings don't need me to explain the intricacies of court, what matters and what doesn't."

Her tutor was right. Arsinoe's tenth birthday had come and gone, and no one had mentioned it. She hadn't even minded: she knew what mattered in the court. She forced herself to look out the window again. Below, Aspasia had surrendered the toy to her fair-haired friend—Hypatia. Arsinoe forced the name to her lips. With delicate fingers, the girl braided the doll's delicate hair. It looked as though it had been cut from a girl, not a beast—the strands were that fine.

"You will go to them now. And you will play. With dolls or with whatever other toys you devise. Perhaps you'll braid your hair and whisper secrets. It makes no difference to me. But they are your confidants now. And they will come to our lessons and learn with you and Alexander. Or with you alone, if you prefer. Alexander need not join us."

Arsinoe's lips tightened. "No, Alexander should come still." She wasn't sure whether her demand had sprung from kindness or cruelty.

As she climbed down the stairs, her heart twisted in her chest. What did these girls know of her now? These children who had been stolen away before the palace fell and had lived for nearly two years feasting in the comfort of their country homes?

"Arsinoe!" Hypatia cried as she stepped outside. The doll fell forgotten at her side.

Aspasia was already on her feet and running toward her. "Arsinoe! How I missed you. I was so worried for you—I prayed for your safety every night."

She should smile. She should laugh. She should speak. Aspasia threw her arms about her neck. Stilted, unnatural.

"We begged our fathers to return here each day," Hypatia added. Her arms now tangled with Aspasia's about Arsinoe's neck.

"I missed you both terribly." Arsinoe forced the lie to her lips. "I can't believe you're real, that you're here with me at last."

Once she'd begun, the false words came easily to her tongue. Lying wasn't difficult—even lying with her heart. Ganymedes had told her that she must befriend these girls. Though he wasn't always fair, he tended to be right. Arsinoe folded her legs and sat on the ground.

"Are you quite well?" Aspasia asked, all earnestness. Her eyes searched Arsinoe's for an answer. "You must tell us everything. All you've done, and all the things you've seen. How have you been treated? How brave you must have been!"

"The queen has treated me with great kindness." Unlike her friends, she knew better than to talk freely. Even in the Sisters' Courtyard, Arsinoe didn't know what ears were listening. Besides, all told, it was the truth: she had been treated well.

Hypatia's voice dropped to a whisper. "But—but tell us: what happened when she seized the palace? Were you very frightened?"

What do you care? What difference does it make to you, you two who were curled up cozy and comfortable in your fathers' villas, far from the city and her woes? Then she reminded herself: *Ganymedes insisted that we be friends.* So Arsinoe answered, "I presented myself to the queen. And she was merciful. You two are brave to return here to me."

"Not nearly as brave as you," Hypatia gushed. "What did you say to the queen? How did you—"

"Aspasia," Arsinoe interrupted. She could bear no more of this needling, of these guileless questions. She shouldn't blame them; they were children still. "Might I see your doll?"

The dark-haired girl surrendered the toy at once. Arsinoe had been right: the hair had come from a human head. She imagined what desperation must have driven some woman to sell such tender locks. There were worse things to lose, Arsinoe supposed. Hair could be regrown.

"She's lovely."

Her friend beamed. "Do you think so? My father brought her back to me from Petra. Her eyes are from dyed glass. That's why they look so real."

A flicker of movement caught Arsinoe's attention. At the far side of the courtyard, in the shadow of her foremother's fountain, stood Alexander. He stared at the scene with cold gray-green eyes. And then he turned back toward the colonnade.

Things grew easier in the afternoons that followed. Her exchanges with her former friends became more natural, approaching closeness at times. She laughed with them, at their stories of their time in the country and the odd folks they'd met there.

"There was one man—he called himself a priest, but I couldn't believe it—who spoke to snakes," Aspasia explained one day, dipping her toes in Poseidon's waves. She'd been living far from Alexandria, south even of Thebes, where her father owned some swaths of farmland—"a thousand stades in each direction, as far as the eye can see," the girl had bragged, although Arsinoe hadn't quite believed her. But she was jealous of Aspasia's mastery of the Egyptian language. The ancient tongue of the Upper Lands came easily to her now, while Arsinoe still struggled to make sense of it.

"He could *not* speak to snakes," Hypatia snapped. Her temper grew testy whenever Aspasia's tales rose too tall.

"He could," Aspasia insisted. "I swear it. He had a vase of red clay, the sort that commoners might use for libations, and he'd take out a wooden flute. And when he played, the cobra would slither through the narrow mouth and dance along with the tune. And then his eyes would slowly close beneath their hood, and it would fall asleep again, as tame as anything."

"Then he didn't *speak* to snakes. He only played to them," Hypatia declared, triumphant.

"But that's not all," Aspasia protested. "He'd whisper secrets to the creatures, and they would whisper back to him. Just like Asclepius. He knew, at once, that I was a great friend of a princess. And that I was fleeing something."

"Of course you were fleeing something, Aspasia," Arsinoe teased. "What else would a noble Macedonian girl be doing in the Upper Lands?"

Her friend laughed. And Hypatia did as well. When Arsinoe laughed with them, part of her wished that she'd been spirited away too, that she'd remained a child and unchanged, not transformed into some not-quite woman with frightful dreams. But games and confidences were easy. It was the lessons with Ganymedes that she dreaded.

* * *

"I wonder what man the queen will marry next." Hypatia sighed as she ran a finger over her copy of Plato's *Treatise on the Soul*. The eunuch had gone to fetch a second set of scrolls, and his four charges were left to entertain themselves. "I hear she's ordered a dozen men brought before her so she might pick the one who pleases her."

"That's just a rumor, Hypatia," Arsinoe answered. "Kings won't send their sons all the way to Alexandria to merely stand before the queen." She didn't think they would, in any event. Berenice wasn't fool enough to pick based on looks. After all, Seleucus had been handsome enough, for what little good that did him.

"Well, I should like to pick among a dozen men, when I marry." Hypatia tittered at her own mischief.

Arsinoe fought the urge to groan. She found the conversation tiresome—she could only imagine what Alexander thought. "A dozen," she echoed. "Whatever should you do with them? Race and wrestle them as Atalanta did so you might always remain a maid?"

"I shouldn't always wish to be a maid," Hypatia replied, tossing back her bronze hair.

Aspasia giggled madly, but Arsinoe looked away. She stole a glance at Alexander. His eyes squinted at one spot on his scroll, as though he was learning something fascinating by staring at a single phrase.

"So," Hypatia carried on, emboldened by Aspasia's laughter. "I wouldn't challenge my suitors to insurmountable feats. I'd merely line them up and pick the handsomest one. The one with the broadest chest and the sharpest eyes."

"You can't then be jealous of the queen," Aspasia cut in.

"Why not?"

"I don't imagine any of her suitors will be handsome," the dark-haired girl said.

"Why shouldn't they be?" Arsinoe said. Their talk irritated her.

It reminded her how little they knew of court, of life. "Her first husband was."

"What do you three care who the queen marries?" Alexander asked coldly. "Why don't you just stick to discussing who your husbands will be? That's the only subject that interests you."

The words cut deep. In that moment, Arsinoe hated him. She hated him for his distance and for naming her as one of them.

"That's not true." Her voice was sharp. He was wrong. "I don't care who I marry, but I care very much who my sister weds. For the man my sister weds will become the king."

"And does it matter if the king is handsome?" Sometimes Alexander thought himself so very clever. "Will that change how he rules?"

"Beauty always matters," Arsinoe snapped. She, too, could be clever. "It matters because it changes your position in the world. The same reason that blood matters. Helen's beauty sailed a thousand ships—and wrecked the city of Troy."

"Helen was a *woman*."

"Helen was a *queen*. And the daughter of all-seeing Zeus. Besides, Paris was a beauty too—the most handsome man in all the world. That's why the goddesses chose him to pick the loveliest among them. And that's why Aphrodite gave him Helen, even though she was already wed to Menelaus." Arsinoe spoke eagerly— she knew that she'd seized on the perfect argument. Alexander wouldn't stand a chance.

"And that was why he was such a coward," he sneered. "Because he didn't want to mar his lovely face."

"Perhaps. But now you're saying he was a coward *because* he was handsome. So, yes, his beauty mattered greatly. You've proved my point." She slapped her hand against the table with satisfaction, but when she looked to Alexander for a concession, he was bristling with anger.

"Why are you defending them?" he shouted. He was almost shaking with fury. His eyes flickered at the two girls, dull in their silence.

"You're just upset because your beauty doesn't matter," Arsinoe taunted. A passion had possessed her. A need to drive him from her, fully and truly. Ganymedes had practically admitted that there was no means to stop her dreams from coming true. The closer she was to Alexander, the greater the risk. The more likely she'd be to suck the life lingering in his corpse, just as she had in her sleep. The thought haunted her morning and night—and her only recourse was to cut Alexander away. "Because your blood doesn't matter," she went on. "And your wife's beauty won't matter, because she'll be nothing. Just like you."

Alexander knocked his chair back hard as he stood, silver clattering on stone. "And of course yours does." His voice barely reached a whisper, but Arsinoe caught every last syllable. "Your beauty matters very, very much. Because you're nothing like Berenice. It's the best quality you've got—the only quality you've got. So you'll need to make use of it."

He stormed from the table and out of the reading room. Neither girl met Arsinoe's eye, and she did not speak. Too much rage roiled in her gut—against Alexander, against her false friends and her false self. She loathed all of them—and Ganymedes for forcing her into lying confidences, for bringing her these useless girls.

It was Aspasia who broke the tension. She squeezed Arsinoe's hand as she passed by to right the toppled seat.

When the eunuch returned, he set fresh scrolls on the table, and made no comment on the taut mood of the three girls. "It's a pity that Alexander has disappeared," he said wryly as he stretched open his papyrus. "Today we'll return to a particular favorite of his: *The Odyssey*."

That was welcome news, at least—a distraction. Arsinoe much preferred Homer's epic to Plato's dialogues, though she knew better than to say it. The eunuch would only chide her for not appreciating philosophy.

"Any child of six knows *The Odyssey*," Hypatia whined. She

never liked much of anything, Arsinoe knew. She was always saying how learning was a waste of time. "What more can we learn from it?"

"What more can three girls of ten learn from the most renowned of poets?" asked Ganymedes. "I'm not certain, Hypatia, but I imagine you'll find something. Why don't you begin our recitation? We're reading from your very favorite book, the one about the Cyclops's cave. You may start: 'Lurching up, he lunged out with his hands toward my men.'"

The fair girl grimaced. "'Lurching up, he lunged out with his hands toward my men and snatching two at once, rapping them on the ground.'" She paused to collect herself, her face contorted in disgust. "'He knocked them dead like pups—their brains gushed out all over, soaked the floor...'"

The child's voice trailed off, trembling, even as the eunuch urged her on. Arsinoe felt strangely grateful for the corpses she'd seen strewn about the palace. Words of horror didn't unnerve her, not when she'd seen true horrors before her eyes. Hypatia reminded her of how she must have been, before she'd become Antigone, before she'd chosen Berenice and death. Arsinoe grew sick, suddenly, of watching Ganymedes toy with her friend, and so she cut in instead: "'And ripping them limb from limb to fix his meal he bolted them down like a mountain-lion, left no scrap, devoured entrails, flesh and bones, marrow and all.'"

"You needn't show off your learning, Arsinoe," the eunuch scolded. "It's not a pleasant quality." It wasn't fair. She wasn't showing off, and Ganymedes knew that.

"*She* doesn't want to recite it. Can't you see you're frightening her?" Arsinoe regretted her last words at once. They sounded more like an insult than a defense, though she hadn't meant them to. Hypatia colored in shame. Aspasia twisted her quill over her scroll, shrinking smaller and smaller with each twirl.

The eunuch smirked. "Aspasia, can you continue? Or does

Arsinoe need to steal your words as well? You may begin again after the Cyclops, now gorged on Odysseus's men, has fallen asleep."

Arsinoe's dark-haired friend didn't even glance in her direction. She straightened her back and pronounced each word with exaggerated care. "'And I with my fighting heart, I thought at first to steal up to him, draw the sharp sword at my hip and stab his chest where the midriff packs the liver—I groped for the fatal spot but a fresh thought held me back. There at a stroke we'd finish off ourselves as well—how could *we* with our bare hands heave back that slab he set to block his cavern's gaping maw? So we lay there groaning, waiting Dawn's first light.'"

"Well read, Aspasia."

Arsinoe eyed the eunuch. He wasn't liberal with his praises. Not without a purpose.

"Now, why doesn't Odysseus attack the Cyclops? The creature killed his men, after all, in a way that our dear Hypatia finds particularly distasteful."

From the corner of her eye, Arsinoe stole a look at the fair-haired girl. She was taking the mocking rather well, everything considered. At least, she didn't look as though she would weep.

"He's scared," Aspasia replied. "And he doesn't see the purpose. He would've been trapped if he killed the Cyclops then. He would have died."

Arsinoe bristled at the words. Aspasia didn't understand at all.

"He wasn't scared," Arsinoe cut in. "He was clever." She retained her child's admiration for this Odysseus. Even if her wily hero turned cold and cruel in the plays of Euripides, here, in the epic poem of old, he was no monster. "He *does* avenge his friends, for in the end he blinds the Cyclops and leaves him for dead."

"And how does that choice work out for Odysseus, Arsinoe? That decision to blind the Cyclops—his great vengeance on behalf of his friends?"

Of course, his revenge against Poseidon's son brought Poseidon's curse, which tossed her hero and his men across the sea for ten long years. She chewed her lip. She saw that she'd set the argument on a faulty truss. Helpless, she replied, "In the end, Odysseus returns to Ithaca."

"And in what manner does he return to Ithaca?"

Arsinoe dodged. "Disguised as a beggar."

"Let me be more exact: how many of his men return with him?"

Arsinoe said nothing. Odysseus returned alone.

"None, Arsinoe. None. After years of trials and torments, after his men are eaten and transfigured and drowned to a one, your great Odysseus, your man of twists and turns, returns to Ithaca. Alone. Because his actions have brought the death of every single one of his companions."

The eunuch's words chilled her. The thought of all her companions dead. But she'd sent Alexander away. That would be enough to protect him. It had to be.

After the lesson ended, her two playmates hurried off, bidding quick farewells, too eager to escape to mind courtesies. Arsinoe made no move to leave. Instead, she helped Ganymedes clear away the scrolls and quills in silence. The other girls would be wary of her for a while now, especially Hypatia, whose listlessness had turned to fury as Ganymedes railed on.

"I didn't mean to embarrass Hypatia," she said at last. "I wanted to help her."

"I know you did," the eunuch replied. "But our intentions aren't always understood. Sometimes the best way to help someone is to let her wrestle on her own."

"I wanted to protect her," Arsinoe whispered in a small voice. "As Cleopatra used to protect me."

Ganymedes looked at her with the same sad eyes she'd seen in the library storehouse. "We can't always protect the ones we love."

She didn't dare argue. What if he proved her wrong?

Her tutor patted her hand gently. "My dear, you have a kind heart. Too kind, perhaps. I worry for you."

"Then perhaps your heart is too kind too."

The eunuch smiled. "Perhaps it is. Here. I even have a present for you."

"Another friend?" she quipped.

"Of a sort." Ganymedes's eyes shifted along the walls. He reached into his tunic and pulled out a small linen bundle. "Be careful."

Eager, Arsinoe lifted one corner. She choked back a gasp at what she saw: a small blade sheathed in leather.

"Hide it," the eunuch warned. "And teach yourself to use it."

That night and many nights that followed, Arsinoe lay awake. She waited until Myrrine's lamp flickered out in the antechamber and her nurse's snores reverberated through the air. Then, when she was sure she was alone—or as alone as she ever hoped to be—she coaxed light into her oil lamp and fetched the knife from among her silks. She liked the weight of it in her hand, and the way its silver licked up the flame. Even the lightest press of her fingers drew a sweet drop of blood, rich and vibrant and red. And then she'd suck the salty venom from her veins. One day soon, she'd learn how to wield the blade.

ELDER

The handwringer standing before her marked the first. Every inch of him—from his sinuous trousers to the sleeves of his billowing tunic—was sheathed in silk, which appeared distinctly ill suited to the Egyptian heat. No doubt the attire was meant to impress her with its opulence, but Berenice would have been more inclined toward him if he didn't keep reaching for his handkerchief to wipe the pooling sweat from his brow. On the whole, he cut a nervous figure rather than an intimidating one. As he recited his plea, he appeared to have little notion of what to do with his voice or feet or hands—save, of course, to use the last to mop the accumulating moisture from his face.

Though Berenice hated to admit it, she felt unprepared as well. She hadn't expected a wooer to come so soon—she'd hoped to solidify her plans for Cyprus first—but she imagined that this Mithradates of Parthia had his own reasons for haste. His bloodthirsty brother Orodes, as she understood it, had driven him from his home, and now he searched frantically for his own army to seize back those lands. How satisfying to sit on the other end of such a negotiation.

"My queen," he began, for the second time. He was a twitchy sort of man—the opposite of Seleucus, who'd been defined by his cruel confidence. From the look of this one, Berenice would guess that he had a few years on her—perhaps five, no more than ten. And he'd spent his time far less wisely than she. He'd lost a kingdom; she had won one. "My queen, I beg to present you a gift, a token of my esteem."

He gestured almost wildly to his men gathered by the entrance arches of the atrium. They looked as surprised as she at their master's command, and when at last two stumbled forward heaving an ivory chest between them, one slipped on the great mosaic paw of Dionysus's leopard, tumbling forward and nearly losing hold of the load. She should be more indulgent. Seleucus had brought no gifts that she could recall. If she'd asked, he would have told her his cock was gift enough.

"Go on, open it," she told the hapless servants. Perhaps Orodes had held on to the better ones. The more practiced of the pair, the one who hadn't nearly spoiled his master's offering, a drab creature of indeterminate years, squinted at her, uncomprehending. She tried again, switching from Greek to Persian. "Open it."

That he seemed to understand, and he gestured to his larger, clumsier comrade to lift the lid. Silks, rich and colorful, spilled from the cedar. Berenice's eyes caught on a lilac garment, a chiton embroidered with gold stitching to form an intricate border of lotus blossoms along the neckline and shoulder. She saw beneath it—the drabber slave sifted through the violets and crimsons and teals— jewels as well: a golden diadem set with ruby and turquoise. These silks were dear gifts—far dearer even than the gold that lay beneath—but useless to her. She didn't need adornments; she needed men, men to expand her kingdom and guard her throne. And this wooer carried too many battles of his own.

Mithradates smiled. "From India and beyond." He ran his greedy eyes over the gifts, as though they still belonged to him. "When we are wed and retake my father's kingdom, we'll control all trade between those far-off eastern lands and Rome."

The Romans had developed quite a taste for silk, as Pieton told it. It didn't surprise Berenice. The Republic lusted after every art it couldn't master: the rich purple cloth of Tyre, the delicate glasswork of Alexandria, the breathing statues of Athens. These trade routes would yield welcome revenue. But dark whispers thronged about this Mithradates, too, ones that didn't share the pleasant scent of silk and coin. He had tried to sell himself as a husband to every princess along the banks of the Euphrates—and had been rebuked by all. If any imagined that he had the strength to recapture his brother's lands, he would already be wed.

"I thank you for your kind gifts."

The man, this lesser son of Parthia, knit his brow, as though he'd expected something more encouraging, though Berenice couldn't imagine how she had raised his hopes. After touting his marital potential across the better part of Asia, he must, by now, have grown accustomed to rejection. His palms slid back and forth against each other. She could hear the dead skin worrying away.

"Will I hear no answer to my suit?" His voice cracked. This boldness was startling. He didn't look the sort of man to press his points. His silks, as well-worn as they were rich; the rubbing of his hands; his pursed lips—he reeked of desperation. Berenice recognized the stink.

Still, she could be direct; the role fit her better than the coquette. And so she replied sharply, "You'll hear an answer since you ask. I've no wish to waste anyone's time, my own least of all. I won't marry Rome's wars in Asia. I've enough of my own worries to attend to at home."

His face fell, all that nervous, jolting energy stripped away to disappointment. His palms stuck together; his lips gaped. Berenice nearly pitied him. Here was his last, his final hope, and she'd dashed it against the onyx. The matter didn't weigh on her for long. When the Parthian shuffled off, her sympathies shuffled with him, and she thought of him no more.

Harvest came, rich and full and warm. The news from beyond her borders remained quiet. The nearest came from Judea, where the Syrian governor, Aulus Gabinius, and his Roman legions had stormed through Nazareth and toward Jerusalem to beat the Judean kingdoms into submission. But the eagle standard never passed south of the Dead Sea. The Republic, it seemed, was content to leave Egypt alone.

And so the only foreigners the early summer winds carried were more suitors. Cotys of Thrace, a frail man old enough to be her grandfather, tried to buy her hand with jewels. And trembling Antiochus of Commagene, nearly young enough to be her son, gave her rare and ancient scrolls plundered from Pergamum—"Gifts for your great library, my queen," he enunciated meticulously, a child practicing his verses. When she gave her rejection, as gently as she could manage, the boy couldn't hide his relief. Young Ariobarzanes of Cappadocia emerged as the best of a bad lot, though she worried over the five years she had on his sixteen, and over the putrid tales that spun about his mother. Athenais of Pontus, Berenice had heard, exerted a strange and unnatural influence over both of her adolescent sons. Having shed her own mother, Berenice wasn't looking to take on a second.

One week ran into the next, and her interest waned. Bright tidings poured in from the Upper Lands: the harvest yielded high. Last Inundation had ripened the fields, and rather than doling out from the storehouses to keep the natives calm, the crown stacked its reserves. Each day, another armada laden with wheat and freshly cut papyrus reeds plowed down the Nile. The grain piled up in the warehouses along the city's southern lake; the reeds were dried and pounded into production to feed the avid bookkeepers at home and abroad. The storehouses overflowed, trade ships swarmed the ports, and even peasant children grew fat.

Pieton convinced Berenice to preside over a citywide jubilee to praise the gods for these gifts, and for five days Alexandria's limestone avenues clattered with charioteers and jugglers, flamethrowers and elephant-drawn wagons that splashed wine into the streets. The people of the city—Greek and Egyptian, Persian and Jewish—

drank themselves into oblivion, slurring out her coronation name in glee: "Berenice the Shining One." And the city itself seemed to shine with her. The great edifices of the Sema and Poseidon's temple, of the gymnasium and the library, had been scrubbed and retouched until their friezes gleamed. The celebration was but a shadow of her father's feasts, but sometimes a shadow outshone its creator. And best of all, throughout the revelries not a peep was heard about the Piper. He remained waylaid in Ephesus, friendless and alone.

When Berenice awoke every morning and gazed over the docks bustling with ships and galleys, she even dared to hope that she wouldn't need to take a second husband. There might be enough men to allow her to conquer Cyprus on her own. Her advisers would chafe at the idea. "You'll always need more soldiers," she could almost hear the eunuch chide. "What chance would your farm-soft men stand against Rome's legions?"

And so Berenice let her councilors fuss over each prospect. "In times of peace," her father once told her, his lips purple with wine, "advisers need to find occupations for their time. Otherwise they think too much. And idle minds always make trouble." Even dull meetings provided useful insights. Thais held the keenest interest in these goings-on; they seemed to kindle some long-forgotten sense of purpose in him. She'd never seen her reedy councilor so eager and bold. Each afternoon he'd bustle through the griffin-embossed doors of the royal atrium with a new set of possibilities.

Nereus, on the other hand, paid less and less attention to the matter at hand. More than once, Berenice caught him drifting off on some divan. Age had caught up with him: his knees and knuckles swelled as the rest of him wasted away. Perhaps he sensed that his death was near. She kept a close watch on him, but the old man seemed to have lost his conspiratorial aspirations. Indeed, with Seleucus dead, he appeared to have lost any aspirations at all. She was no longer sure if she should have him killed, or merely wait for nature to take its unrelenting course. After all, if his treachery became known, she stood to look as much a fool as anyone.

Her eunuch, too, remained more often silent than not during these negotiations, but for entirely different reasons. Pieton imagined that his patience would wear her down, that after the first, or fifth, or fiftieth unsuccessful suit she'd yield to his revolting plan and wed that mewling child who masqueraded as her brother. Pieton still saw her as that soft and pliant girl he'd taught. She would prove him wrong.

"Archelaus, high priest of Bellona at Comana, son of Mithradates the Good Father of Pontus." The herald struck his staff three times against the stone.

In interest, Berenice glanced up, her eyes flicking over the wine god on his dancing leopard to where the trio of ivory-hatched arches opened into the atrium. The pedigree, if nothing else, intrigued her. After all, it had been *this* Mithradates, not the one from Parthia that she'd already dismissed, who'd proved the last great threat to Rome. And she saw that the owner of the name was pleasing enough. He wore an openmouthed lion headdress just like his famed progenitor, but beneath its jagged fangs Berenice noted a bright and playful set of eyes. His broad chest sheathed with a breastplate of gleaming silver, he looked everything a man should. Not that she cared about such things. As he bent his knee on the leopard's mouth, a dark lock freed itself from the lion's jaws and fell across his eyes. A better start than most.

"Rise, my friend." A playful note had struck her voice. She tempered it. She was a grown woman of twenty-one, not some love-struck girl of fourteen. "I'll hear your suit."

Carelessly he tossed a curl from his face; his eyes, black and bright, bore into hers. An impish smile teased his lips to reveal a set of white teeth—*And how well I play this game.* The moment she noticed his grin it vanished, and he was all earnest courtesy.

"You are gracious, my queen, as well as beautiful. And I've heard tell often of your cunning, both on the battlefield and off."

He paused, and Berenice couldn't tell whether he mocked her. She liked to be ready with a witticism to deflect false compliments, but her wit failed her now.

"I daresay many others have come before you with a similar plea," he continued. "I won't insult your intellect by dancing about the matter. You already know the nature of my suit: I come to wed you."

"You're far from the first." Again, that odd flirtation in her voice. Much as she wanted to, she couldn't fully drown it out.

"I don't wonder at that. Few women could equal you in loveliness, and from what I hear, not one equals you in will."

Berenice raised her brow. "Is that so?" She could play this teasing game too. "What dreadful tales do they tell of me in Cappadocia?"

"No dreadful tales. Only glorious ones. All reflect the same claim: that you rule with twice your father's strength and thrice his wisdom."

If he knew her father, she thought wryly, he'd not think that such a compliment. She knew better than to be won over by pretty words. She wasn't some besotted girl.

"Do you see my court, Archelaus?" Berenice gestured to the bowed buttresses of the ceiling with their gold- and ruby-leaf lotus flowers, to the glistening mosaic on the floor wrought from glass and lapis lazuli, to the silver chairs that held her advisers on enamel-studded claws.

He nodded, though his eyes did not shift to look. Instead, they dug into her very soul.

"I shall tell you a secret, then," she whispered in her most conspiratorial tone. "The worst-kept secret of Alexandria. The city is chock-full of flatterers. From the moment I rise in the morning to the moment I sleep, praises ring in my ears. I don't need to wed another honeyed tongue."

She could see that his soldiers, great oafs of men in crimson-edged robes lurking beneath the largest doorway, eyed her warily.

One bent to whisper something to his companion, but then thought better of it. Their master, though, laughed loud and heartily.

"You catch me out on flattery, my queen. I can't help but admire that. And you're not wrong." He paused to study her a moment, as if testing how she might react. "That comes as a relief, for there are other, more disagreeable rumors that surround your name."

"And what might those be? I admit that they sound more intriguing."

Pieton shifted in the chair at her left. He coughed into his arm. She ignored him.

"That you think no man is worthy of your marriage bed."

She blinked in amazement. She'd not expected that. She imagined tales of murder to swirl, but not of vanity. That, too, was a form of softness, one that she particularly despised, and one that she'd never dreamt she would stand accused of. Beauty had never been her gift, nor her aspiration. It would have been a foolish exercise in defying fate. Her mother had ensured that she would have no illusions on that front.

"It seems you've come on a fool's errand, then." Berenice laughed brightly. "All the way from Comana to Alexandria too. A long and dangerous way to come to try to wed a woman who refuses to be won."

Archelaus smiled. "I relish a challenge. I'm fool enough to think I might prove my worth."

He snapped his fingers. Two servants straining beneath a silver chest appeared in the grand ivory-inlaid arch. He watched their progress fixedly as they lumbered through the room, clinging so close to the corners that their backs brushed against the battle tapestry that Berenice had had hung to hide a few of her father's preferred satyrs. Alexander and his rearing horse swayed at the intrusion, but the great general, sword hoisted above his head, was otherwise unperturbed. The men gave the arrow-pierced Persians and their thrashing steeds a wider berth and shuffled on without further incident.

Once before her, the smaller of the two servants, a delicate, amber-eyed youth, coughed and lost his grip. His partner stumbled forward to keep the box from falling, but the chest and its contents still hit the stone with a heavy thud. The son of Mithradates winced at the sound.

"A small token, my queen."

More silks, Berenice expected, or else gold and precious gems. She'd no use for such trinkets. She needed men, arms, and horses. The dainty servant opened the chest to retrieve a small gold box from its innards. With a smile, he delivered the gift to her. It weighed heavy in her hands. It wasn't gold plate—every inch was hewn from solid metal. She ran her fingers along its carvings: a young Jason sailing with his Argonauts. With care, Berenice eased away the top. Within lay the expected: a necklace, a hundred pearls dripping from a web of golden threads. A lovely piece. His slaves had fine taste. Her fingers twitched to caress it.

The eunuch spat his poison in her ear. "My queen, you shouldn't be the first to touch."

Too cool, Pieton, too cautious. She wasn't a eunuch but a queen. She wouldn't quake like some divested, unsexed thing.

"My eunuch thinks you mean to kill me with this gift," she told her suitor. "So come, Archelaus, and prove him wrong. Fasten your necklace about my throat."

His men murmured at her words. The tallest of the Galatian guardsmen reached for the ax he belted at his side, only to remember, too late, that he'd abandoned his weapons outside the atrium. Her own advisers looked no happier. Pieton fumed at her side, muttering curses under his breath. Berenice ignored all that; it was noise and nothing more. She watched her suitor's act instead. Seleucus would have reeled at such a request. "Do you mistake me for a slave?" he would have spat.

But Archelaus merely blinked at her in interest. That rid him of any hesitation.

"It's a great honor, my queen."

His voice was low, a coo, but it echoed through her head. He strode toward her, his bearing brash. His fingers brushed her throat as he crossed the jewels over her breast. A shiver twitched down her spine as he fastened the clasp at the nape of her neck.

"I hope you find it worthy of you," he whispered. His beard scratched behind her ear. Her heart stirred, and her loins too. So this was what it was to be charmed.

Archelaus addressed her advisers. "I bear other gifts as well, now that no man here can accuse me of ill intent." Dryton leaned forward in feigned interest. Thais scribbled away at his lists. He recorded every gift with precision, down to the smallest bauble. "An emerald diadem, a set of golden bracelets to adorn the queen's wrists, a silver-studded bridle, a saddle wrought from the skins of the finest heifers in Cappadocia," Archelaus recited. "My land is known for its well-blooded horses; of these I have brought three hundred as gifts for the queen. And if my suit proves successful, I shall add another twelve thousand men to the three thousand who sailed with me. Of these, some one thousand have chargers of their own."

Berenice's men sorely needed horses to face Rome's cavalry. And the soldiers of sea-starved Comana certainly knew how to fight on foot and steed alike. Fifteen thousand was no paltry number. Seleucus had offered only six to buy his place at her side.

"These are generous gifts, Archelaus."

"And there is one more as well." He smiled, giving a discreet nod to one of his serving men. Two guards stepped forward, a cedar chest inlaid with enamel and pearl balanced between them. "It's not proper to call it a gift, for by rights it belongs to your house more than it ever did to mine."

Such a cedar chest had once belonged to the House of Ptolemy. How often she'd heard tell of such a box. *No,* she scolded herself. *It isn't possible.* Her father's legends of what he'd seen as a guest in the Pontic court could hardly stand as truth.

"My father loved it well, this treasure that he stole," Archelaus went on. "He wore it in many a victory over Rome. He used to say that it gave him the strength of its first wearer."

Even now, even when he'd all but said the words, Berenice couldn't believe that the talisman of her house would be returned— to her. It was bright portent, the sort around which dynasties were formed. She didn't dare trust it. And so she bit her tongue and said nothing at all.

"Queen Berenice the Shining One, it is an honor to present you with the cloak of Alexander the Conqueror." Taking a few steps back, Archelaus threw open the chest.

Berenice leaned in close to examine the worn and weary purple garment, as threadbare as any she'd ever seen. The cloak of Alexander had been stolen from her family by Mithradates himself, and now, at last, it was returned. This was no paltry bauble.

The eunuch cleared his throat. "How strange. I thought that the cloak was found among your father's treasures in Talaura when Pompey decimated Mithradates's armies and destroyed his lands. It is said that the Roman general wore that very garment in his third triumph as he paraded your sisters through the streets."

Berenice suspected that Pieton was driven by some relentless desire to ruin any match for her other than to her brother. The eunuch clung dearly to his jealousies.

Archelaus smiled in return, as though Pieton's impertinence had been a simple pleasantry. "Pompey is a man of many tales. What man would not wish to claim that he wore the great conqueror's cloak?"

"What man indeed..." The eunuch studied her suitor with tight lips. "Tell me, son of Mithradates, bringer of so fine and great a gift: who was your mother?"

"She was a concubine," he answered, his tone light. "You wouldn't know her name."

"I might. Your father was a great man. Even the concubines of great men may become legends. Chryseis, for instance, has had her name passed down for generations upon generations. And she didn't share your mother's fortune: she never whelped a son for Agamemnon."

Berenice felt her irritation rising at the eunuch's insistence. Archelaus, to his credit, remained calm.

"But my mother had no priestly father begging for her release. I fear it's a rather different tale. A sadder one."

Pieton pressed on, impervious to Berenice's glares. "Every story has its intricacies. I'd quite like to hear yours. Let us at least begin here with a name." The eunuch overlooked her anger, intent to irk her with his disregard, and her patience wore thin.

Archelaus's voice grew terse. "Metis was my poor mother's name. Few have bloodlines as pure as the queen's." He had no reason to feel shame, Berenice thought. Neither of her own parents had been born by either of Ptolemy the Savior's wedded wives.

"Metis." The eunuch tasted the word carefully. He was reaping far too much delight from this. He was, Berenice saw, a twisted creature, spurred only by his envies. Perhaps she should have heeded her mother's warning. "I do recall that name," Pieton continued. "But I was under the impression that she bore Mithradates only daughters. Not a single son."

Her suitor shrugged. "That I stand before you contradicts your claim."

"That you stand before me contradicts nothing. I could just as well myself proclaim to be a son of Mithradates. I've no less proof of it than you."

The eunuch's mockery made a mockery of her; Berenice would stand for no more of it. "Pieton, silence," she snapped. "Archelaus has brought worthy gifts. I'll hear his plea."

The man grinned. There was a certain mischief, a boyishness, beneath that lion-headed hood. And when he spoke, his words rang with measured charm.

"My plea is short, though not for want of sentiment. I come to wed you, to join my power in Comana to yours in Egypt. We're a small power, but a brave one. And I swear I will fight for this kingdom as if it were my own. My father battled hard against the Romans for many long years; they called him King of Kings and said he would unite the East against the She-Wolf's spawn. There are those who say his death marks the end of that great campaign against the Republic's greedy talons. That we should all bend our knees, and kiss their purple hems, and be content to rule as client kings. That there can be no fight against the encroaching eagle without my father at the fore."

Archelaus paused. The quiet throbbed in Berenice's ears. The whole hall hung breathless on his words.

"But I've come to tell you that those men are wrong. I proclaim loud and clear before this court, and before any court you choose: in Queen Berenice the Shining One, I see Mithradates reborn."

Mithradates was dead, his kingdom lost, his family slaughtered. Archelaus's words sounded more like a curse than like praise, though Berenice knew that he had meant them favorably. She opened her mouth to object, to cast aside the damning compliment. But it was too late. First one guard cheered, and then another. Then a third. The full set of twelve who attended her banged their sword blunts against the onyx floor.

"*Kore Mithradatou,*" they cried out. Daughter of Mithradates.

"He does speak rather prettily," Pieton allowed after her suitor and his men had left. "It's a pity his words have no truth in them."

"You might have kept your insults to yourself." Berenice scowled at the eunuch, her heart still rippling, the strange words still ringing in her ears. To have a husband such as that, one who could inspire the fight in men, in her—no, perhaps it was too dangerous, that intoxicating charm. She turned to Pieton, to find him unyielding, his hands folded in his lap.

"I don't stand for liars," the eunuch answered. "He's no son of Mithradates. And he's no enemy of Rome."

"Thais." The shrinking adviser trembled at her voice, which, she hated to admit, trembled too. "You deemed him a worthy groom. What say you? I trust you took a passing glance at his lineage."

"I did, my queen. I did. Of course."

"And? Is he who he says he is?" Blood pulsed at her temple, at her throat. It unnerved her. A poor idea, to mix matters of the heart and head.

"He—he is the high priest of Bellona. He rules Comana and the surrounding lands."

Thais had skirted the question. Berenice knew that didn't bode well. She should abandon this desire to wed and be loved. It sprang from the softness rotting inside her.

"And tell us, Thais," the eunuch drawled. "Under whose auspices does he rule? By whose sword did he win that position?"

The land minister's eyes darted quickly to the floor, as though he hoped Dionysus's leopard might unhinge its jaws and swallow him whole. "By Pompey's sword. He rules under the banner of Rome."

Was there a man in this world who didn't bend before Rome? Her fingers reached for the faience chalice at her side. It sickened her, this feebleness of her generation. The weakness her mother had purged bubbled up once more.

Dryton broke in. "My queen, there are many who rule only at Rome's word. If you dismiss each of them, you'll have few suitors indeed."

Berenice felt her lips twitch. The handsome minister of war had his moments. And he was right in this. The world might be weak and cowardly, but she would show Rome what it meant to be strong. "You do make a point. Do you disagree, Pieton? Is there some secret set of kings who seek my hand? Perhaps there's an Indian prince who has not yet bowed to Rome. Some Ethiop?"

"I've told you a thousand times, Bere—"

She cleared her throat. No more of his cloying familiarities. He'd been her tutor once, but that had been a lifetime ago. He'd lost the right to call her by her name.

"I beg your pardon, *my queen*." He stressed her title with distaste, as though she hadn't earned it. "But I believe you know my advice. Wed your brother Ptolemy."

"I told you not to mention that again." Her anger mounted in her chest. Not only did the eunuch plot with the concubine; he defied her explicit commands. Her mother's warning haunted her. *Do not trust the eunuch.* It wasn't natural for Pieton to press her marriage to that useless child. Not when he'd seen how wedding the Piper had destroyed her mother. She could think of only one reason for his obsession: he had already betrayed her for the concubine. Just as her own father had. "But since you continue to ignore my wishes, I can't help but conclude that you have some other motivation. Which of us do you serve, Pieton: me or that whore?"

Pieton turned pale—paler than Berenice had ever seen him, the sun sucked from his skin. When he answered, his voice quaked.

"Imply what you like, my queen, but don't imply that. I'm no traitor. You look in all the wrong places for those. I alone have stood by you these long years. I've taught you from the cradle, and advised you as you plotted to assume your rightful throne. Who are these men who surround you now? You trust them for the stick and nuts between their legs? They're your father's creatures to a one. Except for that over there." He pointed to Nereus, whose head nodded closer and closer to his lap. "I'm not sure whom he serves. Is it the Piper?" His arm grew unsteady, as though he'd sunk deep into his cups of wine, and he dropped it back to his side. "Or is it still the ghost of Selene?"

"My queen," Nereus croaked, jerking his drooping chin up. "I serve—"

She ignored the old man. All her fury churned against Pieton, against his eagerness to promote himself at any cost. "You say, Pieton, that you alone have served my claim. Then tell me this: why do you press my brother's rights? None of these men—my father's men, as you call them—beg that I share my throne with Ptolemy." Her voice was shrill, nearly screeching, but she couldn't temper it. She would spawn no monsters. She would not become her mother. "There are other ways. Find them."

Pieton answered sharply. "You won't wed your brother. So be it. Defy reason if you must. But do not wed this man. He lies too well and too easily. He spent the better part of this past year begging for a commission from Rome's governor in Syria."

"You're set against him for your own foolish prejudices. There's no more to your objection than that." In that moment, the full blunt of her anger turned against the eunuch. Berenice never should have trusted him. His kind was known for its fickleness.

Pieton bristled as he stood. His every motion made her blood burn in her veins. "Believe what you will about my motivations, but do not marry him. Or do, and suffer for it."

She let the words—the warning—echo in the empty air. Her other advisers sat in stunned silence as Berenice let her rage mount and fade.

"Is that a threat, Pieton?" Her words came cool and calculated. Just as the eunuch had taught her.

That wiped away his confidence. His body, puffed with anger, seemed to deflate vertebra by vertebra, his frame folding in on itself. Everyone knew the penalty for threatening a queen.

"I—my queen—" The eunuch had become the stammerer.

"Get out." Her voice scarcely rose above a whisper. He hadn't earned her screams. "Get out, and don't show your face in this court again. Any *man* would lose his head for this offense. Count your blessing that you've already lost your balls instead."

The eunuch stilled his quaking. He never got caught up in emotions for too long, not the way she did. Eyes fixed on hers, he bowed. Deep and graceful. A dancer's bow. As a child, Berenice used to think he could have been a dancer in a different life. Now she'd given him the chance in this one. From the smallest archway, he met her gaze once more.

"When you catch a man in a lie, it's only because he's already fooled you with a thousand others," Pieton said stiffly. "That Archelaus is no son of Mithradates. He is no enemy of Rome. And he is no fit consort."

"Another word, eunuch," she spat, "and I'll change my mind and have your head upon a spike, balls or no."

Fury blinded her once the eunuch left her presence. She'd blindly relied on his advice for too long. After her mother's death, he'd been the closest thing she had to family. Softness lay in that. And even now, she knew she couldn't steel herself enough to order his death.

Slowly, she became aware of her other councilors: Thais trembling his quill over his inkpot, and Nereus nodding slowly, though she couldn't tell if the gesture came from weariness or agreement. Dryton watched her with removed interest, one finger leisurely tapping at his chin.

"Thais."

"Y-yes, my queen?" He shook so violently that she feared he'd wet himself. Or perhaps jolt the inkpot from its stand. At least that would break the tension.

She asked the question as simply as she could: "Is Archelaus the son of Mithradates, or is he not?"

Thais looked to Nereus for aid, but the old man made no move to rescue him: his own situation was far too precarious for heroism. Her shaky minister of lands gasped and spoke so quickly that Berenice strained to separate his words.

"He's not, my queen, the son of Mithradates—nor did I claim he was. The eun—um, the—it seems that all known sons of Mithradates are accounted for—and dead."

"Then why did you trot him out all spiced for the slaughter?" An image rose to her mind in sour satisfaction: Thais's tongue lolling out, eyes rolled back, his neck a bloody stump mounted on a spear.

"He—he is, however, by all accounts, the *grandson* of Mithradates, my queen," Thais explained, tripping over his words. "His mother, it seems, was one Eupatra, a daughter that Mithradates sired on his concubine Metis. And his father, his trueborn father, is said to be Archelaus, the general to Mithradates."

So he'd traded a father for a grandfather. A pragmatic lie. Not a fatal one.

A knock sounded against the stone. If the eunuch dared return—

"My queen." The servant's voice was muffled against the ivory. "There is a messenger from Ephesus. I didn't wish to disturb you, but he insisted it was urgent."

News from Ephesus meant news of her father, and that was not the sort of news that would wait.

"Let him enter."

A winded youth emerged between two guards. When they loosened their grip on his shoulders, the child tumbled toward the ground, catching himself with his wrists before springing back up. Dazed, he blinked a half dozen times. When he finally managed to open his mouth, his words rushed forth.

"My master sent me here at once. He said I could put this letter in your hands alone, no one else's." He panted, clutching a piece of parchment.

"Who's your master, boy?"

The child trembled. "I—I'm not to say."

Is that how you address your queen? Pieton's words were still imprinted in her ears. Even when she dismissed him, Berenice couldn't rid herself of his counsel.

"Think, next time, how you speak to a queen," she snapped. "Come. Discharge your duty. Hand me the letter."

On dainty steps, the boy crossed over Dionysus's attendant satyrs. He eyed the leopard warily as though he feared it might spring to life. He knelt as he handed over the letter.

Red Artemis, head high, drew her bow across her chest. The mark of the Ephesian priests—that didn't bode well. Berenice cracked the goddess in two and read: "Queen Berenice the Shining One, I write at great peril to my person. Pompey has overturned the Senate's decrees. He has given the governor of Syria leave to send his men in aid of your father. The Piper sails to Antioch to join him at once. Please forgive me if I sign only, a friend."

A friend. What friends did she have in Ephesus? The Piper must have made his enemies there, even as he bought back his Roman allies. She'd been lulled by the soothing tidings from Judea, by the fact that no legions had crossed her borders. But in the end, the Republic would support her father, and send its men reeling against her phalanxes. Weeks, perhaps even months, might go by, but the battle would descend on Alexandria. Berenice thought of all the grain she'd stored, of all the men she'd gathered to recapture Cyprus. They'd die fighting Rome here instead. And perhaps she would die with them. She bit her lip and swallowed the bitter taste in her mouth.

"Leave us, boy."

The messenger nearly ran to escape the atrium, as though its very air was poisoned. Perhaps it was. This day had brought its share of misfortunes.

"What news, my queen?" anxious Thais asked. "What news from Ephesus?"

"No matter of great concern." *It cannot be. Not yet.* She would not breathe a word of this to anyone.

Berenice took in the faces that remained: Thais, pretty Dryton, world-weary Nereus. A fresh fury erupted as she gazed at the last, his fingers worrying away at his throat. She needed someone else to turn on. "Nereus, you've remained rather silent on this matter of my marriage."

The old man looked up in surprise, but recovered himself with another tug at his whiskers. "In such delicate topics"—he cast a withering look at Thais—"old men know it's best to show reticence."

Berenice shook her head. Those had been the wrong words. "I don't recall *reticence* as your defining quality when last it came time for me to wed."

"My queen, what the eunuch—"

"It makes no difference. A casual observation, nothing more." She smiled. "Don't concern yourself with lofty goals of reticence. I beg your opinion: what do you make of Archelaus? What is your opinion on Thais's accounting of his lineage?" She tried to see the brighter side: Nereus might even prove more valuable to her now that she knew in which directions his treachery lay. Selene was dead, and Seleucus too, while the Piper remained very much alive. Alive and leading a Roman army. She and Nereus might well be stuck with each other.

"His accounting matches my own," the old man answered. "I've no reason to believe that this young Archelaus is not the son of that Archelaus the Pontic general, and the grandson of Mithradates on his mother's side."

She nodded slowly, thoughtfully. Her eyes wandered from Nereus to Thais to Dryton. Each dodged her gaze. Thais pored over his account of Archelaus's gifts, and Nereus pulled nervously at the skin around his throat. Even Dryton managed to busy himself by fixedly adjusting his signet ring. They'd all tread warily for some time now.

"I'm glad you agree, Nereus." Berenice grinned, too wildly. No one would dare voice an objection. And it was this news from Ephesus, she reminded herself, that pushed her hand. Even though she planned to tell no one of the tidings, word would spread. The palace wasn't renowned for keeping secrets. She needed to wed Archelaus before he realized what war he might be wedding. "It promises to be a good union, this joining of the Houses of Ptolemy and Mithradates."

"M-my queen," the old man stuttered. "Are you certain—"

"What happened to your reticence on delicate matters of the heart?" Her mind cleared and she rushed to cover her words. *Matters of the heart?* What drivel had worked its way into her speech? She could not—would not—let whatever slight tenderness she might have felt for Archelaus cloud her judgment. He had a handsome face—nothing more. He also had horses and soldiers. Those were what she cared about. "Dryton, you are now my minister of coin. Make preparations for the royal marriage. I'll wed within the week."

That afternoon Berenice set out for Antirrhodos to clear her head, taking a skiff to cross the small harbor that separated the abandoned palace from its fellows. Her suitors and their entourages choked the other royal lodges and their gardens, but no one stayed out on these forgotten banks. The palace had fallen quickly into disrepair after its builder's ignominious death, and it was too removed from the goings-on of Alexandria to hold much appeal for her visitors and their men. That was what she loved about the island, which was disturbed only by the few priests of the Isis temple and the flagging sphinxes that lined the remnants of its main avenue. Beyond these gasps of civilization, her father's menagerie had dwindled—only the giraffes lingered, and a few scuttling peahens—but there was no better spot to clear her head. Eyes closed, she could even imagine herself alone. Or imagine how it might feel to be alone.

Emergence's blushing hues had become bright Harvest greens. Even in Alexandria, where rain fell from time to time, the Nile's flood still left its mark. Last year, Berenice had been able to see through the trees during this season, but now the leaves grew thick, and she could imagine herself in some wilderness of Ethiopia. Through the overgrown foliage, she spotted a glint of marble, a monument to Hathor, the horned cow goddess of the ancients. For generations, her forefathers had tended to the shrine to varying degrees, and as she climbed toward its apex, an idea sprang to mind: once she'd achieved her victory, she would build her new palace here, upon the stones of the overlooked lodges of Ptolemy Alexander, the ill-fated brother of Ptolemy the Savior. She used to worry that the land carried curses—the furies of forgotten gods—but that was a child's nightmare, not a queen's.

Behind her, a branch snapped. Alarmed, she spun around. Her guards walked as silent as the desert night. They were born trappers from Ammon or thereabouts, stalkers by nature. Their feet didn't know how to take a misplaced step.

"My queen." Archelaus sank to one knee. How quick he was to assume a position of supplication. But Berenice didn't think it sprang from weakness. It stemmed from some deeper game he played. "I didn't realize—I didn't mean to disturb you."

He did disturb her, though she hated to admit it. The look of him, his playful smiles and disarming eyes—she could feel a bead of sweat gathering between her breasts. Her hands trembled. An unfamiliar sentiment lurked in the wake of his lingering glances. The blood rushing to her face named it "desire." Flustered, Berenice willed herself to walk away, but her feet remained firmly planted in the grass.

"I meant what I said earlier." His tone was quiet, almost musical. "You do remind me of my father reborn."

It was a strange thing to say a second time: that she reminded him of a doomed man. His father, no less. She wasn't sure whether to be flattered or offended.

"You may drop the ruse now." Berenice kept her voice cold. She wouldn't be taken in by his act—and it must be, she chided herself, an act.

"What do you mean?"

"I know that Mithradates wasn't your father. You couldn't have thought I wouldn't tease out the truth."

"I do not—"

"Hush." She placed her finger over his lips, and then drew it away at once, as though she'd touched something scorching hot. "It doesn't make a difference to me whether he was your father or your grandfather. But I won't be made a fool."

"I'm glad to hear that, then." His eyes bored into her, and she turned away. "I would never want to cause you displeasure. I do envy you your parentage."

She choked back a laugh. "You are full of odd compliments for the woman you want to wed."

It was better to speak to him like this, with her back to him, when she didn't have to look upon his face, and guard against his hungry gaze.

"Would you rather I praised your eyes and your lips, your neck and thighs?" His sandals crunched on the sapling grass. "That I tell you you're the loveliest woman I've ever seen, that your face would launch a second thousand ships, that Aphrodite herself would pale before your beauty?"

"Then I'd call you a liar. I know there's little enough in my face to praise. But I can't imagine why you compare me to a man who fought Rome and died for it."

More footfalls. Soft steps, mindful ones.

"I didn't mean to recall his history, but his essence. Did you ever chance to meet Mithradates of Pontus?"

All at once, he was behind her, scant inches from her flesh. His breath was hot against her neck. She dared not move or breathe. All thoughts of reason fled.

"There was a quality to him, an intangible quality. Some say it was his bearing, others say it was his spirit, but either way there was a spark in him, an ethereal and undeniable spark, that made other men eager to follow. And I see the same in you. What greater compliment is there than that?" Boldly, he ran a finger through her hair, along the tender edge of her ear.

"I don't inspire easy confidence in men." She stepped back to face him. To keep his hands at bay. "The confidence they have in me is earned, hard and rough and coarse. You don't know me, Archelaus of Comana."

"No, Berenice." Her name danced upon his lips. "I can't claim to know you, but I'd very much like to."

She blinked her eyes and shook away his mawkish words. She wouldn't succumb to meekness, not after everything she'd endured. "Is this how all men speak in Cappadocia? With honeyed whispers and not a bit of sense?"

He cocked his head, and his dark curls kissed his lashes. "In Comana, we speak as we see. How do men address you here that it shocks you to hear praise?"

"They address me with due respect. And fewer cloying compliments."

"Would you rather I insult you, then?"

A step erased the space between them. He towered over her; for once, Berenice felt so very small. Unnerved, she looked down, but he cupped her chin and brought her eyes to meet his. She could feel his heart beating through his chest. Its pounding matched the hammering of her own.

"Tell you that you are nothing, no one? Underestimate you as every other creature has done—man, woman, and eunuch?"

He kissed her, long and soft and sweet. She didn't slip away.

"No." The sun glinted in his eyes. "I'll not betray your worth."

What does that mean? her reason begged. But her thoughtless heart silenced her objections. For that moment, she bathed, fluttering, in his warmth.

YOUNGER

S tiff linen scratched her skin. Unworn, the garment rubbed
and stuck in places, just as she'd told Myrrine it would when
her nurse pinned the new robe beneath her arms and
wrapped it about her frame. At least she couldn't get too cozy in it.
The temple's heady incense made her sleepy, and the prickle of dis-
comfort kept her alert. Squinting against the sun, she twisted to
watch the procession of nobles shuffle onto the benches. Deep reds
and purples had returned to fashion, and it seemed that every high-
born Alexandrian worth his salt had draped himself as richly as a
rose bloom. Beyond the adornments, the faces were familiar. Thais
and Nereus, Dryton and Laomedon. Arsinoe even caught sight of
Hypatia's father, his auburn beard kissing his comrade's ear as he
whispered some amusing secret.

And then came Berenice, all white and gold and glowing. Arsinoe
tried to snare her sister's gaze, but the bride didn't even glance in
her direction. No, the queen had eyes only for Archelaus. Arsinoe
squirmed and shifted against stone to inspect this second bridegroom.
He was tall—taller than Seleucus, for certain. Taller even than her
Achilles had been before Berenice's men had struck him down.

At the high altar, the royal pair met before the stone-faced god.
The priest joined their hands. Arsinoe's knee jangled against the
bench. It helped to banish her anxieties to one part of her body; she
liked to watch it spring to life.

"I accept you." Archelaus's voice rang no different than Seleucus's once had. Would her sister murder this one too? She'd no rea-

son to think this Archelaus would betray Berenice. But she hadn't suspected Seleucus either, not at first, not until she'd overheard his man plotting with Nereus. She liked this plan: wed men, murder them, and steal their soldiers. That would be her course, when she ruled. *How would you come to rule, Arsinoe?* the serpent's voice teased. *How many are you prepared to kill?*

"Stop twitching." Ganymedes's hand stilled her leg. "And pay attention."

She *was* paying attention. It wasn't her fault that the ceremony was so like the last that she could mouth along with every word.

"Before the great god Serapis, I join these two humble suppliants in body, in spirit, and in mind." The high priest's voice echoed shrilly, which somewhat ruined the effect. He sounded comical rather than solemn, at least to Arsinoe. "Their union shall be blessed by sons, sons who will rule Egypt until the day Serapis rises from the dead."

Myrrh filled her nostrils and her lungs, along with the salt and a trace of some other scent. Her eyelids drooped. She soared as a vulture over blinding sands. The stench of death lulled her circles lower, lower, lower . . . and then she saw the carcass unattended. Young and fresh with blood. Her lids snapped open. All around her men were rising, only to sink to their knees in deference to the queen and her consort. This time Arsinoe didn't try to catch Berenice's eye.

"What did you note?" the eunuch asked as his firm grip led her from the temple. Outside, a mob of commoners had gathered along the street, swarming the columned porticoes of the nearby houses to catch a glimpse of her sister and her second match.

"My sister likes this husband better than the first."

"How could you tell?"

"I could see it in her eyes, the way she looked at him," Arsinoe answered brightly, though she found the questions wearisome. There was little to learn from second ceremonies, second weddings— seconds in general.

"You'll have to do better than looks and glances," the eunuch told her as they turned onto the vast Canopic Way. The crowd grew rowdier here, often spilling into the avenue, as though their distance from Serapis's temple spared them any thought of decorum. A drunken man lurched toward them, casting off the warning hands of his wiser friends. Quickly, a guard emerged and knocked him back, striking him with the flat of his sword. Arsinoe winced at the blow, and Ganymedes steered them closer to the street's center after that. At times, they passed so close to the pools that dotted the median that she could dip her fingers in their depths.

"Keep your dirty hands out," Ganymedes scolded her. "Common folk draw their drinking water from there. Now pay attention. Tell me: what else did you see?"

That wasn't fair. Her hands had been scrubbed clean that morning. But she didn't bother to object. The eunuch didn't seem to be in the mood to listen.

"The ceremony was much like the first." Arsinoe shrugged. "The stalls were more crowded, though, and I saw Hypatia's father in attendance."

"Indeed," Ganymedes said thoughtfully. "And why do you think the noblemen of Alexandria were eager to see the queen wed a second time?"

"A good wedding means good wine," she quipped. She'd heard that somewhere—from Myrrine, perhaps? The entrance to the palace loomed at the avenue's end, the gold-plated gates thrown open to admit the line of emptied wagons that lurched ahead. When they'd left that morning, each cart had overflowed with wine and grain, coins and sweetmeats. Wedding gifts for the subjects from their queen.

Ganymedes spoke sharply, shattering her reverie. "When I ask you a question, you'll take a moment to consider, so you stand a chance of answering it wisely."

Arsinoe bit her lip, hard. But not hard enough for blood. She did that sometimes, when she was alone. She liked the jolt of pain, the iron taste on her tongue. "They don't believe my father will return."

"You can be very wise, Arsinoe." Her tutor smiled widely, and she could see the blackened gums along his upper teeth. "Now tell me: have you learned to use that present I gave you?"

She practiced—she did. Each night when she was alone, Arsinoe gouged the blade into her writing desk and hurled the knife against the wall. But in truth she couldn't say she'd made much progress: the dagger wouldn't stick when she threw it, and she wasn't sure whether her skill at skewering a slab of wood would help much if she should have to skewer a man. Besides, Myrrine had discovered the scratch marks on her furnishing, so she had to be doubly careful not to be discovered.

"I have learned," she lied. She'd find someone to teach her.

"Good, very good indeed." The eunuch pursed his lips.

As they entered the palace, Ganymedes pulled her aside, ducking into the small rotunda—Alexander's shrine. Within, a marble figure of the great man, naked and large as life, clutched a sword in one hand and a scepter in the other. The curved walls were covered with frescoes from the Conqueror's life: his birth, his blessing at Ammon, his defeat of the Persians. Arsinoe wondered how her own altar might look, how she would feel if her likeness should live forever surrounded by her memories, living them over and over again. That was foolishness. There would never be a shrine to her.

She felt Ganymedes kneel beside her. His knees creaked beneath his weight. "I've been sent word that your father has left Ephesus," the eunuch whispered so near to her she could taste his breath. "He shall return to Alexandria. And soon. With many men."

Her mind jolted at the news. Her father would return—with soldiers. A thousand pressing questions sprang to her tongue. What would happen to Berenice? Would her sister flee the palace—or stay and fight? And would her father welcome her? Or was she tainted now—a traitor?

"Ganymedes," she began, "what will—"

"Hush, Arsinoe. Now is not the time." Ganymedes put a hand to her lips. "Go find your friends, and bring them to the library. It's a feast day, but that doesn't excuse you from lessons."

She hated that sort of answer. Hated how grown-ups still treated her as a little girl, as though she hadn't aged a thousand years since she'd been abandoned in the palace. But she held her tongue—that, too, she'd learned. And so she merely nodded. But she didn't do as she was told. Aspasia and Hypatia would only sully her mind with petty concerns. She didn't want to recount each moment of the wedding, every stitch of her sister's robes. The eunuch would tell her nothing with the others lurking about anyway, and she needed time to think on her own.

Arsinoe shunned the great courtyard, where the servants busied themselves in preparation for the evening's feast, and wandered up through the gardens, looping back in circles to make sure no man followed her. The news of her father's rise troubled her. More bloodstained stones to wash away with rain. She didn't want Berenice to die.

The Alexandrian sun beat hard upon her shoulders; her skin burned to summer's bronze. Myrrine always scolded her for spending so much time basking in it—"a princess shouldn't be as brown as a farmer's daughter." Arsinoe liked how she assumed a new color each season. She pictured herself as one of winter's dull birds that brightened when the temperature warmed.

She approached Aphrodite's fountain, the site where her vision had come true. She slipped off her sandals and stepped in. The water rose first to her ankles and then, with another step, to her knees as she squeezed behind the statue. Squatting, back flush against the shell, she waited. The gods would send new images to cloud her eyes, ones that would reveal the outcome of the war, and teach her how she should act and feel and how to wield a knife. But she saw nothing—only the statue's stone back and the sky beyond. The trees reflected in the pool, and her own hands, brown against the water.

In time, she stood, a fool.

"Arsinoe."

Hypatia's voice. She ignored it.

"Arsinoe."

Again.

"Arsinoe. What're you doing there?" Hypatia snickered at the fountain's lip. Dark-haired Aspasia stood silent at her friend's side. At least she didn't laugh.

"What do you care?" Arsinoe glared at the girls. She hated them, their lighthearted giggles and easy smiles. How could Ganymedes think them suitable companions for her? What could they teach her of the world?

"Ganymedes asked us to fetch you."

"You do the eunuch's bidding now?"

Nervous, Hypatia shifted under Arsinoe's gaze. Arsinoe knew she should be kinder. The girl wasn't to blame for her father's homecoming, or for the poison images that corroded her thoughts.

"Come. Linger awhile. It's a feast day, after all." Arsinoe grinned. "The eunuch can't expect us to hurry to our courses."

The fair-haired child hesitated, but Aspasia tossed off her sandals and skipped into the pool, splashing wildly about the stones. Arsinoe kicked up water too, and soon they were both collapsed, soaked in water and laughter. Only when the slopping subsided did Hypatia approach.

"What was the wedding like?" she asked shyly from the fountain's edge.

"Archelaus *is* rather handsome," Arsinoe teased. "You might like him after all."

"My father said the same." Hypatia sighed. "I wish he'd taken me too." She eyed Arsinoe's ruined silks. The girl's fingers twitched at her side. "I'd never hear the end of it if I played in clothes like those."

"I'll give some to you, if you'd like," Arsinoe offered. Glancing back to Aspasia, she added, "To both of you."

"Will you? Will you truly?" Hypatia squealed. Arsinoe shied away from the sound of the girl's delight. She couldn't imagine what it must be like to have so few worries that clothes could soothe her wounds.

"Why does he watch us like that?" Aspasia's voice cut in, harsh with disgust. Arsinoe followed her dark-haired friend's gaze to the fountain's edge and across the marble walkway. And there he was, leaning against a column: Alexander. Watching.

"I don't know." Arsinoe shrugged. "Perhaps he's lonely."

"Perhaps he's in love with you," Hypatia teased, singsong.

"Don't be stupid." Arsinoe's temper reared. She hated how Hypatia could think of love and lust, of weddings and finery, when her world had begun to crumble again. "Not all of us think only of marriage. Some of us have more important dreams."

Yet the nights that followed turned her dreams to darkness, dreams of the dead, of Cleopatra and Alexander and Berenice. A cobra, a vulture, a lioness, Arsinoe stalked the fallen to their graves. In the dwindling Harvest afternoons, she ignored her night terrors as best she could. She distracted herself with knife lessons, teaching herself to cut and toss and jab. Even the throwing grew easier with practice: sometimes she'd get the blade to stick, quivering, in the wood. Her fingers sprouted first cuts, and then scabs. If Myrrine noticed Arsinoe's scrapes and scratches, the nurse kept it to herself.

But Arsinoe couldn't shake the visions, no matter how many times she struck her target carved into a tree. Against her better judgment, she started to keep a record of the signs, a mark for each corpse she saw. And though she saw less and less of Alexander as the air grew cooler, his was the body that haunted her mind most often. More often even than Berenice's. And only on his bones did she feast.

* * *

Sun bright overhead, Arsinoe hurled her knife against the bark. The blade stuck, trembling a moment, before it bounced away, useless. She cursed her clumsiness. How much longer would she have to practice before her arm grew strong enough to stick the knife each time? She glanced behind her in time to catch a few guards circling toward her on their rounds; irritated, she hid the weapon in her robes. She hated stopping during a bad streak, but she'd practice all the more diligently when the men had passed.

Slumping against the tree, she unfurled her papyrus scrap, the record of her nightly sins. Menelaus's name—scratched out with a heavy line—leapt to her eyes. She drew another mark next to Alexander's. Thirteen now. Thirteen times she'd seen his corpse rotting in her dreams. But still he lived—he and Cleopatra and Berenice and Ganymedes. What had made her vision of the fire-bearded guard different? She'd seen through a cobra's eyes, but there was nothing remarkable in that. At night, she was a snake, a bird, a leopard. "Turn your mind from these gruesome sights," Ganymedes had told her. "Don't choose Cassandra's fate." But how could she "choose" a fate? Wasn't the whole point of fate that she wouldn't have any choice at all?

Beyond the guards, a solitary figure sauntered by. Silhouetted against the sky, it might have been a small man or a tall boy. Arsinoe couldn't be sure. His strides were long and careless. His hand tousled his black locks. And then he turned his gaze on her. He started at her stare, thrown by the shock of being watched. The sun passed behind a cloud, and she realized with a jolt that this changeling was Alexander. No matter how often she saw him lurking in the shade, she always expected him to look like a boy. Quickly, she folded the papyrus in her hand.

"What is that?" Unshaken, he approached her. Their time apart had turned him bold.

She tossed off his words. "What do you care?" She wouldn't show him her list, and her insolence would—she hoped—drive him away.

"Come on, let me see." He reached for the paper. She jerked it from his grasping hand.

"I said it's no concern of yours." Her face burned; she couldn't say why.

"Don't be such a child, Arsinoe." His voice cracked over her name—another unwelcome aspect of his metamorphosis. She didn't know him now at all. In her distraction, he grabbed her wrist and snatched away the papyrus. His eyes grazed down the page. "What's my name doing here?"

"It's—" The words died on her tongue. She wanted to tell him what she'd seen, but she couldn't bear the ridicule, the pity. Not from him, of all people. And if she breathed a syllable, how could she deny the rest of what it meant? Then Alexander would know the truth: that she would kill him. He'd shrink from her in fear. Perhaps that would be easier.

"You're right," he jeered. "It's better not to tell me. I don't want to hear about some silly game you and Hypatia are playing. Just leave me out of it."

Alexander let the scrap slip from his fingers, and watched as it fluttered to the ground.

Arsinoe couldn't bear for him to think of her like that, to lump her with those simpering girls. "It's not—"

"No, I see it now. You're no different from them, cooing over Archelaus and any man who stumbles onto your path. Go braid your hair, or play with dolls, or pick which man you want to wed." The anger mounted in his voice, and she could hear the relish in his final words, as though he'd practiced them a hundred times before: "Some man who matters, as you say."

Alexander stormed off. His stride lost its preening quality; he became a boy once more. Arsinoe shouldn't follow. It would be better to let him leave and forget her. All she could offer him was death.

Her feet rebelled against her wisdom, and she raced after him.

She grabbed his shoulder. He tried to shrug her hand away, but she only tightened her grip.

"I can—I'll tell you what the papyrus means."

His shoulder rose and fell beneath her palm. She could feel his breath in her fingers. When he turned to her, his voice was cool. "I don't care, Arsinoe. Just leave me alone."

Helios's chariot blazed behind him, and even as Arsinoe squinted, she could see him only as a shadow. His gray-green eyes obscured, he looked a stranger, an angry Adonis curdling into a man.

"I haven't changed," she said. "You have."

"Me?" Alexander's voice cracked again. He didn't bother trying to hide it. "Tell me: what about me has changed?"

Arsinoe took a deep breath. Half-truths and worse had become her element. The right words would salve the wound. How well she'd learned that lesson in court. But with Alexander, the task was harder. The lies and platitudes didn't spring to her tongue as they did with Ganymedes and Berenice.

"You avoid me," she began slowly, stalling for time, shifting the blame. But even that couldn't help her. She was too flustered; her confidence flagged. "You've stopped coming to lessons. You've lost interest in our games. Ganymedes warned me that you'd change."

"Oh, Arsinoe." Alexander let out a cruel laugh. "Don't ply me with your poison. I've heard you lie to others too many times to be tricked myself."

He walked into the sun. Ganymedes had been right: Alexander would leave her, as Cleopatra and her father had, as her mother and two little brothers had. Each had abandoned her in the end, and for all her honeyed words she couldn't call them back.

"They're the names of the dead." Her voice burst across the yard.

Alexander stopped. "What do you mean?"

"The dead. It's a list of the names of people I've seen die." She turned her gaze to the ground. She shouldn't speak of her visions; she didn't even know if she could trust this changing Alexander. But it was too late now. She couldn't unsay what she had said. Those words would always stand between them. But better that he think her mad than lump her with her frivolous friends.

When Arsinoe glanced up, she realized that her recklessness had been rewarded: his eyes were in her thrall.

"I saw the queen this morning—she must have met a quick demise," he taunted.

"That's not what I mean, and you know it. Don't play dumb."

"Explain it to me, then. Slowly. I'm not as quick as your new playmates."

"You're twice as quick," she snapped. She dropped her voice to a breath, a whisper, forcing Alexander to take a step nearer to catch her words. "They're the names of those I have seen dead in my dreams—my visions."

She nearly swallowed the final syllables as she cast an eye about for eavesdroppers. So many skulking pairs of ears. She could count the four guards she'd seen before along the garden gate, and a pair of servants trimmed the bushes beneath the cypress trees.

"Go on," he prompted.

"This isn't the place to speak of this. Come." Arsinoe enjoyed borrowing Ganymedes's lines, sowing her own infuriating mysteries.

Alexander followed quietly. She was grateful for his silence. Her mind was busy, racing from chamber to chamber, but she didn't dare admit that she didn't know where to take him. Ganymedes would often conduct private talks in the library, but she imagined that Aspasia and Hypatia were lurking there. The kitchen's use was in listening, not speaking; two chatty children drew attention, whereas quiet ones didn't. And she couldn't trust the gardens of Ptolemy the Benefactor anymore. But her feet went on, unbidden, across the marble walks and between the cypress colonnades, by the lotus-studded archway that opened into the royal courtyard and past the piping satyrs that graced its walls. Alexander's footfalls came to match her own, so soon they two sounded as one grown man instead of a pair of children. Only when she saw the other Arsinoe at her fountain did she realize her destination. She turned and put a finger to Alexander's lips. She had to stand on tiptoe to whisper in his ear.

"There will be two guards outside my rooms."

"Your rooms?" Alexander repeated dumbly. There were few sacred spaces in the palace, but their adventures had never brought them to her chambers.

"Yes, my rooms," she replied, delighting in his awe. She liked that she could still surprise him. "Myrrine will be waiting in the antechamber. When I go in, I'll shriek. That'll get the attention of the guards. You sneak in behind while everyone's distracted. Go hide under the golden bed in my room."

Alexander nodded.

"And take off your—"

"Sandals. I know, Arsinoe. We've played this game before."

It's not a game, she nearly snapped, but she held her tongue. "We must be careful. Wait here for my signal."

"You mean your scream?" He gave her an odd look.

She let her feet slam hard against the wood as she raced up the stairs. She wanted her approach to draw attention. This dance was familiar; she'd played it out in her head a hundred times. In her imaginings, it was Cleopatra she had to sneak into her rooms. Her sister returned from Rome in secret, boxed in a wine cask, perhaps, or rolled up in a carpet. Word would come of her passage, and it would fall to Arsinoe to keep her safe until their father returned. In the meantime, she'd steal extra food from the kitchens, and every evening the two sisters would whisper their dark exploits to the dark night. But that was back in the days when she longed for her father's return, when she was sure he'd embrace her with open arms.

By the time Arsinoe reached the threshold to her rooms, her heart was pounding in her throat. The two guards loomed taller, more menacing in life. And though they often smiled at her, today both of their faces were grim. Even their vulture helms looked as though they were scowling.

Within the chambers, voices battered; Arsinoe had not anticipated this. In her imaginings, it was Myrrine, and Myrrine alone, who waited in her rooms. But those had been mere dreams, fantasies. Through the door, Arsinoe could hear Ganymedes's falsetto, though she couldn't make out the words. Startled, she wanted to turn back, to tell Alexander that they should slip off to some other hideaway, but she did not. *Fortes fortuna adiuuat.*

When she opened the door, the eunuch cut off his speech. Myrrine smiled in relief.

"There you are," Ganymedes shrilled.

"These are my chambers. Why are you here?" Arsinoe looked to Myrrine for aid. Her nurse bore no love for the eunuch—"the man who lost his balls," the woman called him behind closed doors. But she said nothing now.

The eunuch chuckled. "I thought you might wish to hear your father's plans." His broken teeth were stained purple. He'd been drinking. Arsinoe could read it on his blotchy face. He had never held wine well.

"What—what of my father's plans?" She stumbled, thrown.

"I'd hoped that you would know the answer by now. Or are you afraid that Nereus lurks behind every bush? Your father marches from Ephesus to Antioch with Aulus Gabinius's army as we speak. It seems that your sister thinks this putative son of Mithradates will lead her men to war. But I suppose you know that's why she wedded and bedded him."

This time, wine had turned Ganymedes talkative; Arsinoe had seen it drive him to both extremes. This, she realized, was the ripe and perfect moment she'd been waiting for, the moment to ask about her visions and her father. To ask why some came true and some vanished into nothing. To ask whether the New Dionysus would count her among the traitors. The eunuch wanted to engage her; she could hear it in his swift and lulling slurs. She might ask anything. But there was Alexander to think of, still and silent by the stairs. In time, he'd realize that she'd lost interest in their game—he was the one who had called it that: a game. And then, afterward, he'd grow cool toward her again. But he'd come around. He always did. Or at least he always had before. The two desires tore at Arsinoe, claws kneading her chest.

"Ganymedes. I need to speak with Myrrine alone." Arsinoe spoke quickly, before she could take back the words.

"Why's that?" her tutor scoffed. "What secrets do you share with your slave?"

A thought sprang to her, an idea half born. Arsinoe squirmed from one foot to the other and cast her eyes to the ground. "It has to do with women's troubles."

"Women's troubles." The eunuch laughed outright. "Surely you're too young—"

"Ganymedes, leave her be. Can't you see when you're not wanted?" Myrrine had come to her rescue, and Arsinoe was grateful for it, even though she knew she was too old, by far, to rely on her nurse.

"The child is lying," Ganymedes grumbled. "I don't want to encourage such behavior."

"Look at her. She's quaking. She wants her nurse, not her eunuch. Leave us."

Ganymedes glared at Myrrine for a long, hard moment. And then he shrugged. "So be it," he drawled. "If you've lost all interest in the outside world, Arsinoe, far be it from me to bore you with it."

His words stung, but Arsinoe held back her venom as he lumbered from the antechamber. The moments stretched thin as Arsinoe listened to his footsteps trudge on, and she prayed that Alexander had thought to slink behind some corner. Not that the eunuch was in a state of mind to notice much of anything.

"All right, my dear." Myrrine gave Arsinoe a kindly smile. A pinch of pity rose in her chest, a tinge of guilt for the trick she was about to play. "What is it? It can't be your moon blood yet."

Through the side of her mouth, she gasped until her lungs were full of air and opened her lips as if to speak. Myrrine drew near, and Arsinoe let out a terrible scream. The sound pierced the walls; her nurse clasped her hands over her ears. In her haste, Myrrine knocked over a vase of roses, and the shatter of terra-cotta added to the cacophony.

"What's the matter, child?" Myrrine grabbed Arsinoe by the shoulder and shook her violently. "What's wrong?"

It didn't take long for the guards to charge in, one furious man followed by his twin. Arsinoe wondered whether they were indeed twins, they looked so much alike—the same tight black eyes and bulbous noses. They looked less fearsome now, with their fingers plugging their ears. Between their stomping and Arsinoe's shrieking, no one noticed when Alexander crept through the door. She was sure of it.

"Can no one shut this child up?" the angrier of the two men shouted above the din.

Arsinoe strained her voice until she saw that her friend had stolen into her bedchamber and slipped under her bed. Then, just as suddenly as she'd begun, she fell silent.

"What madness came over you, child?" Myrrine shook Arsinoe again as if to make sure that whatever spirit had possessed her was truly gone.

All three stared at her in wonder: the two guards and her nurse. In time, the one who'd yelled about shutting her up shrugged at his companion.

"I—I—" Arsinoe stammered, as though startled by her own outburst. "I thought—I thought there was a snake. Over there, behind the divan."

"A snake?" Myrrine gave her a narrow look. "Heavens, child. I thought you'd seen Zeus himself climbing through the window, for all the racket you made." Her nurse shook her head over the rose petals strewn about the pottery shards.

"I was frightened. I *am* sorry." Arsinoe did her best to look distraught.

"Go to your room," Myrrine chided, "and think about what a mess you made and how many people you've disturbed."

Arsinoe bit the smile from her lips as she obeyed her nurse's order. Once she'd shut the door behind her, she grinned. She could feel her heart pounding at her ribs. She was alive, free. Creeping from beneath her bed frame, Alexander met her smile. For a long moment, they stared at each other dumbly, each sizing up the other. Then they collapsed on the mat and laughed together as they had not done in ages.

After the giggling subsided, Alexander sat up and scooted toward the far end of the bed, as though he still wasn't sure where they stood with one another. Hastily, Arsinoe moved away as well, watching as her friend's face tightened and his lips grew small. He looked as serious as Arsinoe had ever seen him. And what she wanted was to jump on top of him and make him laugh, to tickle him until he begged her to stop. But she owed him more than that, and better too.

"So you saw me dead," he said flatly.

She nodded. No more lies, no more denials.

"How—how did I die?" He spoke in a thin voice, quiet and brave. "Was it—will it happen soon?"

"I don't know, Alexander. I saw only your corpse." She did not add, *It had already been picked over by scavengers, and then by me.* Even the truth had its decencies. She hoped.

"And the gods—they sent this vision to you?" His eyes were wide and earnest.

"I—" She bit her lip. "I've had others come true."

"The one you had about the guard—the one who gave you food when you were hiding . . ."

Alexander remembered—and he believed her. It almost made her want to weep. He was the one friend—maybe the one person—

who listened to her and trusted her. Arsinoe shook her head. There was no point in wandering down that path.

"There's more." She forced herself to continue. She couldn't leave the worst unspoken—not when she'd already told him so much. "I didn't only *see* your body." Her eyes fixed on the ground, on one patch of shimmering onyx. She could almost make out their reflections in its sheen. She took a deep breath that filled her to her toes. "I feasted on it."

"You—you what?"

She ignored the horror in his voice, the sinking in her stomach. "I was a bird—a vulture—and that's when I saw it. That's when I always see it. I see a carcass from above, and I circle down to find that it's you. And—and—" Her tongue stumbled, but she pressed on. "And that's when I dig my beak into your flesh."

Alexander said nothing. Arsinoe looked at him because she couldn't force herself to look away any longer. He sat frozen, unblinking. He reminded her of a river snake she'd once seen in the menagerie. The creature hadn't belonged there, and when the gardener cornered him, he didn't hiss. He merely drew up his body and stared until the servant struck him with a club—and he fell dead. The silence wore against Arsinoe's eyes, threatening to consume her. She shattered it.

"And so—so now you see why we can't...why we mustn't spend time together. Why you should leave my rooms at once, and never return. I should have told you all that before."

"Yes," he answered finally. "You should have told me before."

So he agreed with her. That was worse, almost, even though it would make their separation easier. Arsinoe's heart beat in her throat so fiercely that she didn't dare open her mouth for fear it might escape. But she swallowed and forced herself to speak. "I'm glad you understand, then, why we can't be friends."

Alexander laughed, wildly and suddenly. "No, that I don't understand at all. What does your dream have to do with our friendship?"

Why was he playing dumb? She wanted to shove him, to make him realize what was at stake. This was serious.

"But don't you see? The dream means I'll bring your death. I'll feast upon your flesh. You have to stay away from me. For your own protection."

He laughed again. Her fist clenched at her side.

"How dare you." She forgot herself and almost shouted. "Alexander, how dare you laugh at the gods and the Fates? There's nothing funny about this!"

"What else would you have me do but laugh?" He shook his head slowly. "If you're destined to bring about my death, then you'll bring it. 'You'll never find a man on earth, if a god leads him on, who can escape his fate.'"

Arsinoe opened her mouth to object, but she couldn't argue against that point. The gods wouldn't change their minds about which strings to twist—not even at Berenice's will. And she—she was no queen. Not yet. Not ever.

"And besides," he went on, bold, brazen, this new Alexander, "there's nothing here for me but you. Let the gods rain down their horrors. It won't frighten me away."

His gray-green eyes dug into her dark ones. She thought he might keep his gaze fixed on her forever. And then, ashamed, she looked away. Even now, even after she'd confessed and told him all, she couldn't face him.

A stone was sticking into her side. No, it was no stone; it was a sheath. She looked up.

"Tell me, Alexander." She caught his burning eyes. "What do you know about knives?"

ELDER

Berenice gazed over the practice fields. On this scarred patch of dirt, straw sacks rose on straw steeds from the dust. Opposite, live ones faced off against them, two dozen men seated unsteadily on horses. "Recruits," Archelaus called them, but that term sounded overly generous. Soon they'd be worth no more than the arrow-pierced sacks that served as their adversaries.

One man, his arm sagging under his javelin's weight, kicked his mare toward a particularly pathetic-looking straw soldier, his stuffing already hanging out in clumps. Berenice bit her lip. She hoped he'd hold on long enough to strike the target. His compatriots, too, watched with trepidation as they struggled to rein in their own mounts. At least half of the horses seemed to be nags dragged from their riders' farms; a stiff sea breeze might send them off their spindly legs. Not one among them, man or beast, would stand a chance against a Roman sword. They were arrow fodder, nothing more.

"What do you make of our new men?" Berenice asked, glancing over at her companion. She started to find Dryton's stubbly face rather than the eunuch's smooth one. Though long weeks had passed since she'd dismissed Pieton, she still expected him to appear at her side, as though her plight, her desperation, would call him back in spite of her threats and his better sense. She recognized that another of her advisers had betrayed her. What else could explain these paltry excuses for soldiers that had arrived instead of her husband's battle-tested men?

"Your eyes are as sharp as mine. I've not seen one throw his javelin to hit the mark." Dryton kept his tone light—but it didn't fool her.

"They'll be better at getting struck by them," she answered coolly.

A golden band jangled at her wrist. Her body had sharpened, as though her bones might break from her flesh. It worried her, the way the fat had melted off her frame. A married woman should grow round, ready for a child. Even in this, her body had betrayed her. Had she been struck by some illness or, worse, fear?

"My queen, these boys are lucky we bought their swords," Dryton went on. "Otherwise, they'd be slaving over some Roman's farm in Cappadocia. Here they get to fight and drink and fuck—and get paid for it in cold coin."

"I see they have the better end of the bargain," Berenice replied. She should turn her mind from those other worries—the deeper concerns that gnawed at her, the same fears that kept her tossing at Archelaus's side each night. *Where were they?* she wondered. *Where were those promised men?* Her father already neared Pelusium, the Nile's easternmost port. The Piper was no great warrior himself, but with this Roman terror, this Aulus Gabinius, leading his army ... This governor of Syria had already shown his mettle in Judea. But she couldn't admit these concerns. A queen must be hardened and fearless in the face of death. And so instead she quipped, "I see what little my coins buy me: a few hundred men who can't unhorse a bag of straw. Perhaps I should take the straw to battle in their place."

"What they need, my queen, is time." Dryton offered his phrases patiently whenever he wanted to propose something she wouldn't like. She'd begun to fear that he thought her unhinged. "We don't have the strength to fight first for Pelusium, and then again for Alexandria."

That was lunacy.

"A victory in Pelusium would mean no battle for Alexandria," Berenice replied. She'd spoken too soon, she realized: her words outstripped her reasoning. And then slowly, surely, she reached the same dull insight. "There is, then—you believe we won't have a victory in Pelusium."

Against all sense, she hoped that Dryton would smirk and toss aside some careless remark about queens and battles, and the one never being able to predict the other. But her minister of coin said nothing, and that was worse, far worse than teasing. It meant he'd given up, accepted defeat and failure.

She channeled her fears into rage. "That's your plan, then? Your brilliant strategy? To wait, impotent, as Rome seizes our eastern stronghold? To do nothing until the dogs snap at our flanks?"

Once roused, she could cling to this fury. It might shield her from all else. By sheer force of will, Tryphaena had forced the world off its axis. Perhaps Berenice would do the same.

"My queen." Dryton's voice was brusque. "What else would you have us do? Gabinius has sixty thousand soldiers at his command. By the time he marches from Antioch to Pelusium, he'll have added ten thousand more to those. These men under your husband's command"—he gestured to the would-be soldiers clashing with their mock enemies—"they can't win a battle against rested legions. Let the Romans tire themselves out fighting farmers. Their slow march will buy us time. Weeks, perhaps . . ."

"Weeks before what?" Berenice glared at Dryton, but he refused to meet her eye. "Weeks before *what?*"

"Before your men would have to fight . . ." Her adviser stared out over the practice field to where it met the sea, as if the answer lay in its depths.

"And then what, Dryton? What will happen when, outnumbered three to one, they face Rome's hardened soldiers? Will these weeks of practice make a difference?"

"I've seen worse men win under worse odds."

"Don't lie to me. I can't stand it when men lie." Her tone was final, and Dryton fell silent. He had no gibe for that.

Across the field, her husband galloped to join his recruits. He took an astonishing interest in each set of men. With every arriving wave, Archelaus would divide them into small groups for exercises based on their skills and weaknesses, as if they were sons of kings, not lowly arrow marks. Perhaps they'd fight better if they believed themselves sons of kings. Berenice didn't know what swayed men's minds in battle, though the gods knew that she wished she did.

As she watched Archelaus throw a spear into the straw target at the center, she felt that she hardly knew her husband at all. Had he been plotting with Dryton? He must have been: her minister of coin would hardly have proposed such a plan without talking to her general first. Fifteen thousand men, her husband had promised. But she'd never seen more than three thousand. She wanted to hate him for this, for his failings. But no matter how clear they were in her eyes, she could not stoke her anger against him—not fully.

"*Mithradatou,*" the recruits cried out to greet their king. He was, in truth, no more than their consort; Berenice had seen to that. But on the battlefield he ruled. Son of Mithradates.

That same lie again. *When you catch a man in a lie, it's only because he's already fooled you with a thousand others.* Pieton's words came back to haunt her. *But he cares for you,* a small, soft voice whispered. *He wouldn't betray you.* Had she been a fool to trust Archelaus? To marry her fate to his?

No. The fault lay with her advisers. They should have taken other measures to ensure that his men arrived. Nereus knew the treacheries of Poseidon better than anyone—he should have predicted that some ships might be lost this time of year, especially ships commanded by the landlocked men of Comana.

And what did she know of Dryton, her newly cast minister of coin, who always had a sneer on his face? That he was Nereus's nephew, either by birth or marriage, but little else. What did she know of any of these men who claimed to serve, to advise, to fight? Archelaus, for all his faults, she knew. She knew his touch and his body and his breath. She knew his heavy arms wrapped around her in the morning and his fierce kisses at night. If she couldn't trust that, the steady beating of his heart by hers, what could she trust? And so, each afternoon, she rode down to the battlements, watching and worrying. If she wished it hard enough, and held her breath, and said her prayers, surely they'd begin to improve. But it was no use. For all her waiting, Berenice saw no progress.

That evening, when Archelaus, sweating and stinking, came to her, she turned away, shunning his embrace. Even after weeks of warmth and kindness, she still expected him to tear her legs open as Seleucus would have, to force himself on her and remind her with blood and seed that he was still a man. But Archelaus made no move to hurt her. Instead, she felt his body ease beside hers on the bed. Time twitched onward until its marching grew too much for her to bear.

"Did you intend to tell me?" Her voice stayed even. She stared fixedly at the far wall. In the corner of her eye, she caught her reflection and winced.

"Did I intend to tell you what?"

"About your secret plot with Dryton."

"What plot is this?" he asked, so gently that she looked back at him. To check his face for deceit. But Archelaus looked as he always did, except his eyes wrinkled with concern.

"That you planned no defense against my father and the Roman legions that march on Pelusium," she answered crisply. "That you meant to stand idly by as my people were slaughtered and my fields were ravaged."

"*Our* people. *Our* fields," he stressed. He held her in his steady gaze; it made her cheeks burn, even now. She hated that. She should have fled from it at once, this power he had over her. "And no,

I don't plan to stand idly by. I plan to fight once the recruits are ready."

They would never be ready. She watched each day, and no matter how much they loved their general, that love didn't transmute into better target practice. "And will that be before or after Gabinius captures Alexandria?"

"You must have patience, my dear." Archelaus stroked her hair tenderly. "Soldiers are not molded in a day."

Berenice pulled away from his touch. "Don't talk down to me, Archelaus. You won't like how I respond."

She sat bolt straight, tough as stone, and stared at him, his soft curls and dark eyes. He wasn't so different from Seleucus, nor from any man. He merely tried to wrench her kingdom in another way, through gentleness and caresses. She had been soft to trust him. How her mother would have cursed this incipient weakness that gripped Berenice's throat and settled in her chest.

"What happened to the men you promised me? Fifteen thousand of your city's soldiers? Perhaps they wouldn't need so much training."

"My love, the storms—"

"Don't lie to me about storms. If my father's ships could pass unhindered, why couldn't yours?" She knew her question was unfair. Her father had merely sailed along the coast from Ephesus to Antioch, not across the depths of the waves.

"Berenice." Her name sounded so sweet on his tongue. He always spoke it slowly, as though savoring each morsel. "What else can I say but the truth: I wouldn't lie to you. I love you."

"We didn't wed for *love*." She spoke the word with disgust, as though its very mention might taint her.

Archelaus arched his brow in interest. "Didn't we? Tell me, Berenice: what then compelled you to choose me? You might have waited longer. There would have been other men, better men, men with greater armies than I could ever offer. Even if every ship had sailed safely across the waves."

No, not for love, she repeated to herself—who else would listen? But she had to admit that foolishness had played into her choice. There'd been something in his looks, his manner, that pleased her. Something in the way he spoke to her that made her eager to be near him. That still did. She'd never felt that way about a man before. She couldn't dwell on it.

"We wed because I needed a consort. Your timing was favorable, and your birth . . ." She didn't mention the doubts cast upon his lineage. It didn't matter if he was the son of Mithradates, or his grandson, or his servant's cousin. It only mattered that the men revered him as though he was. She'd enough royal blood for both of them. Just not enough soldiers.

"Your shame flatters you. You didn't want to wed for—"

"I wed to protect my kingdom." Berenice's anger flared. He had no claim on her—no one did. She would not be weak in this. "If you don't know that, then you've never heard a word I've said. You don't know me at all. And now I ask you: how do we stop the Roman army?"

She stared at him hard. His eyes darted off to the side before he returned her gaze. A tell, a slip. Her father had taught it to her long ago, when he was still sober enough to explain the rules of dice and the other games that swallowed up his nights. *Don't look to see how a man rolls: his eyes will tell you so much more.* How she'd trusted her father then. She'd been eager to drink in his words as proof of love.

"I know Gabinius better than he knows himself," Archelaus avowed, holding her eye. "I spent two seasons feasting and fighting at his side. He'll march on Pelusium, and when he takes it with ease, he'll grow cocky. He's beloved by his men, and he'll let them run wild after a victory. They'll drink too much, and fuck too much, and raid too much. And then, in time, weary with merriment, they'll cross the Nile's mouths to take Alexandria. And there, in the swamps, our men will battle the oncoming horde, and emerge muddy and triumphant."

Her furies quieted. It was a plan, maybe even a good one. And who could predict Gabinius's movements better than her husband? That intimate understanding had value too—as much as soldiers and gold. Berenice's burning fury cooled. Perhaps she hadn't been so foolish after all.

"Our men will fight better along the swamps than the Romans will," she allowed. "And we might make use of our advantage on the sea."

Heartened, Archelaus went on, almost cheerfully. "Precisely, my queen. Your father and Gabinius are confident that we'll meet them on the dry lands between Antioch and Pelusium. They won't be prepared to fight us in the swamps. And there we won't hand them their victory on a platter."

Their victory. Berenice's heart thudded and then slowed. She understood the second meaning of those words: even her husband didn't believe that she could hold the throne. But he was wrong. He didn't know how long she'd fought, how hard she could be. He knew only her softness, as she knew his. And so she didn't flare and rail against him as she would have against Dryton or Thais, if the latter ever dared object to a word she said. She leaned over and gently kissed Archelaus on the lips. He had nothing more to say that she needed to hear.

Dryton didn't receive such pleasant treatment. As the weeks passed, Berenice refused to offer him either punishment or reprieve. She instead picked pliant Thais as the adviser to dog her steps and check up on the progress of her soldiers. She was weary of men with strong beliefs and hidden agendas. Thais had no beliefs, or at least none that he was bold enough to voice. And when the reports came in, one after another—"The Romans have reached Jerusalem"; "The Romans have reached Rinokoloura"; "The Romans have taken Pelusium"—he offered no opinion beyond a sad shrug of his bony shoulders. It was acknowledgment of what they

280 . EMILY HOLLEMAN

both knew: that he could hardly be expected to put on a brave front. Whereas Pieton would have cursed and Dryton would have slammed his fist against some stone, Thais remained steady and laconic. "It'll turn out in the end, my queen."

As another afternoon drained into evening, Berenice asked for Leda to attend her. The old nurse beamed brightly, honored by the task. Of late, Berenice had been favoring Merytmut. The girl had served as the first midwife of Berenice's strength; perhaps she might help her tame this second husband too. But Leda, as was her wont, had grown jealous and protective, murmuring jabs about Upper Egyptian rebels each chance she got.

"Run a bath with scented oils, Leda," Berenice told her loudly. The woman's hearing wasn't what it once was.

The old maid's hands trembled as she scrubbed Berenice's back; her fingers had lost much of their nimbleness. Tangles that had once unraveled with a look now required earnest tugging.

"Leda, what do you make of the coming war?" Berenice asked, feigning carelessness, as though she had merely asked after the arrival of olive oil from the south. "What chance does my husband stand in battle?"

"In—in battle, my queen?" Leda stammered. The woman might advise on men easily enough, but she knew better than to involve herself in politics.

Berenice wished for the other sort of confidence, though—confidences from a wife, a woman. As her father's army neared, she found herself filled with a tenderness toward Archelaus, no matter how she tried to quench it. She wanted to be at his side in peace as in war. Was she looking for absolution, then—for a reason to call Archelaus to her? How her mother would have sneered that she sought justification for weakness from her nurse. Like some child in changing clothes. Berenice shook her head in disgust. "Never mind, Leda. It doesn't matter."

The nurse looked at her intensely, as though she might be able to read her mistress's mind. Berenice could make out the shadow of the young woman, the girl Leda must have been. Hers had been a thoughtful face once, with no small hint of beauty.

"Men who win on the battlefield must first win in the bedroom," her servant told her quietly.

And there it was—her pardon. She could summon her husband not for herself, not from any desire to sleep once more, while time was left, with the one man she'd ever cared for. No, there was a grander purpose: he needed her for victory. She would sacrifice her body. Her machinations sounded pathetic. She had grasped at straws and Leda had handed her one.

Oiled and coiffed, Berenice welcomed Archelaus to her chambers that night. As he reclined upon the divan, she looked at him with fresh eyes. From a distance, bronzed with the sun's heat, he gleamed, a painting quickened off the palace wall. But when he was near at hand, her eyes sharpened at his wears. The skin around his knuckles cracked from the wind, his eyes squinted even when the sun was bent, his gait lagged from some injury she couldn't name. He scarcely looked like the same man who'd wooed her in the menagerie that day. That man had shone with hope. And yet this one needed her—he did. She saw that clearly in his eyes. He might lie about many things, but not that: the aching in his gaze.

"My love." She knelt beside him. "My love, what troubles you?"

"It's poor luck," he murmured, running a hand along her waist, "for a general to share his wife's bed before battle. I should be out in the elements with my men."

They shared this too, she realized, this lying about what they needed. That gave her courage. Perhaps this lying might reveal another sort of strength.

"Your men," she teased, "sleep on soft mats in the lodges of my forefathers. For many, these past weeks have been the most luxurious of their lives. There's no shame for you in indulging as well. Tomorrow, you march. Tonight, we should enjoy each other."

He turned away. Berenice felt him slipping from her grasp, his worries creeping up on him.

"My love." She aped Seleucus's patterns, invoking words to force sentiments. "My love, what frightens you?"

She slipped her hand down his taut stomach. His body tensed beneath her fingers.

"Nothing frightens me." His tone belied his words. When he looked at her, whatever truth had crossed his face was hidden. It didn't matter. The truth didn't live between them anymore. "It's Aulus Gabinius who should be frightened now."

"I'm sure he quakes within his tent, lying on the hard, unwelcoming ground." With her finger she traced his mouth. It, too, was lined with cares. He bent to kiss her, and her lips met his eagerly. The sweat still lingered on them. He lifted her as he stood; his heart pounded against her own as he laid her on the bed. Warm fingers slipped along her sides, teasing the cloth from her skin. The room was hot, too hot; the fire blazed too bright. Its heat prickled at her flesh. In one swift motion, Archelaus lifted the chiton over her head, letting its pins fall where they may. And then her trembling began. She couldn't help herself—no matter how many times they made love, the beginning frightened her. That lurking threat of Seleucus, of pain and spite—that she could never quite forget.

Archelaus's kisses grew more urgent. Berenice fixed her eyes upon the hearth. She hoped it might calm her quaking form. *He won't hurt you,* she whispered to herself. *He never has.* He'd freed himself from his robes. Her pupils burned against the flames. He entered her. She did not cry out in pain. A dozen separate licks consumed the fresh sycamore, in yellow and orange, a taste of blue. With crackling fingers, the flames lurched onward, devouring branch after branch. Their appetites insatiable. The dead man twitched on top of her and collapsed.

Time stretched thin before he stirred. And when he did, there was a strange look in his eye, an intensity that Berenice hadn't seen before. He sat back on his knees. His gaze fell slowly from her eyes down to her belly. Impulsively, he kissed her stomach, and whispered to her womb.

"May the gods let a child blossom here."

"May they indeed," she echoed back.

And then he nestled against her, his head buried in her breast. She stroked the hair curling on his head and neck until his body twitched and his breathing slowed with the quiet rhythms of sleep. And for a long time afterward, she lay stiff and frozen, fearing that the slightest motion might disturb him. This was love, she realized, for she loved him deeply then, with a ferocity she hadn't felt before. She was desperate to protect him, willing even to trade his death for hers. When dawn pried open her lids, she was surprised to find that she'd slept at all.

Morning brought other changes as well. Weary Archelaus had been rekindled as a raring, burgeoning version of himself. There had been some truth in Leda's words: her husband had needed her and this—it had restored his vigor. This bold and jumpy creature had stolen the worn one's place and was pacing back and forth across her onyx floors. With a quick kiss, he slipped from her, anxious to rejoin his men, his mind already flitting over his new plans.

From the eastern portico, Berenice watched the army ride into the rising sun. When the last packhorse disappeared over the horizon, she turned to Merytmut. She had known this moment would come, though she hadn't wanted to admit it. Not even to herself. Not when she could still feel the remnants of his seed spilling out between her legs. The maid's eyes were blank and unreadable. Better her than Leda.

Berenice spoke harshly to mask her regrets. "There are methods to ensure that a child won't latch onto the womb. You're familiar with such potions?"

The girl nodded.

"Good. Brew some for me tonight. And bring me a tonic to help me sleep."

Berenice walked back into her chambers. She would not weep. She'd known this too, this price she would pay for loving him, for wanting him. If Archelaus returned, they'd make another. But she could not be saddled with a dead man's babe.

YOUNGER

The library's great reading room was drained clean of men. The sardonyx pillars that, like Atlas, heaved up the limestone sky made for dismal companions. The lion-clawed benches clustered about the meeting tables looked lonesome, crying out for the scholars' return. Arsinoe wondered where they'd gone. Had they returned to the refectory to weather the coming tempest, or had they fled Alexandria entirely? Did the city stand empty too? After all, the void reverberated to every corner of the royal complex. Only her sister Berenice remained, shuttered away in her private rooms, as a skeletal set of guards, slowed by wounds and years, haunted the halls and courtyards.

Here, Aspasia and Hypatia lingered too, slouching on one side of the table, whispering secrets as though nothing had changed, while Arsinoe and Alexander sat across from them, knowing full well that everything had. The chamber was warm, the air close and sticky, her eyes bleary with sleep. But then a page would crinkle or a quill would scratch, and she turned all ears: alert. And the guards burst through the ebony doors.

"Arsinoe."

They dragged her screaming from the room.

"Arsinoe."

She fought them, tooth and nail and talon. She tore away their flesh, and feasted on it with her beak.

"Arsinoe."

A claw pinched her skin above the knee. Alexander.

"Ouch," she mouthed to him, rubbing the red mark on her thigh. His eyes darted anxiously to Ganymedes.

The eunuch swelled when angry, and he was swollen now. As swollen as she'd ever seen him. When he phrased the question again, he pronounced each word with exaggerated care: "Tell me, Arsinoe: why does Electra respond as she does to her brother's appearance? Why won't she believe he is who he says he is?"

She sucked her upper lip. What did it matter anymore why Electra believed her brother's claims?

"That's simple, Ganymedes," Arsinoe stalled. "Any child knows why Electra, daughter of Agamemnon and Clytemnestra, doesn't believe that her brother, Orestes, is who he says he is." Repeating the query was her favorite dilatory tactic. They'd been discussing Aeschylus—she remembered that much. But whenever she read that early version of the tale, she skimmed over the brother-sister bits. She was too eager to reach the description of the dreams, first of Cassandra, and then of Clytemnestra. Arsinoe clung to the hope that these might shed light on her own.

"Tell me, then, if it's so simple."

"Electra, daughter of Agamemnon and Clytem—"

"We know who her parents are. Stop stalling."

"I'm not stalling!" She hated when the eunuch caught her at her tricks. "Electra is surprised to find that her brother has visited their father's tomb. She thought she was the only one, the only one who mourned Agamemnon's death." Shorn of embellishment, her words wandered on, listless, daft. Like this lesson. Why did Ganymedes insist on pretending that nothing was wrong?

"Indeed, she did suspect that. But any child, as you say, with a passing knowledge of the myth might give the same answer. We study Aeschylus's interpretation, it would behoove you to recall." Ganymedes's eyes bent to the other children. Hypatia picked studiously at her nails, and Alexander fixed his eyes on the unbound scroll before him. But Aspasia smiled and met the eunuch's gaze.

"I know why Electra didn't believe it was Orestes at once," she answered in her lesson voice, prim and proper.

"I didn't ask you, child," Ganymedes chided. "I asked Arsinoe. As our princess seems to be too distracted to attend her lessons, the rest of you may go. Arsinoe alone lacks understanding of this work."

His words stung. It wasn't fair to shame her before her friends. "I understand——" She started to object, but the eunuch cut her off with a glare.

Aspasia looked disappointed—she'd grown ever more determined to show off. But Hypatia could scarcely conceal her delight. Of late the fair-haired girl had been looking especially eager to rush from their lessons. Arsinoe suspected that there was some secret reason for her playmate's glee. Some boy, perhaps. But she'd never know the truth of it. The two girls, her sworn companions, were distant with her now. As though Alexander's nearness polluted her royal blood. She didn't mind. She didn't care for them either.

"Go," Ganymedes barked. "Now." Hypatia and Aspasia fled.

Alexander lingered, rolling his scrolls slowly and meticulously, one letter at a time. He, too, had perfected the art of stalling.

"Alexander," the eunuch snapped. "What are you doing?"

"I'm minding the scrolls, Ganymedes," the boy protested. "I know they're very old." The eunuch only glared, and under his watchful eye, her friend finished his business quickly and fled the room.

"Your studies don't wait upon your leisure, Arsinoe," Ganymedes scolded loudly, as though he wanted the whole library to hear. "You must pay closer heed to the lines in question. Begin by reading Electra's antistrophe with the chorus. The one that starts 'What should our prayers be saying.'"

Arsinoe cleared her throat. "'What should our prayers be saying, that we suffer the pain of our parents? She tries to fawn, we'll not be charmed, like savage wolves, we'll not be tamed, no mother comfort soothes our rage.'"

That line gave her pause. She liked the ring of it. And that was how she was too: savage and uncharmed. Her mother had abandoned her, the stranger that she was, and she would not be soothed. Not like her weak-willed brothers, reared on mother's milk, nor like Hypatia and Aspasia, who'd never understood what it meant to be alone. Only Alexander did. He'd been left by his mother first and then his father too.

When Arsinoe looked up again, she was surprised to find her tutor still there. Usually, he prompted her quickly when she got lost in her musings. But now he watched her from across the table, matching her in silence and stillness. And then, all at once, long after her companion's footsteps had faded, he seized her wrist. His voice cut in a hoarse whisper: "Follow me."

Heart pounding, Arsinoe did as she was told. The other flight, their failed one, flashed vividly before her eyes. Achilles with his throat split, fading in the servants' corridors. But she had no choice: her tutor's comfort was as close to a mother's as she would get.

Ganymedes tramped through the library, farther and farther from the halls that bordered the palace grounds. Arsinoe knew that there was an entrance that adjoined the street as well, but she'd never passed through it herself. Surely that must be their destination—why else go through these strange halls and atria she'd never seen before? These rooms looked shoddier than the ones on the royal side. The benches here were hewn from ordinary wood, ungilded. She suspected that common citizens might even be allowed to visit on occasion.

She panted, racing to keep up. "Where are we going?"

"You tire of our cloistered lessons, Arsinoe, so the time has come for practical ones." Ganymedes spoke in the strange, breezy voice he used when she was certain he was spinning excuses from the ether. "There's no better way to see which way the wind blows than on the city streets."

"The city streets?" she repeated dumbly. "But I am—there are—"

"Guards, yes, I know. Do you take me for a fool?"

Her mouth opened and closed like one of the gold-flecked fish in the garden ponds. "No, Ganymedes," she muttered softly.

"Then follow me, and hold your tongue."

Arsinoe nodded. She could be quiet; she could cloak her fears. The eunuch turned and led her along the winding corridors that snaked toward the dormitories. Maybe she'd misheard his words, and he'd said "between scholars' sheets," or some other oddly turned phrase of his. At each bend, she glanced back to see whether her sister's sentinels pursued them. Sometimes she saw none, but here and there one would emerge. An aging man, with the rough-spun tunic of a servant, appeared time and again. She knew better than to be tricked by his simple garb. He must be among Berenice's spies. What else would bring him scurrying after her?

She caught up to Ganymedes and gasped at his shoulder, "There's a—"

"I know, child, I know. Hush."

But Arsinoe couldn't hush—her heart thudded too loudly. Surely the guard could hear its pounding as clearly as she could. And with each step she had to fight the urge to peer back at him. She forced herself to count to five, to ten, fifteen, twenty before she twisted her head. And each time she looked, he loomed closer, quieter, more terrifying. At first she'd taken him for an old man, but she now saw that was a guise. His face might be bent over a walking stick, but that was another part of the spectacle. Beneath that hooded cloak, some tall, broad-shouldered soldier loomed. *The wolf.*

After turning back on their steps a half dozen times, Arsinoe and Ganymedes arrived at the dormitories. And here the eunuch dropped the ruse. He attacked the tower steps madly, pausing only when they'd reached the very top. The corridor above looked drab to Arsinoe's eyes. The muses on the walls had grown so dark with dust that she could hardly tell one from the other. When they reached the far end, Ganymedes pounded on a shabby wooden door.

But that's Kleon the Argive's cell, Arsinoe wanted to object. She and Alexander had learned that lesson from harsh experience, ages ago, when they'd been playing king of the mountain. "Everyone knows the king has to be at the highest spot," she'd told him, laughing, as they'd crept up to the top of the scholars' residence. Most of the men had indulged the royal girl and her friend, but not Kleon. He had named them a nuisance and swatted Alexander with his switch until he bled. Yet much as Kleon frightened Arsinoe with his milky eyes and stony dedication to each task, the bent man who dogged their steps scared her all the more. If the eunuch thought they might escape this way, she wouldn't question him.

The door swung open, and Ganymedes hustled her inside. The chamber itself looked as bare as a priest's—but the good sort of priest, the sort that Myrrine sometimes told her of, not the ones who tended to Serapis and crowded their chambers with gems and gold worthy of a king. Arsinoe had expected something grander, more mysterious, but she knew better than to voice her disappointment. She knew better than to speak at all.

Kleon sat, blind eyes sealed shut, on a small blanket spread over a cold bit of stone. As far as Arsinoe could tell, he hadn't gotten up to open the latch. The door, it seemed, had welcomed them on its own.

"My apologies," Ganymedes murmured, and Kleon's white eyes blinked open. *He won't know it's me,* Arsinoe told herself. *He can't even see that I'm here.* "I didn't mean to disturb you at this hour, but we find ourselves in need of the scholars' passage."

Time stretched, and the blind man said nothing. He didn't move. Arsinoe wasn't even sure he breathed. But then, ever so slightly, his chin angled downward, a mere fraction. She couldn't say whether he'd actually nodded, but Ganymedes was already shuffling her forward, lifting a rotted tapestry and ducking her head through a hidden door, and then prodding her onto another, steeper set of steps into the black.

They climbed down for a long while—far longer, Arsinoe

thought, than it had taken them to ascend, but it was hard to tell, for the upward scramble had been well lit. And still deeper they plunged into the bowels of the tower, until Arsinoe swore that they must be beneath the earth itself. When the ground flattened out, she stubbed her toe, hard, so accustomed had her steps grown to falling down, down, down.

"Quiet," Ganymedes chided her, though she had hardly cried out at all. "It's not much farther now."

The floor was damp. The water soaked through her sandals, into the soles of her feet. She was weary, suddenly, and despite everything, she wished herself back in her chambers.

"Do you have your knife?" the eunuch asked.

By habit, Arsinoe kept the blade fastened at her waist, but she checked her belt just the same. The hard leather scabbard met her hand. She breathed a sigh of relief.

"Yes."

"Good. You may well need it."

"Ganymedes." She clung to his hand, to the darkness, to the lost spaces between indoors and out. "What should I expect upon my father's return?"

"Your father isn't the most forgiving of men," her tutor told her quietly. "But I imagine in your case, given your youth, he shall make an exception. I'll ensure that he does."

Arsinoe tried to parse *what,* precisely, she must be forgiven for. She only had told Berenice about Nereus, and he'd been Seleucus's man, not her father's. She hadn't spilled any other secrets—there hadn't been any others for her to spill. But before she had a chance to ask Ganymedes what he meant, they emerged. The daylight bit her eyes; in their haste, she'd forgotten the hour. The rest of the world had not. The agora buzzed with buyers and sellers, children and thieves. They'd hardly walked five paces before Arsinoe saw the truth of the eunuch's words: the peasants had no qualms about which way the wind blew over the palace.

An ancient crone, gnarled fingers clenching a gnarled cane, scolded a clean-shaven youth preening at his curls: "Gabinius won't stand for such girlish vanities. The Romans, they prefer real men." The old woman shook her stick in anger, but her eyes lit up when they fell upon Arsinoe. The beldam searched her stall, knotted fingers grazing over yellow baubles and cheap jewels until she found what she was looking for. A turquoise beetle, true in its stone, opened in her palm.

"This gave fortune to the ancients," she crooned. "I can see, my dear, that you'll soon need it."

Arsinoe's ears piqued at the warning. She was about to ask Ganymedes about it when she was distracted by another sight. A throng of gritty street rats, eyes white and wide on filthy faces, stared at her. They moved as one, a single mass of flesh, until fights broke out and separate creatures emerged: a tangle-haired girl dragging her wailing brother by the hand, a sticky-eyed boy pushing another to the gutter, a mud-caked youth smirking as he snatched a hunk of bread from a babe.

"Ganymedes," she began. "Who are those—"

"Hush, child. Listen." Ganymedes pointed.

Her eyes followed his finger to where a fishmonger, a hunch-backed man of some unknown years—forty or eighty, she couldn't tell—hawked his wares: "Buy before the Romans drive up the price. When the Piper returns, you'll be begging me to sell you a sickly squid for three times the cost of this fine cod."

"Why'll the army up the price of your squirming worms?" a fruit-laden woman teased. "Gabinius most like wants to keep his soldiers alive, not poison 'em with these maggots you call fish."

A second peasant, this one middle-aged but clothed in the bright hues of youth, laughed, and Arsinoe got the sense that such scenes played out often. The commoners spoke with a freedom unknown within the palace walls. There everyone talked of the great and glorious victory the queen would strike against the Roman legions.

Arsinoe wondered whether Berenice ever snuck into the streets. She imagined not; it would be even harder to creep unnoticed as a queen.

The fruit-laden woman bent her head over the fishmonger's goods, prodding at a few fish with her thick fingers. The seller took no offense at this rough handling of his wares, which Arsinoe found strange. Perhaps this, too, marked a common practice. She'd rarely seen food before it reached the table, and then only in the royal kitchens.

"My child." The eunuch knelt at her feet, before the square's small temple of Serapis, a miniature of the great one at the city's southern end. His fingers dug circles about her wrists. "There's somewhere I must go now."

Arsinoe's voice shrank. "I'm not coming with you?"

Ganymedes shook his head. "No, my dear. You must wait for me. You must wait for me here."

"Here?" she echoed, glancing about the marketplace.

"Yes. I will come back for you."

"Will you be long?"

His eyes were lined and sagging. The eunuch looked as he might in twenty years, when he was old, and tired, and spent. "No, my sweet, not so very long."

"But where—"

His finger silenced her lips. Gently, he kissed her hand, and then, more quickly than she could have imagined, he vanished into the throngs. *Wait,* she wanted to cry out. *You can't leave me here. Not you as well*... She swallowed her protests. They'd make no difference. If Ganymedes said that she must wait, he'd have a reason for it. And no amount of bargaining on her part would change that. He would come back for her. He always had.

Arsinoe's stomach grumbled, though she couldn't say if it was from hunger or nerves. Perhaps she would be sick. The crowd wiped against her; she could taste the peasants' sweat, their stink upon her skin. Desperately, she needed to run, to rid herself of these vermin, or she'd become one herself. Barreling forward, she used her shoulders to cut out a path to the edge, to a great stone temple that turned out from the agora, gazing over the sea. She scampered up the stairs, taking them two by two. Up close, she recognized the designs on the sky-blue pillars: the swirls of fish and mermaids, ships and sailors, climbing the heights. She was at the Temple of Poseidon, though she'd only ever entered through its broad colonnade across from the beach.

Poseidon, Earth-Shaker, Lord of the Seaways, I beg you . . . Her thoughts trailed off. Hard as she tried to summon one, Arsinoe didn't know the proper prayer. Should she beg for her sister's safe passage? She'd said those words often enough, but now she wasn't sure. If Cleopatra arrived, then surely her father would come too. And then what would become of her? Of Ganymedes? Of Myrrine? Of Berenice? She'd been a girl of eight when her sister had seized the throne, but Arsinoe remembered the day's bloodshed well, and *that* had been named a bloodless coup. She didn't wish to see what a bloody one looked like, didn't wish to add those visions to her haunted nights.

Stares tore at her skin. The children's gazes weighed heaviest of all. A clutch of them sized her up from the far side of the square. *What can I snatch off her?* those eyes demanded. *Is she as feeble as she looks?* Much as Arsinoe liked the breezy plane of the temple portico, she'd left herself exposed. Only a solitary beggar lingered here, too old and ragged to have anything to steal. And so she snuck back down into the agora. She'd have to find Ganymedes there at any rate. And she shouldn't keep him waiting.

She needn't have worried. The eunuch wasn't at the fishmonger's stall, nor was he waiting by the scarab-peddling crone. Her legs were weary and she wanted to sit down, but she didn't dare. The crowd nearly swallowed her when she stood; she'd be lost if she sank any lower. How would her tutor find her then?

Dusk had fallen violet, and Arsinoe shivered with night's first chill. And still, no Ganymedes. As the dark crept in, the crowds began to clear, and she could see well enough across the marketplace. She stood on her toes and gazed in each direction, but she could make out no sign of her tutor. What, she wondered, could possibly be taking him so long? Slowly, she realized the truth: he wasn't coming back. She'd known that he'd abandon her; she'd always known. Or at the very least, she should have known. What other certainties were there? Her father and her mother, her sister and her brothers, had all turned away from her when Berenice stole the throne. It had only been a matter of time before the eunuch did the same.

Shaking, Arsinoe wrapped her coral mantle more tightly around her shoulders. Her clothes shone garish in the crowd, the sapphire tunic beneath an even greater affront than the shawl. The fabric was far too finely woven as well; the clothes of her companions were all rough-spun. Her tutor hadn't merely abandoned her: he'd left her marked an outsider, tainted by her royal garb.

Too many eyes, whichever way she turned. Arsinoe darted through the lingering throngs, slight as an arrow, and, eager to escape their gazes, raced down the first alleyway she saw. Her pumping blood, fresh with fury, warmed her body and stirred her mind. With no purpose but to run, she turned and twisted down smaller and smaller lanes. She was done waiting for people who weren't coming back.

Winded, she skidded to a stop and dropped her head between her legs. It had been silly—childish, she saw—to race off like that. But still, not all was lost. She could retrace her steps to the palace. She'd visited the agora and the lesser temples and even the Temple of Serapis, which lay across the southern edge of town, enough times to be able to find her way back home. The salty scent of the sea reached her nostrils; the docks couldn't be far. Arsinoe circled back through the narrow lanes. Helios's dying rays kissed her left cheek. She knew that she was walking north and true. Eyes set on the stones in front of her, she raced onward through the avenues. She'd rid herself of alleys now. Her feet opened onto the beach, hitting on soft sand with relief.

Suddenly, she realized that she shouldn't have come back this way. She'd run back to her rooms once before. And already something had changed. Too still, too empty, too quiet. On most feast days, these fields flooded with children, running, screeching, clamoring. Not only street urchins, but the honest sons and daughters of merchants and even low noblemen crowded the gated gardens. But now the expanse lay empty save for a small cluster of Jews, either too old or too young to fight, who'd gathered to bear witness. A gust of wind filled Arsinoe's nostrils with smoke; she coughed into her elbow and squinted at the palace gate. It was bolted shut.

On careful toes, she approached the group of men. "Strange beliefs or no, Jews hear all," Ganymedes had told her once when she'd grown tired of learning Aramaic; she could only hope that his words would prove correct. Head hung nearly to her chest, Arsinoe tried to make herself as small as possible. When one of the quorum glanced back at her, she squatted and pretended to search for some lost jewel in the sand. Massaging the cool grains, she strained her ears to listen. The act was comforting in itself: eavesdropping came as naturally to her as breathing.

"Romans? The House of Ptolemy?" the youngest one, a boy of fourteen or so, spat. He went on, but Arsinoe could not make sense of the rest of his quick words. Her ears rang with the one: *Romans.*

An old man—the boy's grandfather, perhaps—growled a correction. The only phrase she caught was "at the Canopic Gate." Arsinoe needed no further bidding. She raced back through the gardens and toward the smaller streets. She couldn't return to the palace now, perhaps not ever. Soon the royal grounds would swarm with Romans. *Your father isn't the most forgiving of men.* She saw the eunuch's meaning now. Two years—more—she'd spent in

Berenice's court. She'd shared her sister's food and table, even her counsel. Enough to taint her a traitor too.

Arsinoe's feet carried her through the market and by the Temple of Tyche and into the belly of the city. She ran past drunken men and fat donkeys and women selling fabrics and grapes and beans. She ran past grand homes with red-tile roofs and terraced temples with friezes of the gods, along knotted alleys stinking of fish and lush boulevards lined with drinking pools, by stone houses that slowly gave way to wood-roofed shacks. She ran until she could no longer smell the sea.

Even the hovels grew thin. Before her stretched an empty field of green dotted with stone markers and marble hutches. Tombs. The city of the dead. She'd heard of this lesser settlement that held the bones of lesser men, but she'd never seen it with her own eyes. Her own forefathers were buried by the palace, glass eyes gazing toward Macedonia across the sea. These modest graves marked the corpses of sundry Jews, Assyrians, and Africans who flocked to the great city on the delta. The dead brought quiet with them. As Arsinoe crept between their houses, she shivered. The last specks of sun had sunk beneath the horizon. The chill of night took hold.

Her belly growled—loudly. She recognized it as hunger now, but she could ignore it for a while longer. She hadn't forgotten the lessons from the early days of Berenice's rule. She knew that she could last for whole days with scarcely any food at all; she'd need to grow accustomed to such rumblings again. And this time, she was on her own. Myrrine didn't know where she was, Ganymedes had left her to rot, her fire-bearded guard was dead.

So much death, she thought as she looked over the tombs upon tombs that lined the field. The next one was full of corpse markers too; they stretched as far as she could see in the dying light. *Will Berenice soon join them?* The morbid thought pulsed in her ears as though she'd spoken it aloud. Arsinoe cast her gaze about, willing herself to forget, to cleanse the dark thoughts from her mind. Her eyes caught on a darkened spot, the maw of a cavern. She squinted at it until she could make sense of what she saw. It wasn't a cavern at all, but something far better: an entrance to the catacombs. She caught her breath, but she didn't run. Rushing might draw attention, but here, she knew, she might pass the night.

A torch blazed merrily below, lighting the way for the dead's visitors, she supposed. Her own ancestors' tombs were sealed and guarded, but these simple folks had few valuables worth protecting. She'd likely find little more than bones.

And stink. The putrid stench of decay rose to greet her as she began her downward climb. These bodies, clearly, hadn't been prepared for second life, embalmed with the deathless juices of the gods. Tunic clutched over her nose, Arsinoe crept down the sandstone steps into the homes of the dead, like Odysseus descending into the shade world of the damned.

The torch's flame licked away some ten paces of the dark, but no more. She curled just outside its warming reach. Weariness weighed her down; she needed rest. Rest or food, and she wouldn't eat until the morning came, or longer still. Arsinoe's mind wandered over the city streets, over the eastern wall, over to her father's camp. There she would explain to Cleopatra what had happened under Berenice's rule, how she hadn't betrayed Father, how she'd merely done what . . .

"That all you got?" a boy's voice cracked. Arsinoe's eyes opened to blackness. "What 'm I supposed to do with six coppers?"

"I thought—I thought—I thought them's gold." A trembled squeak.

"How many times I've got to tell you? Gold don't stick when you bite."

"We—we might buy a bit o' food with it."

"Food?" the first replied. "Where d'ya think we'd get food for *that?*"

Their accents lashed against Arsinoe's ears, but she forced herself to listen. She'd have to learn to speak that way as well. Otherwise she'd never pass for a gutter rat.

Their voices hushed. The older slammed the younger aside. "Shut your trap," he hissed. "Someone's about."

In the darkness, Arsinoe's fingers fumbled for her knife. She turned and drew it from her scabbard—but not quickly enough. A coarse hand knocked it away.

"Grab that," the boy ordered his friend—his fingers struck against her shoulders. "That's a nice knife for a mouse. And those 'r' fancy clothes. What's a stinking girl like you doing with such finery?" he sneered. "Ajax, seems the gods smile at the likes of us af'er all."

From the corner of her eye, Arsinoe caught the other boy—a child of eight, perhaps, not a half-grown youth—nodding timidly. His hands shook where he held the knife.

"Give us the clothes," the older boy told her. "And maybe we won't kill ya slow."

Wild, impulsive, Arsinoe sank her teeth into his flesh. A string of curses, only half of which she understood, escaped his mouth. He socked her hard across the lips. On hands and knees, she groped across the grainy earth. Her fingers struck what felt like a stone, long and narrow. She wrapped her fingers around its weight, and swung it hard. This time she wasn't too slow. Her elbow braced as she struck the youth's temple.

Her assailant collapsed. His young accomplice shrieked and dropped the knife.

"Shut your trap." She flung the new words at him. Her hand trembled but her voice did not. Crimson streaked the older boy's brow. He looked younger than before. Perhaps he'd seen only eleven summers, the same as her.

"You killed him," the little one whispered.

Her heart pounded in her head. For the first time, Arsinoe

looked down at the weapon clutched in her fist. It was no stone at all, but a bone—a femur, by the look of it. Ganymedes had made her learn the parts of the body after he'd found her thumbing over Hippocrates. She'd traced the illustrated skeletons with her adorned fingers. How different she must look now, seizing bones as weapons, like the savages who lived far up the Nile and didn't speak a word of Greek. A day out of the palace and already a murderer. She wasn't sure whether to be proud or ashamed.

With a timid foot, she nudged the fallen boy. His body was warm and heavy against her sandaled toes. "I just knocked him out. He'll be all right," she declared with a confidence she didn't feel. A strange energy pulsed through her as she looked back at the younger child. Frightened, he shrunk away from her gaze.

"I won't hurt you," she offered with a shrug. The boy nodded quickly, in silence. She was suddenly afraid he might cry.

"Come. He wasn't so kind to you to begin with." Arsinoe nodded at the creature at her feet. He showed no signs of stirring; perhaps she had killed him. Shouldn't boys die harder than that? If killing was so easy, why write songs in praise of it? What honor was there in Achilles's slaying of Hector if souls were so prompt and skittish in flight?

"He was my cousin," the child murmured, eyes fixed on the dirt.

Her stomach growled. She'd no answer for that. "Do you want something to eat, Ajax?" She was glad that she remembered his name. There was a power in naming things.

"You have food?" he asked, eager. Arsinoe could see the hunger in his eyes, wide and open to the whites.

"No, but I know how we might get some." Her fingers caressed the smooth bone in her hand. She liked the weight of it, the heft. And it was easier to wield than a knife. "D'you know where I might sell these clothes?"

He nodded, wary eyes still fixed on the ivory in her hand. "I do. I know a woman who buys those fine sorts of things."

"Take me to her. And hold on to that knife."

With a last glance at his cousin's body, the boy grabbed the blade and scampered ahead toward the steps and the newly breaking day. *Hunger runs deeper than blood.* Her first lesson. One she'd learned all on her own.

As they neared the blink of sunlight, the boy turned back to her, like Orpheus to Eurydice. He stopped and gaped, openmouthed.

"What now?"

"You can't bring that." He motioned toward the bone still clutched in her fingers. "Ya know: bad luck to bother the dead."

Of course. It would be bad luck. Arsinoe knew the curses that fell upon grave robbers and cretins who disturbed the tombs of good men.

"The dead don't need it," she said, beaming at her own irreverence. "I do."

ELDER

The battle limped on, creeping toward Alexandria's gates. At first, Archelaus's letters had sounded sanguine enough. He detailed the army's successful crossing of the Nile's western mouths, even joking about how one of his men had fallen from his horse in midstream and completed the journey clinging to the creature's tail. In all, he seemed proud of his young recruits. His scouts, he mentioned, suspected that the rumors of the size of Gabinius's army had been overblown. But once her husband had confronted the Roman legions in the flesh, his tone changed. Despite his attempts to cloak the bad news with good, Berenice found it easy enough to read between the lines: her infantry had been decimated, and while her cavalry may have won a few meager victories, more often it, too, suffered defeat. She was outmatched. That much was clear. Each day, she awaited Archelaus's carrier pigeon with a jumble of impatience and dread.

And at night, she could not sleep. Her body writhed in the darkness. Though Merytmut promised that her illness was unrelated to her brew—"I swear it on my life, my queen"—Berenice didn't believe it. She'd been soft to take her husband to her bed, to long for closeness when she deserved none. And she was being punished for it. Poison claws wrenched her baby from her womb. She didn't deserve to be a mother; she wasn't fierce enough for that.

It was only when dawn dragged her nails across the sea that her mind quieted at last, and she wished for nothing more than to spend the whole morning sleeping away her troubles. But she did not.

She'd already revealed her weakness by retreating to her chambers for a few short days. Now she had to be strong. Alexandria had to be reminded that she still had a queen.

Berenice crossed the chamber and cast aside the curtains. The sky cloudless, the sun drained over the horizon, soaking the sea crimson. *Blood.* If she believed in omens, she had to admit that this was a poor one. A pang struck her stomach; her fingers clutched the phantom pain. But it was nothing. An echo of what had lived and died inside her. Nothing more.

"Merytmut," she cried out. The girl should be by her bed. She'd promised not to leave her side. "Merytmut!"

The copper-faced maid scampered in. If either the early hour or the foreboding that lingered over the palace bothered her, she gave no sign of it. She looked as fair and fresh as ever. Perhaps that was true fortitude—the ability to sail through adversity unmoved by hunger or fatigue.

"My queen." Merytmut bowed. Throughout her nearly two years at court, the girl had flouted all its courtesies, and now that she'd embraced them, it was too late. There was a bitter irony in that.

"Did any messages come in the night?" Berenice's desperation coalesced around that question. She should have insisted on facing her father's forces in battle, rather than agreeing to rot away here in the palace. In camp, she would have known the outcome at once, not be forced to watch for fire signals and messenger birds.

"None, my queen," Merytmut answered. "All silent."

The need to act—to do something, anything—overwhelmed Berenice even though she knew there was nothing to be done here in Alexandria. Nothing that mattered, at least. She grasped at the empty air.

"Summon my councilors," she told the girl. "In an hour, they're to attend a meeting in the atrium."

"Your—your councilors," the maid stammered.

"My councilors, yes. Are you deaf or simply dumb?" She cursed

Merytmut, and her own softness too. She'd asked for the potion with good reason. Why dwell on the life that had drained from her? What fate would have met the son she might have borne after her father stormed the city? The boy's head would be smashed against the stone, if he even lived that long. Regret was an affliction of the weak.

"But my queen, Dryton rode with Archelaus to the battle." The girl answered gingerly, as though addressing a child or someone of feeble mind. "And the eunuch . . . you've banished him from your sight. And—"

"Bring Thais, then," Berenice snapped. She didn't need this accounting of who'd left her already and who merely intended to. She cared only about those who remained.

"I'm afraid Thais has not been seen since the army marched against Gabinius's men."

"Damn him," Berenice spat, more for effect than for any other reason. She could hardly feign surprise. Her reedy adviser had shown no backbone in the easiest of times; of course he'd fled when the breeze changed. "He's no great loss. Send for Nereus, then, and be done with it." Fitting that the last man who remained to her was the one whose underhanded loyalties she knew for certain.

Merytmut's voice trembled as she answered, "The old man is no longer with us."

The blows came quickly now, one after another. It had begun with Pieton plotting with the concubine. And now the rest had left her—for her father, or for the underworld.

"What do you mean?" Berenice tried to recall how Nereus had looked when last she'd seen him. He'd appeared hardy enough, though she supposed a man of his years might die at a moment's notice. "Why didn't you tell me at once?"

"It happened while you were ill," the girl protested. "And I thought it best to spare you."

Berenice brushed away her hurts with callous words. "Men

die. Old men die often. What does it matter—" She cut herself off. Merytmut's face, so often blank with mystery, told the plain truth now. "He didn't die, then. He deserted me as well." She should have foreseen this—one treachery always wrought another. Her father had taught her that lesson long ago. First he turned against her mother and then against her, the first child of his loins.

"It's said that he fled to Antioch. To tend to some bastard babe of Seleucus."

"Of—of Seleucus," she stammered, unbelieving. Old men were plagued by foolish fits of devotion too. After all these years, he still loved Selene, dead Selene, enough to wed his fortune to her infant grandson.

What had she done to earn such little loyalty? Did they sense the softness in her, the weakness she'd fought so hard to hide? She'd inspired men—inspired soldiers to fight for her. What happened to that woman riding among Seleucus's men, men who had hated her with every fiber of their being? She'd won them over with her words; she'd amazed them with her strength. She'd hoped that one of her advisers would stand by her still. That thought, too, reeked of regret. Only one had ever cared for her: Pieton. And she'd cursed him and sent him away. There was no use in dwelling on that. She would be strong—she would show Alexandria her queen.

"Run a bath and dress me for court," she told the maid. She couldn't stand another moment alone with her own thoughts.

Though Berenice had steeled herself for silence, the quiet of the great courtyard stunned her. Some guards remained, men withered deep into their years, but they numbered few enough to make her uneasy. And they did not shift nor spit nor laugh the way their younger comrades had. Their spirits had already been worn away. Resigned to their fate, these men merely stood, watching and waiting for the end. The two who looked after her were not much better, though at least they had a proper number of teeth between them. Archelaus had begged her to let him leave fitter guards, but she had dismissed the idea. She wouldn't have the tales say that the battle was lost on account of her delicacies.

As she neared the royal atrium, the palace grew lonelier still. A few courtiers lingered about the further colonnades, but even they shunned this place. For the first time that Berenice could recall, her father's splendid floor mosaic was on full display. Dionysus, his copper curls crowned with ivy, sat on his leopard, a gourd of wine in one hand and a staff of fennel in the other. Satyrs danced, hands clasped together, whirling madly about the god. In the far corner, set off from her divine consort by a solid border of rolling blue waves, lay naked Ariadne, her dark hair drifting over her breasts. Forsaken and useless. Like the woman that she was.

As Berenice climbed up to her throne—and it was her throne, not the Piper's—she wondered whether it would be the last time. Ever since she'd watched the bloody rise of dawn—even before, when she'd first seen the blood leaking down her thighs—she'd known that her husband wouldn't win this battle. His recruits couldn't stand against so many men, so many *Romans*. She'd taken her pleasure—and sent him to his death.

The hours ticked slowly onward. The sun slid through the windows at ever-changing angles, as though this day was no different than any other. Berenice's seat grew numb. She shifted on the gold-plated ivory; it was never meant to be a comfortable chair. Even her father had known better than to swathe its harshness with cushions. Not that he'd much cared for public audiences. The lightest excuse—a hunt, a banquet, a woman—always proved enough to send him on his way. "A good king," he'd told her once, "knows when to send an adviser to do his bidding." She wondered at her memories of him, of the foolish lessons he'd imparted to her about what it meant to rule. Could she trust those recollections? All those years ago, as her mother birthed those monstrous babes, had her father truly regarded her as his heir? Or had that, too, been part of some childish dream?

"Queen Berenice the Shining One." The herald's voice cut off her musings. "A messenger begs an audience."

"Show him in," she answered. From the corner of her eye, she could make out her nervous guards sizing each other up, deciding who should move first to defend the queen. Or, more likely, they were merely bored, preoccupied with the minutiae of their own small lives. She couldn't imagine that they cared much whether she lived or died. Not even her sometime councilors did.

The boy who stumbled through the greatest archway looked even younger than the usual ones. He quaked with each passing step. These commoners were always quaking when they bore the messages of their betters. A few sprigs of hair—the beginnings of a beard—trembled on his chin. He must be nearing manhood, Berenice supposed—older than she'd first thought.

"What news do you bring?" she prompted.

"My queen, I—I—" he stuttered. "My queen, I . . ." His voice trailed off. His eyes lingered over the barren atrium. Even this low-born child recognized her peril. "I didn't wish to disturb—"

"Do I look disturbed?" Berenice gestured about the empty room.

"No, my queen. I—"

"I look to be quite alone. I can't imagine why your presence would be a disturbance to me." Her feeble heart wished to delay his words—to cling to her last moments of hope, to ignore the truth, the knell of death.

He flushed purple. *Never show them you are soft.*

"Out with it." She pushed the reluctant words from her mouth. She clutched at strength.

"My queen, the battle's lost. Archelaus is gone—dead, it's thought. The Romans surround the city walls." The boy dispatched his words quickly. And then, shaking, he left her too.

It had come to this. She was encircled by Romans, by blood and death. And she could do nothing to stop the onslaught. It would take someone far harder and braver to halt Rome's inexorable rise and return her dynasty to its lost glories. No regrets, no weakness here. And yet she could not sit still and be patient. Instead, she paced about the atrium, taking a strange delight in kicking at Dionysus's face. Her footsteps shuddered through the palace; she took pleasure in the sounds as well. These pounding steps as the battle soured would be her last remembered act as queen. Servants would tell their children and their children's children how the dreadful Berenice had seethed and roared in the last days of her reign. "Take care," they'd warn as they tucked in their little ones at night. "I hear that fearsome creature still haunts these halls, howling for Archelaus."

"Archelaus!" She keened for him, for the dead man who'd shown her that paltry bit of love. Had it been love, as he called it, or simple folly? And whose fault was it but hers that he lay on some battlefield, gasping his last breaths? The moment he quit her halls, she'd marked him as a corpse. *I will not bear a dead man's son.* She'd bear no sons at all. Not even monsters, as her mother had.

An outside scuffle reached her ears: the sound of flesh on flesh, a servant's yelp, and then a creaking door. Berenice's heart calmed; none of it mattered. She was prepared to greet death. She savored this moment before she turned to look her killer in the eye. But it wasn't her death who stood before her, at least not the one she'd expected. No, it was a far more familiar figure, as shrunken by defeat as she.

"Pieton?" Her voice strained and broke. "What are you doing? Why have you come?"

"My queen..." He hung his weary head. The familiar sadness flickered in his eyes as he shrugged his shoulders. The little girl inside her wanted to run to him and weep, the way she had those years ago when her mother had been driven from the palace and he'd promised her that, one day, she would be queen. But she was not a child anymore. Her tutor had betrayed her, and his treachery cut deepest of all. He'd plotted with that woman—that concubine who'd first turned her father's eye. No, she did not need his comfort.

"Berenice." Her name—not "my queen," not her title, but her given name alone—sprang from his lips. He spoke it as gently as he had when she was a child. She couldn't bring herself to chide him for the closeness. "Berenice, you must listen to me. I beg you, Berenice. You must flee."

"Flee?" The sound escaped her body as a sob. "Flee? Flee? *Flee?*" Each repetition stripped the word of its meaning. "*Flee* my throne, my city?" There was no sense in it, in a plea for flight.

"Berenice"—again that name, that wretched, besieged name— "I beg you. There's no hope left. I—even I have . . ." Pieton's voice trailed off. Then he straightened up and met her eye. "I've sent word to your father. I've offered him my services, such as they are."

His lips moved, but she couldn't make sense of the phrases that escaped them. So many times they'd spoken here, the queen and her eunuch. She couldn't recall a time when he hadn't lurked at her side, a shadow and a protector. Even when he'd spoken to the concubine, she'd known somewhere in her heart that he'd been acting for her. For what he imagined were her best interests. After she'd sent him away in anger, she'd never believed him truly gone. But he, too, had betrayed her in the end. She couldn't even hold his loyalty.

"Did you think that your treachery would shock me?" she asked cruelly. She had to be cruel now. "When did you turn against me? Don't pretend that this marks the first time."

"Berenice, I have never betrayed your trust. Of all your advisers—"

"Of all my advisers," she spat. She clung to fury, as though it would stave off weakness. It had in the past. "You're the only one to come before me and confess your deceit. What a remarkable way to distinguish yourself."

"And what have the others done?" Pieton asked. "Dryton fought in the battle with Archelaus. Where is he now? Did he come rushing back to rescue you and defend you to the death? And what of Nereus, that wretched old man? Is he lurking about? Or has he, too, scampered off into the night?"

The eunuch knew—he always did, as though he'd been blessed by some second sight. No, she would not marvel at him. She'd curse him and send away his temptations. His promises of life.

"You're right. I should be grateful that you've come to taunt me, that you lacked the decency to merely desert me as the others did." Berenice bit her lip. She tasted blood upon it. Her skin had begun to crack all over these past few days, around her eyes and her mouth, down even to her toes. Her army's flaws made manifest.

"I haven't come to taunt you, Berenice. I've come to offer you your last chance. Your father means to execute you. If you don't leave, you will die."

The truth—she could still recognize that. And she would cleave to it.

"Then I will die. And I will die a queen. I'm no eunuch—my womanhood was not cut away. I will not be remembered as the Ptolemy who *fled,* who abandoned her subjects to the sword."

"Berenice." Pieton stared back at her with his sad, sad eyes. "I am so sorry. I am so sorry to leave you here alone."

This was too much to take. She would not accept his pity.

"Be gone!" A harpy, she shrieked at his retreat. The sound of her voice rebounded off the walls long after the eunuch had deserted her.

His words haunted her deep into the night. *Flee, flee.* That advice was foolish too: where could she go? She wasn't her father; she would receive no warm reception in Rome. Did Pieton imagine that she'd sail up the river to Nubia? Or perhaps she'd drag her ships across the desert sands and chart a course to India? No, even if she wanted to run, there was no point in it. Rome's talons stretched too far.

When Leda came to put out the candles, Berenice turned her away. She'd given up all hope of sleep. The wax stained the saucers, and even dripped onto the onyx floors. As she'd done when she was young, she let the wax coat her hands, allowing her fingers to linger on the stalks as the hot droplets scorched her skin. Later, she'd pick away the residue. If she wasn't dead by then.

Desperate, Berenice clasped the vulture at her chest. What nonsense had driven her to put on that necklace? Mut, the beleaguered mother goddess, would not protect her, just as her own mother could not. She moved to tear the amulet from her throat, but something stopped her hand.

Why hadn't she seen it before? Her thoughts sizzled in fits and bursts. The woman raped and weeping in Thebes. Her husband still and strangled on his bed. *Perhaps someday you might linger in the southern kingdom* ... Berenice could send for Merytmut. Her servant would know the twisting ways to escape the palace undetected. Here lay the solution to the eunuch's words: *Flee, flee.* There was a place that would shelter her, that still lay beyond Rome's reach.

Her finger ducked across the flame, lingering just long enough to feel the fire's scream. Berenice could picture herself in Thebes, among the alabaster of that dying city. *And what would you do there?* that other voice sneered, the voice that haunted her darkest moments, that recalled her mother's hacking breath. *What sort of peace could you find, you who have been queen?*

A drop of wax melted onto her skin. *Never show them you are soft.* It burned hotter than the flame, this last taste of scalding fire. Her hands were red and blotchy. The sight turned her stomach to bile.

Would you be content to pray and kneel and bend among the priestesses? Are you your father's daughter after all? The voice transformed. It did not belong to Tryphaena, long dead and destroyed. It was Berenice's own. *What comfort would you find in flight?*

That was what they expected—Pieton, Nereus, Dryton, even Archelaus. They imagined her a spineless woman still. She wouldn't slink away in the darkness; she wouldn't beg to cling to some shadow of life. What torture could death bring? She was a queen, a goddess, a Ptolemy.

When Rome's soldiers tore into her chambers, she did not scream. She did not thrash at their harsh hands or beg for foolish mercies. Head high, she went to meet her fate as had the pharaohs of old. To embrace death with dignity.

YOUNGER

Little Ajax licked the pomegranate juice from his fingers, savoring its sticky sweetness. At first, it had disgusted her, how he'd milk the last remnants of his food from his filthy hands, but now she almost admired his tenacity. Arsinoe had never seen anyone enjoy meals the way this street boy did, though she'd attended feasts where she had tasted the most opulent of dishes, rich heifer meat and figs dipped in the sweetest honey that lingered in her throat for days. But now that she thought back, it seemed that all the courtiers had merely picked at their plates, toying with the entrails and sipping at the sauces. This child had the way of it, embracing the sheer relish all those pompous nobles eschewed, smacking his lips with each bite and grinning from ear to ear.

"Where should we go now?" he asked, his feet swinging back and forth over the canal. "Where should we sleep tonight?"

He trailed Arsinoe everywhere, this little boy whose cousin she had killed. At first, she'd tried to rid herself of him, waking in the middle of the night and creeping out on her own. She didn't know how to care for herself; how could she be expected to look after him? Besides, he'd lived his whole life on the streets—surely he should know more of their workings than she? But Ajax always found her in the end, rushing to her side, all slights forgotten, as though she'd never meant to abandon him at all and had merely misplaced him as she might a shawl on a warm day. Arsinoe wondered if Big Ajax had tried similar tricks on his cousin before finally giving up and accepting him as a hanger-on.

*** *** ***

The sun had slipped lower in the sky—so low that its rays barely crept over the Temple of Serapis to the east. Beyond that, Arsinoe knew, the orb would soon be plunging into the sea. It had been days since she'd seen the waves, though she could still taste the salt on her tongue, even here beyond the south wall, in the underbelly of the city. Squatting with her back flush against the stone fortification, she felt almost safe: a quick hop over the canal would bring her back to the cover of the catacombs. Besides, she'd learned quickly enough that the northern parts belonged to the wealthy, and it was better to stay here, near the canal and the fresh water that it carried. Salt water was the province of the rich, the luxury of those who had access to the pure variety at the twist of a knob. It was better to hide here, far from that other life, far from the Roman soldiers— her father's soldiers—who pounded at the palace gates.

But there remained one place that she couldn't make herself avoid: the agora. Each afternoon, she'd lead Ajax there. Early on, when her money pouch had still been heavy from the coin she'd earned selling her palace clothes, it had been easy to come up with a pretense. Once they arrived at the market, Ajax would vanish into the crowd. Raised on the streets, he knew more people—buyers, sellers, street urchins—than she could count. And she'd wander through the stalls, past the old woman hawking scarabs, who hardly paid her any mind now, and on to the fishmonger, whose prices, Arsinoe noticed, had soared when the Romans came, just as he'd predicted. After all, food had started to run scarce—there were another ten thousand mouths to feed.

At the end of each visit, she'd grow desperate and climb the steps of Poseidon's temple to look out over the square, scanning for that hulking, familiar form. *I will come back for you.* Ganymedes's parting words echoed in her head, but each time she heard them they shed a bit more of their meaning. Now that the coins had dwindled to the last few, Arsinoe could no longer sustain the same tired excuses of things they might buy. They couldn't afford to run through the rest of the money—not for things that they could beg or trade for or steal. And she knew, deep in her heart, that the eunuch wouldn't return for her.

"We should go back to the catacombs," she told the boy. Every night she'd spent outside the palace she'd spent there, shielded from the wind and the dangers of prying eyes. Not in the one where she'd struck Big Ajax, but in a nearby cavern where the two cousins had set up a haphazard sort of home.

Ajax, who'd grown tired of squatting and was now sitting cross-legged on the filthy ground, glanced up at her, his dark eyes squinting with confusion. But if he objected to the plan—or wondered why she'd decided not to pass through the market as they had each afternoon before—he knew better than to say anything. He merely nodded, and scrambled to his feet. "There are those who were born to lead," Arsinoe remembered Ganymedes telling her once, "and those who are meant to follow." Ajax clearly belonged to the second category.

When she reached to retrieve her bone from beneath her legs, the boy frowned, as he always did.

"It's not too late to put that back, ya know," he told her sternly. "Like I told ya, it's no good, stealin' from the dead. An' it makes you stick out, besides."

Arsinoe's fingers tightened on the femur. It must have belonged to some mighty soldier, she imagined, or perhaps some seer practiced in the mystic arts. A great power resided in the relic, and besides, she felt more comfortable wielding it than the knife that Ganymedes had given her. Though she'd practiced with that blade for ages at the palace, none of what she learned seemed to carry over to this new world. What difference did it make if she could throw a knife hard enough to stick in a tree? She was more worried about what might come in handy in a close-range fight. And from the moment she'd closed her fist around this new weapon, her body seemed to know what to do—when to strike Big Ajax, and how hard. She wouldn't part with her bone. Never mind Little Ajax's silly superstitions.

"It's brought me good luck so far," she snapped, though she knew that wasn't fair. And from Little Ajax's face, she could tell that he, too, was thinking of his cousin, of the fate he'd met at the end of her lucky bone. The boy was smart in that regard: he never spoke of Big Ajax. But Arsinoe knew that he must think of him. Just as she thought of Alexander and Ganymedes, of Myrrine and Cleopatra. And even, though she fought hard not to, of doomed Berenice.

She turned and walked on. Let him follow or not. It didn't make a wick of difference to her. But he did, as he always did, skipping behind her on the stones. Perhaps she'd been unfair to him, to taunt him that way. But he looked to her for protection, and she gave it, however begrudgingly. Arsinoe couldn't provide even that without her bone. This, she imagined, was what having a little brother must be like. A real one, not like the two blood brothers her mother had stolen, the ones she'd hardly ever seen except on ceremony.

"I din' mean to make you mad," Ajax said as they neared the catacombs. "I jus' don' want rottin' luck, is all."

"I know," she reassured him so he'd keep his mouth shut. Something felt wrong, out of joint. The city of the dead tended to be quiet, save for the sounds of a few other street children like herself, like Big and Little Ajax, who'd taken up residence in the winding catacombs. But this silence was of a different quality. She could hear her breath, slow and steady, outmatched by Ajax's faster pants. Arsinoe's heart thudded dully in her ears. And then a shout pierced the air.

That voice—she knew that voice. She would have known it anywhere. Even here, where it made no sense at all. The voice—the yell—belonged to Alexander. He'd come for her, when everyone else had forgotten, and he'd sought her here. She broke into a run.

"Wait!" Ajax cried out. "Stay back."

And he was right—Arsinoe saw that—because what could she do, she with her bone and her knife, against whatever it was that attacked her friend? But that didn't matter. She had to reach him—he'd come so far for her. *The Fates don't often send friends such as that.*

Defying her wiser nature, she followed the scream's course, darting between the great mausoleums, their facades brushed in mimicry of colonnaded houses, complete with cobalt pediments. As she slipped by her favorite frieze, where a horse-high Ptolemy the Brother-Loving slung his sword into a fallen Persian's throat, she eked out a whispered prayer to Serapis between her rapid pants. And on she ran past the smaller tombstones, the early ones carved with images of their occupants giving way to those marked only by crude drawings: a man reclining on a red divan, a woman clutching a babe to her chest. Arsinoe ran as though she had no choice, as though she were reeled in against her better will.

As she twisted beyond the last of the stone markers, to the spot where the ground sprouted only wooden stakes, she saw them: a man, or very nearly one, stood over Alexander. In his hand the man clutched a knife.

"You don't steal from me, boy," he hissed.

Arsinoe couldn't make out what Alexander said in return, but it didn't matter. She darted toward his assailant, and struck him across the knees with the femur as hard as she could. His legs crumpled, and his knife went spinning from his hand. A string of curses escaped his lips, half of which Arsinoe hardly recognized as Greek. With surprising speed, Alexander darted for the fallen blade, and plunged it into his attacker's throat. Blood spurted from the wound in rapid bursts as the man gasped and twitched against the grass. And then his body stilled, and the liquid ran dry.

"Alexander." Arsinoe turned to embrace her friend.

He wiped the blood against his stained tunic before looking up at her. His eyes were wrong. They weren't the gray-green of Alexander's, but as dark and murky as her own.

"What'd ya call me?" he asked, his head cocked to one side. From here, she saw, he looked nothing like her palace friend. The same age, perhaps, around the same build, but not even a glint of resemblance beyond that. He didn't even *sound* like Alexander. She'd been a fool to think that her childhood companion, spoiled by court life, had followed her out here.

"Nothing," she murmured.

"I'm Cerberus." The boy grinned.

Cerberus. Hades's three-headed hellhound. Arsinoe would have smiled at the name if her insides didn't feel rubbed raw. Not all street children took on gruesome monikers, but she'd discovered that many did. Even the ones who didn't adopt grisly names rarely went by their birth ones. Ajax, he was Little Ajax, and his lost cousin had been the "Big" of the pair. Two warriors of the great poet's songs. Arsinoe doubted that their mothers—whatever lowly sort of women they might have been—would have had the gall to name their children after such lofty figures.

"You got a name?" the boy asked, staring at her with interest. He wasn't shy about looking at her. There was an impudence to it.

Arsinoe shook her head; she had no answer to that question. She didn't even have a name. "I'm no man," she said. Like Odysseus.

"I got eyes to see that." He laughed. "You got quite a swing on ya, no man. What's that you got?"

She held out the bone to show him, but not too close. Who knew what sort of boy he was, this boy who caught himself up in trouble among the catacombs?

"You're not no man." He whooped with delight. "You're Osteodora."

Osteodora. The bone bearer.

* * *

Snug between the bodies of her two companions, she was safe. The easy rise and fall of breath calmed her heart. She'd no reason not to be content. She was warm. Her belly was full, or full enough. No one could touch her in this place. As the moon climbed higher against the black, her mind wandered through the darkness, out of the catacombs and back to the palace, to those who had died and those who soon would. She no longer soared at night; she only slithered.

"Osteodora." Bony fingers poked her ribs. "Ya can't sleep all day."

She sealed her eyes tighter, as though that might stall the dawn. Lying here, she felt cozy and unwound. Once she rose, she'd have to face all the dangers of the day.

"Dooooo-raaaaa," Ajax cried in that frightful singsong voice of his.

"Dora, I've told ya a hundred times over. I'll slog 'im if you don't shut 'im up."

"Dora!" the little one squealed.

Her eyes shot open. Cerberus had caught Ajax by the ear and was pinching his flesh so hard that it began to redden.

"Don't torment him," she chided.

The older boy groaned. He didn't understand why she kept Ajax around, why she fed him and taught him to use her knife. "He was passed to me," she'd tried to explain. It was no use, but she'd no other way of telling of the guilt that plagued her. Cerberus wouldn't understand. As far as she knew, he had thought nothing of the man he'd slain the day they met. But even as days bled by, the boy's cousin haunted her, the image of his head smashed in the crypts. On cool nights, when her comrades slept easy, her wounded heart would hope that Big Ajax still lived. And then the sun would rise, and she'd be grateful for his death, for the luck it had brought her, and for Cerberus.

As the three picked their way through the bustling street, Little

Ajax ran out ahead. He was friends with twice as many people as she and Cerberus put together, which made him useful—she would remind the older boy of that. Ajax, with his sweet and easy smile, fetched the day's news for them, sussing out which merchants were absent, and which had hired new guards, and which had received fresh shipments of goods. That bit mattered most. More Romans meant more mouths to feed—mouths more important than those belonging to beggar children like herself.

"Today'll be a good one. I feel it, y'hear?" Cerberus whispered.

"Why d'ya say that? Why's it different from yest'day?" She aped his voice's rhythms, the lulls between jammed-together words.

"You still talk funny." He smirked.

"I talk better than you."

"Ya call th' be'er?"

She laughed at his voice, and at his beaming face. He exaggerated his accent sometimes to test her, to see if she'd take her own too far. But he didn't ask her about it; he had his secrets too. Like how he'd learned to kill a man with a swift jab of a knife.

"Come." Her eyes scanned the crowd. "Why's it got to be such a good day?" Hunger gnawed at her. On good days, they found food before famine's fingers clawed their bellies and sucked away their strength.

"'Cause I got a secret. I know where we'll get our next meal."

Her ears perked. "How do you? Half the merchants don't even have food to sell."

"I know o' one who does." Cerberus's voice dropped to a whisper. "We steal from Bes's shop. He's gone each day. I know what time. And I heard his best guard's got sick."

She shivered. Bes frightened her. A hefty man whose family hailed from the Upper Lands, he had established himself as one of the city's most prominent merchants—and the most ruthless. She heard that he cut off the hands of a young assistant who dared steal from him, and gouged out the eyes of a street boy for staring too lustily at his wares. And besides, Cerberus was many things, but prudent wasn't one of them. *People let all sorts of idle gossip stand unchallenged,* she reasoned with herself. She should know. Even so, Bes wasn't the sort of man she was eager to cross.

"I don't—" She cut off her own protest when she caught sight of Ajax, skirting back through the crowd. His head hung low; his whole frame hunched in on itself. She knew that face, that walk. No news, no shipments—no luck. She met Cerberus's eye and shrugged. "It sounds like a good enough plan."

Entering Bes's shop was easier than she had imagined. Cerberus stood guard, Ajax sprang the lock, and soon she and the younger boy had crept into the store. While the other shopkeepers had been picked clean, the merchant's wares were plentiful: fruits, nuts, sweetmeats. Anything she could dream of. She rushed first to the cashews. Nuts filled bellies like nothing else; she'd learned that lesson quickly enough. Ajax hurried over to gather dates. He was still plagued by a child's sweet tooth.

"Ajax, don't fill your arms with those. Steal something useful."

"These are useful." His mouth squirted juice.

"Hurry, though. We can't stay here long."

She scraped another armful of almonds into her cloth. Deftly, she tied its ends around her bone. She no longer wondered about who its previous owner had been. Now it felt as much a part of her as her own fingers.

"Dora," her companion squealed.

"Shut up," she snapped. The shop door creaked open. She held her breath.

"You've come to the right spot, my friend." The man addressed an unseen patron. Osteodora pressed herself against the wall. "I've supplied many an excellent feast. And I imagine there'll be many now to celebrate the king's homecoming."

In the edge of her sight, an object tumbled to the ground. For a moment she was sure it was Berenice's head. Osteodora shook away the sight; her visions came upon her at strange moments now. With so much death, the gods refused to spare even her days. And no sooner had Berenice's face turned back into a pomegranate than another portent rose: carrion crows slain and guards tearing up her chambers. Myrrine weeping. Myrrine beaten. Myrrine dead. Crimson spilled beneath the bed frame. Blood spread before her eyes and her sight blurred red.

"You filthy thieves," a voice hissed.

"Run," Ajax whispered, shaking her already unsteady frame. "Dora, run—now!"

Her comrade dashed forward. The man grabbed his wrist, but Ajax twisted away. Osteodora dug her nails into her flesh. She wouldn't be haunted by Berenice's death, nor by Myrrine's. Those women belonged to another life.

The shopkeeper loomed before her, his mouth curled into a snarl. "Where's your courage now, girl? Come, give me what you've stolen, and perhaps I'll cut off only a few of your fingers."

He held out his hand; that was his mistake. As the shopkeeper reached for her bundle, Osteodora wrested it away and sank her teeth into his fleshy palm. Her knee sprang up, hard and fast, and crashed into his groin. As the man doubled in pain, she slipped out the door into the street.

Her eyes darted one way and then the other. She couldn't return to their meeting place—not at once, at any rate. And so she rushed headlong in the opposite direction, away from the canal and the catacombs. Her feet knew the twisting lanes as well as that other girl had once known the palace plazas and porticoes.

A man swore as her bundle struck his cart. She wove and darted through the onslaught of passersby. Every street, every alleyway, every boulevard was swarming on this first warm day of spring. *Persephone returns, and the world blooms with life.* There was another return as well: the return of her father and her sister to Alexandria.

But Osteodora wouldn't think of that. That was Arsinoe's family, not her own. And they'd abandoned her.

When she was sure she wasn't being followed, she doubled back through the streets, slowing her pace to a walk. Still too many eyes picked her out. No matter how hard she tried, she couldn't disappear. A youth walking with his lover gave her a lingering look, and an older man wearing the white robes of a priest stared at her for a long while. Perhaps Ajax was right: the bone did draw glances. But she took pleasure in them. It was better to be seen as a threat, looked upon with fear and disgust, than as another shrinking street mouse. The bundle dug into her shoulder. Her rough-spun clothes scratched against her skin. And slowly the crowds began to thin as she approached the canal. Ajax, reliable Ajax, sat waiting, his legs dangled over the clear waters.

"Here." She tossed him a pomegranate. He tore into its peel with his teeth, not bothering to open it with his knife.

Teeth mottled pink with seeds, Ajax peered up at her and mumbled, "Shouldn't we wait for Cerberus?"

"I'll tell him you already wolfed down half your bit, if it makes your eating easier."

Her eyes scanned the three streets that opened onto the canal for Cerberus's skinny form. Her weight shifted from foot to foot. She fingered the coin belt she wore knotted against her skin. Its denizens bore the face of her—Arsinoe's—father. When she'd sold her palace clothes, she'd stared in awe as the shopkeeper handed over gold piece after gold piece. Ajax had kicked her and hissed, "Bite 'em or put 'em away." And then he'd shown her how to cut a stretch of cloth and stitch it beneath the filthy tunic she now wore. "That way," he'd told her proudly, "the coins won't fall out, and won't get stole neither." Their numbers had dwindled there against her waist. She wouldn't use the remaining ones for food, only for favors or for tonics—things too hard to steal.

She watched as her friend ate his share as ferociously and joyously as he always did. She wondered, as she often did, how he'd ended up with Big Ajax, what had brought him to the streets. For a long while, she'd been waiting to ask him—and now, with him so utterly jubilant, the moment felt ripe.

"Ajax," she asked quietly. "Where's your mother?"

The boy blushed to his neck. He must be ashamed of the woman, then, of whatever had happened to lead him to this place. Osteodora realized that many of the street children weren't orphans. They couldn't be. The city hadn't seen plague or war in years; their parents couldn't have all died off. Many of her new compatriots, she imagined, had been raised on the streets. And when they reached the age when their smiles no longer helped their mothers beg, they were turned out—or they fled. Cerberus had mentioned it once: "Why shoul' I steal for that old hag when I coul' steal twice as good for me?"

"I—I don't remember her," Ajax stammered, eyes cast out over the still water.

"Not anything?" she pried. Curiosity overwhelmed her. She'd never been good at holding her tongue. And besides, she was crafting her own account. Sooner or later, she imagined, someone would ask.

"Not much, Dora. I don't remember much of anything, really, before Big Ajax took me..." He shrugged his bony shoulders. He looked so little huddled against the great canal. Had he seen even eight summers? She couldn't tell. Street children ran small for their age, and most took her for older than she was.

Bundle clutched to her chest, Osteodora sat down beside Ajax. He looked up at her with his gap-toothed smile.

"What about your mother, Dora?"

"Ran off. Took my two brothers, left me to fend for myself." She told Arsinoe's story, in broad strokes. How she was betrayed and left behind. A lump formed in her throat; it was strange that the tale still affected her. "She always wanted boys anyway," she added, harshly, coldly. *And what of Ganymedes, then? Did he want boys too?*

The sound of feet scraping against stone. She leapt up: Cerberus. And there he was, bruised and beaten, walking across the boulevard—staggering, more like. He couldn't keep his steps in a straight line. He favored his left leg with each stumbled stride.

"Dora, don't," Ajax protested. She ignored his warning. He was always frightened of something. The bigger boys already teased him for being a craven. Bone over her shoulder, she rushed to her wounded friend.

"Dora." Cerberus spat milky blood. "Run."

But the warning came too late. Guards, thick with armor, descended from all sides. Ajax had vanished back into the streets. And Cerberus collapsed on the stones.

"Arsinoe." One of the soldiers knelt by her side. "It's time to return to the palace."

That name. How did they know her here?

"You've got the wrong girl," she shouted, backing away.

The man shook his head. "I know your face. Don't be frightened of me."

Fear pounded in her veins. She eyed each of the three palace men. Had they always been so hard and menacing? She feinted to the left, and then dove to the right, slipping between two sets of legs. But forceful fingers snatched her wrist and dragged her back.

"Arsinoe." Again, the first guard called her by that other girl's name. "No one's going to harm you."

She screamed and kicked and lashed, though she knew that it wouldn't do her any good. Cerberus didn't move; perhaps he was dead. There was blood—so much blood.

"What d'ya do to him?" she cried in anger, though she knew it was her own fault. It had only happened because he'd befriended her. Everyone who cared for her left, or turned to dust. That was her curse.

"Arsinoe," the guard repeated. "Calm yourself."

He clamped his hand over her mouth and scooped her into his

arms. She writhed and flailed, struggled and shrieked, but she could not free herself. As they neared the city gate, she redoubled her efforts. She twisted right and then quickly left again. Free, she fell hard against the stone. But before she could scamper up, two sets of hands set her upright and marched her to the waiting litter. She recognized its silver-plated cedar, the gold handles and violet curtains. A thousand times Arsinoe had ridden in it before. But no amount of prodding could convince her to enter quietly now. With guards towering at each side, she'd no hope of escape. But that was no reason not to fight.

Clawing and screeching, she thrashed against their hands. And still the soldiers twisted her body into the carrier. Her head went last. She thought she caught a glimpse of Ajax, tears welling at the prospect of a second cousin lost. But perhaps she'd only imagined it.

As she was trundled into the litter, she heard someone cluck, "Osteodora? I can see why that name fits you now."

She knew that voice. It belonged to no man.

"Ganymedes?" she asked in disbelief as she looked up at the person opposite her. The eunuch wouldn't have come to bring Arsinoe to her death. Or at least she didn't imagine he would.

The tutor reclined calmly on the pillows across from her, and he answered in an idle tone, as though no time had passed at all since their last encounter. "Yes, my dear, it's only me. Though I'd scarcely recognize you on the street."

"Why should you? You left me." She spat the words.

"Yes, for a time, I did. As I warned you I would."

You said you'd come back. She wanted to scream and curse him to the stars. But she knew better. Such a display would only show her to be weak. And she wasn't weak—not now. She'd survived outside the palace with no more than a knife and a bone. She didn't need Ganymedes; she didn't need anyone. So instead she asked, "How—how d'ya find me?"

"'How d'ya find me?'" The eunuch tutted. "Scarcely two

weeks gone, and already you've picked up some pidgin form of Greek."

"How did you discover my whereabouts?" she asked with a careful clip.

"My dear." He squeezed her hand. She didn't recoil. She'd learned to hide her emotions better. "I live in the palace, yes, but I still have my connections in other corners. And . . . there are those who keep a close eye on the denizens of that world, the children in particular. I heard someone speaking of a newly arrived girl, Osteodora. It didn't take long to determine that it was you."

Staring through the litter's curtains, she watched as the houses grew large and stately once more. A few dozen street rats had gathered round to follow the gilded carrier, but soon they lost interest and scattered. Perhaps they whispered the tale of Osteodora, snatched from their midst. Or perhaps not. Perhaps they'd already forgotten her. Ajax hadn't, but he would. He never mentioned his cousin, after all. And he would survive; she had to believe that. He'd find some other protector. Perhaps Cerberus would take him on. If he lived. She had to believe that too. They'd been her last friends, her only friends.

Ganymedes studied her but she wouldn't return his gaze. She swallowed her berating words. "I could have died when you abandoned me," she wanted to scream. And also, "I wish that you'd left me there." But she'd learned patience. She wouldn't give him the satisfaction of seeing her squirm. She pursed her lips and spoke with all the ease she could muster. "And what news comes from the palace?"

"Your father rules. Your sister rots in a cell. You can't be surprised by that. But Ptolemy the New Dionysus wishes to welcome you, his youngest daughter, with open arms."

"My father sent for me, then?" The blood pounded in her temple.

Almost imperceptibly, the eunuch shook his head. "Cleopatra is very anxious to see you, my dear."

It had been her sister, then, who'd saved her. As she always had. But she couldn't draw any comfort from that.

As they neared the palace, she grew painfully aware of her body: her knotted hair, her grimy face, her filthy fingers. With a surreptitious thumb, she tried to work away the worst of the dirt under her nails.

"A maid will wash and scrub you clean before you are presented. No need to bother yourself with that."

A maid—not Myrrine. That vision had proved true.

"You're oddly quiet, my dear. I thought you would be bursting with tales from your rough days on the street."

Her eyes—Arsinoe's eyes—caught on the dried flecks of blood that were spattered across her prized possession. "A bone bearer keeps her secrets."

The eunuch's gaze followed hers. "And to think that I feared you might be too kind, too gentle for the alleyways."

Scrubbed and plaited, Arsinoe stared over the great courtyard. It looked larger than she remembered it. Her stomach churned violently. She hardly dared take a step, let alone cross the whole length. The dancing dolphin mosaic that marked the place where the two central paths met looked stades away. Not even a thousand paces would carry her there.

Arsinoe no longer felt brave. Ganymedes had taken her bone from her. "It's not a proper plaything for a princess," he'd said. Perhaps he'd stolen her courage along with it. Behind her, a guard cleared his throat. It startled her, to be watched and prompted. All the same, she took the first step, treading lightly on the marble as though her newly sullied feet might destroy its elegance.

Nothing about the palace seemed right. It felt too big, open and treacherous. Arsinoe missed the nooks and crannies of the catacombs, places where people could attack from only one direction. Even the smells disturbed her. The cloying scents of roses and sandalwood, of lilies and honey, stung her nostrils. She'd grown accustomed to earthy odors: the stench of dirt and sweat, her two unwashed friends curled up next to her.

Already she'd reached the dolphin's nose. Arsinoe stared down to where her sandals met the vibrant pebbles. She squinted at the image until it no longer formed a fish at all, but instead broke into countless disparate dots of blue and green. She couldn't linger here either. Time marched on, and—as the guard had said—her father waited for her.

With only a little urging, her feet bore her forward, toward the great atrium where she had been called before Berenice on so many occasions. A hand grasped her shoulder. She spun around, swallowing a shriek. It was just the soldier, the throat-clearing one, shaking his head slowly.

"Your father will see you in the royal dining lounge," he told her gently.

Arsinoe nodded. She remembered now. Her father didn't care for the atrium, the throne. He preferred to conduct his meetings lazing on a silken couch. And so she turned down the path to her right. She watched the waves of blue shingles ebb and flow along the steps. The dread mounted in her chest. She turned her attention to the bushes in full and regal bloom. Their name flickered at the tip of her tongue. Dilaty? Ditivy? Dittany. That was it: dittany.

Set off to the side, the gold-laced doorframe loomed, its twisted carvings hung with grapes, a promise of the bounties held within. Arsinoe took a breath, steeling herself for whatever would come, and crossed through the threshold.

Twin divans were set head-to-head, and on each lay a familiar figure. Her father, all in purple, his diadem askew, reclined languidly against the silken pillows. He barely glanced up at her entrance. Posed on the other couch was Cleopatra, a changed Cleopatra, with widened hips and sprouting breasts. A thousand times Arsinoe had imagined this moment, this reunion. How she would rush into her sister's arms.

But her feet were glued to the onyx. It was only when Cleopatra looked at him and whispered "Father" that any of them moved at all. And then the New Dionysus, the Piper, Arsinoe's father, the king, slid his feet off the divan in order to sit and beckoned her to approach. The gesture should have been one of warmth, but he looked as cold and distant as he did on his coins. Arsinoe approached, and in dutiful silence he wrapped and unwrapped his icy arms about her frame.

Once freed, she saw that her sister had rushed to her side.

"My dear, sweet sister," Cleopatra whispered, her voice trembling. The Macedonian, the sacred, secret language of their house, sounded strange, unfamiliar to Arsinoe's ears. "I can scarcely believe you're real."

Arsinoe felt nothing. Only emptiness. But she forced herself to weep.

ELDER

It was the darkness that threatened to break her. The thirst, the stink, the scratch of rats—all that she could have borne. If only she could see. But the four walls of her prison were solid and impenetrable. Though reason told Berenice that the sun still rose each morning, she saw no evidence of it. Alexandria might as well have been cloaked in endless night for all the difference it made here.

At odd hours, the door would creak and release a slit of light. An unknown servant—never the same—would enter with a stale heel of bread or a rotting date. By turns grateful and sickened, Berenice devoured whatever she was offered. Imprisonment had begun to take its toll: her bones ached and her fingers shook. Her thick hair fell out in clumps. At least no one forced a mirror on her.

Sometimes she'd barter for information. A silver bracelet loosened even stubborn tongues, and so she discovered that Dryton, her lofty military adviser, was dead. Brought down by arrows as he fled the battle, white banner in hand. She shouldn't have trusted that one; he couldn't even surrender properly. Her vulture amulet bought more secrets. Arsinoe, too, had betrayed her, she learned from some ugly wisp of a slave. But soon the rumors dried. She'd no more jewels, and a mantle, no matter how finely woven, didn't command the same attention as gems. And so one night she found herself shivering by her chamber pot, weeping over Leda's death. But she dried her eyes, and asked no more questions after that.

Berenice heard boots banging against stone. She heard them

often enough; sometimes she wondered whether the soldiers stomped back and forth to taunt her. But this time their pitch had a different cadence. She could almost hear them crying out: "The time has come, the time has come to die."

A piercing ray ushered in a pair of guards: one tall, one stout. By their vulture helmets, Berenice could see that they were Alexandrians, not Romans. That was a cold sort of comfort, to be led to her death by her own countrymen. With their unlined faces, they looked too young to be soldiers of any kind, a thousand years younger than she'd ever been. All the same, she stood, smoothing her robes along her legs. She ran dirty fingers through the ashes of her dirty hair. Filthy and reeking, she held her chin high. She blinked against the blinding oil lamps as she emerged, but she didn't shield her eyes. *Never show them you are soft.*

Their silent procession clambered up a slanted corridor and through a set of unfamiliar colonnades, paved only with plain and rough-hewn stone. Here and there, she caught sight of a chipped painting; the nymphs still smiled even when they'd lost their arms and legs and teeth. Would she? In death, would her lips curl into a mirthless grin?

Too soon, her feet were crossing into the great courtyard. There the banked colonnades swarmed with the half-forgotten faces of noblemen who had come late to her cause, and had returned quickly to her father's. Pieton's face was not among theirs. Of course it wasn't. No amount of begging could wash away his sins.

She searched the crowd for the dearer dead: Archelaus, Leda, even Dryton. But she knew she'd never see another friendly face, just as she knew she'd never bear a child or lead men into battle or build a palace of her own. As she stepped into the atrium, her knees turned weak, and all the stories of gods reborn were as flaked as flimsy child's tales. *Never show them you are soft.*

High above the throngs sat her father, bolt straight upon the inlaid throne. His hair had receded farther from his broken nose, but otherwise his face looked exactly as it had in her childhood. His concubine lounged to his left, on full display, reclining in Tryphaena's silks stitched with amethyst and jade. The creature's youngest child, scarcely more than a babe, played with the pearls about her neck. The older boy, a round child of five, eyed Berenice with greedy interest. Her own gaze turned to the two daughters. Cleopatra, almost a woman now, had the decency to avert her eyes. There, beside her, perched Arsinoe, knees drawn up to her chin. Even at a distance, Berenice could make out her welling eyes. The child hadn't forsaken her, not in the end. "Don't cry," she whispered to herself. "They'll see."

The heart of the chamber had been cleared of men. A hunk of granite reared from the ground, blotting out Dionysus's smiling face. A lump swelled in her throat. Beside the block stood the largest man she'd ever seen. His neck strained against his breast-plate's collar, as if it had been crafted for some properly sized soldier. His fingers clenched and loosened on the handle of his ax. All eyes were fixed on her, but her toes melted into the stone. She urged them on, but her feet wouldn't listen. No one would watch her sweat; she wouldn't give them that satisfaction. She nearly spoke the words aloud: *Never show them you are soft.*

"The traitor wishes to make a sort of speech," her father said.

She did, she did. She'd tell them how Rome's rise augured Egypt's death, and how the goddess Mut held sway over their neutered deities, and how the concubine who stole her father's bed would never match her mother. Her brave words would echo on— the daughter who died with venom on her breath.

"Father." She found her tongue. "Father, please."

Long years washed away, lonely years of strength and strife, and she was a child of nine once more, begging for her father's love. She cried and wailed—every woman's weapon that she despised—to cling to this wretched life. Her father's eyes brimmed with disgust— the look he reserved for his grotesque and stillborn babes.

The Piper's voice cut through her screams. "Guards, go on. Put an end to this creature's mewling."

Rough hands dragged Berenice forward. It was too late—she knew it was too late—and yet she pleaded on. The stone smashed up against her knees, and her words abandoned her. Tears streamed down her face, and she looked up to catch her father's gaze. The blade glinted in the torchlight.

Soft.

ACKNOWLEDGMENTS

So many wonderful people helped me bring Arsinoe's and Berenice's stories to the page. In particular, I would like to thank my dear friend Meghan Flaherty for believing in this book from the very beginning and for reading more iterations of this manuscript than I dare count. My sister, Julia, for her astute critiques and her unwavering support. My mother for inciting my love of literature and my father for kindling my interest in history. Julia Kardon and Ivan Lett for answering the questions I was too embarrassed to ask anyone else. David Goodwillie for connecting me to my amazing agent. Sam Kahn, Leah Franqui, Jenny Nissel, and Brian Denton for their kind and careful reads of early drafts of this book.

Enormous thanks to Alexis Hurley for placing this manuscript with the perfect publisher and holding my hand when I needed it. To my brilliant editor, Judy Clain, for her tireless passion for this project and her keen editorial insights. To Amanda Brower for her hard work on everything from editing to production. To Nell Beram for flagging any lingering modern idioms and correcting my rampant overuse of the subjunctive. To Karen Landry, Lisa Erickson, Heather Fain, Meghan Deans, and Miriam Parker for their outstanding production and marketing efforts. To my publicist, Morgan Moroney, for trusting me in front of an audience and a video camera. To Reagan Arthur and everyone else at Little, Brown for publishing this book.

I also owe a debt of gratitude to the many cultural institutions of

New York City that made much of my research possible, especially to the New York and Brooklyn Public Libraries for their exhaustive collections of history, art, and architecture books, and to the Metropolitan Museum of Art and the Brooklyn Museum for their stunning sets of Greek, Roman, and Egyptian artifacts.

CLASSICAL CITATIONS

9 *"Can anyone be so indifferent... within a period of not quite fifty-three years?"*: Polybius, *Histories,* Book 1, line 1.

12 *"The one named mother is not the child's true parent... woman is a stranger fostering a stranger"*: Aeschylus, *The Furies,* lines 657–660.

38 *"Now look at the two of us.... You're so rash—I am so afraid for you"*: Sophocles, *Antigone,* lines 70–74, 80–81, 96.

38 *"Deserted so by loved ones, struck by fate"*: Ibid., line 1011.

62 *"I'm not ashamed to sail through trouble with you, to make your troubles mine"*: Ibid., lines 608–609.

63 *"I have no love for a friend who loves in words alone"*: Ibid., line 612.

95 *"You'll soon show what you are, worth your breeding... for all your royal blood"*: Ibid., lines 44–46.

99 *"It wasn't Zeus, not in the least, who made this proclamation... could override the gods, the great unwritten, unshakeable traditions"*: Ibid., lines 499–505.

125 *"Dreams as well can come our way from Zeus"*: Homer, *The Iliad,* Book 1, line 73.

127 *"But Death overtakes even the man who runs from the battle"*: Simonides, fragments.

150 *"Surely, of all creatures that have life and will, we women are the most wretched"*: Euripides, *Medea,* lines 228–231.

197 *"It appears to me a most excellent thing for the physician to cultivate Prognosis"*: Hippocrates, *The Book of Prognostics,* Book 1, lines 1–2.

198 *"Men regard its nature and cause as divine... and a cause whence it originates"*: Hippocrates, *On the Sacred Disease,* lines 3–5.

216 *"She had terrible dreams.... She dreamed she gave birth to a snake"*: Aeschylus, *The Libation Bearers,* lines 523–524, 527.

226–227 *"Lurching up, he lunged out.... So we lay there groaning, waiting Dawn's first light"*: Homer, *The Odyssey,* Book 9, lines 324–343.

271 *"You'll never find a man on earth, if a god leads him on, who can escape his fate"*: Sophocles, *Oedipus at Colonus,* lines 266–268.

287 *"What should our prayers be saying... no mother comfort soothes our rage"*: Aeschylus, *The Libation Bearers,* lines 420–422.

SOURCES

Aeschylus, *The Furies* in: P. Meineck (trans.), H. Foley (intro.), *Oresteia* (Indianapolis/Cambridge, Massachusetts: Hackett Publishing Company, Inc., 1998).

Aeschylus, *The Libation Bearers* in: P. Meineck (trans.), H. Foley (intro.), *Oresteia* (Indianapolis/Cambridge, Massachusetts: Hackett Publishing Company, Inc., 1998).

Euripides, *Medea* in: P. Vellacott (trans. & intro.), *Medea and Other Plays* (Baltimore: Penguin Books, 1963).

Euripides, *The Trojan Women,* trans. R. Lattimore, in: D. Grene & R. Lattimore (eds.), *The Complete Greek Tragedies: Euripides III* (Chicago/London: University of Chicago Press, 1958).

Hippocrates, *The Book of Prognostics,* trans. F. Adams (http://classics.mit.edu//Hippocrates/prognost.html: The Internet Classics Archive, 1994–2009).

Hippocrates, *On the Sacred Disease,* trans. F. Adams (http://classics.mit.edu//Hippocrates/sacred.html: The Internet Classics Archive, 1994–2009).

Homer, *The Iliad,* trans. R. Fagles (New York: Penguin Books, 1990).

Homer, *The Odyssey,* trans. R. Fagles (New York: Penguin Books, 1996).

Polybius, *Histories* in: E. Shuckburgh (trans.), A. Bernstein (intro.), *Polybius on Roman Imperialism* (South Bend: Regnery Gateway, 1980).

Simonides, Fragments in: D. Campbell (trans. & ed.), *Greek Lyric,*

Volume III: Stesichorus, Ibycus, Simonides, and Others (Cambridge, Massachusetts: Loeb Classical Library, 1991).

Sophocles, *Antigone* in: R. Fagles (trans.), B. Knox (intro. & notes), *The Three Theban Plays* (New York: Penguin Books, 1984).

Sophocles, *Oedipus at Colonus* in: R. Fagles (trans.), B. Knox (intro. & notes), *The Three Theban Plays* (New York: Penguin Books, 1984).

ABOUT THE AUTHOR

Emily Holleman, a graduate of Yale University, spent several years as an editor of *Salon*—a job she left to follow Arsinoe and her quest for the throne of Egypt. Holleman is, like Arsinoe, a younger sister, and she has devoted the past four years to reading and writing about the Ptolemies. She is currently at work on the second novel in the Fall of Egypt series. She lives in Brooklyn.

CLEOPATRA'S SHADOWS

QUESTIONS AND TOPICS
FOR DISCUSSION

1. Throughout her childhood, Arsinoe has always felt closest to Cleopatra. Over the course of the novel, though, Cleopatra is mostly absent from Arsinoe's life. How is it revealed to us that Arsinoe may have more cause for allegiance with Berenice? What about their circumstances and experience bonds them?

2. Consider the author's decision to narrate the book from two perspectives. How did it affect your perceptions? Did you feel more drawn to one voice over the other? If so, why? What purpose does the dual narration serve?

3. Compare how Arsinoe and Berenice handle death and tragedy. Why do you suppose they process it in this way? What do their reactions to trauma, violence, and loss say about their characters?

4. At any point in the novel, did your allegiance switch from Arsinoe to Berenice? Did you come to feel sympathy for Berenice? If so, why, and at what point in the story? What shifted your feelings toward or against her?

5. On page 93, Alexander comments, "I don't think that being unafraid is the same as being brave.... I think bravery is when you go on even though you are frightened." How do you interpret

his comment? How does what he says help Arsinoe to see herself in a new light?

6. Did you expect Ganymedes to abandon Arsinoe in the agora? Were you surprised when he returned for her? Do you trust him, and should Arsinoe trust him? Why or why not?

7. Do you think Arsinoe and Cleopatra's relationship will resume with the same intensity and loyalty now that they have reunited? How has what Arsinoe endured during Cleopatra's absence changed her and potentially turned her away from Cleopatra? In your eyes, did Cleopatra have a choice in her abandonment of Arsinoe?

8. The role of mothers—and betrayal by them—features prominently in the book. On page 91, Arsinoe remarks, "What good were mothers, anyway?" And on page 106, during her last conversation with her dying mother, Berenice is troubled by her mother's fixation on her rule. Then she realizes that, just maybe, there's caring in her mother's worry, even if it's not the caring that Berenice would have wanted. "But it was the sort that her mother had to give." Have you ever experienced something similar? How would you handle being in Berenice's—or Arsinoe's—shoes?

9. Arsinoe has dark and prophetic dreams, and when she tries to tell her tutor, Ganymedes, he rebukes her. Why are these dreams so important to Arsinoe? What role do you think they play in her understanding of the world? Have you ever experienced a dream that came true, or that clarified something for you in your waking life? Do you think dreams have a predictive or symbolic power?